A
FATAL
CELL PHONE
VIDEO

GARY REED

A Fatal Cell Phone Video

Great New Legal Thriller
By **John Bercaw, author of <u>A Pink Mist</u>**
This is a page-turner, closely related to current events, and
I hated when it ended.

Excellent Legal Thriller
By **Michele Wyan, author of <u>Night Stranger</u>**
This is an enjoyable read for legal thriller fans. The plot is
filled with suspense and twists and turns and the characters
are deftly developed. Reed is an author to watch. I highly
recommend this book.

Great Legal Thriller Set in Cincinnati
By **Mike Chlanda, author of <u>The Heist</u>**
Great legal thriller set in my new hometown of Cincinnati.
Reed brings to life courtroom characters as only a trial at-
torney can. Looking forward to the next one! I especially
liked the Weary Dunston character.

Held My Interest from the Beginning
By **Good Reads reader**
I had to force myself to put it down and go to sleep, as I
just kept wanting to know what happened next, and how
the dilemma would be resolved.

I Really Enjoyed This Book!
By **Amazon Customer**
I really enjoyed this book. It was hard to put down. I recognized a lot of the places mentioned in the book since it is
set in the Tri-State where I live. The story is so close to real
life and the events happening in today's world.

A Fatal Cell Phone Video

This Is a Must Read For Americans
By Amazon Customer

A gripping legal thriller with a dose of politics. The character development was great and very realistic. I couldn't put it down until I reached the end. Thank you, Gary Reed, for this lesson on bias and bigotry while keeping us enthralled with a great murder story.

Timely Legal Drama
By Amazon Customer

This is a suspenseful, quick read. Great legal drama and writing, and I particularly enjoyed the local color from Cincinnati (since I live here). The book also is very timely, tying in much of the current debate about profiling and how legal events are turning on cell phone videos
Very thought provoking!

Great Read!
Loved That It Was Set In Cincinnati
By Amazon Customer

Great read! Loved that it was set in Cincinnati. I like that he writes strong women characters … well, except for the reporter. Could not put it down!

An Enjoyable Read!
By Amazon Customer

Set in my "second home" city, I was comfortable in this place and with the people who live in this novel. The plot is both as old as the hills and new, while providing a unique twist to messages on the nightly news. And, the TV broadcasts are a great comic relief to a tense storyline.
An enjoyable read!

Top Quark Publishing Co.
Union, Kentucky 41091

ISBN:

FCPV070220

A
FATAL
CELL PHONE
VIDEO

GARY REED

"Decades of research have proven that expectation is a powerful force. It acts on our perceptions much as gravity acts on light, bending them in ways that are measurable by others, but, at least to us, imperceptible."

Joseph T. Hallinan, *Kidding Ourselves*

PROLOGUE

SUNDAY, JULY 12, 3:20 A.M

The red pickup truck slammed to a stop midway across the 8th Street Viaduct, the half-mile-long bridge that connects Cincinnati's downtown business district to the distressed, post-Appalachian neighborhood of Lower Price Hill. Even at 3:20 in the morning, stopping on the busy thoroughfare was risky. The drizzling rain and fog only made things worse.

The two men moved quickly. In the truck's cargo bed, a sheet of plastic wrapped around the body of the dead woman. Grabbing the plastic sheeting, they removed the body and rested it momentarily on the viaduct's concrete and metal side rail. Working together, they lifted the sheeting from one end and allowed the body to slide out of the plastic and plunge the 200 or so feet to the railroad tracks below.

The men returned the sheeting to the bed of the truck and secured it. They would dispose of it separately in case it bore fingerprints or other telltale evidence. They climbed back into the truck and slammed the doors shut. As the pickup sped away, the two men, both twenty-one-years-old, let out a series of shouts – releasing some of the tension they felt.

The truck's Confederate flag flapped in the wind.

PART I: THE VICTIMS

The heavyset man burst through the Inn's doors and confronted the blonde woman. "What the hell are you doing?" he demanded. Glancing at the video camera mounted on a tripod, he asked, "Why are you photographing my inn?"

The man had black hair, mahogany brown eyes, and a strong Hispanic accent. His skin was the color of a UPS deliveryman's uniform. Given what she knew about the inn, the blonde woman assumed the man was Mexican. He wore a cheap plastic name tag that said, "Manager."

"I'm Ann Lindsey Medawar," the woman said. "I'm a film student." As she spoke, she slid her cell phone into her pocket. She gave the man her best smile. "I'm getting some video of my husband and a friend entering and leaving the inn." Her husband, Rafiq A. Medawar, M.D., was a surgeon at the nearby Trauma Center.

"I did not give you permission to use my place for your movie," the manager insisted. "Get the hell off my property."

"I don't understand the problem," Ann said, stalling for time. "Most businesses would like a little free publicity."

"I don't need no goddam publicity. Get lost!"

"What if I pay you?" Ann asked. "How much does it cost to rent a room?"

"Are you with the police? Immigration?" the man asked. "Who told you to film my place?"

"I'm not filming your place," Ann said. "I'm filming my husband."

"Where is this husband?"

"He's putting on his costume," Ann fudged, rationalizing that her husband's surgical mask, gloves, and stethoscope were a costume of sorts. He and Angelica Rios, a nurse on his surgical team, were visiting an undocumented woman, hiding inside in the inn with two sick children. According to Angelica, the woman recently arrived from Mexico.

The manager looked around as if expecting to see a platoon of FBI, DEA and ICE agents preparing to swarm the inn.

"What's your name?" Ann asked.

"Diego," the man said, warily. "I want you to get out of here. Get lost!"

"Diego," Ann countered, "what if I give you a hundred dollars? I video my husband and his friend leaving, and then I go."

"You sure you're not Immigration?"

"I'm a film student, that's all. This is for my class."

"If you're lying to me, I will break your camera, and then I will break both your arms. You understand?"

Ann dug into her wallet.

"Here's fifty," she said, offering the money to the man. "It's all I've got on me. My husband will give you the rest when he comes out."

"Five minutes!" The man grumbled, taking the money. "If you're not gone in five minutes, I'm going to shove that camera up your ass."

He stormed back into the inn.

Ann was thankful Diego had not touched the tripod or the video camera mounted on it. She had used that camera to record Rafiq and Angelica enter the inn. Then, she had carefully re-positioned the tripod so that the camera mounted on it would capture Rafiq and Angelica as they emerged from the inn. She had also found a spot where she could use her cell phone to make a backup video, without being captured by the mounted camera.

She had even had a stroke of luck. After she had the camera re-positioned and ready, two men had left the inn, then another, and finally, a few minutes later, a fourth. She had been able to check the video. It had captured their faces fine. One of the men looked upset at being caught on video leaving the sleazy inn but didn't say anything. Importantly, she had not filmed herself.

Ann moved back to the spot where she would use her cell phone to video Rafiq and Angelica when they came back through the door. She reinserted her cell phone and arm into the sling-like device that would steady her cell phone camera. And waited.

A few minutes later Rafiq and Angelica came out. Ann checked the video on her cell phone and didn't like what she saw. She asked them to re-do their exit.

Rafiq and the nurse complied, but then Rafiq called it quits. "Last night was brutal," he complained. "I'm not used to working the night shift anymore. I really need to go home and get some sleep."

"The manager tried to run me off," Ann said, stowing the camera and tripod in the trunk of her car. "I promised to pay him, but I'm tapped out. Give me some money, and you can go."

"How much do you need?"

"Fifty."

"Ann," Rafiq said, shaking his head, "you let everyone take advantage of you." He pulled out his wallet and removed all the cash he had.

Ann kissed him on the cheek, took the money from his hand, and thanked him. She went into the inn as he headed for his car. Angelica had already left.

9:00 – 9:05 A.M.

Rafiq Medawar pulled his car from the Sleep Cheap Inn's parking. He had had misgivings about this little adventure from the beginning and was glad to be heading home.

Angelica was involved in helping immigrants and had asked him to check on the woman's children. She hoped he could persuade the woman to take her kids to the hospital.

Even if he couldn't, she had argued, he could make sure they didn't have cholera or something else as deadly and contagious.

He hadn't wanted to get involved. Without being able to run labs or other tests, he would not be able to diagnose the kids. But Ann had urged him to go. She reminded him that she and her class were making a documentary about the plight of the undocumented in their city. She wanted to get video of the inn and of him and Angelica entering and leaving the inn. He could never say "no" to Ann. But he had put his foot down and insisted she could not enter the room where the woman was staying. He didn't want her exposed to whatever the kids had. Besides, it would be unprofessional, and the poor woman would likely be spooked.

It had all turned out pretty much as he had expected. He didn't think the kids had cholera, but he couldn't rule out hepatitis or a lot of other possibilities, and he hadn't been able to convince the poor woman to let him take her to the hospital.

Move on, he told himself.

He turned on his car radio, hoping to catch the news. The announcer reported that the Cincinnati Police were raiding the Heidelberg Sausage plant in Queensgate. The police had detained 76 workers with suspicious citizenship papers.

He sighed. When Ann heard the report of yet another immigration raid, she would be livid. He turned up the volume a little. Ann would want to talk about it. He wanted to be sure he got the details.

"Behind me," a reporter narrated, "police officers are hauling away computers and email servers from the company's offices, along with boxes of records."

Pam Sprecher, the spokesperson for Hamilton County Prosecutor Richard Warren, gave a brief statement. "The police," she said, "are investigating allegations that Heidelberg Sausage Company knowingly hires undocumented workers with phony citizenship papers. Today's raid is the result of a six-month investigation into the company's hiring practices."

For context, the reporter explained that in recent months, Hamilton County Prosecutor Richard Warren had directed high profile raids on several Mexican restaurants, a warehouse in Northside, and other businesses. "Today's raid," he said, "is the largest to date."

The reporter also noted that Warren was expected to run for the district's Congressional seat. Critics, the reporter said, complain that the raids are publicity stunts.

Medawar nodded. That's exactly what Ann would say.

9:05 A.M. – 9:07 A.M.

Driving a red, late-model Mercedes 350 sedan, Emily Goessel, age forty, was hurrying through Clifton on her way to her kids' school. The school nurse had called with the news that her daughter, Brittany, had the measles. The nurse had all but demanded someone pick up Brittany as soon as possible, implying that Brittany was putting other kids at risk. Goessel didn't understand the fuss. When she was a kid, everyone got the measles. It was no big deal.

She – *not her husband* – had picked up their son, Dylan, a week ago, when he too came down the measles. She – *not her husband* – had to put up with the nurse and school principal demanding to know if her kids had been vaccinated. *And have them end up autistic? Not a chance.* And she – *not her husband* – was the one who had to deflect their questions about how she had procured certifications that their kids had been vaccinated when, obviously, they hadn't been.

She felt it was her husband's turn to do the school run and put up with the vaccination Nazis. But her husband refused, claiming he had clients in from out-of-town and couldn't possibly leave. *Why was his job always more important than hers? She had meetings too. Granted, he made several times what she did, and they couldn't afford him getting fired, but they were his kids too. He needed to act like a father once in a while.*

Caught up in her own thoughts, Goessel did not notice the police cruiser following her with its light flashing. It was only when the policeman briefly turned on the cruiser's siren that she realized she was speeding – and about to get a ticket.

She turned down the aptly named Travelers Lane, three blocks of fast food restaurants and the like, and began looking for a place to pull over. None of the fast food restaurant parking lots on either side of the street seemed suitable. *Just her luck, someone she knew would see the whole humiliating thing.*

When the cop turned his siren on again, she cursed and abruptly pulled into the next parking lot. After she did, she realized she had pulled into the parking lot of the Sleep Cheap Inn. *Only the worst possible place on the whole street.*

When she parked her car, the policeman turned the cruiser's siren off. Before searching her glove compartment for her registration papers, she glanced back at the police car and its occupant. *The cop*, she thought, *looked like he was twenty-something.* It was beyond annoying that some kid was about to give her a ticket and a lecture on speeding.

It was her too-busy-for-his-family husband's fault. If *he* had picked up Brittany, *she* wouldn't be getting a ticket.

9:06 A.M.– 9:09 A.M.

Assigned to patrol duty in the city's Fifth District, Cincinnati Police Department officer Eleanor Billington was making her way down McMillan Street when she saw the police cruiser turn into Travelers Lane with its siren on. She recognized the patrolman. He was Peter Browne. Tall, good-looking, handsome-in-his-uniform, no-wedding-band Peter Browne.

Billington flipped on her own siren and followed Browne's cruiser down the side street. She pulled into the parking lot of the hot sheets motel and parked alongside Browne's black and white.

Billington was almost thirty, which likely made her a few

years older than Browne. That might or might not rule out a long-term relationship, but since she had first met Browne, he had intrigued her. For the moment, however, she was just wondering if he would be available later for lunch. She turned her siren off and got out of her vehicle. Browne, she could see, was noting the license plate number of the red Mercedes and going through the usual protocols.

Billington gave Browne a big, flirtatious grin. "Thought you might need some backup," she greeted the good-looking, slightly younger cop. "She looks pretty dangerous to me."

Browne smiled. "I like my women dangerous."

9:09 A.M. – 9:16 A.M.

Emily Goessel saw the two officers chatting – and taking their time about it. She fumed as she watched the lady cop flirt with the patrolman. She was frustrated that there was nothing she could do about it – until it occurred to her that, actually, there *was* something she could do.

She pulled her cell phone from her purse, rolled down the car window, and ostentatiously began videoing the two officers. She knew her video wasn't going to be as sensational as all those videos of white police officers beating some black man while he lies on the street or sidewalk trying to cover his head. *But,* she told herself, *that wasn't the point.*

She figured once the cops saw her making a video of them chatting and flirting, they would hurry up and get this over with. *Who knew,* she thought, warming to the topic, *rather than have me email the video to their superiors or post it on the internet, maybe they will let me off with a warning?* As the two cops continued their conversation, she became more certain. *There was just no way they would want the world to know that a mother was delayed from picking up her sick child while they leisurely shot the breeze.*

The officers didn't notice.

Goessel tried to hold her cell phone steady, but it wasn't

as easy as it sounded.

And then, just because it was one of those days when nothing goes right, some jerks walked between her car and the police cars, inserting themselves into the video she was trying to make. They were two tough-looking Mexican men, a young Mexican woman, and her two small kids. Goessel had heard all sorts of rumors about the inn, from it being a transit point for drugs to being a favorite waystation for illegals. These people just seemed to confirm all the rumors she had heard.

Perfect, Goessel thought. Everybody knows this inn is nothing but trouble, and these two cops are so busy talking, a bunch of illegals go walking right by, and they don't even notice.

Her camera followed the Mexicans as they crowded into a worn-out, blue Honda and drove off. She turned her camera back in the direction of the police officers, but their conversation had ended.

As the young patrolman approached her car, Goessel kept her video running. She wanted to be sure the cop understood that she was not happy — and had him on video flirting with the female cop.

"Sorry for the delay, Ma'am," the young patrolman said.

His way, she supposed, of letting her know he could see what she was doing with the cell phone.

"My child is sick," Goessel said, reaching for the moral high ground. "The school called and said my daughter is very sick. They asked me to come and get her as soon as possible."

"I'm sorry to hear that, Ma'am, but —"

"My child is sick and crying and begging for her mother," Goessel asserted with no more exaggeration than she thought was her right, "and I'm sitting here while you have a gabfest with your cop friend. I want —"

"Ma'am," the young cop interrupted, "you were going well over the speed limit. Those speed limits are set to keep people safe. It wouldn't help your daughter if you had an accident and were seriously hurt or killed. Or if you injured or killed some other kid's mother."

"Oh, for Chrissake, no one had an accident, and no one's been injured or killed. I want you to know that —"

"Ma'am," the patrolman interrupted again. "I need to see your license, registration, and proof of insurance."

"I've been sitting here with them in my hand for five minutes," Goessel fired back, even though the actual time was not half that. It galled her no end that the patrolman wanted to see her papers, but ignored the illegals who had walked right by him.

She surrendered the papers to the patrolman. "I want you to know," she said, "that I'm going to make sure your superiors see my video of you and that woman officer taking your good time while my daughter is sick, begging for her mother."

"You do what you have to do, Ma'am," Browne responded. "Let's just get this done as quickly as we can, so you can get your daughter. I'm going to be right back."

Five minutes later, Goessel had her ticket and was on her way — mentally preparing for the day's next battle.

Just one word from the school-nurse busybody about vaccinations, she told herself, and she's going to wish she had minded her own business.

AFTERNOON

Devin Garner had not heard the news reports of the raid on the Heidelberg Sausage plant. And even if he had, on this day, he would not have paid those reports any attention.

He had his own problem. He was in the Hamilton County Courthouse in the midst of the trial of two young men — Jonas Trottel and an immigrant kid, Pablo Sanchez. Both were nineteen years old, and one of them, Jonas Trottel, was his client. An old gasbag, Weary Dunston, represented the other kid.

The prosecution charged the pair with stealing a gun from the owner of a hole-in-the-wall convenience store in Lower Price Hill, the neighborhood where both kids lived and where Garner had his office.

Lower Price Hill was a depressed area, long populated by folks from Appalachia, who migrated to Cincinnati during and after World War II for jobs. In recent years, however, the neighborhood was changing, as blacks and Hispanics migrated in, and descendants of that earlier generation of Appalachians migrated out. The hillside community was close to the downtown business and entertainment areas, but thus far, its high crime rate had stymied sporadic efforts at gentrifying the neighborhood.

Garner had located his office there out of a desire to do well by doing good. Defending a kid like Jonas Trottel was part of that commitment. Mrs. Trottel, the kid's mother, had asked him to help her son but could not afford his usual rates. He had agreed to represent Jonas for the pittance the state would pay him if he were court-appointed counsel, and then he had even discounted that.

Devin Garner was a stark contrast to his client. Just shy of six foot, he had unruly, curly blonde hair and the lanky body of a runner. His navy suit fit his frame well, and a new, sky-blue silk tie stood out against his crisp white shirt. But his most noticeable features were the intense blue eyes that suggested a keen intelligence and the quick and mischievous smile that made him immediately likable.

At five-foot-four, Jonas Trottel was short and pudgy, and his gaze seemed to dart about in a perpetual state of confusion. Mrs. Trottel had somehow found the money to buy her son a white shirt, and Garner had given Jonas a tie, but along with the white shirt and tie, Jonas had worn Dockers and sneakers to court. Sartorial matters, however, were the least of the problems Jonas Trottel presented as a client.

His IQ was not low enough for him to escape criminal responsibility, but he was clearly more than a little "slow."

As a result, Jonas was not much help in his own defense. Garner wasn't even sure Jonas fully understood the peril he was in. A kid like him wouldn't fare well in prison, and a felony conviction would bar him for life from government programs he might need when his mother could no longer help him.

His codefendant, Pablo Sanchez, lived in the Nuestras Casas Housing Co-Op, three blocks down the street from where she and Jonas lived. He was new to the neighborhood and spoke little English, making him not much help either. Both kids insisted they hadn't taken or even seen the store-owner's gun.

The prosecution itself was a simple affair. The prosecution would present just two witnesses, Enoch Tate, the store owner, and the police officer who made the arrest. Ordinarily, the police officer would testify first, but he was testifying in a drug case in another courtroom.

***

Liz O'Malley, the newest Assistant Prosecuting Attorney for Hamilton County, was at the podium leading the storeowner through the details of the theft. She was in her first year out of law school and handling the trial by the book. Tall and gangly with long black hair, she wore heavy eyeglasses and dark suits that made her look both professional and concerned about being taken seriously.

The witness, Enoch Tate, was a short wiry man, who spoke with a bit of an Appalachian accent. He testified that Jonas and the "Mexican" kid entered his store just as he got a phone call. "I turned my back just one damn second," he complained, "to check something on the wall behind me, and when I turned back around, Jonas and that Mexican kid were gone. And so was my gun."

"Where was your gun before it disappeared?" O'Malley asked.

"Well, see, like a damn fool, I'd left it right there on the counter where they could grab it." His face twisted in disgust.

"What, if anything," O'Malley asked, her wording a model of direct examination, "did you do when you realized your gun was missing?"

"I called 9-1-1," Tate said, shaking his head at how dense O'Malley was. "I'm sick and tired of people stealing from me. What the hell was I supposed to do?"

Garner smiled as O'Malley struggled not to react. He'd had his own share of difficult witnesses and could empathize.

"Was this right after the defendants disappeared from your store?"

"Of course," Tate said. He looked around, as if hoping to find someone who knew what they were doing ready to take over the prosecution. "I wasn't gonna wait till they came back and stole the rest of my store."

Garner was on his feet before Tate had that final sentence out of his mouth. "Objection, Your Honor," he said in a loud voice. "Nonresponsive and prejudicial. Move to strike."

Judge Seiler glanced at O'Malley. When she didn't respond, he said, "Sustained. The jury will disregard the witness's last statement."

"It might help," Garner said, "if Your Honor were to instruct the witness to confine his answers to the questions counsel asks." He was sympathetic to the problems the witness presented O'Malley, but he had his own job to do, and part of that job was to throw O'Malley and the witness off stride if the opportunity presented itself.

Judge Seiler instructed the witness to limit his answers to the questions asked by counsel, but his resigned tone of voice suggested that he didn't share Garner's view that it might help.

O'Malley dealt as best she could with a topic defense

counsel were sure to raise on cross. The police had arrested the kids a short distance from his store. Neither kid had the gun, and both denied taking it. She asked Tate if he ever got his gun back.

Tate shook his head and said, "No, and that gun cost me $500."

O'Malley had Tate identify the receipt showing what he paid for the gun and moved the receipt's admission into evidence.

Garner didn't object. Neither did Weary Dunston, the attorney appointed by the court to represent Pablo Sanchez.

With that, O'Malley returned to counsel table and said, "Defense witness."

Garner stood to cross-examine Tate, but so did Dunston. Garner wanted to conduct his cross-examination first, before the long-winded Dunston tried everyone's patience. Ignoring Dunston, Garner picked up his trial notebook to take it with him to the podium.

Weary Dunston complained. "Mr. Garner," he said, "if you don't mind, I think I should go first. My client is the first-named defendant, and as you know—"

"Weary," Garner interrupted, "I think I can shorten this if you'll let me—"

Dunston stepped in front of counsel table. "I'm the more experienced attorney here," he said in a voice easily loud enough for the jurors to hear. "I think, young man, if you observe, you just might learn something."

"But Weary," Garner began. "I —"

Dunston turned and "accidentally" knocked over the water bottle on the table in front of where Garner had been sitting. The bottle rolled across the table and dropped onto the floor. "Sorry, sorry, my bad," Dunston said, but when Garner bent over to pick up the bottle, Dunston made his way to the podium.

Garner shook his head in disbelief. He sat back down and resigned himself to watch the show. He did not know how Dunston had come by the nickname Weary, but it fit. The old man's eyelids drooped, the bags under his eyes fell in folds, and creases lined his long face. A certain lassitude suggested he had seen and heard it all. In a word, he looked weary. But a longstanding courthouse legend attributed the moniker to a well-known judge. In that account, early in Dunston's career, the judge grumbled that Dunston's long-winded oratory made judges and juries weary, and the label stuck.

For thirty minutes, between bouts of intense, chest-rattling coughing, Dunston cross-examined the store owner. Among other things, Dunston's questions seized on a statement in the police report that Tate had blamed the theft on an "alien." After showing Tate the police report, Dunston demanded that Tate admit he had told the police a space alien had taken his gun.

Tate responded with indignation. "That's horse pucky! I never said nothing about space aliens. I said that boy was a foreigner. The cop must have put that down as 'alien.' You know, like in the post office, where they say aliens have to register."

"Isn't it a fact," Dunston persisted, "that you thought the thief was a space alien?"

Garner winced. The question was stupid, but it was just the sort of thing he had been afraid Dunston would come up with.

"No, but your client ain't from around here that's for sure," Tate said. "He lives down there in that New Ass Tacos Co-Op. He's probably one of them illegals. Wouldn't surprise me none if he were a drug dealer or something."

Dunston moved to strike the outburst as non-responsive.

Judge Seiler granted the motion and once again instructed the witness to confine his responses to the question asked.

Unwilling to give up on his line of questioning, Dunston

asked if Tate thought his client's co-defendant, Jonas Trottel, was an "alien" from outer space.

"Might be," Tate allowed. "From Planet Stupid."

Another paroxysm of coughing overcame Weary Dunston.

When Dunston recovered, Judge Seiler, who had limited Dunston to thirty minutes for his cross-examination, suggested that Dunston give Garner an opportunity to question the witness. Judge Seiler said that might allow Dunston an opportunity to get his breath, but as he said this, he repeatedly clicked the ballpoint pen in his hand open and shut. It was obvious to Garner that Dunston had irked the normally patient judge.

"Precisely, precisely," Dunston said, as if the suggestion had been his own idea.

As Dunston sat down, Garner glanced at the jurors. The expressions on their faces had turned from bored to irritated. He suspected they would be even more irritated when he finished his cross, but for a different reason.

***

Garner had been solicitous of the courthouse staff from his first day as an attorney. He knew each by name. He unfailingly asked not only how they were, but how their sick spouse was doing or how their grandchild was getting along in school. His interest had been genuine – he liked the folks who worked in the courthouse. They did their thankless jobs well for too little pay and were every bit like the folks he'd grown up with.

Today, all that had paid off.

Before Enoch Tate had taken the witness stand, Scott Greene, the bailiff assigned to Judge Seiler's courtroom, had shared with Garner an interesting bit of news. Tate had brought a gun with him to the courthouse. Security was holding it.

"It's not the gun he claims my client stole from him, is

it?" Garner asked.

Greene had shrugged and checked his watch. It was time to call the courtroom back to order.

Garner asked a favor of Greene.

Greene had agreed but stood and motioned for Garner to take his place, cutting off any further discussion.

***

Now, as Garner moved to the podium, he glanced at the bailiff, and when he had his attention, nodded. Greene picked up his phone and dialed a number.

Garner turned his attention to the witness. "Mr. Tate, my name is Devin Garner. I'm counsel for Jonas Trottel. My office is in Lower Price Hill. I'm not sure you remember me, but I've been in your store a bunch of times."

Tate folded his arms and glared at Garner.

"If it helps, Mr. Tate," Garner said, "I promise to be brief."

Enoch Tate continued to glare at Garner, but Garner ignored the hostility. He had meant the comment for the jury anyway.

"Mr. Tate," Garner began his direct, "as you know, when the police caught up with Jonas and Pablo a short distance from your store, they didn't have your gun." Garner used the boys' first names, instead of calling them "the defendants," to remind the jurors they were kids, not abstractions.

Tate unfolded his arms and frowned, but said nothing.

"Is it possible, sir," Garner asked, "that you didn't leave your gun where you thought you did, that you simply mislaid your gun, and these boys didn't steal it?"

Tate puffed himself up and spat out his answer. "I ain't saying I made a false report to the police. I ain't fixin' to go to jail just to save your stupid client."

Garner tried a different approach. "After the police arrested Jonas and Pablo, did you find your gun?"

Tate folded his arms again.

When the witness didn't answer, Garner repeated his question.

Anger contorted Tate's face. He looked at the jury and shook his head in disgust and said, "No."

Garner heard someone entering the courtroom. He glanced behind him. A deputy sheriff made his way forward, a small security bag in his hand.

"Your Honor," Garner said, "a moment please."

The deputy sheriff entered the area in the front of the court reserved for the parties, counsel, and court officials. He went straight to the bailiff's desk.

Greene removed a gun from the security bag and examined it. He checked something in his records and then looked at Garner and nodded. The deputy put the gun back in the security bag.

Garner, a sly smile on his face, turned his attention back to the witness. "Mr. Tate, did you bring a gun with you this morning, when you came to the courthouse?"

Tate raised his chin and said, "What if I did?"

Judge Seiler spoke. "Mr. Tate, just answer the question, and we'll all get through this quicker."

"Did you," Garner repeated, "bring a gun with you to the courthouse this morning?"

Tate glared at Garner for a long moment before saying, "You bet I did. Ain't safe around here."

"When you got to security, they took custody of your gun while you're inside the courthouse?"

"That's their job."

"Your Honor," Garner said, "I request permission for the deputy sheriff to approach the witness."

Looking at the deputy, Judge Seiler said, "Please state your name for the record."

"Deputy Sheriff Peter Workman, Your Honor."

"You're on the security detail assigned to the court?"

"Yes, Your Honor," Workman said, standing erect, his

brown uniform crisp. "Not usually. Just today."

Judge Seiler looked at Garner and said, "Proceed."

"Deputy Workman," Garner said, "if you would be so kind as to give Mr. Tate his gun."

The deputy carefully removed the gun from the security bag, removed the gun's magazine, and checked to be sure a round was not chambered. He then handed the gun to the witness.

Enoch Tate took the gun and examined it.

"Mr. Tate," Garner said, "please read the gun's serial number, so we have that for the record."

Tate found the number and read it.

Garner jotted the number down in his trial notebook next to the serial number of the gun his client had supposedly stolen from the store. Garner asked Tate to read the number again, slower, "to be sure the court reporter got it correctly."

Tate read the number again.

Garner checked his own notation to be sure he'd gotten it down right. He had. He tried to suppress another smile, but couldn't. He looked up at the witness and asked, "Is that your gun? The one the deputy sheriff took custody of when you entered the courthouse?"

Tate adjusted himself uneasily in the wooden witness chair. He glared at Garner and said, "Looks like it."

"The prosecutor, Ms. O'Malley, gave you a copy of the receipt for the gun you allege someone stole from you, Prosecution Exhibit 12. Can you find it there in front of you?"

Tate shuffled through the papers in front of him and found the exhibit.

Garner glanced around the portion of the courtroom inside the bar. The jurors were watching him to see where he was going with this. Judge Seiler had stopped working on the papers on his desk and was paying attention. Scott Greene had laid aside his crossword puzzle and had a smile on his face. Liz O'Malley, the prosecutor, wasn't smiling.

She tossed her pen down and crossed her arms.

"Mr. Tate, for the record," Garner said, "would you read from that receipt the serial number of the gun someone allegedly stole from you."

As Tate read the number, Garner looked again at the number in his trial notebook, the number he'd copied from the exhibit and put there before the trial. He returned his attention to Tate.

"The serial number on the gun the deputy sheriff took from you today and the serial number on the gun you say someone stole from you are the same," Garner said. "Isn't that right?"

Tate's face reddened and his body tensed. "So what?"

"So, the gun you brought with you today is the same gun you claim my client stole from you?"

"You heard me read the serial numbers."

Garner gave the jurors a knowing glance, as if he and they had a shared secret. "Yes or no, Mr. Tate. Is the gun you brought with you today the same gun you say Jonas and Pablo stole from you?"

Tate rubbed his nose and stared at Garner before answering. "They must have got scared and returned it to the store after the police arrested them."

"Where did you find it?"

Tate raised his hand in front of his mouth. "I don't remember."

"You have a security camera in your store?" Garner asked.

Tate folded his arms and glared at Garner again.

"Did the security camera show these boys stealing your gun?"

Tate looked down and mumbled, "No."

Garner made Tate repeat his answer so the jury could hear his response. He paused a moment to let the answer sink in before asking, "Did the security camera catch these boys returning your gun?"

Tate stuck out his chin in defiance. "It don't see every-thing."

"Mr. Tate," Garner said, "the truth is, these boys didn't steal your gun and then risk sneaking back into that little, tiny store of yours to return it. The truth is, you mislaid it and mistakenly thought they took it. Isn't that right?"

"You want the truth?" Tate said, his voice loud and belligerent. "The truth is, we don't need no illegal aliens in this country, and we sure as hell don't need them in this neighborhood."

One of the jurors shook her head in disbelief.

Garner closed his trial notebook on the podium, a signal to the jury he was wrapping up. "Mr. Tate," he said, "you found your gun shortly after you reported what you thought was a theft to the police?"

Tate rubbed the stubble on his face and hesitated. "I ain't implicating myself in making a false report to the police. I ain't gonna get myself arrested."

Judge Seiler cleared his throat.

Garner waited to see what the judge was about to say.

"Mr. Tate," Judge Seiler said, "no one is going to arrest you for making a false report if you honestly believed what you told the police, even if you were mistaken."

The witness rubbed his stubble again. His hand was short and arthritic.

"Do you suppose it's possible," Judge Seiler asked, "that you mislaid your gun and you were mistaken when you told the police someone stole it?"

Enoch Tate hesitated and rubbed his leg before responding, "Yeah, maybe."

"'Yeah, maybe,'" Judge Seiler prodded, "as in, 'Yeah, you probably just mislaid your gun and the defendants didn't actually steal it?' Or as in, 'Anything's possible. For all you know, maybe little green men from Outer Space took your gun'?"

"If them space things was little green men," Tate grumbled, "that damn security camera would catch them. They must be invisible or something."

"Mr. Tate," Judge Seiler repeated, "do you think you were mistaken?"

As Garner watched, Tate seemed to deflate, like a punctured tire going flat. After hesitating for several moments, Tate turned to look at the judge and said, "Yeah, maybe."

Judge Seiler looked at Ms. O'Malley. "Is the prosecution willing to dismiss?"

O'Malley stood and removed her glasses. "Yes, Your Honor," she said. "The prosecution moves for dismissal of the charges."

She shot an angry look at Garner. It was the third time he'd bested her in court.

Judge Seiler turned to defense counsel and said, "So ordered. I'm dismissing the charges."

Weary Dunston jumped to his feet. "Thank you, Your Honor, for bringing this travesty to a speedy conclusion. If I may say so, Your Honor—"

"Save it," Judge Seiler snapped. He turned to the jury and began the usual little speech he gave to thank and dismiss jurors.

As Judge Seiler went about that, Garner returned to counsel table and whispered to his client. "Jonas, we won. You're not going to jail."

Jonas didn't smile or look happy. "Can you tell the Judge," he asked Garner, "that I'm not from Planet Stupid?"

"He knows," Garner said.

FRIDAY, OCTOBER 16

6:00 P.M. NEWS

Queen City News Live: Bringing you the news you want to hear.

News Anchor Bob Bunker: Hamilton County Prosecutor Richard Warren held a press conference this afternoon to discuss this morning's raid on the Heidelberg Sausage plant in Queensgate. Sheriff's deputies arrested 76 individuals suspected of being in the country illegally. [Video shows police hauling away computers and boxes of documents.] Tiffany Albern has this report.

Tiffany Albern: Thank you, Bob. I'm at the William Howard Taft Center, where Hamilton County Prosecutor Richard Warren just held a press conference. Warren described Heidelberg Sausage as an "egregious violator" of U.S. immigration laws. He said his office would pursue criminal charges against the company and its officials if it finds evidence of fraud, falsification of documents, or other crimes. Here's some of what Warren had to say:

Video Clip Plays, Warren speaking: We're going to look wherever the evidence takes us. No one gets a free pass. I hope this raid sends a message to other employers. In this county, you can't ignore the law and go unscathed.

Tiffany Albern: In response to questions, Warren said that federal immigration agents were not involved in the raid and were not informed in advance. Warren added that if his office determined any workers arrested at the plant were undocumented, it would turn them over to ICE – Immigration and Customs Enforcement – to be deported.

I asked Warren if employers should expect more raids.

Video clip plays, Warren speaking: Yes, absolutely. If we find evidence of illegals in our community, we're going to take action. Like I said, we can't have these people taking jobs from decent, hard-working Americans, and we can't have them selling drugs, committing violent crimes, and what have you. The American taxpayer is tired of paying taxes to support those people.

News Anchor Bob Bunker: Tiffany, we've heard reports that demonstrators tried to interrupt Warren's remarks.

Tiffany Albern: That's right, Bob. A group of immigrant-rights protesters briefly interrupted the press conference. They unfurled a banner reading, "No human life is illegal." Deputy Sheriffs escorted the protestors from the building.

News Anchor Bob Bunker: A nineteen-year-old immigrant, Pablo Sanchez, won acquittal today in the Hamilton County Court of Common Pleas on charges of stealing a gun from a convenience store in Lower Price Hill. But as he left the courthouse, Immigration and Customs Enforcement agents were waiting and took him into custody for deportation proceedings. A spokesperson for the local ICE office said Sanchez was in the country illegally.

Co-Anchor Ashley Gelb: Cincinnati's Over the Rhine neighborhood is changing quickly. After the break, we have a special report on how much it costs to live there now.

FRIDAY – SATURDAY, OCTOBER 16 - 17

5:00 P.M. – 2:30 A.M.

At home, Rafiq Medawar took a sleeping pill and slept through the day, waking around dinner time. Ann was not home when he woke. Medawar was not all that surprised – Ann kept busy and often tried to stay out of the house when he had to sleep. He took a shower and tried to revive himself.

At 5:45, Ann was still not home. He tried to reach her on her cell, to touch base and find out when to expect her. Ann didn't answer. That was unlike her, but at first, he didn't think anything of it. He sent her a text, checked his own email, and began looking for something he could fix for the two of them for supper.

Half an hour later, he tried Ann again and still got no answer. He left another voicemail. He looked around the usual places for a note from Ann. He found none. He was concerned.

By 7:00, he was worried and called Ann's sister, Kate, but she had not heard from Ann. He called Ann's parents and spoke to her mother. She had not spoken with Ann all day.

At 7:30, he tried Ann's cell again but again got no answer. He left a voicemail letting Ann know he was worried. He double checked his cell for messages or voicemail. He found nothing.

He called Carolyn "Carrie" Hixson, Ann's partner on her documentary film project. Best friends, the two had talked incessantly since beginning work on their documentary. She too had been trying to reach Ann without success.

Calls to several more of Ann's friends turned up nothing.

Medawar called Ann's sister and parents again. They

hadn't heard anything, but with this second call, they were now worried too.

He checked news reports for major traffic accidents or anything else that might provide a clue. He called the Trauma Center. She was not a patient, and no one had seen her.

He couldn't imagine anything happening to Ann, but when he had still not heard from her by nine that evening, he called the Cincinnati Police to report Ann missing. He was impatient with the irrelevant questions. His answers were unnecessarily abrupt and testy.

Not convinced the police were taking his report seriously, he decided to press the issue. Leaving a note on the kitchen table telling Ann he was worried about her and asking her to call him the minute she got home, he headed to the Trauma Center.

At 9:30 p.m., when he got there, the evening's first gunshot victim had already arrived. As the victim headed into surgery, Medawar introduced himself to the police officers who followed the victim to the Trauma Center. He asked for their help.

The cops made a few calls and assured him that officers were being sent to the Sleep Cheap Inn and that other steps were underway to locate Ann.

He continued to watch for Ann at the Trauma Center. As the hours passed, he began to despair. He wanted news but dreaded what he would learn.

At 2:30 a.m., fearing the worst, he left for home.

SATURDAY, OCTOBER 17

9:30 A.M. – 11:30 A.M.

The knock on the front door came at 9:38 a.m.

Two Cincinnati Police Department detectives asked Rafiq Medawar if they could come in. In a direct and dignified way, they broke the news that his wife was dead. Her body had been found at the overlook in Eden Park. The officers explained that her wallet and cell-phone had been found on her body. There were no obvious signs of sexual assault.

"How?" Medawar asked. "How did she die?"

"She was shot," Detective James Chilton said. "It appears death would have been instantaneous."

Medawar hesitated a long moment before saying anything. When Ann hadn't come home, he had braced himself for terrible news. As a Trauma Center surgeon, he had had to deliver bad news to the families of whose loved ones had died suddenly. But still, he was having trouble accepting what the officers were saying.

"You have to forgive me," he said finally. "This is hard to absorb. Ann is the most vital, loving, giving person I have ever known. I'm having trouble believing something like this could have happened to her."

"Do you know anyone who might have wanted to harm your wife?"

"No, Ann's not that kind of person. Everybody loved her."

"When did you last see your wife?"

"Yesterday morning, about 9:00."

"Was that here?"

"No, at the Sleep Cheap Inn in Clifton."

Detective Chilton and the officer accompanying him exchanged glances. "What were you doing there?" Chilton asked.

Medawar briefly explained the reasons for their visit to the inn.

"Did you talk with your wife after that?" the detective probed.

"I worked the night shift," Medawar replied, "and as soon as I left the woman and her kids, I headed home to get some sleep. The hotel manager had hassled Ann about taking pictures, and she offered to pay him. I gave her some cash, and as I was leaving, she was headed inside to pay him. When she didn't come home, I reported her missing."

"We need you to go to the morgue and confirm the identification," the detective said, offering Medawar a brochure that explained the procedure and provided directions to the morgue.

When the police officers left, Medawar called Ann's parents and repeated what the police had just told him. He spoke with Ace Lindsey, Ann's father, and promised to call back as soon as he left the morgue.

Mr. Lindsey insisted that he and Mrs. Lindsey would meet him there.

The procedure at the morgue was like something out of a television drama. Ann's lifeless body, covered only with a white sheet, lay in a refrigerated drawer in the morgue. He and the Lindseys quickly confirmed that *yes, this was the body of Ann Lindsey Medawar.*

Only one thing didn't follow the script: Mr. and Mrs. Lindsey were as cold as the morgue itself. Rafiq Medawar had never been close to Ann's parents, but they had always been cordial. He did not know if their reaction was how they dealt with something like this, or if they somehow blamed him for Ann's death.

He tried not to think about that. He also tried not to think about what lay ahead. But he knew that Ann's body — her cadaver — would remain in the refrigerated drawer until

Monday morning. Then, a pathologist would carefully examine the bullet wounds in her chest and head, before examining her body's other orifices. He would cut a Y-shaped slit in her torso and remove and weigh her organs. He would saw off the top of her skull and remove her brain and weigh it.

When his work was done, the pathologist would record his findings in a report written in language as sterile as the steel instruments in the autopsy room.

The autopsy report would not mention the white sheet that had covered the once vibrant woman's body as it lay in the refrigerated drawer over the weekend. The report would also not mention the stunning white dress Ann wore on the day she and Rafiq first met, or the beautiful, white wedding gown she wore at their wedding. Nor would it mention the white roses Rafiq had given her each year on their anniversary.

It would also not mention her husband or say that this was the worst day in his life.

11:30 A.M. – 12:05 P.M.

"It's Saturday, guys. This better be important," Hamilton County Prosecutor Richard Warren bellowed to the trio waiting in his office.

Decorated in a style that might be called "20th century legal," his office was lined on three sides with bookcases filled with old legal volumes. The wall behind his desk was the exception. It was his vanity wall, covered with awards and pictures of Warren with various notables.

Warren settled into the oxblood-leather executive chair behind his expansive, dark-cherry desk – the desk the morning newspaper described as "not as large as an aircraft carrier." Three individuals – his top two aides and a police detective – were sitting before his desk in stiff-backed chairs.

"Boss, the police found the body of Ann Lindsey Medawar this morning," Assistant Prosecutor William Bradford said. "Shot to death, two bullets, point blank range."

Bradford was the office's most seasoned trial attorney and heir apparent to Warren if, as everyone expected, Warren ran for Congress and won. One of the few African-Americans in a leadership role in Hamilton County, Bradford was forty-years-old, tall, handsome, smart and ambitious.

"She's Ace Lindsey's kid?" Warren asked, referring to the wealthy and politically powerful Cincinnati businessman, whose backing or opposition could make or break a Cincinnati politician's career.

"That's right, Dick," Pam Sprecher, his press liaison, chimed in. "She was pretty well known around town – well liked. I've actually met her a couple times. She moved in all the right circles – something of an activist. This is going to be all over the news."

"Do we know who did it?" Warren asked.

"Too early," Bradford said.

"Okay, okay, what do we know so far?"

"Boss, this is Detective Jim Chilton. He's leading the investigation. I thought he could brief all of us."

"Chilton?" Warren repeated.

"Yes, sir," the detective responded.

"Nice to meet you. What do you have?"

"Her husband reported his wife missing last night," Chilton said. "He said he last saw her at the Sleep Cheap Inn in Clifton. That was Friday morning, about 9:00 a.m.

"This morning," Chilton continued, "joggers found her body at the overlook in Eden Park. Somebody dumped it there, and like I said, joggers found it there early this morning. We're waiting for the time of death from the Coroner's office, but sometime yesterday or very early this morning."

Chilton flipped a page in his notebook before continuing. "She still had her wallet and cell phone, so it doesn't look like a robbery. Her car is missing, which means we can't rule out a hijacking. Again, we're waiting for a report from the Coroner's office, but it doesn't look like sexual assault either."

"She was at the Sleep Cheap Inn?" Warren said, shaking his head. "I know that place. It's a dump, lot of Mexicans, drugs, prostitution, what have you. It should have been shut down years ago. What the hell was she doing there?"

"Her husband says she was making a documentary," Chilton said. "Something to do with illegals."

"If I can jump in," Sprecher, the press liaison said, getting up from her chair. "Dick, the police found some video on her cell phone you need to see. Detective Chilton had their forensics person email it to me."

Sprecher, an attractive woman in her mid-thirties, placed her laptop on Warren's desk so he could see it.

"In this video," she said, "there are two individuals entering the inn. The man is Ann's husband. He's a surgeon, works at the Trauma Center. The woman is a nurse. Filipino, I think. The nurse apparently works at the Trauma Center too.

"Here's the next video," Sprecher continued. "This is Ann's husband and the nurse leaving the inn sometime later."

"So, her husband's a surgeon, and he goes to a hot-sheets motel with a nurse," Warren summarized, chuckling. "That's a story we've all heard before. His wife follows him, or was waiting there for him, and she catches the son of a bitch on video going into this place and coming back out a while later?"

"That's what it looks like," Sprecher agreed.

"Who's the husband? What do we know about him?"

"His name's Rafiq Medawar," Sprecher said. "His family's from Lebanon or Syria. I've heard rumors the Lindseys weren't happy about Ann marrying him."

"If he's a Muslim," Warren said, "I'm sure Ace Lindsey was none too happy."

Warren glanced at his wristwatch. "Basically," he said,

searching for the bottom line, "it looks like her husband and a hot little Filipino nurse went to this inn for some extra-curricular activities. The jealous wife gets him on video going into this place with the nurse. She hangs around, films him again when he leaves. He sees her there, or she confronts him later. Her husband's some kind of Middle East-erner, Syrian or whatever, and he doesn't put up with that from a woman. He goes nuts and kills her.

"Yeah, Christ Almighty," Warren concluded, "this is going to be *all* over the goddam news."

Detective Chilton spoke up. "Mr. Warren, if I may, Dr. Medawar says he went to this place to check on a Mexican woman, an illegal. He says this nurse wanted him to check on the woman's kids, to make sure they didn't have cholera or something."

"Anything to back that up?" Warren asked.

"We haven't found the nurse yet," Detective Chilton replied. "She's not answering her phone, but we're still working on that."

"She'll back him up, of course," Warren groused. "Do your best to find her, but she'll be a waste of time."

Detective Chilton looked at his notes and continued. "I talked with Diego Olivar, the guy who manages the inn. Of course, he denies that there are any illegals there. He says it's not the kind of place that attracts families with kids."

"He's lying about the illegals," Warren said, "but he's got a point about it not being a family-friendly place. Anything else?"

"We haven't found the gun yet. We're just getting started, so that's about all I have so far."

"Keep up the good work, Detective," Warren said as if reading from a bad script. "Let's get a search warrant and see if we can find the gun or anything else useful in the husband's car or home. I'm going to call Ace and offer condolences. I'll promise him that we're going to be all over this, so keep me updated. And guys, we can't let the press get out ahead of us on this thing. Let's stay focused."

Turning back to Bradford, he added, "Bill, I want you to handle this case personally. Okay? You can have any help you need, but I want *you* on this."

Bradford acknowledged the assignment.

As people rose to leave, Warren barked one last instruction. "Hey, let's figure out how to shut down that goddam inn. Can we do that, *please?*"

3:30 P.M. – 6:30 P.M.

Devin Garner was still in his office at 3:30 Saturday afternoon when his cell phone signaled he had a call – it played the opening music from Law & Order. When he answered, he heard a familiar voice with an unexpected message.

"Devin, it's Rafiq Medawar. Someone has killed Ann. Shot her and dumped her body in Eden Park. The police are at my house now with a search warrant."

Garner was stunned to learn that Ann had been killed, but forced himself to remain professional.

"Did you let them in?"

"Yes, I told them they could search the whole house, I have nothing to hide."

"They're searching the house now?"

"Yeah," Medawar said. "But while I was standing here watching them, it occurred to me – maybe I screwed up. I should have called you."

"No, you did the right thing. If they have a search warrant, you have to let them do their jobs. And you don't want to give them the impression you're trying to hide anything."

"Good, because they wanted to test my hands for gunpowder residue, and I let them."

"That's fine too. Maybe it'll help convince them you're not the shooter."

"I can't believe they think I killed Ann."

"They may just be trying to eliminate you as a suspect. When they catch who did this, they don't want him saying the police didn't explore the possibility the husband did it."

"It doesn't feel right."

"I'm going to leave now and come over to your place. Let the cops do their search, but don't discuss Ann's death with the police until I get there. If they want to interview you, tell them that's fine, but I insisted you wait until I get there."

...

Garner had met Medawar when they had been among the twenty-five or so individuals who participated in the previous year's Leadership Cincinnati program. As in similar programs in many cities, they and the others chosen for the program had participated in a series of all-day events, spread over several months. During those sessions, they got a crash course on the issues facing the city from public officials, business executives, and nonprofit leaders. They also spent time working together at a homeless shelter and on other projects.

He and Medawar had quickly become friends. Not close friends, but he and a date had gone to dinner with Rafiq and Ann, and he and Rafiq had gone hiking together a couple times. Mainly, however, they had stayed in touch through Facebook and the occasional lunch.

In light traffic, it took Garner only about fifteen minutes to reach his friend's home. The house was an old Tudor-style home on a tree-lined street in Hyde Park, a neighborhood on Cincinnati's east side favored by professionals. As Garner approached the house, he could see several Cincinnati Police Department vehicles parked in front of the home. He also noticed several neighbors discretely monitoring events.

Garner chatted briefly with Medawar, again offering his condolences, before turning his attention to the team conducting the search.

Garner introduced himself to the lead officer and gave

him his business card.

"We've already met," the officer said, his expression belligerent. "Detective James Chilton, if you don't remember."

Garner flashed a smile of recognition. Some months previously, he had gotten the better of the detective during cross-examination. Obviously, the detective hadn't forgotten.

After a brief discussion, Garner returned to Medawar and pulled him outside.

"Do you or Ann own a gun?" Garner asked.

"No. You met Ann. No way!"

"Neither of you have a gun registered in your name, even if you no longer have it?" Garner probed.

"No, never."

"I'll let them know."

Garner returned to Detective Chilton. "I've talked to my client, and he says neither he nor Ann own a gun."

"If they don't own any guns," Chilton said, "then I think we're about done here."

"I will need an inventory of everything you took," Garner said.

The detective glared contemptuously at Garner.

Garner refused to back down. Instead, he smiled and offered to make coffee for the detective.

Chilton snorted. "I'll have someone get the inventory for you," he said.

When Chilton and the other officers left, Medawar asked the obvious question. "Do they think I killed Ann?"

"The cops who were here?" Garner asked, hoping to deflect the question. "They're just doing their job."

"Somebody had to send them here."

"You're the husband," Garner said. "Somebody downtown may suspect you of killing Ann. There's no way to know, but for now, we have to assume they think you may have killed Ann."

"That's stupid. I told them what happened."

"Look, I could be wrong," Garner said. "Maybe they're just being methodical, so no one can criticize them later for not considering all the possibilities. But for now, we have to assume they want to pin this on you, close this case out, and move on to the next one."

Medawar protested again that it would be idiotic for the police to focus on him instead of trying to find the real killer.

Garner let his friend blow off steam for a while, before talking him down and forcing him to come to grips with the fact that, for the moment at least, the cops might well be working on the assumption that he killed Ann.

"That's stupid," Medawar insisted. "I loved Ann, I would never hurt her. They're not going to prosecute me for something I didn't do."

Garner delivered The Lecture. It's the lecture defense attorneys always give. "Whether or not the government prosecutes, or a jury convicts, doesn't turn on guilt or innocence," he explained. "It turns on the available, admissible evidence."

"In some ways," Garner explained, "a mobster who can produce three witnesses to say he was beating them at poker when the crime occurred may be better off than an innocent man who was at home alone, sound asleep."

He and Medawar had even had this discussion before when it had merely been an abstract discussion about Garner's job as criminal defense counsel.

"You just gave me 'The Lecture,'" Medawar said.

Garner smiled.

Not tonight, but sometime, he would explain to Medawar that the criminal justice process was actually more complex and uncertain than The Lecture implied. Judges and juries filter evidence through their own experiences, beliefs, and prejudices. They believe testimony and evidence consistent with their preconceived views, and — unless the evidence is overwhelming — disbelieve evidence that runs counter to their preconceptions. But without exculpatory evidence, things could get simple quickly. As simple as a prison cell.

Garner laid a yellow pad on a Medawar's kitchen table and removed a pen from his shirt pocket.

"The first thing we have to do," he said, "is identify any evidence that may be available right now, but that might not be available later. Physical evidence that might get thrown away. Records that might be deleted. Memories that might fade."

Medawar slumped into another of the kitchen chairs.

Garner asked his friend to recount everything he could recall from the day before.

SATURDAY, OCTOBER 17

6:00 P.M. NEWS

Queen City News Live: Bringing you the news you want to hear.

News Anchor Bob Bunker: Our lead story tonight: Cincinnati Police are investigating the murder of Ann Lindsey Medawar. Ms. Medawar, whose family is well known in Cincinnati, was an activist in several causes. Tiffany Albern is on the scene and has this report.

Tiffany Albern: Thank you, Bob. As you can see, I'm here in front of the Sleep Cheap Inn in Clifton. Ann Lindsey Medawar was last seen here yesterday morning. Joggers found her body this morning in Eden Park. Police officers told me she had been shot twice at close range. She does not appear to have been the victim of a robbery or sexual assault.

Her husband, Dr. Rafiq Medawar, reported her missing last night. He claims he last saw his wife here yesterday morning at about nine o'clock. Dr. Medawar is a surgeon at the Trauma Center.

According to the statement he gave Cincinnati Police, Dr. Medawar claims he came here to check on the sick children of an undocumented woman. He told police that a nurse who works with him at the Trauma Center asked him to check on the children. He says his wife is working on a documentary about illegal immigrants. He claims she met him here hoping to make a video for her project.

Police sources tell us that they have reviewed videos that Ms. Medawar made here yesterday morning. They show her husband and a nurse entering the inn and then leaving together some time later. The videos do not show the mother, her children, or *any* undocumented immigrants.

Police say they cannot rule out the possibility that Dr.

Medawar and the nurse were here a for a sexual liaison. Police theorize that Ms. Medawar suspected her husband of infidelity and followed him from the hospital to the inn, without his knowledge.

I spoke with Diego Olivar, the manager of the Sleep Cheap Inn. He denies that there are any undocumented immigrants – or any children – staying at the inn.

A spokesperson for the Trauma Center said it would not have been part of Dr. Medawar's duties at the Trauma Center to visit undocumented immigrants.

So far, police say they have been unable to locate the woman or her children. They have also not been able to reach the nurse to corroborate Dr. Medawar's account. Police are investigating and will not say if Dr. Medawar is a suspect.

Tiffany Albern reporting live from Clifton.

Co-Anchor Ashley Gelb: Scientists have found a surprising new use for coffee filters. Our consumer affairs reporter will tell us more after this.

SUNDAY, OCTOBER 18

NOON – 1:30 P.M.

On Sunday, Devin Garner arrived at the Medawar home just after noon. He brought pizza and a determination to get out ahead of the police investigation.

Rafiq Medawar was unshaven, and his eyes were bloodshot. He apparently hadn't slept much and was on edge – jumping in response to noises. He ate little of the pizza.

"I've been trying to reach Angelica Rios," Medawar told Garner. "She's the nurse who talked me into going to that damn inn."

Garner listened.

"I've called her several times and left voice mail messages. I've sent her text messages. But she hasn't gotten back to me. I even called the Trauma Center, but she's not scheduled to work again until Monday."

"That's not good," Garner said.

"She will back up my story," Medawar insisted, "and then the police will *have to* believe me."

"Rafiq, I'm sure when we find her, she will back up what you told the police," Garner assured his friend. "But I don't want you to be too invested in the hope that the police will take her word for it and move on. If they think you and this nurse are having an affair, they are going to view anything she says pretty skeptically."

"We have to find her!" Medawar insisted.

"They found Ann's body yesterday morning – that's more than twenty-four hours ago," Garner said. "Given Ann's family, the cops had to know from the start that this case was going to get a lot of attention. What I'm saying is – the police have probably found Rios by now. They had a big head start. If they talked to her, she's already told them why you went to this inn. If they haven't been able to reach her either, then we have to wonder why."

"I don't think I gave them her name," Medawar said. "Maybe they haven't identified her?"

"Maybe," Garner allowed, "but all they had to do was go the Trauma Center with the video and start asking around. It shouldn't have taken them more than a couple minutes to identify her."

Garner watched as Medawar stirred his coffee, lost in his own thoughts.

"Last night, you said Rios was involved with her church," Garner said. "I could try to contact them."

Medawar shook his head. "I tried to reach the pastor this morning. He didn't answer, and he hasn't called me back. He must be conducting services."

"Why don't you give me the information," Garner urged. "If you don't hear from him, I'll keep trying. There are some people I may need you to contact, to tell them to expect me to be in touch, but we can't have you doing much more than that. As your attorney, I can work with people and try to get them to cooperate. But if you do that, we risk having the police or prosecutor claim you're trying to create an alibi or intimidate witnesses."

Medawar picked up the tablet on which he had written the name of the church and its phone number and tossed it across the table to Garner.

Garner sipped his coffee, allowing a moment for the tension to spend itself.

"I can only imagine how frustrating this must be," Garner said. "But try thinking about it like this. I'd trust you to operate on me. I wouldn't insist on helping or try to tell you how to do the surgery. Well, this is what I do. You have to trust me on this. I'll keep you informed and involved, but we have to be smart."

Medawar nodded, but it was clear he wasn't content with that.

"Here's something you can do," Garner said. "You can help me find that woman whose kids you saw. I don't know if we can convince her to help, but you're the one who went to see her kids when you didn't have to. If anyone has a chance of convincing her to help, it would be you. What do you say we drive over to the inn and see if we can find this woman and her kids?"

"Do you really think she's still going to be there?"

"Probably not, but I don't see where we have anything to lose by trying."

"She's afraid of the police," Medawar said. "Where she comes from, the police are nothing but trouble, and she is terrified she is going to be deported."

"The worst that can happen is she tells us to go away."

Medawar nodded. "Give me a couple minutes," he said and walked from the room.

Garner heard water run in the bathroom and the sound of a couple drawers opening and shutting. When Medawar returned, he had shaved and combed his hair and was wearing a clean shirt.

Medawar obviously had not had much sleep. He was still in shock at his wife's death, and he was frustrated that no one would confirm what had he told the police.

In short, he was an emotional mess.

Garner wondered if taking Medawar to the inn would be a mistake. He wanted to give Medawar something to do, but maybe he should have sent an investigator to the inn.

Still, if anyone had a chance of convincing the woman to help, it was the kindly physician who had gone out of his way to help her.

2:35 P.M. – 2:45 P.M.

When Garner and Medawar arrived at the Sleep Cheap Inn, the parking lot was nearly empty. They went directly to the room where Medawar visited the Mexican woman and her kids. Medawar knocked several times but got no answer.

He identified himself but still got no answer. He and Garner then tried several nearby doors but got no answers from those rooms either.

They retreated to the registration desk, where Medawar rang a bell on the counter for service. A heavy-set, dark-skinned man, who appeared to have been dozing in the back office, made his way to the counter.

"Is the manager here?" Medawar asked the groggy man. "We'd like to speak with him if he's available."

"I'm the manager," the man replied warily. His English was heavily accented.

Medawar introduced himself and Garner.

The manager said nothing.

Medawar asked the man his name.

The man hesitated, then replied, "Diego Olivar."

Medawar explained that he and his wife had visited the inn on Friday morning to see a woman newly arrived from Mexico and her two children. Both of the children were ill.

The manager did not respond.

"You will remember my wife. She stayed by the door. She was making a video – a documentary. You spoke with her. She agreed to pay you for permission to use images of your inn in her video."

"I never saw her," the manager said. "And we don't have any woman with kids staying here."

"Were you here Friday morning? Maybe there is another manager?" Medawar asked.

"*Sí, Sí*, I was here. I am the manager, but I did not talk to anyone about a video."

"Look, I'm not the police. I don't care about the immigration status of your guests," Medawar pleaded. "My wife was killed. I'm just trying to find out what happened to her."

"I don't know nothing about your wife. You should leave."

"Is that what you told the police, you lying –"

Garner grabbed Medawar's arm.

"Mr. Olivar," Garner interjected, "you have to forgive my friend. Someone killed his wife, and he is very upset. Is there anyone else his wife might have spoken with?"

"I don't know anything about his wife. Now, get out of here, or I'll call the police."

"If you killed my wife," Medawar said, but stopped when the manager lifted a gun from behind the counter.

Garner grabbed Medawar and pulled him away. "Let's go, Rafiq. This isn't helping."

"He's lying," Medawar said, refusing to be pulled away.

"And he's got a gun. Come on, Rafiq, this isn't helping anything."

Medawar jerked free of Garner's hold, turned abruptly, and headed angrily toward the door. Garner followed a step behind.

When they reached Garner's car, Medawar exploded. "He's lying. He had something to do with what happened to Ann."

"Maybe, but he's not going to talk to us about it. Losing your temper and getting arrested – or shot – isn't going to solve anything. We'll figure this out another way."

Medawar reluctantly got into the car.

Before either spoke again, they were nearly back to Medawar's home.

When he did speak, Medawar said quietly, "I'm screwed."

"I know it's hard," Garner said, "but you can't think that way."

"The police think I did it. Angelica won't respond to my calls. Maybe someone killed her too. That slimebag lied to the police. Nobody's going to believe me. Even Ann's parents are acting weird."

"Rafiq, we'll figure it out."

"What's to figure out? Somebody killed my wife, and the police are going to hang it on me. I'm screwed."

MONDAY, OCTOBER 19

8:25 A.M. – 8:35 A.M.

Detective James Chilton was 5' 10" and 235 pounds of bellicosity. This Monday morning, like every morning, he was angry and frustrated. He was angry at having too much work. He was angry at the lousy pay. He was angry at the paperwork. He was frustrated because none of it would improve. It would only get worse.

Something else made him angry. Just because he was a cop, people automatically assumed he was a social dinosaur. People assumed he would rather be sitting on his ass downing coffee and donuts. He was frustrated because – well, because he *was* a dinosaur. He actually cared about right and wrong and catching the scum bags who killed people. And, *yeah*, he *would* rather be grousing over coffee and donuts. *Who the hell wouldn't?*

But deep down, he suspected those things did not truly explain why he was angry. Maybe his first wife had been right. When she left him, she said he wasn't angry because she was leaving. She said he was angry because that's how he was put together. He was angry and frustrated, she said, at the molecular level. *She was right about the first part. He wasn't mad that she left. Maybe she was right about the rest too.*

He filled his coffee mug and located his District captain. "Listen, I wanted you to know that I met with Prosecutor Warren on Saturday. In his office."

"What did *the Dick* want?" the captain asked.

The police rank and file and almost everyone else referred to Warren as "*the Dick*." But still, it surprised Chilton to hear the captain do so.

"His people wanted me to brief Warren on the shooting of Ace Lindsey's kid."

"First time you've had to brief Warren?" the captain

asked.

"Yeah," Chilton said.

"You need a better class of victim," the captain said. "*The Dick* isn't going to ask for a briefing if the victim is some poor schmuck. But if some rich guy's kid gets shot, he's all over it."

Chilton filled the captain in on the details of the investigation, including the open ends that needed to be run down. "Warren's got his mind made up that the husband did it," he concluded.

"What do you think?" the captain asked.

"I'm old-fashioned," Chilton grumbled. "I liked it better when we investigated a case before we decided who did it."

The captain chuckled. "Stick with the case and do what you think is necessary."

That suited Chilton fine. This was a high-profile case, and he wanted to stick with it.

The captain glanced at his watch, a sure sign he felt sufficiently briefed.

"One more thing," Chilton said. "Warren also wants someone to find a reason to shut down the Sleep Cheap Inn. I was thinking Vice should handle that."

"I'll talk to Vice," the captain said, "but I want you to stay involved. You need to make sure nothing the Department does undermines the prosecution of whoever killed Ace Lindsey's daughter. If we start stepping on our own feet, Warren will go ballistic."

Chilton still thought Vice should handle investigating the Sleep Cheap Inn. They didn't need his help. "You taking anything off my plate?" he asked.

"Just do the best you can," came the inevitable response.

Chilton left the briefing angry and frustrated.

10:00 A.M. – 11:30 A.M.

Garner heard the front door open. He had a desk for a receptionist but had not hired anyone to sit behind it. He got up from his own desk and stepped from his office to the small reception area. As he expected, it was Rafiq Medawar.

"Hey, good morning," Garner said. He had asked Medawar to come to his office to discuss next steps.

"Hey yourself," Medawar retorted.

"How about some coffee?"

"Sure."

Garner pointed to his office, which he had straightened up, and told Medawar to have a seat.

Medawar ignored the suggestion. "How much space do you have here?" he asked as he followed Garner to the little kitchenette at the back of the office.

"The reception area, two offices, a conference room, and this kitchenette." Garner poured two cups of coffee. "Plus, I use the upstairs for storage. Old files mainly."

"Nice."

"More room than I'd have in space near the courthouse, but not nice," Garner said. "You want nice? Go to any of the big law firms downtown. From their conference rooms, you'll have great views of the river, the stadiums."

Medawar shrugged.

"How are you holding up?" Garner asked.

"I got some sleep last night, so I'm doing a little better."

Garner could see that his friend was still processing Ann's death and was only beginning to work his way through the usual stages of grief.

Garner showed Medawar into his office. "I'm afraid what I'm about to discuss with you," he said, "is only going to add to the stress you're feeling."

Medawar studied Garner. "Let's hear it."

"I'm concerned," Garner said, "that unless we can head him off, the prosecutor is going to come after you for Ann's murder."

Medawar started to say something, but Garner held up

his hand. "Let me get this out. This isn't easy for me either."

Medawar folded his arms but said nothing.

"Anyone who knows you knows you didn't kill Ann. But Dick Warren doesn't know you. All he knows is that the media, for some insane reason, are describing you as a Syrian Muslim. For Warren, that's like blood in the water for a shark."

"Why don't we do an interview with him? Or with one of the television news shows?"

"That's worth talking about," Garner said. "But I think the first thing we should talk about is whether I'm the one who should be giving you that advice, whether I should be the one to represent you."

"You don't want to represent me?" Medawar asked.

"No, I'm *not* saying that. I want to handle your case. Defending an innocent client against an unfair prosecution is not something a lawyer gets to do very often, but it's the only thing that makes criminal defense work worth it, at least for me."

"Then, what are you saying?"

"I'm saying I'm just five years out of law school. I've tried more cases than a lot of lawyers at this point in their careers, but there are plenty of criminal defense lawyers who have more experience and have tried more and bigger cases than I have."

"I know that," Medawar said.

"Hear me out," Garner said. "I've been second chair in three homicide cases, but I've never been the first chair."

"First chair, second chair," Medawar interrupted. "That's like a lead surgeon, assisting surgeon?"

"Right." Garner collected his thoughts and continued. "Ann was not just your wife. She was also Ace Lindsey's daughter. If you get indicted, your case is going to get a lot of media attention, at least locally. You need to think about whether you'd be better off with someone who has been lead counsel in a high-profile case."

"Are you saying you can't represent me?"

"No, but you have to consider what is best for you. I want you to think about whether you would be better served by hiring someone with more experience, someone with big case experience. You should think about whether you want to hire one of the big-name guys."

Medawar unfolded his arms. "Are you telling me I *should* do that, or that I *should think* about it?"

"I'm saying you need to think about it and decide what's best for you."

"Wouldn't hiring one of those guys signal that I'm guilty? Wouldn't one of those guys just attract more attention?"

"It might, but that brings me to the second thing I want you to think about."

Medawar pushed his chair back an inch or two.

"I wanted you to come to my office," Garner said, "to make a point. I wanted you to see where my office is. I wanted you to see the boarded-up buildings you passed on your way here. I need you to understand, really understand, that I'm not in one of the big downtown law firms. My office isn't even downtown. Or on the east side. My office is in godforsaken Lower Price Hill."

Garner took a sip of coffee.

"If you get indicted, and I hope you don't, but if you do, your family and friends are going to follow your case on the news. So will Ann's family. Christ, Rafiq, everyone in town will be paying attention. And second-guessing."

Garner looked straight at Medawar. "If I'm your attorney, every time my name comes up, you know what they're going to say? 'Lower Price Hill attorney Devin Garner.'"

Garner got up and began pacing.

"That's what they're going to say, 'Lower Price Hill attorney.' But you know what your family, friends, and everyone else are going to hear when they say that? 'Some lower price lawyer nobody ever heard of.'"

"That bothers you, doesn't it?"

"I'm afraid it's going to worry you, your family, your friends. I'm afraid that you're going to think you made a mistake hiring me. You know how Cincinnati is with the whole east side – west side thing."

"I never pay any attention to that."

"Maybe not consciously, but I-75 runs down the middle of Cincinnati like a bad scar, and there are constant remarks, jokes, whatever, about how the better educated, wealthier, classier folks live on the east side, and your blue-collar, pink-collar and no-collar people live on the west side. You can't live in this city and not be affected by that.

"You know how it goes. The people who go to the symphony and the Playhouse in the Park live on the east side. Pete Rose fans live here in Price Hill."

"Oh, come on. You belong to the Playhouse."

"You people on the east side listen to public radio," Garner continued his rant. "The people who live on the west side listen to talk radio. Or hip-hop."

"You listen to public radio," Medawar said. "I know you do."

"Doesn't matter. Your friends and family and the people you work with won't know that. They'll think I listen to Willie Cunningham. They'll wonder if maybe I listen to Pete Santilli."

"Why the hell *did* you locate your office here?" Medawar asked, a bit of irony in his voice. A small smile struggled to make an appearance on his face.

"I thought we talked about that," Garner said, sitting down again. "When I graduated from law school, I didn't have any good options. A friend and classmate, Rachel Burns, suggested that we open our own practice. She thought we should locate somewhere underserved, somewhere where we could make a difference. Basically, she convinced me we could do well by doing good. Lower Price Hill fit the bill. It was also the only place we could afford."

"What happened to her?"

"She stuck it out for a couple years, but she never felt safe here, and she couldn't get used to not having a steady income. She took a job with the prosecutor's office."

"Can you call her and tell her I'm not a Syrian Muslim murderer?"

"Already did. She couldn't say anything, but she left me under the impression that Warren has already made up his mind."

Garner watched his friend react to that news. He thought Medawar was not just going through the usual stages of grief over Ann's death. He was reacting to the police investigation in much the same way.

Medawar was someone who had always earned and enjoyed praise for his accomplishments. He had been good at school, he had become a doctor, he was a highly regarded surgeon. And now, his reputation was being shredded. For many, he would always be that doctor who killed his wife.

Garner thought his friend was mourning the loss not just of his wife, but of his reputation. Garner thought Medawar was going through something like the usual stages of grief for that loss as well. He could almost see his friend move from denial to anger.

"Devin," Medawar said finally, "I trust you. I want you to represent me." Medawar raised his hands, palms up. "It's that simple."

"You sure you don't want time to think it over?"

"I understand what you're saying about the guys with big names and more experience," Medawar responded, his voice more assertive than it had been. "In the medical field, we have the same thing. There are surgeons with big reputations and a lot of experience. Some of them are terrific, and some are overrated or past their best years. Surgical skills aside, most of them are incredible assholes.

"I've heard you and others talk about some of the big-name lawyers. Their fees are outrageously high, their egos are so big they have their own gravitational fields, and they have large numbers of clients fighting for their attention."

Garner couldn't remember the conversation, but he was sure he had said something like that. It was an open secret in the profession.

"I'd rather have you represent me," Medawar concluded. He was looking directly at Garner as he spoke. He wasn't rubbing his nose or glancing around the room, the way some people do when they're not being candid. Garner took all that as positive.

"But even if I wanted someone better known, with more experience, to represent me" Medawar continued, "I couldn't afford what they would charge.

"As to the big downtown law firms, this isn't the kind of case they handle. You told me that yourself. And Ann was Ace Lindsey's daughter. I doubt any of the big firms would even be interested, but I know I sure as hell couldn't afford them."

Garner nodded. Medawar was correct. The big downtown law firms seldom did criminal law, and when they did, it was white collar stuff. And they would be even more expensive than most experienced criminal defense attorneys.

"I'm still paying off my student debt. Ann and I just bought a house. If what you told me yesterday is correct, her life insurance won't pay until this is cleared up.

"I'm going to have to go to my relatives to raise the money for your fee – and for bail, if it comes to that. Some of my relatives have offered to help. They're pretty well off, but they're nowhere near the same bracket as the Lindseys. There's only so much I can ask of them."

"What about the Lindseys?" Garner asked.

Medawar shook his head. "No, I don't think so. They weren't happy about Ann marrying me, and I've never been able to make much progress with them. Besides, I think they blame me for Ann's death. I had to ask them for help with Ann's funeral and burial expenses. They agreed, but they looked at me the way you look at the bottom of your shoe when you've just stepped in dog shit."

"They think you killed her?" Garner asked. He tried to mask the concern in his voice but didn't succeed.

"I hope not," Medawar said. "I just think they believe that if Ann married someone else, this wouldn't have happened."

"I promise you," Garner said, "I'm not going to let you down. I hope we can convince the police to get their heads on straight and go look for whoever actually did this. That's the important thing now. But if the police, or Warren, have their minds made up already, I'm going to work as hard and as smart as I can to get this turned around."

Garner stood and offered his hand. Medawar stood and accepted it.

His client was obviously feeling overwhelmed, but it was important to press ahead. Garner discussed what they needed to do to try to head off an indictment, and if they weren't successful, what the defense would entail and what it likely would cost. He watched Medawar take in everything he was saying. He was extraordinarily smart and processed information quickly.

He had Medawar sign a formal fee agreement and a variety of other papers – mainly, releases to obtain information. He also asked him to collect his birth certificate, grade school report cards, diplomas, childhood pictures, anything that would help to establish that he grew up in town and was not raised in the Middle East.

Finally, Garner asked Medawar to compile a list of his friends and teachers from grade and high school, who could help verify his ties to the community. On second thought, he expanded the request. He also wanted to know about college and medical school friends and teachers and anyone else who might be willing to give a statement about his character. He tasked Medawar with providing their current contact information if he could find it.

Garner had to get those things out of the way, but he hoped that his business-like approach conveyed to Medawar the impression that he knew what he was doing. He wanted his friend to feel confident he'd made the right decision. And maybe, he was also trying to convince himself as well. After all, this would be the most important case he had ever handled. He knew he was taking on a lot of responsibility.

But his biggest concern was whether the available, admissible evidence would be enough to forestall the forces aligning against his friend.

11:30 A.M – 12:30 P.M.

When Medawar left, Garner contacted the private investigator he usually worked with and tasked him with finding and interviewing anyone and everyone Medawar had encountered at the Trauma Center, especially the police officers.

It wasn't clear when Ann had been killed, but if the Coroner's office put her time of death while Medawar was at the Trauma Center, he would have an alibi. Even if Ann had been killed earlier, before Medawar got to the Trauma Center, the exercise would be important. He needed to make sure none of the people Medawar encountered had anything harmful to say about his appearance or demeanor. Most of all, it would be important to make sure no one Medawar encountered that evening would later claim he had said or done something inappropriate or incriminating.

Next, Garner tracked down Joan Adams, the University of Cincinnati professor who taught the documentary-making class Ann had been taking. He explained why he wanted to meet with her.

Professor Adams had a better idea. "You should come and meet with the whole class," she said. "It's a graduate level course, and there are only eight in the class." She hesitated and corrected herself. "Well, seven now."

"They were all involved in the same project as Ann —

the documentary about undocumented immigrants in our area."

Garner got the details on when and where the class met.

He had barely hung up from that call when his phone rang. It was the pastor from the evangelical church where Angelica Rios was a member.

"I'm afraid I've got bad news," the pastor told Garner. "Angelica was in the country on forged papers. She panicked when she learned that someone killed Ms. Medawar and the police were looking for her. She drove to Dayton and flew back to the Philippines."

"Why Dayton?" Garner asked. He didn't really care, but he wanted to keep the pastor on the line, trying to give himself time to think of anything he needed to ask.

"They have a sanctuary for undocumented immigrants in Dayton. She was familiar with it. That, and she was probably afraid to fly out of Cincinnati. She may have been afraid they would be on the lookout for her."

Garner found the news disappointing, but a new question occurred to him. "Dr. Medawar and Angelica went to this inn to see an undocumented woman with two sick kids. Do you know what happened to them?"

"No, but I'll see if I can find out. But just so you know, I'm not going to do anything that will get them deported."

"I understand," Garner said. "I'll appreciate anything you can do."

Garner headed downtown for a court appearance. Later, when he returned to his office, he had a voicemail message to call the pastor.

"I spoke to a friend at the sanctuary in Dayton," he said when Garner reached him. "Somebody drove the woman and her kids to the sanctuary the same day your client and Angelica visited them. The sanctuary staff helped them relocate."

"Where?" Garner asked.

"I didn't ask, and they didn't say. And, just to save you

some time, they won't tell you. Even if you could somehow force them to tell you, she will have moved again by then. Probably several times."

"The new underground railroad?" Garner asked.

"Something like that," the pastor agreed.

"What's her name?"

"Same story. I honestly don't know, and I wouldn't tell you if I did."

"I appreciate the help you've given me."

"You're welcome at our services," the pastor said. "It sounds like your client could use some prayers."

"Amen to that," Garner said. He wasn't trying to be funny. He just didn't know what else to say.

TUESDAY, OCTOBER 20

10:00 A.M. – 11:30 A.M.

The next morning, for the first time since graduating from law school five years earlier, Devin Garner found himself back in a classroom.

If he was to keep the prosecutor's office from charging Medawar, he had to find corroboration for Medawar's story. He did not need to go back to school to understand that. But getting that corroboration was becoming worryingly difficult. Ann was dead. The manager of the Sleep Cheep Inn was denying everything. Angelica Rios had panicked and returned to the Philippines. That left her "Making A Documentary" class at the University of Cincinnati.

When the class began, Professor Adams provided a brief overview of the course for his benefit. "The course," she said, "included classroom sessions devoted to lectures and discussion of best practices."

"But the most important part of the course," she stressed, "is the practical experience of actually making a documentary. That involves everything from doing research, conducting interviews, and recording other material for the final product.

"Later," she said, "the class will cull through the recordings, write and narrate the script, and pull together the finished product."

Professor Adams made a point of the fact that she did not pick the subject of the documentary. The class did.

"The whole class is involved in gathering video of anti-immigration gatherings and overheated political rhetoric. But they are also working, in pairs, on some of the ways being undocumented affects individuals and families."

One pair was focusing on the difficulties the undocumented encountered in obtaining health care. Another two-person team was looking into the difficult working conditions the undocumented often face.

The third pair was exploring how the constant risk of deportation affected immigrants. They were especially interested in those who had come into the country when they were very young and for all practical purposes, had never lived anywhere else.

Ann and her partner were – well, had been – looking into violence aimed at immigrants and in particular at the undocumented.

Professor Adams asked each team to explain in greater detail what they were working on.

Ann's partner, Carrie Hixson, went first. "Ann and I," she explained, "were trying to track down immigrants who had been singled out for violence because of their ethnic or religious background – or simply because they were immigrants." She hesitated as if trying to decide how much detail was necessary. "We were focusing on some incidents in which Hispanic women had been abducted and killed."

Garner was surprised. Medawar had not mentioned that.

Each of the other teams described what they were working on in a similar bare-bones fashion.

"You may already know this from the news reports," Garner said, "but Ann met her husband, Rafiq, at the Sleep Cheap Inn on Friday morning. He and a nurse were there to see an undocumented woman and her kids. The kids were sick."

Garner couldn't read the faces of Ann's classmates. They were simply listening to what he was saying and taking it all in.

"Ann got video of Rafiq and the nurse going into the inn and coming back out. To me, that sounds like access to health care, not violence. Why would Ann have been making that video?"

A Chinese-American woman, Nancy Wong, responded.

"Ann was probably just trying to grab some video that we might be able to use," she said. Wong was the one who described what the healthcare issues team was doing. Several people nodded in agreement.

"This probably came up at the last minute," someone else said. "Besides, it involved her husband. Maybe he wouldn't agree to anyone else making a video of him doing this."

The group seemed to agree with that point as well.

Garner moved to a delicate question. "Ann used her cell phone to record Rafiq and the nurse," he said. "Here's my question. Is it possible to use a cell phone to get video for your documentary?"

"We're all using our cell phones!" several people said at once. Garner was surprised.

His surprise prompted a lively discussion.

Several people wanted to tell him about Tangerine, the movie recorded almost entirely on iPhone cameras that was a hit at Sundance. Something about transvestite prostitutes. Garner didn't think he was going to rush out and rent that one.

Others explained that lots of people were making documentaries and short movies entirely or almost entirely with iPhones.

"There's an annual competition. You can look it up online," Wong offered.

Someone else threw in the thought that a number of professionals have made some really cool commercials with cell phones.

One of the guys in the group decided to do a demonstration. Everyone called him "Cam" – whether short for Cameron or camera, Garner couldn't tell, but he suspected it was the latter. Cam was a tall, thin guy with large ears and his hair pulled into a ponytail. He showed Garner the iPhone he was using for the project.

"We're all using iPhones," someone interjected.

Cam attached a gadget – with its own lens – to his cell phone. "With this," he said, "you can capture a much wider view than usual with a cell phone camera, without a fishbowl effect around the edges."

"What's that called?" Garner asked. "I need the exact name."

"It's called a '1.33x Anamorphic Adapter Lens for iPhone.' Cam answered. "A company called Moondog Labs makes it."

"Would Ann have been using that when she was making video for your documentary?"

"Yes," Cam said. "I'm sure Ann had this on her cell too. We all did."

Garner could see others in the class nod in agreement.

"Here's something else you need to know," Cam said. "We've all downloaded a software program onto our cell phones to get better quality pictures." He rattled off the name of the program.

Garner wanted to capture the name of the software program and had Cam repeat it.

"FimicPro, version 5," Cam said. "It costs about eight bucks."

Cam wasn't done with his demonstration.

"The big problem with a cell phone is jiggle," he said. "It's impossible to hold a cell phone video cam steady for any length of time.

"That used to be a problem for other cameras too, but somebody invented equipment to stabilize the larger cameras. They called that rig a 'Steadicam.'

"As newer, smaller cameras came along, they came up with smaller and smaller versions."

As he spoke, Cam removed a device from his camera bag.

"For the iPhone," he said, "the stabilizer is called the 'Steadicam Smoothee.'"

Cam held the device up for Garner to see. It wasn't

much bigger than the sling for a broken arm. Cam attached the device to his cell phone and demonstrated how it worked.

Garner was relieved the group wanted to be helpful. He explained that when a married woman – like Ann – is killed, the police almost always suspect her husband.

Several in the class nodded along as he said that. It was a truism for anyone who has watched TV crime shows. Everybody knew that.

"I'm afraid the prosecutor is going to try to hang Ann's murder on her husband," Garner told the class. "They seemed to have latched onto the theory that Ann went to the Sleep Cheap Inn to catch her husband with the nurse." Garner didn't think he was telling them anything they didn't know.

"Let's assume Ann was using a cell phone with this extra stuff on it," he continued. "If she was, would you say it's pretty clear she was recording a video for the class project? And not because she thought her husband was cheating on her? Have I got that right?"

There was an awkward silence.

Cam, who seemed to be the least inhibited by social conventions, spoke up. "Sorry man, but no. She could have just been getting really good quality video of the son-of-a-bitch cheating on her."

That prompted an uproar.

Cam backpedaled. "Hey, I don't think that's why Ann was there," he protested. "If a guy was lucky enough to be married to someone like Ann, he'd have to be crazy to go banging some random nurse.

"Ann was probably trying to get some video for the documentary, but she already had the equipment. The equipment doesn't care what you record. If Ann was trying to catch her husband cheating, there was no reason for her not to use it. I'm just saying, if that's your best argument – you're in trouble."

Garner could feel the wind go out of his sails.

"Hang on!" Cam said. He opened his camera bag and pulled out a collapsible tripod and assembled it. He mounted a camera on top.

"We want to use our cell phones for this project," he explained. "But for most things, you don't get a second chance doing what we're doing. Say you're recording a demonstration, or an interview, or whatever. There are no dress rehearsals, no do-overs. So, we all agreed, whenever possible, we would also use a camera as a backup. That and to get a different angle.

"If Ann was recording some video for our documentary, she would have used a camera like this for back-up. I mean, probably, assuming it was feasible, and I don't see why it wouldn't have been.

"Think about it. If she didn't want her husband to see her, she wouldn't have been using her cell phone. And she wouldn't set up a camera on a tripod by the entrance door. And she certainly wouldn't have asked her husband and his little nurse friend to be sure to walk in front of it. She would have used a regular camera with a telephoto lens and shot from a distance."

Garner nodded. That was useful. Maybe even crucial.

"What I'm saying is," Cam concluded, "did the police find her camera and tripod? Did Dr. Medawar and this nurse walk in front of her camera as they were going into this place? If they did, then you got the police by the short hairs."

His classmates weren't sure it was so simple. "What if whoever killed her stole the camera?" someone asked.

Someone else repeated Cam's question. "Mr. Garner, do the police have her camera?"

"Excellent question," Garner conceded. "I haven't been able to get access to what the police recovered from the crime scene. The prosecutor will make me work for it."

Deciding things were now open for discussion, someone else offered the theory that the inn manager, or someone associated with the inn, must have killed Ann. Several people agreed.

Keesha Neave, a short, heavy-set, black woman, turned to Professor Adams. "Some of us were talking before class. We want to know if we can change the subject of our video and have it focus on who killed Ann?

"What we're thinking," she explained, "is maybe we could take turns watching who comes in and out of that inn and maybe try to interview some of them. That inn has been trouble for years. Maybe we could, you know, get some video about its history of problems. We could ask the police, the health department, whoever, why they haven't shut this place down."

Professor Adams quashed that idea in a hurry. "Under no circumstances are any of you to go near that place," she said, emphatically. "We've had one person killed, and that's too many. It's up to the police to find out who killed Ann. This a University class, and a University project. The University cannot accept that risk, and I won't stand for it. Understood?"

The rebuke was met with some grumbling.

Garner stepped forward. "Guys," he said, "I really appreciate the offer. Honestly, I do. But I agree with Professor Adams, and I'm sure if Rafiq were here, he would say the same thing.

"Frankly, I'm not sure Rafiq could handle it if one of you started snooping around there and got killed. Or got arrested for interfering with the police investigation. If you want to honor Ann, then finish the video."

Despite the nice speech, Garner knew what he would have done when he was a student, had he been in their situation. And it would not have involved taking sober advice.

"If you want to help find out who killed Ann, and why," Garner said, "how about this?" He handed his legal pad to

Cam. "Write down your name, phone number, and email address. If anything comes up where I can use your skills, I promise I will reach out to you." Garner found some of his business cards in his briefcase and passed those out as well.

"In the meanwhile," he said, "there is something you can help me with right now. I've got a couple questions that are terribly important."

He had their attention.

"Did Ann discuss going to this inn, or getting a video of her husband and this nurse with any of you?"

No one recalled Ann mentioning it.

"Did Ann tell any of you that she thought her husband might be having an affair?"

No, they assured him, from what they could tell, Ann adored her husband.

The bell rang, but Garner did not have that "saved by the bell" feeling. He thanked Professor Adams and the class. The class members scrambled for the door, and he followed them out. As the door closed behind him, he felt that the last chance to head off an indictment may have closed as well.

WEDNESDAY, OCTOBER 21

9:00 A.M. – 11:30 A.M.

On Wednesday morning, Devin Garner attended the funeral Mass for Ann Lindsey Medawar at the St. Anthony of Padua Church in Cincinnati's East Walnut Hills neighborhood. He greeted Rafiq Medawar near the door to the church, expressed his condolences, and stepped aside, so others could take their turn offering him what words of sympathy and loss they could muster.

Medawar seemed to be holding up reasonably well, but Garner noticed that when his friend thought no one was looking, he appeared a bit at a loss, as if he could not understand where Ann was and why she was not at his side. Garner felt for his friend, but he was also representing him in connection with the police investigation. He was concerned his presence near him would only remind people of the cloud of suspicion the media had created. Besides, nearly everyone else at the funeral had known Ann or Rafiq longer than he had.

Garner moved from the vestibule into the interior of the church. He was early and took some time to walk along the church's bright white interior walls, taking in the stained-glass windows, the stations of the cross, and other icons of the faith. On either side of the altar, there were large portraits of Saint Maron and Saint Rafga. Garner did not recall either being mentioned during his years in parochial schools.

Large numbers of German and Irish immigrants settled in Cincinnati in the 19th Century, and as a result, the city was home to a surprising number of Roman Catholic churches. St. Anthony of Padua was a Catholic church, but not a Roman Catholic church – or even an Eastern Orthodox Catholic Church. It was a Maronite Catholic church – the small arm of the Catholic church that arose in Lebanon and drew followers primarily from Lebanon and its diaspora.

The Maronite church in the United States pre-dated the brutal civil war that tore Lebanon apart from 1975 to 1990. But its presence in the United States grew significantly during that civil war, as people – more than a million in all – fled that small country. As has happened so many times when sectarian and ethnic strife have ravaged foreign lands, some of those who fled the violence in their ancestral home sought refuge and new lives in the United States. If they ended up in Cincinnati, and if they were Maronite Catholic, they would find their way to St. Anthony of Padua.

From his conversations with Medawar during the Leadership program and since, Garner had learned that Medawar's family was among those who fled Lebanon during that country's prolonged civil war. Medawar's father had been a physician in Beirut with a substantial practice, and his mother a university professor. Their lives, before the civil war, had been cosmopolitan and prosperous. Their relocation to the United States had not been easy or happy, but it was less difficult for them than for many. Rafiq had been born in Cincinnati.

But if the prosecutor were determined to charge Rafiq with Ann's murder, none of that would matter. His future would be on the line in a criminal justice system that was tilted in favor of the prosecution.

The church began to fill. Garner found a place in a pew near the back and thumbed through the hymnal. The words to the prayers and hymns appeared in English on the pages on the left, and in Aramaic and sometimes Syriac on the right-hand side. In a different time, in any of the Roman Catholic churches in the city, the words might have been in English and Latin, or even, before the World Wars, in German and Latin.

Father Joseph Zaidan, the pastor, took his place, and the pallbearers rolled the carriage containing Ann's casket down the center aisle. The priest blessed the coffin, wafted it with burnt incense, and began the service.

When it came time for the sermon, the priest acknowledged that Ann had been raised in the Baptist faith and had converted to Catholicism only after she met Rafiq. But, he said, she had quickly become a beloved member of the St. Anthony community. He recounted that in recent weeks, before God called her to his side, Ann had been working with him on a response to the recent, highly political wave of concern about immigration.

She pointed him to this verse from Deuteronomy 10:19, and urged him to write a sermon based on it: "And you are to love those who are foreigners, for you yourselves were foreigners in Egypt."

She also thought he might draw on Exodus 22:21: "Do not mistreat or oppress a foreigner, for you were foreigners in Egypt."

And finally, she suggested a passage from the New Testament – Mathew 25:35: "For I was hungry, and you gave me something to eat, I was thirsty, and you gave me something to drink, I was a stranger and you invited me in."

Ann was troubled that politicians and others were ranting against allowing refugees from Syria to come into the country. She was deeply concerned, Father Zaidan recalled, that some were even threatening to drive millions of Hispanic immigrants from this country.

Ann wanted him to speak out and remind people that the Holy Family had once been refugees in Egypt – and that, indeed, God's chosen people had once been immigrants there without rights of citizenship. *If God tells us to befriend the alien and instructs us not to oppress the alien*, she wanted to know, *why were politicians, who claimed to be Christian, acting the part of the pharaoh?*

Father Zaidan promised to give that sermon someday soon. He said he hoped God would inspire him to write a sermon up to the standards Ann would have insisted on.

But he went on to make the point, inevitable at a funeral

Mass, that all of us are – in some sense – immigrants in this life, for one day our souls, like Ann's, will leave this life and go to our eternal home. If we are as full of God's love as Ann, Father Zaidan assured the mourners, our eternal home will be at God's side – as he was sure Ann's was.

When the service ended, Garner followed the other mourners from the church. As he did, a slender woman in a long, black dress approached and asked if she could have a word with him. "I don't know if you recall me," she said, "I'm Carrie Hixson. Ann and I were working on the documentary together."

"I do remember you," Garner said. He remembered her not only because she was Ann's partner, but also because she was attractive, engaging and smart – the sort of person one remembers. "This must be hard," he said.

"It is hard. Ann and I were really close friends."

It was clear Hixson had been crying during the service, and she appeared to be on the verge of doing so again, but collected herself and got directly to the point.

"You're defending Rafiq," she said. It sounded to Garner almost like an accusation. "I didn't want to discuss this in front of Joan – Professor Adams – but there are some things you should know."

Garner felt a sinking feeling.

"For you to understand, for you to believe me, I need to show you some video."

He agreed to meet her the next afternoon.

Even more sober now than when the Mass had ended, he joined the funeral procession to the cemetery. As Ann was laid to rest, he stood near the back of the small gathering of relatives and friends at the graveside. He watched Ann's parents, the Lindseys, with particular interest. They were formal, correct and sober, but seemed to keep a certain distance – physical and emotional – from Medawar.

When the burial service was over, Garner once more said a few brief words of condolence to Medawar before leaving. He had been too young to remember his mother's death. But as he drove away, he thought about his father's more recent death and funeral.

Thinking about how he felt then, he understood why so many in his family would drink themselves into oblivion after a funeral. He had no intention of doing that to himself, but he had his own way of not dealing with painful emotions. He would bury himself in his work.

But first, he had another commitment.

12:10 P.M. – 1:30 P.M.

Reya's Authentic Mexican Restaurant was about twenty minutes south of Cincinnati in Florence, Kentucky. Devin Garner had read that the restaurant served some of the most authentic, and maybe the best, traditional Mexican food in Greater Cincinnati. But that's not why, after leaving the cemetery, he went to the worse-for-wear restaurant. He went to see his uncle, Hank Bremen. Actually, his father's uncle, but like his father, he had always called him "Uncle Hank."

Garner regretted that he had seen little of Hank over the previous three years since Hank married Reya Sanchez, the restaurant's owner. Hank's marriage to Reya had roughly coincided with Rachel Burns' departure. Hank had immersed himself in his new marriage and in running her restaurant, and Garner had immersed himself in building his practice.

When Garner entered the restaurant, Hank was standing in the dining room, keeping an eye on the service. They exchanged greetings and slid into a booth. Hank waved one of the waitresses over, ordered lunch, and gave her special instructions to give the cook.

"Hank," the waitress asked, "is this your nephew, the one who is a lawyer?" She spoke English with a heavy accent. Looking at Garner, she added, "All the time, he talks about you."

Hank did introductions. The waitress, Alejandra, told

Garner in a stage whisper, "We love your uncle. We call him 'Hank Habanero.'"

Garner laughed and said he loved it. The waitress grinned and hurried away.

"You're representing that doctor they think killed his wife," Hank said.

"I'm representing him, but I don't know why anyone would think he killed his wife. Rafiq is a friend of mine, and he was madly in love with his wife."

"Where did you meet him?"

"We went through Leadership Cincinnati together. We hit it off and stayed in touch. He's a great guy, and his wife was terrific."

"He's a Muslim? From Syria, right?"

"I don't know where the media got that. He's Catholic. I just came from the church."

"You've got your hands full. The news media make it sound like he's practically on the terrorist watch list."

"I know, but it's not like he grew up in some madrassa in the Middle East. He was born right here in Cincinnati. He went away to college, but before that, he went to school here in Cincinnati. I mean, he went to Summit Country Day. How many terrorists you think they have there?"

"I don't know," his uncle said. "How many third graders do they have?"

Garner chuckled. "I miss talking with you."

"What kind of doctor is he?"

"He's a surgeon. With his credentials, he could have gotten a job anywhere, but he chose to work at the Trauma Center. He doesn't talk about it, but when I pressed him once, he just said he wanted to give back to the community that took his family in."

The waitress was back at the table with drinks and chips and salsa.

"Where is Reya?" Garner asked when the waitress left.

"She's in Mexico, doing missionary work."

"Missionary work?"

"Yeah, that's what she calls it. She goes down there, way down in Mexico where she's from, and finds people who want to come to the States. She helps them get across the border."

"She's a coyote?" Garner asked.

His uncle ignored the pejorative term. "I've been down there. You wouldn't believe how poor the people are. The government has always been corrupt. Instead of focusing on education and jobs, the government protects the rich from the poor."

"You traveled through Mexico?"

"Yeah. Reya has a camper, and we traveled all over down there, but mainly, where we went, it was rural, and the people were dirt poor."

"Weren't you concerned about the drug cartels? I mean, of being kidnapped or robbed or something?"

"As long as I was with Reya, I wasn't worried, but I did almost get robbed once."

Garner helped himself to some chips and salsa and waited for the story to unfold.

"We were staying in this adobe house, just like in the old cowboy movies, and Reya was off somewhere. I was bored and looking for something to do, so I decided to sharpen this knife I had with me. There were no windows in the house, and it was hot, so I went outside.

"I'm standing there on the porch sharpening the knife, and I see this woman across the street looking at me. I'd met her but couldn't remember her name. Anyway, I start goofing off. I acted like I was pulling a hair from my scalp and pretended to drop it onto the knife. I acted like the blade split the hair in two.

"Later, she came over and asked if I had seen the two men. I didn't know what she was talking about. She said that two men were sneaking up on the house where I staying, one coming from either side. She said they were going to rob me – and probably beat me up or kill me. And then I walk out and start showing how sharp my knife is, and they apparently decided it wasn't worth it and left."

The waitress brought their food to the table, and "Hank Habanero" explained what each dish was and how he had the cook tweak it.

As they ate, Hank talked about Reya's kids – all grown now. Reya, he explained, had been married twice before. When she was quite young, she married someone from the town where she grew up. "They had one child – Diego. He kept his father's name – Olivar. So, Diego Olivar. I'm not sure how that marriage ended – Reya doesn't like to talk about it.

"But after that, she and Diego came to the States. She married a Mexican-American guy in Phoenix. Sanchez. His family had lived in the States for generations. They had two kids – Hector and Maya. He died, and somehow Reya and her kids ended up here.

"I've gotten really close to those two kids. Hector is in college. He's studying political science at UK in Lexington. Maya didn't go to college. She usually works here, but she's in Mexico now with Reya."

"You said her oldest is Diego Olivar?" Garner asked. "The guy that manages the Sleep Cheap Inn?"

"Yeah," Hank said. "That's what I wanted to talk to you about."

The waitress started to approach, but Hank shook his head, and she busied herself checking on her other tables.

"How much do you know about that inn?" Hank asked.

"Not much, except it's got a bad reputation. It was built in the 1950's and hasn't been kept up well. I checked the real estate records on Monday, and somebody new bought it a couple years ago. A company called Aqua Caliente, Inc. I wasn't great in Spanish in school, but even I know that means 'hot water.'"

"That's Diego. That's his company. Reya's lawyer set it

up for him."

"Reya's son owns the Sleep Cheap Inn?"

"On paper. Reya may have put some money in it, but I think he's fronting for one of the drug cartels."

"Oh, geez."

"I don't know much about it, but he has to be into something off the books. I know he has illegals working there. I hear rumors that drug dealers use the inn to do deals. But it's all vague. Reya won't talk about it or let anyone else talk about it."

Garner took a bite of his food and chewed on what Hank was telling him. "The last time anyone saw Ann Med-awar," he said, "she was going into the inn to pay him for using video of the inn in the documentary she and her class were making. So, I'm interested in anything you can you tell me about Diego."

Hank nodded. "Reya dotes on him. She thinks he can do no wrong, but I don't trust him. What do you call those people who don't have a conscience?"

"A sociopath?"

"Psychopath. Yeah, I think he's a cold-blooded psycho-path. If you've been around Reya, you know how every-thing's 'Jesus this' and 'Jesus that.' So, about three or four years ago, Diego decided he wanted to be a minister. He went to some Bible school in Cincinnati for a couple months and then tried to set up his own congregation."

"Didn't work out?"

"He was spending a lot of time with the ladies in the choir. It turned out, he was sleeping with several of them, and that was the end of that."

"It doesn't sound like you were surprised," Garner said.

"Reya kept telling me how hard Diego was working, es-pecially with the choir, and how Jesus was working through him. I told her that when a minister spends that much time with the ladies of the choir, he's getting more than 'amens.'"

Garner laughed.

"Next thing I know, he's running that inn, and Reya is sending him some of the women she brings into the country to work. The pretty ones."

"What happens to the rest of the people she smuggles in?"

"She usually keeps them here until they hook up with someone in the community they know – usually a relative – or until they can get a job."

"That's always mystified me. How does someone with no English, no papers, no contacts, not much education, find a job? We've got people who grew up here, speak English, graduated from high school, maybe even have some college, and can't find jobs."

Hank ignored Garner's question. "I just wanted you to know that Diego owns that inn, at least on paper, and that you can't trust him. I want you to be careful."

"Actually, I met Diego," Garner said. "I went to the inn to see if I could locate any witnesses. He told me to get lost."

After he finished eating and listened to more stories of Hank's travels in Mexico, Garner said he had to get to the office – he hadn't been to work all day.

As Garner prepared to leave, his uncle insisted on walking out with him. Once they were outside, his uncle pulled him aside.

"Be careful," his uncle said. "I don't know what all Diego's involved in, or who he's doing business with, but watch yourself. I know you have to represent your friend, your client, and all that, but don't get yourself killed."

THURSDAY, OCTOBER 22

11:30 A.M. – 2:30 P.M.

The next morning, a little after 11:30, Devin Garner answered the phone in his office.

"Have you had lunch?" a woman asked.

Garner couldn't place the voice, but it sounded familiar. "No," he said, "not yet." His reply was tentative and conditional as if he reserved the right to amend his response based on further evidence.

"Sorry," the woman laughed. "This is Carrie Hixon. We spoke yesterday at the church. I just finished my classes, and I'm headed to your office. I was going to stop and grab something for us to eat if you don't mind working through lunch."

Garner protested half-heartedly, saying she didn't need to do that, he could have something brought in.

"I know where your office is," Hixson scoffed. "You've got a better chance of having somebody deliver cocaine than lunch."

"It's not that bad," Garner said. "Things are actually improving here."

She insisted.

Half an hour later, Carrie Hixon made her entrance — carrying her laptop, cans of diet cola, and a large bag of Chinese take-out containers. Garner directed her to his conference room. Hixson sat her computer and lunch on the table, slid off her jacket, and flashed a bright smile as she surveyed her surroundings.

These were all prosaic things that people routinely do. But Carrie Hixon was young, slim, blonde, beautiful, vivacious, classy, and obviously intelligent. She was for Garner the embodiment of a kind of idealized woman — a goddess.

Or at least, an east side goddess.

Women like her, he believed, lived in a universe far, far removed from the one he inhabited. There was something utterly improbable about her presence in his dusty office, in this part of town. It was like going into a Subway in a bad neighborhood and finding Martha Stewart behind the counter, ready to take your order.

Garner wished he had arranged to meet her somewhere else. Somewhere nicer.

"Take whatever you want," Hixson said, pointing to four containers with an assortment of Chinese foods, several boxes of white and fried rice, plus another of egg rolls, and yet another of desserts and fortune cookies. "I didn't know what you like, so I overdid it."

Garner ignored the food offering.

"You gave me the impression yesterday," he said as he took a seat across from her, "that you had something to share with me that I needed to know, but that I wasn't going to like."

He hesitated a second before continuing. When he did, he noticed that Hixson did not interrupt, but waited for him finish his thought. She was instinctively polite in the way that only people brought up in upper-class surroundings are. It was something instilled – like perfect posture – at an early age and carefully nurtured. *GMO*, he thought. *The rich have Genetically Modified Offspring, engineered to have perfect manners, perfect posture, perfect lives.*

"Did Ann go to the inn," he asked, "because she thought Rafiq was cheating?"

Hixson looked at him directly, not avoiding his eyes. Then, she looked down and rubbed her index finger on the table top, as if trying to rub out a spot, before responding.

"You're a criminal defense attorney?" she asked finally. "You mainly defend people who are accused of crimes?"

"That's right."

"You must live in a pretty dark world. I guess you always

have to wonder if your client is lying to you, if the person who claims to be a witness is exaggerating, if the cops are hiding something, if you can trust what anybody says."

"It comes with the territory."

"I believe," Hixson said, "Rafiq went to the inn to try to persuade that poor woman to take her sick kids to the hospital. I believe Ann went there to get some video footage for the documentary, not because she thought Rafiq was cheating. I'm sorry if I worried you."

Relieved, Garner reached for one of the cartons of food. "Did Ann say anything to you about going to this inn?" he asked. "Did she discuss any of this with you before she went?"

Hixson shook her head. "No, I wish she had. We talked all the time, so this must have come up at the last minute."

"What was it you wanted to discuss?"

"I wanted you to understand what Ann and I were working on. Let me walk you through it, and then you can decide if it's helpful."

Garner gestured for her to continue.

"For our part of the project, Ann and I were supposed to try to come up with something about violence against undocumented immigrants in the Greater Cincinnati area. When we started, all we had to go on were some scattered news reports that we found doing Google searches. Mainly, they were just reports of some incidents here in Lower Price Hill. The news reports were pretty sketchy, no real details.

"We found a social services organization on State Street. The Toribio Romo González Center. We met the director and spent a lot of time talking to him. He told us that there had been a lot more of that stuff than made it into the news, some of it pretty ugly. But his bigger concern was that some young women from the Hispanic community were being killed.

"He had a couple names, but not much more. Some of it was just rumor. But someone dumped one of the bodies at his doorstep. Literally, right in the entrance to the Center.

"Ann and I tried to track down family members, neighbors, friends – anyone who might shed light on the names he gave us. As we talked to people, we came up with a couple more names. It's pretty scary."

Garner pushed his food away and replaced it with a legal pad. "Rafiq didn't mention any of this."

"Ann kept most of it from Rafiq, so he wouldn't worry. She didn't want him to ask her to stop."

"Some Hispanic women have been killed," Garner recapped what he thought she had just told him. "That's disturbing, but I'm having trouble connecting the dots. What does that have to do with Ann's death?"

"Do you know who killed Ann?" Hixson replied.

"No."

"Do you have a theory? Somebody you think may have killed her?"

"Not really," Garner admitted, "but I assume it has to have been someone associated with the Sleep Cheap Inn in some way. I don't think this inn was just providing a hiding place for undocumented people. I suspect the guy who runs it is forcing women into prostitution to pay for a place to hide. He may be forcing those women to deliver drugs. Maybe – well, who knows? The prosecutor is raiding places left and right, looking for illegals and –"

"And headlines," Hixson offered.

"And headlines," Garner agreed. "Rafiq and this nurse show up, and then they see Ann outside taking videos. Someone – maybe the manager, maybe someone else – panicked. Or they just decided not to take any chances."

"You're probably right," Hixson said, "but that's not what I was thinking."

Garner was surprised to see that – at least for the moment – Hixson looked unsure of herself. He didn't know that people like this woman ever had self-doubts. It made her seem less like a goddess, less like a Hollywood movie star, more like a real person.

"I don't have any proof," Hixson said, "but I think whoever killed these other women may have killed Ann."

Hixson again rubbed her index finger on the invisible stain on the table. "I'm thinking of the people who are wrapped up in all this anti-immigration rhetoric. I'm not talking just about the politicians. The things the politicians are saying are bad enough, but there's some really horrible stuff on the internet and talk radio. Apparently, some people buy into that. There are also meetings and rallies and speeches. I think that's behind some of the ugly incidents we heard about. So did Ann."

"You think they spend too much time with this garbage and then decide to do something about it?"

"Sure, you've got all of these school shootings, and all those other shootings —"

"All done," Garner interjected, "by loser white guys."

"Right," Hixon nodded. "My first thought was someone like that might be responsible for killing these women. They see Ann and me at some of those anti-immigration rallies, and then they see Ann at the inn or wherever she went from there. They decide Ann is investigating them. They grab Ann and kill her. That gets rid of Ann. And, whether on purpose or not, it draws police attention to this shady hotel with a reputation for drugs, prostitution, and undocumented immigrants."

Garner smiled at Hixson. "And you think *my* world is dark?"

"I want you to look at some of the video Ann and I took. You don't have to look at all of it. Just some of it. And then you can tell me just how dark the world can be."

For the next hour, Hixson walked Garner through a series of videos she and Ann made, explaining the background for each and answering — as best she could — his questions. When the interviews were in Spanish, she provided simultaneous translation into English.

At the end, Garner was stunned. By the videos. By the possibilities they raised. And by Caroline – Carrie – Hixson.

As Hixson left, she flashed her goddess smile at Garner. It was the kind of smile that that could do more than light up a room. It could change how a young man saw the world.

FRIDAY, OCTOBER 23

MID-AFTERNOON

Devin Garner met his uncle, newly nicknamed "Hank Habanero," at an Irish pub in Price Hill. The lunch crowd was thin, the food heavy.

"What's up?" Garner asked his uncle after they settled in and placed their drink and sandwich orders.

"I'm thinking about leaving Reya, and I want to know if you can represent me."

"You and Reya live in Kentucky, so you have to do the divorce proceedings over there. I'm licensed in Kentucky, but I don't get over there often. But if it's just a No-Fault divorce, sure, I can handle it."

Garner was puzzled, but he waited for the barmaid to serve their drinks before probing. Hank had a beer. Garner restricted himself to a diet soda.

"I thought you were happy. You obviously love running the restaurant, and you said you were close to Reya's kids. It's none of my business, but what's going on?"

"I'm afraid Reya is getting in over her head in some stuff I don't want any part of. You know me, I'm not exactly Sunday Bible School material. I don't care if Reya wants to help people come here from Mexico. Where she's from, most of the people are dirt poor, the government is corrupt, and you've got all that violence going on."

The barkeep returned and delivered their sandwiches.

"We've got all these people in this country who want drugs," his uncle continued, "and you've got people down there who have nothing. Unless they want to go into the army or can get into the police, the only opportunity most of those people have is if they can get on with one of the cartels. There's not much else. People want to come here to get away from that, to get their kids away from all that."

Garner just listened, sure this was going somewhere he wasn't going to like.

"I made four or five trips down there with her. When we came back across the border the last time, we had one girl – young woman – crawled up in a ball under the seat in the back of the camper. I don't know how she stood it. We had two more on the roof under a canvas, surrounded by boxes of peppers and other supplies for the restaurant. The border people ran mirrors under the camper and let us through. All the dogs could smell was the peppers.

"Like I was saying, I'm not that fussy about a lot of things. I think Reya charges those people too much, but that's none of my business. I don't like the way she treats the people she helps across the border. She treats them like dirt, but again not my business."

Hank took a bite of his sandwich and washed it down with a sip of beer.

"We've always got at least a couple of them living in the basement. Once, she had half a dozen people crammed together down there."

Garner interrupted. "How do they get jobs? Find a place to live? That's what I don't understand."

"Some already have family or friends here, and they hook up with them. Reya has a contact that provides phony documentation. Most of the time, he can get them jobs and a place to live. He has companies lined up that will take undocumented workers and workers with questionable papers because they pay them almost nothing."

"Nice," Garner said. "Twenty-first-century sweatshops."

"Yeah, well, like I say, not my business. But now Reya is thinking about bringing back drugs. I think her son, Diego, is feeding her a line about how much more money she can make, but maybe whoever she has to deal with in Mexico is leaning on her."

"You don't want to get involved in that," Garner told

his uncle. "You just don't."

"I know, I know. That's what I keep telling Reya, but she's headstrong. She always thinks she knows best. She doesn't think she'll get caught, and she thinks if she does, she can just slip the cop or the DEA agent some money — like she did when the Mexican police caught her with guns."

Garner hadn't heard about that.

"Oh, and you'll love this," Hank continued, shaking his head. "She says Jesus will protect her."

Garner groaned. "I'm not someone who studies the Bible, but I had to read plenty of it in school. I don't remember the part about God protecting drug traffickers."

"I told her the restaurant is doing fine," Hank continued, warming to the topic. "I told her we don't need the money, but she won't listen. Before she left for this last trip, I told her, if she's going to get involved in that shit, I don't want any part of it. You and Jesus can do what you want, but I'm not getting involved in drugs. It's not right, and I'm too old to end up in prison."

Garner nodded in agreement. "When you make up your mind that you're going to leave," he said, "just let me know. A No-Fault divorce is easy — as long as you don't have issues over the property division." As he said that, it occurred to Garner where this conversation was headed.

"When you sold your bar," he asked his uncle, "you kept that money separate, right?"

"No, see, that's the problem. We just put all of our money into a joint account."

"Can't you just withdraw what you had?"

"No. That's why I need your help. Reya bought some property in Over the Rhine years ago when it first looked like the area was going to be — what do they call that —"

"Gentrified?"

"Yeah, she thought that whole area was going to be the next hot thing. They were going to kick out all the poor people, the hookers, and druggies and renovate the old build-ings, or replace them with new buildings. You know, for your professionals and better-off folks.

"She bought a building over there right before the riots in 2001. Those riots put the brakes on everything. She's just been renting the property, but that area is finally taking off."

The barmaid came back to see if they needed anything. When she left, Garner picked up where his uncle had left off. "Sounds like Reya had the right idea." He was feeling for solid ground, wondering when he was going to step into something squishy. "I wish I owned property there. In fact, I'd love to relocate my office there."

"Lot of people wish they owned property there now. Reya always wanted to open a restaurant in Over the Rhine. About six months ago, she got the tenants to leave, and she had contractors begin work renovating the place."

Garner still wasn't sure where this was going, but he re-mained certain he wasn't going to like it.

"I told her she needed to hire a lawyer or somebody who knew what they were doing, to make sure she got all the building permits and whatever else she needed. But she wouldn't listen. In Mexico, where she's from, you just pay off the building inspector."

Hank took a bite of his sandwich, grunted to show that he liked it, and washed the food down with a drink of beer.

"So, about a month ago," he continued, "the building inspector comes in and shuts the work down. She's going to have to pay some fines, and it looks like she's going to have to rip out some of the construction and have it done over. She's bleeding money right now."

"That's not your problem," Garner told his uncle. "You just need to take your money and get out, before things get worse."

"That's the thing. I can't take just take my money and get out because she's sunk it all in this new restaurant. There's almost nothing left in our account."

"Can she take out a loan against the restaurant in Florence to pay you back?"

"She's negotiating a refinancing package to get over the hump on the new restaurant, and she's going to use the restaurant in Florence as collateral."

"If she does that, you're screwed."

"I figured that. That's why I thought we should talk."

"It's actually worse than that," Garner said, thinking out loud. "If she decides to get into the drug business to make some extra cash, and the feds catch her with drugs in the restaurant, or in this new place, they can seize the property, and you'll never see her or your money again."

Garner watched his uncle take another sip of beer. He was beginning to regret not ordering one too. "When is she due back?"

"I expect her back Sunday night, late, but with travel, you never know."

"Are you ready to leave?"

"Yes. I'm not packed if that's what you mean, but I've made up my mind."

"Okay, you need to move out this weekend. I'll have the papers ready Monday morning for you to sign, and I'll get them filed right away. I'll see if I can force her to deal with you before she gets everything tied up."

"She is going to fight like hell," Hank said. "She needs the money for the new restaurant, and she doesn't see why I should get anything. It's how she thinks."

"Well," Garner said with conviction, "it's not how I think."

FRIDAY, OCTOBER 23

6:00 P.M. NEWS

Queen City News Live: Bringing you the news you want to hear.

Anchor Bob Bunker: This morning, the Cincinnati Police Department raided another local business, looking for undocumented workers. Tiffany Albern is on the scene.

Tiffany Albern: Bob, I'm here at the corporate offices of local home builder, The Bauherren Company. Cincinnati police officers arrived here early this morning and at several of the company's building sites around the city with search warrants. Police officers on the scene declined to comment, referring us to Hamilton County Prosecutor Richard Warren, who requested this morning's raids.

Pam Sprecher, the spokesperson for Warren, told me that the Prosecutor's office is looking for evidence the homebuilder knowingly uses subcontractors who have long track records of employing undocumented immigrants. She refused to say if she expects charges to be brought against The Bauherren Company, but she said the Prosecutor's office intends to follow the evidence, wherever it leads, and to bring charges where appropriate.

Co-Anchor Ashley Gelb: The measles outbreak at the William Howard Taft Academy continues to spread. Seven children have come down with the condition so far. One student has been hospitalized.

We contacted the Hamilton County Health Department. Officials there say that numerous studies have shown that the measles vaccine is safe and does not cause autism. A number of parents here and around the country disagree. They argue that too many children have developed autism after receiving the measles vaccine. We hope to have more on this developing story at 11:00.

MONDAY, OCTOBER 26 – SUNDAY, NOVEMBER 1

On Monday, Garner filed a divorce petition for Hank Bremen in the Circuit Court for Boone County, the Kentucky county that included Florence. That was where both Reya Sanchez and Hank lived and where Reya's restaurant was located.

In the petition, he alleged that the division of the parties' property should take into account that the restaurant had significantly increased in value during the marriage, short-lived as it was, largely due to Hank's contributions. The allegations were aggressive, but not altogether unreasonable. Hank had run other restaurants and since he and Reya married, he had spent more time in the restaurant than she had. Importantly, the allegations were enough to provide a basis for Garner to file a notice of lis pendens – a notice in the county's real estate records that his uncle claimed a lien on the restaurant.

By Friday, the bank's attorneys found the lien and notified Reya's attorney, Carl Anwalt, that the bank could not go through with the refinancing until she sorted things out with her husband and got the lien removed. When that had been resolved, the lawyers explained, the bank would need to re-evaluate – depending on how much that cost her. By day's end, Anwalt explained the new development to his strong-willed client.

On Saturday afternoon, two Hispanic women – one in her mid-fifties and the other in her early twenties – entered the grounds of the Second Amendment Hunting and Fishing Club in Boone County, Kentucky, where Hank had his own camper and was living temporarily. The older woman wore a knit cap – something like a ski cap. The younger woman wore Dockers, a sweatshirt with a brand name logo, and a pained expression.

The gate to the club grounds was locked, and a sign on the gate warned: "Private Property. No Trespassing."

Using a hacksaw to remove the lock, the two women made their way past the locked gate to the club grounds.

After making sure Hank was not around, the two women put a pound of marijuana in his camper and left. Ninety minutes later, Deputy Sheriffs from the Boone County Sheriff's office showed up with a search warrant, looking for the camper of one Hank Bremen.

Hank Bremen was away for the weekend with some friends on a fishing-and-drinking trip, but two of the younger members of the club returned from a hike just in time to see what the two Mexican women were up to. They knew about Hank's divorce – after Hank's latest bender, everyone in the club knew – and they knew Hank refused to have anything to do with drugs. So, when the two Mexican women left, the young men removed the stash, tossed it in their pickup truck, and took it to a small cave at the far end of the club grounds for safekeeping.

They made it back to the campsite in time to inform the Deputy Sheriffs of Hank's pending divorce – and to assure the uniformed gendarmes that the tip about drugs was just harassment by his ex. "Everybody knew it was a mistake for him to marry that woman," they explained. "She's plum loco."

When Hank returned on Sunday night, club members filled him in on what he'd missed. Out of curiosity, he asked what happened to the marijuana.

"On Saturday night," the Club president said, "we got together all the members who were here for the weekend, and we got rid of it. You could say it was a joint effort."

"The evidence," someone else chimed in, "went up in smoke."

TUESDAY, NOVEMBER 10

After her husband pointed out that her speeding ticket was her third moving violation in less than a year, Emily Goessel was beside herself. She could not have her license suspended. If she had to, she would attend those awful classes, but really, she didn't see why she should even have to do that. She had a friend who had to go to those classes, and she said they had been dreadful. Most of the people there were riff-raff. Her friend said it was worse than shopping at Walmart. *She* had nothing in common with *them*.

Tired of listening to his wife grouse about why her traffic tickets were his fault, Larry Goessel contacted the law firm his company used. The law firm was one of the city's top firms, with offices in the downtown business district. He spoke with the corporate lawyer with whom he usually worked and asked her if there was anything the firm could do to help his wife.

She, in turn, contacted the head of the firm's litigation section, Hayden Lassiter Barrington, V, whom everyone called Quint, to see how the firm handled such requests. She assumed the firm would send a litigation associate to traffic court with the client. But Quint had no desire to have the firm's young lawyers pulled off profitable matters to deal with a client's traffic ticket. He knew from bitter experience the client would be unhappy with the result, and the firm would end up writing off most of the time involved. Besides, traffic court was an awful place, and he did not want his talented young litigators wasting their time there.

After making a call to be sure the pompous old pettifogger was still practicing and would take the case, Quint referred Emily Goessel to Weary Dunston, the "dean" of the traffic court bar. He assured Goessel that Dunston routinely represented the firm's clients in such matters and that there was no one who knew the traffic court personnel better. He would also be much less expensive.

Goessel was somewhat mollified that she would be represented by the dean of the traffic court – a real veteran who knew his way around that madhouse – until she met the old goat and realized having to deal with him would be yet another humiliation. His suit was older than her kids. And to add insult to injury, Dunston had insisted on payment in advance, like she was one of his usual deadbeat clients.

Goessel explained to Dunston the extenuating circumstances – the call from the school that her daughter was sick with a potentially fatal illness.

"The traffic court hears stories like that all day," Dunston explained wearily. "The court won't be impressed. The traffic court judge will want to know one thing, and one thing only," he said. "How fast were you going?"

Goessel could only imagine what traffic court judges might have to put up with, but she thought the phlegmy old litigator was too dismissive of her special circumstances.

"I hope this doesn't come out wrong," she said, "but I can only imagine the sort of people traffic court judges usually have to deal with. I'm not like *those* people. That has to count for something."

Dunston was unconvinced.

"Everything about this is unfair," Goessel complained, launching into her explanation about how, when the cop turned his siren on, she made the mistake of pulling into the parking lot of that fleabag inn. "It was the one where Ace Lindsey's daughter caught her husband having a fling with that Filipino nurse," she said. "And then the young traffic cop, I bet he was still in his twenties, made me sit there while he flirted with some lady cop. My daughter was sick, but *that* came first?"

She insisted Dunston watch the video on her cell phone. As he did, she pointed out the injustice that neither cop had shown the least interest in the Mexicans. "I mean, Christ," she said, "they were probably illegals. But I'm the one who had to show identification? *Whose country is it?*"

Dunston grunted when the video finished and returned the cell phone without saying more.

Upset that the old geezer did not seem sufficiently stirred to indignation, Goessel redoubled her efforts. "You know," she complained, "this was not even fifteen minutes after Ace Lindsey's daughter was last seen, and this is what the police are doing? Flirting? Checking *my* identification."

"What if, for *Chrissake*," she added, trying to get the old man to focus on the injustice of her situation, "that Syrian doctor didn't kill the Lindsey girl? What if one of those Mexicans hanging around that place had something to do with her death? These cops would never know. They were too busy," she argued, "planning a Dunkin' Donuts date to do any police work."

Dunston looked up from his coffee as if surprised to discover that Emily Goessel was still in his office. "This was the same day," he asked, "that the Lindsey girl went missing?"

"From what they said in the newspaper, she was last seen about fifteen minutes before all this. And these cops had nothing better to do than hassle me. Can you at least tell the judge?"

Dunston asked to see the video again. While he watched it, Goessel demanded that he talk with the police and threaten to turn the video over to the news media, or something.

Dunston asked if she had informed the prosecutor's office about the video? Or the doctor's defense attorney?

She had not. She had no desire to get caught up in that. She didn't have the time. She was already dealing with people who were blaming her because their kids got the measles.

"My dear lady, why are people blaming you for the measles?" Dunston asked.

"Long story short," she said, but the explanation that

followed seemed to Dunston more long than short.

"Such a travesty!" Dunston commiserated when at last he could insert himself into the conversation again. "As a businesswoman," Dunston said, "that is not how you want people to think of you."

"What do you mean?" Goessel asked.

"When people think of you, do you want them to think of you as that woman – *wrongly, wrongly, of course, but you know how people are* – who caused those poor kids to get sick? Or do you want people to think of you as the brave woman who selflessly came forward and provided crucial evidence in the trial of a man wrongly accused of killing his beloved wife?"

This was something Goessel had not considered.

"My dear lady, your name will be mentioned in every newscast, in every newspaper. You will be, if I dare say so, the toast of the town!"

Goessel was uncertain. Her own problems were pressing, the problems of some Syrian doctor more distant.

"It is," Dunston declaimed, "after all, your civic duty. Our judicial process, Ma'am, depends on citizens like you. It is, if I may say so, just as much your duty as voting and paying taxes. More so, perhaps, because this poor man's freedom hangs in the balance."

"You really think this is that important?"

"Absolutely, my good woman. It is a basic axiom that the Law is entitled to every man's testimony. And let's be candid, shall we? If the Law is to have every man's testimony, then so much greater must be the need for a woman's testimony. Especially, if I may say so, a woman like yourself. Why Ma'am, your testimony is nothing less than critical if justice is to prevail in this sorry case."

"I meant," Goessel clarified, "do you really think that my testimony would be important enough to make the news?"

Weary Dunston was certain of it. She should just leave things to him.

WEDNESDAY, NOVEMBER 11

11:00 A.M. – 5:00 P.M.

Devin Garner was about to learn just how Reya Sanchez felt about his aggressive representation of her soon-to-be ex. The Postal Service delivered a large package to his office. When he opened the box, inside it he found two dead chickens and two baby chicks, all with their necks wrung. Blood pooled in the bottom of the box.

He immediately called the police. His next call was to his uncle. Hank told him about Reya planting marijuana in his trailer and calling the police. Hank said he had no doubt Reya was responsible for the dead chickens as well.

"But why two dead chickens and two baby chicks?" Garner asked. "There's got to be some significance to that."

"I think she's got you confused with your cousin. He's married, and they have two kids."

"So, she's threatening to kill me and the wife and kids I don't have unless I back off?"

"Devin, I'm sorry. I really am. I don't think she'll do anything. She's just angry and acting out. But we can drop the suit if you're concerned."

"Not going to happen," Garner assured his uncle as the police arrived.

The police said they would take the package and its contents as evidence, but he could tell they lost interest the moment they realized that the incident was related to a divorce. He used his cell phone camera to take pictures of the package and its contents from every angle he could think of.

When the police left, he called his former partner, Rachel Burns, in the Prosecutor's office, hoping she would agree to build a fire under the police. Instead, she suggested he call the Postal Inspectors. The Postal Service, after all, had its own, well-trained police force. He tried that, but once again, as soon as the postal inspector realized the incident arose from a domestic dispute, he too lost interest.

It occurred to Garner that there was only one large, well-known poultry farm in the area. Twenty minutes later, he was there talking with Arnie Vogel, the owner.

"You want to know who I sold those birds to?"

"Right."

"There was two of them, but I don't know their names. I figured they wanted them for church services. We get some of that, every now and again. I try not to ask too many questions."

"Can you describe them?"

"Mexican."

"Women?"

"Yep. One was older, maybe in her fifties, short but big around. And pushy, if you know what I mean."

"And the other?"

"She was just a kid — maybe twenty, scrawny, no meat on her bones."

"Anything else you can remember?"

"Well, the pushy one, she was running the show. The girl didn't say anything. The older woman was wearing a hat, like one of them ski caps, but I don't see why, it wasn't cold."

"Other than that, you have no idea who she was?"

"Nope. Like I said, I try to mind my own business."

Garner pulled out his cell phone and scrolled through the photographs until he found the photo he had taken of Reya when he first met her. In the picture, she was standing next to Hank, but the important thing was, she was wearing the knit cap she apparently always wore.

Garner showed Vogel the picture.

"Yeah," Vogel said, "I'd say that's her."

"You going to be around tomorrow?" Garner asked.

"I'm around here every day. Will be till they bury me."

"I'm going to be back with an affidavit I need you to sign. It will say what you just told me about who bought those chickens."

"Look, I'm sorry this happened, but I don't want to get involved. I didn't have anything to do with what she might have done after she left here. I'm not signing anything."

Garner decided not to force the old man to dig in his heels. He would come back the next day with the affidavit and a subpoena. He'd give him a choice – he could sign the affidavit, or he could appear in court and testify.

But as he was about to leave, he noticed something interesting. "That box over there," he said to pointing to a corrugated cardboard container about two feet on each edge. "What comes in that?"

"Antibiotics. We put it in the feed we give the birds."

"When the two Mexican women bought the chickens, you put them in a box just like that," Garner said.

"Don't remember, but could have. 'Bout the right size."

"Can I have that box?"

"Sure, I don't need it."

Back at his office, Garner Googled the drug company that made the antibiotic and located a phone number for the company. He placed a call to its corporate headquarters and asked to speak to someone in the company's Law Department. He was lucky. The attorney who took his call was sympathetic.

Garner emailed photos of the box in which the chickens had been delivered. The next day, the attorney sent him an affidavit from a shipping manager, attesting to the fact that the box in question had been shipped to the Vogel Farm in Kentucky.

Garner went to work preparing a motion for an order restraining Reya Sanchez from acts or threats of violence or intimidation aimed at her spouse, Hank Bremen, or his attorney.

PART II: THE PROSECUTION

THURSDAY, NOVEMBER 12

12:30 P.M. – 12.40 P.M.

Still dressed in his scrubs, Dr. Medawar entered the Trauma Center waiting room and scanned the people waiting to learn the surgical outcomes of their family member or loved one. Removing his surgical cap, he asked, "Mrs. Freeman?"

"Yes," a short, heavyset black woman responded.

He waited as she struggled to get up. When she stood, her large bosom was more than counterbalanced by her even larger hips, the whole steadied by a thick wooden cane.

"I'm Dr. Medawar," he told the woman.

"And I'm Violet Freeman."

"Your son made it through the surgery. I had to remove his spleen, but I got the bullets out, and I've got everything sutured up."

"Is he going to be okay?"

"We'll know better in forty-eight hours. If he makes it through the next couple days, then I think he'll pull through."

"Give him strength, Lord!" Mrs. Freeman said in a loud voice, looking upward. "And bless this wonderful doctor." Turning her gaze back to Medawar, she added, "Thank you, thank you!"

"Your son is lucky to be alive," Medawar cautioned. "If those bullets had been any higher, he wouldn't have lived long enough to make it here."

"Oh, God!" Mrs. Freeman said.

"He's sixteen and healthy, so we should be optimistic."

Mrs. Freeman began sobbing, but managed to say, "God bless you, God bless you."

Medawar excused himself and approached the two uniformed officers standing nearby. "Are you here on the Freeman shooting?" he asked.

"No," the older of the two officers said. "I'm John Dorman, and this is Pete Workman. We're from the Hamilton County Sheriff's office, and we're here —"

A nurse interrupted. "Dr. Medawar," she called from the door, "there's been a shooting with multiple victims. They're on their way in."

"Oh God," Mrs. Freeman said, "please don't let it be Jeremiah! Please, God, don't take both of my boys."

"I'll be right there," Medawar told the nurse.

"We're here," Deputy Dorman said, his voice more official, "because we have a warrant for your arrest." The other officer removed a pair of handcuffs from his belt and stepped behind Medawar.

In the corner of the waiting room, a skinny young woman with a purple streak through her short hair used her cell phone to video the arrest.

"We're shorthanded today, and we've got injured people coming in," Medawar pleaded. "Can't this wait until we get that taken care of?"

"You have the right to remain silent," Dorman said. "Anything you say can ..."

"What about the rights of the people on their way here?" Medawar asked angrily. "If some of them die because we don't have enough surgeons, what are you going to tell their families?"

"Anything you say can and will be used against you in court," Dorman continued. As he did, the second officer snapped the handcuffs around Medawar's wrists.

The nurse stuck her head back into the waiting room. "They've started arriving, Doctor," she said.

"I can't come," Medawar snapped. "They're arresting me."

"We've got patients who need him," the nurse rebuked

the officers.

"Ma'am, we've got a warrant."

"Tell Dr. Salween what's going on," Medawar told the nurse. "Tell him you need help."

"Oh Lord," Mrs. Freeman cried out to the heavens. "Do you see what's going on here? Sweet Jesus, do you see this?"

The young woman using her cell phone to video the excitement stood and moved to get a better angle.

"You have the right to speak to an attorney," the Deputy Sheriff said. "If you cannot afford an attorney, one will be appointed for you. Do you understand these rights?"

"Can I call my attorney now? Maybe he can talk some sense into you."

"You can call your attorney from the Detention Center."

"I'm in my scrubs," Medawar said. "Can I at least change into my clothes? They're in my locker, with my wallet. You can come with me."

"We need you to follow us," Dorman said, impatiently, pointing toward the patient entrance. His colleague noticed the woman with a cell phone and tried to position himself in front of her.

Just then, a hospital administrator materialized, red-faced and winded, followed by a gray-uniformed security guard. "What's going on?" the administrator asked.

The woman using her cell phone moved to avoid the younger officer.

"We've got a warrant for his arrest," Dorman said.

"The devil has them men's souls," Mrs. Freeman informed the administrator. "Lord," she added, looking upwards, "reach down and cast the devil out of them so this doctor can do your work."

"We've got patients who need to be operated on," the administrator insisted. "Can't this wait?"

"We have our orders," Workman said.

"Lord, you hear that?" Mrs. Freeman shouted between sobs. "Drive the devil out of those men, Jesus."

"Christ on crutches," the security guard said to Mrs. Freeman, "will you give it a rest?"

"That's enough," the administrator admonished the guard. "When we're done here, I want you in my office." Turning to Mrs. Freeman, he said, "Ma'am, I'm sorry."

"Jesus, what is this world coming to?" Mrs. Freeman wailed, looking to the ceiling. "Take me to heaven now, Lord. It's too much! It's too much you're askin' of me, Lord."

Dorman nudged Medawar toward the door.

"Call my attorney," Medawar called over his shoulder to the administrator. "Devin Garner. He's in the phonebook. Let him know what's going on, please. Devin Garner."

"They wouldn't be doing this," someone else in the waiting room chimed in, "if'n it was their kid that needed to be operated on."

The woman with the purple streak in her hair said nothing, but looked up "Devin Garner attorney" on her smartphone. She emailed the video to him, before offering it to a local television station for $100.

12:40 P.M. - 12:45 P.M.

Devin Garner was leaving the courthouse, when he got the call on his cell. He had just completed routine appearances on several cases.

"Devin, it's Bill Bradford. The grand jury returned an indictment against Dr. Medawar." Garner had tried to get an agreement from Bradford to allow Medawar to come in voluntarily, rather than have the police show up unannounced to make the arrest. Bradford had refused, saying Warren had nixed a surrender.

"Okay, thanks for letting me know."

"The Sheriff's office should be making the arrest now,

if they haven't done so already."

"What does the indictment charge?"

"Murder One."

"Bill, that's insane."

"The grand jury didn't think so."

"Bail? Tell me you're not going to keep Rafiq in the Detention Center."

"The arraignment is tomorrow at 1:00. You can ask for bail then."

"Bill, he's not going anywhere. He was willing to come in voluntarily. We've been through this. I've given you everything you need on his ties to the community –"

"Warren insists."

"Then, set something up so I can talk with Warren."

"He's not interested. It's only one night."

"Warren keeps telling the media that Rafiq is a Syrian Muslim. That's not going to play well in the Detention Center. If anything happens to him, if he gets hurt or killed, I'm not just suing the county. I'll make sure Rafiq, or his family, sues Warren personally."

"Threatening Warren isn't going to make him want to do you any favors."

Garner made a face that showed his impatience

"The arraignment is tomorrow at one." Bradford gave Garner the number of the courtroom where the arraignment would take place.

"Just tell Warren. If anything happens to Rafiq, I'll file suit in the middle of his campaign, and I'll do everything in my power to get him as much bad press as I can."

"Devin, your guy is not getting any special treatment. He's getting what anyone else indicted for murder would get."

"If he weren't getting special treatment, you wouldn't have asked for an indictment. You'd be trying to figure out who killed Ann."

"I don't have an ax to grind, Devin. The grand jury

found probable cause to believe Dr. Medawar killed her. It's my job to prosecute."

"Give me a break. It's a ham sandwich indictment."

"You can believe that if you want."

"Have you found an eyewitness?" Garner demanded.

"No."

"Have you found the gun?"

"We've been through all this," Bradford said. "Save it for the trial."

12:45 P.M. – 1:30 P.M.

Medawar fought a swirl of emotions as the Deputy Sheriffs delivered him to the Hamilton County Detention Center. Inside, he watched as the intake officer made the necessary entries in the computer and summoned another officer.

Medawar followed the second man to another room, where he was fingerprinted. He opened his mouth, so the man could swab his inner cheek for a DNA specimen. He could think of half-dozen ways the specimen might have been contaminated, but said nothing.

He followed a different officer into another room for mug shots, and from there to yet another room, where an officer wearing surgical gloves instructed him to disrobe.

"I just got out of the operating room when they arrested me," he complained to the officer as he undressed. "Do you really think I keep drugs stuck up my ass while I'm doing surgery in case somebody shows up to arrest me?"

"They don't pay me to think," the officer replied. "They just pay me to follow procedures."

Realizing it was pointless to argue, Medawar submitted to the full body search.

When the officer finished, he pointed to a package. "Your uniform is there," he said. "Put it on."

Medawar put the jumpsuit on. When he finished dressing, he said, "I want to talk to my attorney."

12:40 P.M. - 12:50 P.M.

Garner contacted the motions judge and requested an emergency bond hearing. The judge's assignment clerk told Garner the judge could hear him at 3:30 and instructed him to notify the Prosecutor's office.

"Who is the motions judge today?"

"Shirazi," the clerk said.

"Excellent!" Garner said. "Thanks."

Judge Amir Shirazi was wicked smart, but was bitter at having twice been passed over for an appointment to the appellate court. He was also a bully, who took pleasure in terrorizing new lawyers. Ordinarily, Garner would have cringed at having to appear before the dyspeptic jurist. But Judge Shirazi had a longstanding feud with the Hamilton County Sheriff. Garner couldn't have hoped for a better draw.

Garner called Bradford and told him he was making an emergency application for bail for Dr. Medawar.

Bradford made it clear he was upset with Garner's move, but said he wasn't surprised. "You're taking this too personal," he warned Garner.

Garner hesitated before saying, "You have no idea."

His next call was to Cam Wiley, the video whiz from the documentary class.

1:05 P.M. – 1:20 P.M.

Garner hustled from the courthouse to the Detention Center. On the way, he got a call from Medawar.

"Devin, I've been arrested. I'm in the Detention Center."

"I heard. I'm on my way. I'll be there in three minutes, maybe less. We can talk as soon as they let me see you."

Medawar thanked Garner.

Fifteen minutes later, Garner sat across from Medawar in a small attorney-consultation room. Garner wore a suit and tie. Medawar wore an orange jumpsuit.

"Obviously," Garner said, "Bradford got the grand jury to indict."

"So I hear," Medawar said, sardonically.

"That's the bad news. The worse news is, the indictment is for Murder One."

"Jesus."

"I know. It sucks."

"You told me to expect this, but it's just unreal. I can't believe this is happening to me."

"Rafiq, I'm sorry about all this."

"It's not your fault. How long do I have to stay in here?"

"That's what I want to talk you about. The arraignment is tomorrow at one, and the court will sort out bail then. But I've arranged for an emergency bail hearing. It's a long shot, but I want to try."

"You'll let me know how that turns out?"

"Actually, they will have you participate by a video hookup from here. You probably won't get to say anything, but at least you'll know what happens and be able to get the flavor of the thing."

"Devin, this probably doesn't get us anywhere, but it really upsets me. When they arrested me, I'd just gotten out of a surgery. We had multiple victims from a shooting on their way in. I asked them to let me take care of that first, but they insisted on bringing me in anyway."

"Who do I need to talk to at the Trauma Center to get the details on how that impacted the Center?"

Medawar gave Garner several names and titles.

"Who would be willing to testify?"

"Go for Dr. Salween. He'll be upset they were left short-handed. The suits won't want to commit to anything until they know for certain which way the wind is blowing. And maybe not even then."

"Got it."

"By the way, if you get to the Trauma Center, my clothes

and wallet are in my locker." He gave Garner his locker com-bination.

"When they led you from the Trauma Center," Garner asked, "was the press waiting?"

"Yeah, they did the whole perp walk thing. My family, everybody at the Trauma Center will see that."

"That shouldn't have happened. It was a sealed indict-ment, meaning no one was supposed to know about it until they arrested you. Someone – I'm guessing from the Prose-cutor's office – leaked the details to the media."

"Ann was right about Warren."

Garner glanced at his watch. "I've got to run to get pre-pared for the hearing."

Medawar looked crestfallen.

Garner decided his client needed a pep talk. "I know we discussed this," he said, "but remember, the old saying is pretty much true. Any prosecutor worth his salt can get a grand jury to indict a ham sandwich. But it's a hell of a lot harder for a prosecutor to prove beyond a reasonable doubt that a ham sandwich shot someone."

"Devin, if I were a ham sandwich, Dick Warren wouldn't be interested in me. Warren thinks I'm a falafel."

Garner laughed. "You may be right, but honestly, I don't think Dick Warren thinks about anybody but himself."

3:30 P.M. – 4:00 P.M.

Judge Amir Shirazi glared down at Garner. "Your client was arrested *when*?"

"Two Deputy Sheriffs arrested Dr. Medawar about 12:30 this afternoon," Garner responded. "If I —"

"And the arraignment is *when*?"

"Tomorrow at 1:00," Liz O'Malley volunteered.

"And *you* are?" Judge Shirazi asked.

"Liz O'Malley from the Prosecutor's office, Your Honor. I'm new."

"Mr. Bradford isn't going to honor us with his presence

this afternoon?"

"This was scheduled on short notice, Your Honor, and he's tied up on something else."

"He wants you to take the blame if the hearing doesn't go right."

"He said I could handle the hearing. He said you were a good judge and would do the right thing."

Judge Shirazi grunted contemptuously. "Did he tell you to say that?"

"No, sir," O'Malley fibbed.

"Mr. Garner, you were about to explain why this couldn't wait until tomorrow. Please edify me."

"Dr. Medawar is a surgeon, Your Honor. He's on the staff at the Trauma Center, and —"

"He's a surgeon," Judge Shirazi interrupted, "and he doesn't think the Detention Center is good enough for him? So that's why this can't wait until tomorrow?"

"He's the best trauma surgeon in town, Your Honor. If some nut job walks into this courtroom five minutes from now, or tomorrow, and pulls out a gun and shoots you, you'd want Dr. Medawar to be the one who operates."

"Unless, in your hypothetical, he's busy committing capital murder?"

"Your Honor, getting shot wasn't a hypothetical today for several young men who arrived by ambulance at the Trauma Center just as the Deputy Sheriffs showed up to arrest Dr. Medawar."

"That was the shooting in the West End?"

"Yes, Your Honor. Dr. Medawar and a Trauma Center official pleaded for the Deputies to hold off until they could get control of the situation with the incoming victims. They explained that the Trauma Center was already shorthanded, and —"

"And our wonderful Sheriff's office personnel couldn't wait?" Judge Shirazi asked, his voice full of sarcasm.

"Your Honor," Liz O'Malley interrupted. "This has

nothing to do with whether the defendant is entitled to bail. Whatever happened earlier today happened. We can't do anything about that now, Your Honor, but that doesn't give Dr. Medawar a get-out-of-jail pass."

"If it's all right with you, Ms. O'Malley, I'll decide whether it does or not."

O'Malley's face reddened.

"Two of the victims died today," Garner said, "one of them on the operating table, and the other waiting for a surgeon. Obviously, I can't say for certain if either or both would have lived, but –"

"One of them was the son of a Cincinnati Police officer?" Judge Shirazi asked, happy to pile on. "I think that's what I heard on the news."

Garner looked at counsel table, where Dr. Salween was sitting next to Cam Wiley. "Is that correct?" Garner asked.

Dr. Salween rose and stood ramrod straight. His hair was chestnut brown and perfectly groomed, his jawline strong and manly. "Yes, that is correct," he said, in a deep voice. Someone whose presence commanded respect, Dr. Salween strode in carefully measured steps to where the attorneys were huddled in front of the bench.

"We lost two young men today," he said. "One of them was the son of a policeman. As I understand it, he was an innocent victim. Just in the wrong place, at the wrong time."

"Your Honor," Garner said, "Dr. Salween is Chief of Staff at the Trauma Center and was there today."

His curiosity about the shootings sated, Judge Shirazi asked, "Mr. Garner, is this your projector and screen?"

"Yes, Your Honor. A young woman in the Trauma Center made a video of the Deputies arresting Dr. Medawar."

"You didn't tell me to bring popcorn," Judge Shirazi grumbled. "Let's see your video."

Garner turned to Cam Wiley at counsel table. Cam was dressed in cargo pants and a grey-and-brown checked shirt. At the last minute, in an effort to be more formal, he had added a blue-and-gold stripped tie that he found in the trunk of his car.

Garner nodded, and Cam hit the play button. He adjusted the sound.

When the video ended, Judge Shirazi shook his head in disgust. "I assume," he said to Garner, "this will be on the evening news?"

"I don't know anything about that," Garner said, "but I wouldn't be surprised. It was a sealed indictment, Your Honor, but somehow the press knew to be waiting outside the Trauma Center when the Deputies left the building with Dr. Medawar."

Judge Shirazi turned to O'Malley. "Will the prosecution stipulate that this is what happened, or do we need to have Mr. Garner call his witnesses?"

"Yes, Your Honor," O'Malley agreed.

Judge Shirazi looked at O'Malley over the top of his glasses, dragging out the look for effect. "Yes, the prosecution will stipulate, or yes, I need to have Mr. Garner call his witnesses?"

"We'll stipulate, Your Honor."

"*We* will, huh? That being you and your tapeworm?"

"The prosecution, Your Honor."

Judge Shirazi looked at the image on the video screen. "Dr. Medawar, are you on call this evening? Are they going to want you to come in and help out if we have a mass shooting?"

"Yes, Your Honor," Medawar said.

"And if I order you released, will you show up for the arraignment tomorrow at 1:00?"

"Yes, Your Honor."

"Dr. –" Judge Shirazi looked at Dr. Salween, but appeared to be struggling to recall his name.

"Salween," the physician volunteered.

"Dr. Salween, I assume you know your colleague, Dr. Medawar?"

"Yes, sir."

"If I release him overnight, will he show up tomorrow?"

"He's a good man, Your Honor. I'm sure he'll be here."

"Mr. Garner, how solid is the case against your client?"

"The indictment charges him with murdering his wife, but the prosecution has no eyewitness, no weapon, no idea where she was shot. They can't even find the car she was driving. Frankly, Your Honor, there's only one reason Dr. Medawar was indicted. Mr. Warren is under the mistaken impression that Dr. Medawar is a Middle Easterner and a Muslim, and that ties in nicely with Warren's election campaign."

"I object!" O'Malley said.

"You *object*, Ms. O'Malley?" Judge Shirazi said, emphasizing her awkward word choice. "So tell me. Does the prosecution have an eyewitness to the murder?"

"No, Your Honor, but—"

"Does the prosecution have the murder weapon?"

"No, but —"

"Have they found her car?"

"Not yet, but —"

"And is Mr. Warren under the impression that Dr. Medawar is from the Middle East?"

"I think he may be, Your Honor, but Mr. Warren didn't indict Dr. Medawar. The grand jury did."

"Ms. O'Malley, my name is Amir Farrukh Shirazi. That's Farsi. Or, as I'm sure Mr. Warren thinks of it, Iranian. I suppose Mr. Warren thinks I'm a Middle Easterner. If someone shoots my wife, is he going to have me indicted?"

"I don't think so."

"You should have let your tapeworm answer that, Ms. O'Malley. It might have sounded more confident."

"I'm confident, Your Honor."

"And Dr. Salween is confident," Judge Shirazi retorted, "that Dr. Medawar will show up tomorrow."

Judge Shirazi turned and looked at the image of Dr.

Medawar on the video screen again. "If I let you go tonight, you're not going to try to be the next Dr. Richard Kimble, the next 'Fugitive,' are you?"

"No, sir," Medawar responded. He had no idea who Richard Kimble was, but his voice was firm and crisp.

"You're not claiming a one-armed man killed your wife, are you?"

"No, sir. I don't know who killed my wife – only that I didn't. I loved my wife very much."

"If Ms. O'Malley gets upset and shoots me, can I count on you to operate?"

"I would do everything I could to save you."

"Here's what I'm going to do," Judge Shirazi said, pausing as if to give his decision one final moment of deliberation. It was something he did just before announcing his decisions. It built suspense, and he believed it made him look thoughtful. "I am going to release Dr. Medawar on his own recognizance overnight, without prejudice to the decision the presiding judge makes tomorrow at his arraignment.

"You are not to leave the county," Judge Shirazi continued. "You can go to the Trauma Center if they need you tonight, but otherwise, you should do what you can to get your affairs in order. At the arraignment tomorrow, the court may remand you to the Detention Center. And just in case I'm wrong about that, I would advise you to bring your passport with you tomorrow.

"One more thing," he added, removing his glasses. "Dr. Medawar, after that video hits tonight's news, I don't think you want to do anything that would give our esteemed Sheriff and his Deputies reason to arrest you on a fugitive warrant. Do you understand what I'm telling you?"

"I think so."

"Good. The 'Fugitive' was a fine television show and movie, but it wouldn't be such a good thing in real life. Do we understand each other?"

"Yes, sir."

"Very good." Judge Shirazi looked at the individuals standing before the bench. "Dr. Salween, thank you for coming in. Ms. O'Malley, nice to meet you. I'm sure the pleasure was all mine. Please give my regards to Mr. Warren.

"The order will be ready in a few minutes. We're adjourned."

THURSDAY, NOVEMBER 12

6:00 P.M. NEWS

Queen City News Live: Bringing you the news you want to hear.

News Anchor Bob Bunker: Our lead story tonight: A running gunfight between rival gangs in the West End left five wounded today, two fatally. One of the victims, apparently an innocent bystander, was the son of Cincinnati Police officer Dwight Johnson. Community leaders are calling for tougher action against gangs. More on that story in a moment.

Also today, a grand jury indicted local physician Rafiq Medawar in the slaying of his wife, Ann Lindsey Medawar. Dr. Medawar is seen here being led away in handcuffs from the Trauma Center, where he is a surgeon. Controversy erupted over the timing of his arrest. Officers from the Sheriff's office arrived to arrest Dr. Medawar just as victims from today's shootings in the West End were arriving. Trauma Center personnel asked the officers to delay the arrest until the shooting victims could be stabilized.

We have exclusive footage of that exchange now, made by someone who was in the waiting room. [Edited version of video plays.]

A spokesperson for the Sheriff's office said the officers' actions are under review.

The Trauma Center refused official comment on the incident, but several sources told us that Dr. Medawar's arrest left the Trauma Center shorthanded and may have contributed to the death of Officer Johnson's son.

Tiffany Albern is at the Hamilton County courthouse and has more on the indictment of Dr. Medawar.

Tiffany Albern: According to a spokesperson for the Hamilton County Prosecutor's office, after completing his shift at the Trauma Center, Dr. Medawar went to a nearby inn where he a met a Filipino nurse, apparently for an affair.

The Prosecutor's office says Ms. Medawar followed her husband to the Sleep Cheap Inn in Clifton and used her cell phone to record videos of her husband and the nurse entering the inn and leaving sometime later.

Prosecutors believe Ms. Medawar confronted her husband, and he became enraged and killed her. The Prosecutor's office says Dr. Medawar does not have any prior arrests or convictions and that it has no reason to believe that Dr. Medawar, who is Syrian, is in the country illegally.

Lower Price Hill attorney Devin Garner, who represents Dr. Medawar, issued a statement denying the charges. He claims that Dr. Medawar went to the Sleep Cheap Inn to check on the children of an undocumented woman, who was afraid to take her sick children to the hospital. He claims Ms. Medawar met her husband there to get footage for a documentary she was making.

News Anchor Bob Bunker: When we return, we will have more on today's West End shootings.

FRIDAY, NOVEMBER 13

12:45 P.M. – 1:30 P.M.

After an indictment, criminal procedure requires the person charged – the defendant – appear in court, be apprised of the charges, and enter a plea. Given the law's preference for words derived from Latin over their simpler Anglo-Saxon counterparts, this typically brief proceeding is called an arraignment.

The arraignment on the Medawar indictment was Friday afternoon. Devin Garner ushered Medawar into the sixth-floor courtroom. As he did, Garner immediately noticed that the courtroom seemed to be bristling with more energy than usual.

Garner scanned the crowd. In addition to the usual assortment of defense attorneys and clients, there were several reporters. The sorting process was easy. The lawyers dressed better than the reporters, and the reporters dressed better than the usual defendants.

Garner smiled at the contrast between his client and the other clients milling around the courtroom. Medawar wore a navy suit, a crisp white shirt with French cuffs, and a silk tie. His cufflinks bore the medical staff insignia.

In contrast, the other defendants in the courtroom seemed to have dressed down for the occasion. Nearly all wore casual clothes. Some wore sweatshirts. Others wore shirts with collars, but left the tails of their shirts hang out in back. Several had handkerchiefs or bandanas tied around their foreheads. And they were the lucky ones. Dressed in orange jumpsuits and shackles, the less fortunate would be brought into the courtroom only when the bailiff called their cases.

Garner spotted William Bradford standing next to the counsel table reserved for the prosecution. Garner started down the center aisle toward the front of the courtroom, but as he did, he got a surprise. Hamilton County Prosecutor Richard Warren was seated at the prosecution table.

"*The Dick* is here," Garner whispered to Medawar. "Let's go introduce ourselves."

Medawar balked. "I don't want anything to do with him."

"Come on, it'll be fun. Besides, we need him to meet you. We've got to replace the stereotype he has with a sense of who you really are."

Garner walked energetically to the front of the courtroom, greeting people he knew as he went, and stepped through the gate or "bar" that separated the area immediately in front of the bench from the cheap seats. Medawar followed, but with less enthusiasm.

"Bill," Garner greeted Bradford as he made his way to the prosecution table. "I want to introduce my client, Dr. Medawar." Turning to his client, Garner said, "Rafiq, this is Assistant Prosecutor Bill Bradford. He'll be handling your case."

As Garner spoke, Warren stood and extended his hand. "I'm Dick Warren," he told Garner. Warren was a big man, tall and broad-shouldered. He had probably been athletic in his earlier years, but now had heavy jowls and a pot-belly. His hair, which he wore in a military cut, was in full retreat.

"Pleasure to meet you," Garner said, shaking the older man's hand. "Mr. Warren, this is Dr. Medawar. Rafiq, this is Dick Warren, the Hamilton County Prosecutor. We don't get to see him in this building very often."

Medawar extended his hand, but Warren ignored him.

"Where are we on the docket?" Garner asked. There were usually fifteen to twenty cases on the afternoon docket, sometimes more. The proceedings typically included arraignments, scheduling conferences and other routine matters. It would likely be late afternoon before the last case would be called.

"We're up first," Bradford said.

Garner wasn't surprised. He assumed Warren was there to grandstand a bit in connection with the Medawar arraignment, hoping to make the evening news. Warren wouldn't want to hang around the courtroom any longer than necessary.

"Mr. Warren," Garner asked, "didn't you go to St. Xavier? That's where Dr. Medawar went to high school. He was in a different year than you, of course, but he was the class valedictorian. You were too, when you graduated, weren't you?"

Warren looked mildly put off. "I didn't go to X, and I wasn't the class nerd. I went to Moeller and played football. We took special pleasure in beating the wusses who went to X."

"All rise," the bailiff called out, signaling that the judge was about to enter the courtroom.

Garner led Medawar to the table for defense counsel, but remained standing. He motioned for Medawar to do the same.

Judge Seiler entered the courtroom, quickly climbed the stairs to the bench, and set down a stack of files. He glanced around the courtroom at the larger than usual crowd and said, "Please be seated."

Judge Seiler was the same judge who presided over Jonas Trottel's trial. Garner counted him a lucky draw. He thought Judge Seiler the best trial judge on the Hamilton County bench. Judge Seiler was Jewish, but Garner didn't think he would buy into the prosecution's theory that Medawar was a Middle Eastern Muslim and therefore guilty. Garner wasn't so sure about some of the other judges.

The bailiff called out, "State versus Rafiq A. Medawar, case number—" The sound of people winding up conversations and moving to their seats drowned out the case number. The news reporters moved forward. Defendants whose cases were further down the docket gravitated toward the back benches.

Bradford stepped forward. He was easily the most experienced and best attorney in the Hamilton County Prosecutor's office. He would handle the actual arraignment.

Garner waived a formal reading of the indictment and had Medawar plead "not guilty" at the appropriate point.

As Judge Seiler worked his way through the formalities of the arraignment, Warren remained seated behind counsel table. As Hamilton County Prosecutor, he was not expected to try cases himself, and in fact, he almost never entered a courtroom. His primary job was to run the prosecutor's office – an obligation he largely delegated. He was also required to represent the prosecutor's office at various meetings and public events. Not one to miss a photo opportunity, Warren handled that part of his job personally.

Judge Seiler invited counsel to state their views on bail. With that, Warren stood and addressed the court. "Your Honor," he said, speaking loudly enough to be heard by any reporters who might be lingering in the back of the courtroom, "the State asks that the court deny bail."

Garner was disappointed. If the court denied bail, Medawar would remain in jail until the trial. He knew that was a possibility, but he had not expected Dick Warren to appear personally to make the pitch.

Garner watched closely as Warren glanced briefly at Judge Seiler and then returned his gaze to the camera recording the proceedings.

"Dr. Medawar stands accused of murdering his wife, a fine young woman from a prominent Cincinnati family," Warren said. "She was a wonderful young woman who had her whole life ahead of her. The indictment charges that Dr. Medawar shot her at nearly point blank range. He then fired a second shot to be certain she was dead. This was a brutal crime.

"As I am sure Your Honor knows, because the media have been reporting this, Dr. Medawar is from Syria, or his family is. Many people have said that. I gather that Mr. Garner quibbles about exactly which country Dr. Medawar is from, so perhaps we should just say he's from the Middle East.

"The important thing here," Warren summed up, "is that the defendant not be allowed to return to wherever he or his family came from. He is a cold-blooded killer and should not be given the opportunity to flee. As I said, we request that bail be denied. But if Your Honor is inclined to set bail, the State requests an amount of at least $2 million."

"Mr. Garner?" Judge Seiler inquired.

"Your Honor," Garner responded, "I frankly have no idea why the media are reporting that Dr. Medawar is from Syria. I am also somewhat surprised that Mr. Warren is relying on erroneous media reports instead of the detailed evidence I provided his office.

"The short version, Your Honor, is this. Dr. Medawar was born right here in Cincinnati. He went to Summit Country Day and to St. Xavier High School. From there, Dr. Medawar went to Harvard for his undergraduate degree and to Stanford for his medical degree and surgical residency.

"Following his medical training, he returned to Cincinnati, where he works at the Trauma Center. With his credentials, he could have worked a less demanding job and made a lot more money. But he chose to work at the Trauma Center, Your Honor, to give back to the community.

"Dr. Medawar is not from Syria, and neither is his family. He's from Cincinnati. He's never been to the Middle East. In fact, except for a brief vacation in Cancun, Dr. Medawar has never been out of the country.

"There is simply no reason to believe that Dr. Medawar will flee the only country he has ever known. Certainly, the murder of his wife was a horrible crime, but he did not commit that crime. He loved his wife. The case against him is a flimsy web of speculation based on the notion he is a hotheaded Muslim from the Middle East. The prosecution has no eyewitness. It doesn't have the murder weapon. It can't even find Ann's car.

"Dr. Medawar is anxious to clear his name. Dr. Medawar is still paying off his medical school loans, and he just recently purchased a home. He has only limited resources. In short, Your Honor, there is no reason to deny bail or to set an excessive bail."

Judge Seiler interrupted Garner with a question. "You provided this information to the prosecutor's office?"

"Yes, Your Honor. I explained all of this to Mr. Bradford in advance of today's hearing. I provided a birth certificate, school transcripts, diplomas, references — the works. In fact, Your Honor, just before the bailiff called the court to order, Mr. Warren and I were discussing the fact that Dr. Medawar went to St. Xavier and was class valedictorian, whereas Mr. Warren went to Moeller and played football."

Light laughter rippled through the courtroom.

Warren's face reddened.

Judge Seiler glanced at the prosecution team. "Mr. Warren," he asked in a slightly exasperated tone, "do you dispute any of this?"

Warren conducted a whispered exchange with Bradford before responding.

"My office contacted the U.C. Trauma Center," Warren said, "and were told Dr. Medawar has been suspended pending further review of his situation."

Garner hadn't heard that. He looked at Medawar. His jaw was clenched, but he was trying not to react.

"Other than that," Warren conceded, "I don't have evidence that would specifically contradict the representations Mr. Garner has just made to the court. It is my understanding, however, that Dr. Medawar's parents immigrated to this country from the Middle East. They may still have family or other ties there."

Warren again adjusted himself so that he was looking directly at the courtroom camera. "As Your Honor knows," he continued, "we have seen too many instances of the children of Middle Eastern immigrants abusing their wives, committing murder, even terrorist acts. And there has been a steady stream of reports of the children of Muslim immigrants becoming radicalized and traveling to Syria, to Somalia, and elsewhere to hook up with ISIS or al Qaeda."

"Thank you for that," Judge Seiler said, cutting Warren off. "Mr. Garner, is your client a Muslim terrorist or terrorist wannabe?"

"No, Your Honor," Garner responded, re-assured by the judge's droll rejection of Warren's grandstanding. "Dr. Medawar's not even Muslim. He's Catholic. He belongs to the St. Anthony of Padua parish, in Walnut Hills."

"Did you apprise the prosecutor's office of that?"

"Yes, Your Honor."

Judge Seiler looked at Warren, shook his head, and set a figure for bail that Medawar would be able to afford. "Dr. Medawar," he added, "as a condition of your release, I am ordering that you surrender your passport, if you have one, and that you remain within Hamilton County."

"Thank you, Your Honor," Medawar said.

"Anything else?" Judge Seiler asked.

"The defense requests a speedy trial," Garner said.

A demand for a speedy trial is routine. Once the defendant has made that demand, unless later waived, the State must – absent a special showing – bring the case to trial within a specified period of time or drop the charges.

There was zero likelihood the prosecutor's office would let a high-profile case like the Medawar prosecution fall between the cracks, but there was also no reason for Garner not to make the almost rote demand. Besides, there were good reasons to insist that the case be tried promptly.

But Garner planned to go further than the usual demand for a speedy trial. By statute in Ohio, the prosecution is allowed 270 days to bring a serious felony case to trial. If the defendant remains in jail in lieu of bond, each day in jail counts as three days. If the court had denied bail, the prosecution would have had to try the case within ninety days.

"Your Honor," Garner said, "the defense requests trial in ninety days. I recognize that you have set bail, and so granting the defense request is entirely within the court's discretion. But I would point out that the prosecution argued against bail. If Mr. Warren was serious about that and not just posturing for the evening news, then his office must be ready to try the case in ninety days."

To Garner's surprise, Warren supported the request. Garner wasn't sure if he had goaded Warren into that, or if Warren was anxious to get the publicity the trial would generate.

"I don't have any openings that soon," Judge Seiler said, looking through his calendar. "The earliest is March 1.

That was much sooner than Garner expected. "Works for me," he said.

"Same here," Bradford added.

"The Clerk will send an order," Judge Seiler stated, "setting the trial for 9:00 a.m., Tuesday, March 1."

2:15 P.M. – 2:30 P.M.

Garner accompanied Medawar through the process of posting bond and being released. Forty minutes later, as he and Medawar left the courthouse, several reporters dogged them with questions, which they ignored. All but one of the reporters gave up the effort when the two crossed Court Street and left the area immediately surrounding the courthouse.

That reporter, Tiffany Albern, and her cameraman followed Garner and Medawar down the street to where Garner had parked his car.

"Dr. Medawar, can you give me one minute, please? I'm Tiffany Albern from Queen City News. I just want to ask you one thing. I want to get your perspective."

Medawar waited for her question.

"The prosecution claims that when your wife confronted you about your affair with the nurse, you became angry and killed her."

"That's not what happened, if that's your question."

"My question is this," the reporter persisted. "Is there something about your Muslim background, about your being from Syria, that may have influenced your reaction? I'm trying to understand this from your point of view."

"Look, we just went through that in court. I'm not from Syria. I was born in this country. I'm not Muslim. I'm Catholic."

"Okay, well my producer wants me to ask you something else."

Medawar was losing patience and wished he had ignored the reporter. Or, that Garner would let him tell her what had really happened.

"My producer wants to know if you or your family have any ties to Syrian President Assad, or to ISIS, or to al Qaeda or any of the other groups fighting over there?"

"You really don't have a clue, do you?" Medawar fumed. He ducked into Garner's car, but the reporter stepped closer so that he couldn't shut the door.

"Back to my question," Albern said. "Do you think being a Muslim contributed to the way you reacted when your wife confronted you?"

"I just told you. I'm not Muslim, and Ann never confronted me. There was nothing to confront me about."

"But do you think your Muslim background contributed to how you reacted?"

Rafiq sighed and gestured for the reporter to come closer, so he could speak without being heard by the camera behind her.

"I thought you just played one on television," Medawar said as she moved in, "but you really are an airhead, aren't you?"

Albern looked startled and stepped back.

As she did, Garner pulled his car forward, allowing Medawar to slam the passenger door shut.

As they drove away, Garner sighed. "Rafiq, I understand where you're coming from, really I do. But that wasn't cool."

"I know, I know. It won't happen again, I promise."

Garner said nothing.

"Are you sure we shouldn't sit down with a reporter — not her, someone with gray matter between their ears — and get my side of the story out?"

"If I were you, I'd be asking the same question. But it won't change the mind of anyone who counts. We'd just be educating the prosecutor's office."

Medawar didn't look convinced.

"Besides, at trial, the prosecution would twist and turn anything you said. They'd tell the jury you all but confessed. Or they would say you've changed your story."

"This whole thing is insane."

"We'll tell your story at trial. Until then, let's try not to give the prosecutor any help."

4:00 P.M. – 4:15 P.M.

Late that afternoon, Garner filed a motion for a domestic violence order in his uncle's case. He attached the drug company affidavit, along with the affidavit he had extracted from Arnie Vogel, and the one he'd had an even harder time getting his uncle to sign. In the court filing, he asked that Reya Sanchez be restrained from further acts of intimidation and harassment.

He had no doubt the court would grant the motion, but he also had no illusions the order would stop someone from doing something stupid if they were willing to risk the consequences. But the hearing and the order would let Reya Sanchez know that she was fighting in his arena now, and she didn't set the rules.

Perhaps just as importantly, Garner believed the hearing would color the court's thinking when it came to argue the

merits of the property division.
He had much to learn.

FRIDAY, NOVEMBER 13

6:00 P.M. NEWS

Queen City News Live: Bringing you the news you want to hear.

News Anchor Bob Bunker: In other news tonight, Dr. Rafiq Medawar was arraigned today in Hamilton County Court. Prosecutors allege he killed his wife, prominent social figure and activist Ann Lindsey Medawar. Tiffany Albern was there. Tiffany, what can you tell us about what happened in court today?

Tiffany Albern: The arraignment today was straightforward. As expected, Dr. Medawar entered a plea of not guilty. He was released after posting bond and surrendering his passport. The court set a trial date of March 1. In view of the indictment, the Trauma Center has suspended Dr. Medawar.

News Anchor Bob Bunker: Did you learn anything that would shed light on why Dr. Medawar killed his wife?

Tiffany Albern: Bob, I spoke with Dr. Medawar after his court appearance today. He denied that his Middle Eastern background or being a Muslim played any role in what happened. But when I tried to ask him whether he has continuing ties to any of the groups fighting in Syria, he lost his temper and became verbally abusive.

News Anchor Bob Bunker: Tiffany, thank you for that report. Can we count on you to keep us updated on any further developments?

Tiffany Albern: Absolutely.

News Anchor Bob Bunker (facing the camera in the studio): I have spoken with several members of the Lindsey family. They tell me that they have been in touch with Hamilton County Prosecutor, Richard Warren. They asked him not to let court proceedings drag on. That may explain the early trial setting.

Co-Anchor Ashley Gelb: Is your cat making you crazy? Coming up next, our medical correspondent has a special report on the controversial reports linking Cat Scratch Disease with mental illnesses.

SATURDAY, NOVEMBER 14

11:30 P.M.

The elite law firms in the downtown business district had twenty-four-hour security, 365 days a year. The Law Office of Devin Garner, P.S.C., did not. Devin Garner could not afford to have old men in cheap security-officer uniforms patrol his office. Instead, he joked, sturdy parking meters stood silent sentry outside his office and never hit him up for free legal advice.

But he did take precautions. He met regularly with the recently established Neighborhood Watch – a group of concerned citizens who promised to notify the police if they saw anything suspicious.

More importantly, he had an arrangement with the men who provided a more informal, but more effective, neighborhood watch – one not sanctioned by the Cincinnati Police Department. Led by Jamal Muhammad, this group was made up of a number of the black men who had moved into the neighborhood in recent years. Determined to turn the neighborhood around, they kept a close eye out for strangers who appeared to be on the prowl for drugs or prostitutes or who were otherwise up to no good.

The fierce men in this more-informal neighborhood watch generally did not call the police. Instead, they would typically confront suspicious strangers and demand that they leave the neighborhood immediately. Armed with steel pipes, police batons, and similar weapons, these men could be very persuasive.

Garner contributed small amounts of cash to the group and allowed them to use his office's conference room for meetings. More importantly, he promised to represent for free any of the men in the group if they were arrested for their activities – as long as they observed the limits he laid down. In return, the group paid special attention to his office.

An early riser, on Saturday night Garner was in bed, asleep, when he realized that his cell phone, which he kept by his bed, was ringing. Well, not ringing. Blaring the theme to Law & Order. When he found the phone and answered it, the caller was Jamal Mohammad.

"A couple idiots tried to break into your office," Mohammad reported. "They were upset you're representing that Syrian doctor and were planning some serious vandalism."

"Did you call the police?"

"No, wasn't necessary," Mohammad said, laconically. "We persuaded them they hadn't thought this through. They apologized and promised not to come back."

Garner was sure that was a rather understated version of what actually happened. "What kind of vandalism?" he asked.

"They had spray paint, some other stuff. They were about to use it when we caught up with them."

It occurred to Garner that the vandals might come back when Muhammad wasn't around. "What happened to the spray paint?"

"After we used up the paint," Muhammad said, "they left the cans behind."

"I'm confused. What did you spray paint?"

"We used it up on them. We wanted to be sure we'd recognize them if they came back."

Garner chuckled. He thanked Muhammad and promised to make another donation to their group.

In the morning, Garner called a security company. He didn't actually think the usual security system would stop a determined burglar, but with the attention the Medawar case was generating, he needed to do something. He was particularly concerned that someone might break into his office and rifle through his client files. If that happened and he had no security system, the Bar Association might think he had been negligent.

He was also concerned that Reya Sanchez or her son, the one Hank had warned him about, might try something stupid.

SUNDAY, NOVEMBER 15

1:30 A.M. - 2:35 A.M.

Sam Scherge couldn't understand why his friend, Roger Storrs, wanted to throw women's bodies off bridges. *That was just stupid!* They should be putting them somewhere that would tell foreigners they weren't welcome.

They'd grabbed this one at the university. He thought they should find that International Student Center, wherever the hell that was, and dump her body there.

But it was Rog's turn to decide where to dump the body, so okay. But then Rog wanted to throw this one off the Brent Spence Bridge, the main bridge from Cincinnati into Northern Kentucky. He'd told him there was way too much traffic. They'd be caught for sure. When they got to the bridge, there were cars and trucks going in both directions. Just like he'd tried to tell him.

That's when Roger had a new idea. He drove across the Brent Spence and went south to the circle freeway, I-275, and took that west, past the goddam airport, to the long bridge that crossed the Ohio River into Indiana. The bridge was out in the middle of freaking nowhere. Roger insisted there wouldn't be any traffic that time of night.

But it turned out that there was more traffic than either of them expected, even at 2:30 in the morning.

There had been a sign, just before the bridge, for the Creation Museum. Sam wanted to turn back, so they could dump the body there. But he hadn't been able to convince Rog.

Now, he was getting worried. They couldn't drive around all night with the body of a dead girl wrapped in plastic sheeting in the bed of the truck. *What if they got pulled over for something?*

That's when they came to another bridge. It went over

the Whitewater River. It wasn't much of a bridge, and it wasn't much of a river, but Roger pulled over to the side of the expressway and waited until a couple trucks passed. When there was no traffic in sight, Roger pulled his pickup to the middle of the bridge and stopped with his emergency lights flashing. They got the body out of the bed of the truck and slipped it over the railing. The river was swollen with rain, and the body floated downstream into a patch of weeds.

As they were getting back into the pickup, a trucker in a big rig blasted his horn and pulled up alongside. The trucker wanted to know if they needed help.

"Thanks, man, but no," Roger said. "Just drank too much beer and had to take a leak."

The trucker shook his head. "You're going to get yourselves killed."

WEDNESDAY, NOVEMBER 18

6:00 P.M. NEWS

Queen City News Live: Bringing you the news you want to hear.

News Anchor Bob Bunker: Hamilton County Prosecutor Richard Warren formally announced this morning. He is running to represent his party in next year's campaign for the congressional district that includes Cincinnati and Hamilton County. Tiffany Albern is at the Warren campaign headquarters and filed this report.

Tiffany Albern: Thank you, Bob. In his announcement this morning, Hamilton County Prosecutor Richard Warren stressed that his campaign would focus on immigration.

Video clip plays, Richard Warren speaking: We have too many people coming into this country illegally. Congress doesn't do anything about it. Some people, people in the other party, support illegal immigration, which is totally detrimental to the fabric of our once-great country. They want those people, because when they and their kids become dependent on welfare, and they will, they are going to vote for the other party.

Tiffany Albern: Tiffany Albern at Warren Campaign headquarters.

Co-Anchor Ashley Gelb: Still to come … Will this weather last?

TUESDAY, NOVEMBER 24

Charged with investigating the Sleep Cheap Inn, Detective James Chilton arranged for the District 5 police, who patrolled the area, to drive through the inn's parking lot often, especially at night. He wanted the patrolmen to record the license numbers of any vehicles parked in the inn's parking lot. Whenever weather and light permitted, he wanted the patrolmen to photograph the vehicles as well.

He hoped to get lucky and find vehicles associated with known drug dealers or vehicles registered to individuals with outstanding arrest warrants — either of which might have provided the basis for a search warrant of the premises.

If the inn was on the up-and-up, its patrons would mainly be low-income travelers from out-of-town, visiting the university or nearby hospitals. That and students looking for a place to hook up. But instead, after a month of monitoring, the patrols were finding mainly the license numbers of local yokels — with only the occasional out-of-area license number. The most interesting had been the license plate of some judge from Northern Kentucky.

The frequent monitoring of the inn enabled Chilton to identify which vehicles were there most of the time — and therefore belonged to the inn's staff. And it had apparently kept the inn's staff on their best behavior.

It was just a matter of time, he believed, until the patrols would find evidence of illegals, prostitution or drug deals or something else he could use to get a search warrant.

WEDNESDAY, NOVEMBER 25

In criminal cases, the pretrial exchange of information and documents that lawyers refer to as "discovery" is more limited than in civil litigation, but Devin Garner was determined to get everything he could from the prosecution.

The prosecutor handling the case, William Bradford, did not object to his requests for the usual matters. Among other things, Bradford produced copies of the videos found on Ann's cell phone and laptop. Bradford also produced the forensic reports prepared by the crime scene investigator and the gun identification expert. And he produced the report of the autopsy performed on Ann Medawar.

Garner studied the videos and documents carefully. The reports revealed that Ann had not been killed where her body had been found. A 9mm Glock fired the slug removed from her body. And when the police searched Medawar's home, they found no signs of blood consistent with a shooting. They also found no gunpowder residue on Rafiq Medawar's hands.

As usual with the Hamilton County Coroner's office, the autopsy report did not address the time of death. He would have to wait until Bradford produced the pathologist's expert witness report to know if Medawar would have an alibi.

But while Bradford was forthcoming with respect to materials relating directly to Ann Medawar's death, he objected to Garner's other requests. Those requests were for autopsy and other reports about the four Hispanic women who had been abducted and killed in the past year.

From what he knew so far, Garner was not convinced those killings were related to Ann's murder, but without more information, it was hard to know what to think. He also wasn't sure it really mattered that he wasn't convinced. If he could present enough evidence of the slayings of those other women, it would give the jurors something to consider. Even if they too were not entirely convinced, those other murders could still be critical. If the jury thought the police hadn't conducted an adequate investigation, or if they were just uncertain, they might well decide that the prosecution had not proven its case against Rafiq beyond a reasonable doubt.

Garner had served formal discovery requests on the Prosecutor's office, asking for police and forensic reports on the slain or missing Hispanic women. He had backed up those requests with subpoenas served on the Hamilton County Coroner's office, which would have performed any forensic analyses or autopsies.

Bradford was required to produce any such materials in the County's possession *if* they were "related to" the indictment *and if* they were "material to the preparation of a defense" or were "intended for use by the prosecuting attorney as evidence at the trial."

Bradford objected and asked the Court to issue an order that neither his own office, nor the Coroner's office had to produce the reports. As Garner had more or less expected, Bradford argued that materials relating to the disappearances and deaths of some Hispanic women were not "related" to the crime charged in the indictment – the slaying of Ann Lindsey Medawar by her husband. The missing and slain women identified by Garner were Hispanics, and Ann Lindsey Medawar was not.

Bradford had not stopped with that. Not only was there no evidence linking the deaths of these Hispanic women to the murder of Ms. Medawar, he insisted, there was no evidence that the same person killed them. They were likely "illegals" and quite possibly drug addicts or engaged in prostitution. If so, their lifestyles put them at risk from any number of predators. The court shouldn't have to sort through evidence about the deaths of four Hispanic women, whose cases had absolutely nothing to do with Dr. Medawar's slaying of his wife.

In the usual case, Garner would simply have filed a responsive brief, explaining why the reports were relevant. In this case, the argument would be straightforward: He intended to show that someone was killing young Hispanic women, and whoever was responsible for those killings, was also responsible for killing Ann Medawar. It was true that Ann Medawar was not Hispanic, but she had been investigating the abductions and deaths of these Hispanic women – and had apparently spooked the killer.

The judge might or might not read the briefs, but counsel would appear at a hearing and repeat – in shortened form – their best arguments. The judge would then make a decision.

Technically, the judge's decision would only address whether or not the Prosecutor and Coroner's offices would have to produce reports responsive to his requests. But as a legal and practical matter, the judge's decision would have more far-reaching consequences.

As a legal matter, if Judge Seiler ruled that the reports were not "related" or "material" to the case, he would likely not allow the defense to present evidence of the other slayings at trial.

As a practical matter, without those reports, Garner would not be able to find out much more about those shootings than Carrie Hixson had – let alone develop a convincing case linking them to Ann's murder. In short, if he didn't get the police and forensic reports now, he would not be able to develop the sort of evidence that might convince the judge to change his mind at trial.

The bottom line was clear. If he lost this skirmish, the jury would likely never hear any evidence about those other killings. Somehow, he had to convince Judge Seiler to allow him room to attempt to prove that someone was killing not only young, undocumented Hispanic women, but may have also killed Ann Medawar, a young *non*-Hispanic woman who was making a documentary about *those* killings.

As he thought about how to convince the judge, he decided to call Carrie Hixson to see if she would be willing to help.

SATURDAY, NOVEMBER 28

2:30 P.M. – 6:30 P.M.

It was only 2:30 in the afternoon, but Devin Garner turned off the light in his outer office and locked the door, so that he and Carrie Hixson could work uninterrupted. This wasn't the time to deal with someone looking for change for the parking meter or needing directions. This was crunch time.

He had invited Hixson to help him think through how he might use some of the materials she and Ann had assembled to convince the judge. She knew the materials better than he did. Could they put together something from the videos to convince the court?

After kicking some ideas around, Hixson decided she could use some help from Cam for his technical proficiency at editing videos and putting them into something slick and professional. Cam summoned Nancy Wong and Keesha Neave, other members of the class, because he knew they would want to be involved.

Along with the reinforcements had come more computers, presentation software, and skill sets. Sandwiches, soft drinks and coffee had materialized as well — and a large canister of pretzels.

Even before the others began to arrive, Garner decided to start by putting together a list of the abductions and deaths in chronological order. They could then add as much detail as they wanted about what the killings had in common.

With luck, once they put all the details side-by-side they might also be able to identify what, if anything, these abductions and killings had in common in addition to the ethnic background of the victims. That in turn might help to convince the judge that these other killings were not just some random deaths among illegal Mexicans, who likely as not were prostitutes and on drugs.

Hixson dug into her notes for the information Garner wanted, and Wong looked through Ann's notes. As they found information about each victim, Garner jotted the information on a series of large poster-sized tablets. Someone else typed the information into a laptop computer.

The earliest case was Natalia Garcia. She had gone missing from the Nuestras Casas Housing Co-Op in Lower Price Hill on the evening of Saturday, June 13. She was tossed over the 8th Street Bridge. She was nineteen years old, had black hair, was 5' 3" tall, and weighed 115 pounds.

The next was Valeria Zuniga. Like the first victim, she lived in the Nuestras Casas Housing Co-Op and had been working at the Heidelberg Sausage Company. She had gone missing Saturday night, July 11. Her body had been found about 8:15 a.m. on Sunday, July 12, at the Saint Toribio Romo Gonzalez Center in Lower Price Hill. She was eighteen years old, had black hair, was 5' 4" tall, and weighed 120 pounds.

Sofia Flores was found August 9. Unlike the first two victims, she didn't live in Lower Price Hill. She lived and worked in the Sleep Cheap Inn in Clifton. She was found in the Mill Creek, apparently tossed there from the South Ludlow Street/U.S. 127 overpass. She was twenty-two years old, had long, dark hair, was 5' 3" tall, and weighed 128 pounds.

The fourth victim was Isabella Ramirez. She was also living at the Sleep Cheap Inn in Clifton, where she was apparently kidnapped late on Saturday, September 12, or early Sunday, September 13. Her body was dumped at the Hamilton County Fair Grounds. The Cincinnati Hispanic Festival was going on there that weekend. She was 5'2" and weighed about 115 pounds.

Hixson had a new case. Camila Suarez was a medical student at the University of Cincinnati and lived in student housing near the U.C. campus. She went missing after leaving a party near the campus about 1:00 a.m. on Sunday, November 15. She was twenty-three years old. She was 5' 5" tall, weighed 120 pounds, and had short black hair. Her body had not been found.

The group sat quietly staring at the list until Cam broke the silence. "Dude," he said, "you're screwed."

Hixson shot Cam an icy look. "We haven't gotten started," she said in a quiet voice. She bit her lip a moment and then asked Cam if she could borrow his projector.

As Cam connected the projector to her laptop, Hixson searched through her files to find the video clip she wanted.

"When Ann and I found a relative – a mother, a sister, whoever we could find – we asked every question we could think of," she explained. "But after the first couple interviews, there was one question we always made sure to ask: *How did she die? What did they do to her?*"

Hixson opened the video clip and projected it onto the wall, so that everyone could see it.

"The first case on our list is Natalia Garcia. This clip is from our interview with her sister." Hixson pressed a key, and the woman on the screen – who had obviously been crying – looked up, straight into the camera. "They shot her in the chest and the head," she said, "Execution style. We came to this country to get away from that. Lot of good it did."

"The next case is Valeria Zuniga. This is her boyfriend." The group heard Ann's voice asking how the woman had died, and Hixson's translation. The boyfriend responded angrily in Spanish, and Hixson translated. "They shot her. Twice. Here" – the young man pointed to the center of his chest – "and then they shot her in the head."

"We couldn't find anyone who knew Sofia Flores," Hixson said. "But the newspaper actually reported her death." Hixson opened an image of a newspaper story. There was a circle around the third paragraph of the short article. "She had been shot in the chest and head, execution style," the article reported.

"Isabella Ramirez," Hixson said as she projected a new clip. "This is her aunt." As the video played, the group could hear Ann ask the woman how her niece had died, and Hixson translate the question into Spanish. The aunt spat out her answer in Spanish. "They shot her like a dog!" Hixson translated. "Twice. They shot her in the chest, and then they shot her in head – to make sure she was dead."

"This is a photo of Camila Suarez. She's the U.C. medical student that just went missing. I got this from her mother," Hixson said. "Camila has not been found – *yet*. But when her body turns up," Hixson said, her voice still icy, "there will be two bullets in it – one to her chest, and one to her head. Just like they did to Ann."

"Holy mackerel!" Cam said. "Let me get to work on setting this up."

"What else do you have?" Garner asked.

"This," Hixson said as she slid a document across the table to Garner. "It's the autopsy report on Natalia Garcia. It says the two slugs were from a 9mm handgun."

"How did you get this?" Garner asked.

"I didn't. Her sister got it from the Coroner's office, and she gave it to me."

"The bullets recovered from Ann," Garner told the group, "were from a 9mm."

"Bingo!" Cam said – inappropriate, as usual, but right on the mark.

WEDNESDAY, DECEMBER 2

11:00 A.M. – 11:55 A.M.

Northern Kentucky is a bedroom community for Cincinnati, much like Arlington, Alexandria, and the rest of Northern Virginia are for Washington, D.C. Just as Washington's Ronald Reagan International Airport is in Northern Virginia, so too, the Greater Cincinnati International Airport is in Northern Kentucky.

Northern Kentucky is divided into three adjacent counties – Kenton, Campbell and Boone. Kenton County is anchored by Covington, and Campbell County by Newport. Both were important Ohio River communities in years past. Boone County was and still is more rural. Its largest city is Florence – ten square miles of suburban sprawl anchored by the Florence Mall.

Devin Garner was in Boone County Circuit Court for the hearing on his motion for a domestic violence order. He wanted an order directing Reya Sanchez to refrain from threatening or committing acts of physical violence against her husband, Henry "Hank" Bremen, or against himself, Hank's attorney.

Garner insisted that Hank attend the hearing, in case he needed to have him testify. He also assured his uncle that the hearing should be straightforward. He had filed more affidavits and other evidence than usual for a motion of that sort. And in this case, the most dramatic threat – the dead chickens – had been against himself. The court was likely to have an even greater concern when the threat was leveled at a member of the bar.

The judge was Circuit Court Judge Dirk Richter. Carl Anwalt represented Reya Sanchez. Garner had not met Anwalt before, but Hank had told him that Anwalt had long represented Reya, and so his appearance in the case was no surprise.

When his turn on the motion docket came, Garner gave a brief explanation of the motion and the evidence supporting it. He offered the judge copies of photos of the box with the dead chickens in it. Garner had the photos printed as 8 x 11 enlargements specifically for that purpose.

When Garner finished, Anwalt took his turn. He began by noting that Devin Garner normally practiced in Ohio – as if that was reason enough to deny the motion. Reya Sanchez, he added, was the owner of Reya's Authentic Mexican Restaurant. Anwalt then argued that Garner had not proven that Reya had made any physical threat. *Maybe* another of Garner's clients had sent the dead chickens. *Maybe* – instead of a threat – it was some voodoo thing.

Anwalt had legal arguments too. The statute that authorized domestic violence orders only applied to violence and threats against members of the same household. Devin Garner was the attorney for Mr. Bremen, but he was not a member of his household. The statue didn't apply to him.

Anwalt also argued that killing Garner would be a crime. Absent the domestic relations statute, he argued, a court may not enjoin a party from committing a crime – citing some very, very old cases.

Garner responded that the notion that a court may not enjoin an act that might also be a crime had indeed been the law, centuries ago, but had not been the law for quite some time. Modern courts routinely enjoin antitrust, securities, and other crimes. They also routinely enjoin violence by labor unions. And most importantly, courts routinely issue domestic violence orders. This court, he pointed out, routinely issued domestic violence orders exactly like the order he was seeking.

Judge Richter announced his decision on the spot, rather than taking it under submission and studying the briefs. "I'm going to deny the motion," he said. "The domestic violence law does not apply to attorneys. And as we all learned in law school, a court cannot enjoin the commission of a crime."

The ruling caught Garner by surprise. "Your Honor, if I may," he blurted out, "the cases cited in my brief make it clear that you may, and should, enjoin a threatened act of violence."

Richter bristled at the challenge. "You have my ruling." He glanced at the motion list on his desk to confirm the young attorney's name. "Mr. Garner, if you're going to practice on this side of the river, you're going to have to learn what the law is over here." Turning to his bailiff, Judge Richter snapped, "Who's next?"

Garner fumed but there was nothing useful he could do about the ruling. He led Hank out of the courtroom.

Hank suggested that they get lunch. He said he knew a good place nearby.

Garner got the name of the restaurant and directions. As he left the courthouse, Garner saw Anwalt headed out as well and approached him.

"Got a minute?" Garner asked. "Hank says you represent Diego Olivar and the Sleep Cheap Inn."

"On most stuff, yeah. What do you need?"

"You probably know I represent Rafiq Medawar – the Trauma Center doctor accused of killing his wife, Ann Lindsey Medawar.'

"Yeah, tough case."

"Any chance of you persuading your client to help? He's the last person to see Ann."

"Diego is not going to testify."

"I can issue a subpoena. But I would rather try to find a way to accommodate whatever concerns he has."

"Diego isn't going to testify. Period. He'll leave town until the trial is over, or do whatever he needs to, but he's not going to testify."

"What's he afraid of?"

"Excuse me?" Anwalt said.

"You heard me. What is your client afraid of? What does he know that he doesn't want to come out in court?"

"Off the record?"

"Okay."

"Diego doesn't know what happened to her."

"Then why won't he testify?"

"Two of the women who work out of the inn have been killed. He doesn't want attention focused on that."

"Did he have something to do with the murders?"

"No, of course not. They were working girls. Izzy Ramirez apparently stepped out behind the inn late one night to get some fresh air and smoke a cigarette. Diego thinks someone grabbed her. He didn't have anything to do with her getting killed. He was pissed when it happened."

"What about the other one?"

"Sofia Flores? Diego doesn't know what happened to her either. He warned the girls not to go out behind the building at night. Apparently, she did anyway, and someone got her too."

"Then, I don't see the problem with him testifying," Garner said.

"Diego isn't going to testify about the Lindsey girl. He doesn't need the attention. He says that's already hurt his business."

Garner nodded to indicate he was following what Anwalt was telling him.

"If you repeat any of that," Anwalt warned, "I'll deny I ever said it. And you'll regret it. And I'm talking about more than dead chickens, understand?"

"You're threatening me?"

"No, I'm just telling you that one of the Mexican cartels is involved, and they play rough."

Garner thanked Anwalt, but left mystified about the whole thing. When the trial came, he would issue a subpoena and see what happened. *Maybe*, he thought, *he'd get lucky and Diego Olivar would show up and plead the Fifth* – that is, assert his right against self-incrimination under the Fifth Amendment to the Constitution. If he did that, the jury would have plenty of questions about who killed Ann.

12:05 P.M. – 1:00 P.M.

For lunch, Garner and his uncle went to a small Mexican restaurant not far from the courthouse. Hank had met the owner a couple times. She greeted him as if he were family.

After they were seated and placed their orders, Garner told his uncle he was still angry about the court's ruling.

"You know why you got your ass whipped, don't you?" Hank asked his nephew.

"Not a clue. Why, do you?"

"Carl Anwalt and Judge Richter are buddies. From what I hear, Richter used to be a drunk, and they put him on the bench to dry out. Anwalt was his drinking buddy, and they did AA together."

"Oh, geez," Garner complained.

"Besides, Anwalt brings Judge Richter to Reya's for lunch every week."

"The judge must like the place," Garner said, aiming for sarcasm.

"The judge loves it. When Reya's there, she fusses over him, and when she's not there, she makes sure the waitresses flirt with him and give him a lot of attention."

"It's not the food that keeps the judge coming back?"

"Well, I think the food's pretty good, but Anwalt brings him there because Reya doesn't charge them. Reya grew up in Mexico, and down there, the cops, the judges, the politicians – they're all corrupt. I try to tell her it's not that way here, but she won't listen."

"So that's why the judge wasn't buying what I was selling?"

"Actually, it's more than that. A couple years ago, the judge's wife was really sick. Cancer. Anwalt talked to Reya, and she arranged for one of the women she brought up from

Mexico to stay at the judge's house – sort of a live-in maid. She did the cooking, cleaning, kept after his wife until she passed. Reya didn't charge the judge. She just had him provide room and board and some spending money for the woman."

Garner shook his head in disgust. "It's not worth rehashing the motion for a domestic violence order," he said, "but that's going to be a real problem if Reya won't settle, and we have to have a hearing on property division. You don't want that judge deciding your case."

"Reya won't settle. I still talk to Maya, her daughter, and she says Reya is being really stubborn. Plus, she can't settle with me without losing the new place in Over the Rhine."

"Are you willing to have me put what you just told me about the free lunches and the free maid in an affidavit? I can ask the judge to recuse himself and let him know I'm willing to file your affidavit and make all this public if he doesn't take himself off the case."

"No, I don't see the point. Reya will deny it. Anwalt will deny it. The judge is liable to end up sanctioning you or filing a complaint with the bar."

"Why don't you let me worry about that?"

"Because you're my nephew. I helped raise you. It's not worth it to me."

Garner watched the older man and realized for the first time how much of the fight had gone out of him.

"Okay, let's put that on hold for now," Garner said. "Let's focus on how we prove that the restaurant is doing better now – since you ran it while Reya was doing whatever she was doing."

Hank poured some more beer into his glass and took a sip. He moved some food from one spot on his plate to another and appeared lost in thought. "I don't know how you're going to do that," he said finally.

"Well, let's start with this. Has the restaurant's business actually increased in the last couple years, since you and Reya got married?"

"Oh, sure. Our sales compared with the same week and same month from the prior year were always better. And they just kept getting better. I convinced Reya to do a little advertising. I talked to the food critic from the *Enquirer* and got him to do a review. I also kept a better eye on food costs and how many people we had working – so profits were up too. Basically, it was just a matter of paying attention to details."

"That's good. What else?"

"One of the things I changed," Hank said, "is I kept the place open longer at night. She used to close by nine, earlier if there wasn't much business. I kept it open until midnight, usually later. Once word got out, we started getting people coming in late – after they had been to a game or wherever. That crowd tends to order a lot more drinks than your lunch crowd, and drinks are more profitable."

"That's good," Garner said, trying to get his uncle to focus on how he could help himself. "That's really helpful."

"Yeah," Hank agreed, "but like I said, I don't see how you're going to prove that."

"If there was an increase in revenue, in profits, it should be in the restaurant's financial statements and its tax returns. I'll serve a subpoena for the restaurant's financial statements, tax returns, that sort of thing."

"Reya didn't want to show the extra revenue, so she insisted that we close down the cash register at nine, and anything that came in after that was off the books."

Garner shook his head. With his uncle, there was always some drama just around the corner.

"Okay," Garner said, "so how do we prove that?"

"I don't know. If I testify to that, Reya will deny it. Or she'll say it was my idea, and she didn't know anything about it, and I stole the money. The waitresses are scared to death of her, so they aren't going to be any help."

Garner studied his uncle. The older man seemed lost in

his own thoughts.

"Hank, I need to know what you're worried about. I need to find out now, not when we're in court."

"Anwalt handles the bookkeeping for the restaurant. You're not going to be able to prove anything."

"I never heard of a lawyer doing his client's bookkeeping," Garner said. "That's weird."

"Maybe he doesn't have enough clients." Hank shrugged. "Maybe he needs the work."

Garner didn't believe that, and he didn't think his uncle did either. "Is he laundering the money Reya gets from her coyote business through the restaurant?" Garner asked. "Is that what's going on?"

"He was, but he got upset when Reya and I got married, and he refused to do that anymore. At least that's what Reya told me. So, when you get the restaurant's financials, they're going to show a drop in revenue after we got married."

"How about I get the records and have a forensic accountant go over the books and see if we can show what they've been doing?"

"Look, Devin, I'm still close to Reya's kids. I don't want to do anything that's going to get Reya in trouble. I understand what you're saying, but how would her kids feel if I did something that got her in trouble with the IRS and she lost her business or went to jail?"

"I understand." Garner said. "Actually," he corrected himself, "after what she tried to do to you, I *don't* understand, but that's your call."

"I know how a lot of people act when they get divorced. I've tended bar long enough to have heard all sorts of stories. All that stuff never helps anyone. They just end up bitter and crying in their beer. I'm not going to do that to myself."

Garner signaled to the barmaid to bring the check. He took his credit card from his wallet and set it on the table.

"Let's go back to your keeping the business open later.

Did that bring in much additional business?"

"Yeah, quite a bit more."

"But that was all off the books?"

Hank nodded, looking sheepish.

"Did Anwalt know what was going on?"

"He had to know," Hank said after mulling it over.

Garner picked up a chip and dipped it in salsa. "Why?"

Hank pointed to Garner's credit card. "Most people pay by credit card. We would run the credit card, but the amount wouldn't show up on the register tape we sent Anwalt the next morning."

Garner grinned. "I don't know if you know what a deposition is," he said, "but it's an opportunity for a lawyer to question a witness under oath before trial. It's usually done in a lawyer's office. There's a court reporter, and she swears in the witness and takes down everything, just like in court, except there's no judge."

His uncle nodded.

"I need to get the books and records first and do some preparation, but before we get to the hearing on property division, I'll notice Anwalt's deposition to testify about the restaurant's bookkeeping. Ethically, Anwalt cannot be a witness and trial counsel both. I should be able to force him to remove himself from the case."

"That still leaves the judge," Hank said. "If you knock his buddy off the case, he may not like that."

"I don't think we'll get to a trial. Anwalt isn't going to want to testify about Reya's accounting. He's going to tell Reya she has to settle."

FRIDAY, DECEMBER 4

2:30 P.M. – 3:45 P.M.

The attorneys for the bank considering the financial package for Reya Sanchez were not the only ones to notice the divorce petition Devin Garner filed on behalf of his uncle. Garner realized this when he received a call from Adam Zhang, an agent with the U.S. Immigration and Customs Enforcement agency or ICE. Zhang said that he had reviewed the divorce file, including the motion for a domestic violence order.

"We're not interested in prosecuting your uncle," Zhang explained, "if we can get his cooperation. We're interested in Reya. As you probably know, she's a coyote. We were hoping you would talk to your uncle and see if he would be willing to talk to us."

"I'm happy to do that," Garner replied. "As you can tell from the papers I filed, I'm not a fan of Reya Sanchez. But just so you know, I'm not optimistic. My uncle is close to her kids, or at least to the two born in this country. He's told me several times that he doesn't want to do anything that would get Reya in trouble. He's concerned about the impact that would have on her kids. I'll talk to him, but I don't think he will be willing to cooperate."

"Do what you can. And remind him that we can only agree not to prosecute him if he cooperates with us."

"Okay, sure," Garner responded, "but since we're doing favors for each other, here's one you can help me with."

He briefly explained what the Medawar case was about and that a critical witness had disappeared. "I've been told Angelica Rios was undocumented and fled back to the Philippines when Ann's murder hit the news," Garner said. "Is there any way ICE can figure out if, in fact, she fled the country?

"Dr. Medawar," Garner added, "is a great guy, a friend. I don't want him getting convicted because the jury thinks this woman's disappearance is suspicious."

"Give me the information you have on her," Zhang said, "and I'll see what I can do."

MONDAY, DECEMBER 7

1:05 P.M. – 1:35 P.M.

Devin Garner slipped off his suit coat jacket and settled uneasily into a hard wooden chair in a conference room in the Prosecutor's office. Carrie Hixson remained standing, setting up her equipment. She was there to run the mini-documentary she and her classmates put together – and to answer questions if the prosecutor was interested in knowing more. The video had been through several iterations and was polished and professional.

Just as Hixson finished her preparations, Assistant Prosecutor William Bradford entered the room, followed like a shadow by a paralegal – a slim, young black woman in her mid- to late-twenties. Bradford bristled with impatience, as if to say, "I don't have time for this."

Garner introduced Hixson. Bradford brusquely introduced Kemi Adichie, the paralegal.

Garner explained that Hixson had been working with Ann on the video their class was doing. "Carrie and her classmates," Garner explained, "put this together for me. I'm going to play it for Judge Seiler at the hearing on your motion Friday afternoon. I wanted to give you an opportunity to see it first."

"What's it about?" Bradford asked.

"It's about the women whose reports I want."

"I'm sorry those women died," Bradford said. "But if you're going to show me a sob piece about how nice those women were, or how tragic their deaths were, I don't need to see it. Sympathy isn't the issue. Those cases have nothing to do with your client shooting his wife."

"I'm here as a courtesy, so you're not caught by surprise in court," Garner said. "Besides Carrie and her colleagues put a lot of effort into this. Sit down and watch it. It won't take long."

Bradford sat down. To make it clear he wasn't going to bother to take notes, he laid his legal pad on the conference room table upside down and put his pen in his jacket pocket.

Garner ignored him and gestured for Hixson to play the video. It was just under five minutes long, but it was impossible to watch without coming away with the impression that the same person had killed the four young Hispanic women whose bodies had been found so far.

The video ended with the mother of the young woman who was still missing. She introduced herself and spoke warmly of her daughter. She said she had read the brief filed by the Prosecutor's office – she held it in her hand. She said she was disturbed at its suggestion that because her daughter and these other women were Hispanic, they must be illegals and prostitutes or drug addicts.

"My daughter," the woman said with real anger in her voice, "was born in this country – right here in Cincinnati. She graduated from Seton High School first in her class. She graduated from Xavier University with honors. When she disappeared, she was a student at the University of Cincinnati medical school. My daughter was not illegal or a prostitute or on drugs."

The woman complained that the police and prosecutor weren't interested in investigating the deaths of Hispanics – they were only interested in raids on employers and getting headlines. In the presentation's final seconds, she begged the judge to let Garner have the files. "At least he wants to know what has happened to my daughter. The Prosecutor, he doesn't care."

Bradford appeared sobered by the video.

"Here's what's going to happen," Garner stated. "On Friday afternoon, when we show up for the hearing before Judge Seiler, the courtroom is going to be packed with Hispanics and other concerned citizens. The press will be there. I'm going to play this video, and the media are going to learn that there's a serial killer loose in this city, but your boss doesn't give a shit, and you and the rest of his office are trying to keep the public from finding out."

Bradford started to object, but Garner cut him off.

"Just to make sure no one misses the point, I'm going to have the parents of Camila Suarez, the young woman that's still missing, there with me in the courtroom. They're going to tell anyone who will listen about their daughter and about your office's lack of interest in her case.

"Ms. Hixson and her classmates are going to provide copies of this video to the reporters who show up, and then they're going to hand deliver copies of it to any TV station that missed the hearing."

Garner stood and put his suit jacket back on.

"Or," he added, "you're going to stop being a jerk and produce the reports on these women. The forensic reports, the autopsy reports, everything."

"Counsel's eyes only?" Bradford asked – meaning would Garner agree to a court order that only Garner could see the reports unless and until they were used at trial.

"Counsel, experts, and my client."

Bradford sighed and nodded.

"I'm not done," Garner snapped. "Plus Carrie and her colleagues. They agree not to publish anything you give me until the case against Dr. Medawar gets dismissed or goes to trial."

Bradford started to object, but surrendered.

"I get everything before the hearing," Garner said as a parting shot, "or this video goes viral."

1:40 P.M. – 1:45 P.M.

"Did you know," Carrie Hixson asked as Garner drove away from the Prosecutor's office, "that I sent his brief – the one that implies that if these women were Hispanics, they were probably prostitutes and drug addicts – to *La Jornada Latina*?

"No," Garner conceded. "I don't even know who or what that is."

"It's a Spanish language newspaper here in Cincinnati," Hixon said, shaking her head. "You were just bluffing in there about packing the courthouse?"

Garner shrugged his shoulders.

"What if he called your bluff?"

"I would have thought of something."

Hixson stared at him, then laughed. "You know what, you probably would have."

"When did you learn to speak Spanish?" Garner asked.

"I was a Spanish major in college."

"You do a semester in Spain?"

"A year, in Barcelona."

"That would explain why you're able to speak Spanish."

"Well, that and I did two years in the Peace Corps in Peru."

"I'd like to hear about that sometime, but tell me, what are you planning to do when you grow up? Are you serious about making documentaries?"

"I thought the documentary course would be fun, but it was more Ann's thing than mine. I'm playing with the idea of trying to get into journalism or the news media. Either that or law school."

"Where did you go to college?"

"The University of Miami — the one in Ohio, not the one in Florida."

"I've never been there, but everyone says the campus is beautiful."

"It is, but if we're playing twenty questions, it's my turn."

"Okay."

"You don't have a ring, so I assume you're not married. Are you seeing someone?"

"No."

"Are you gay?"

Garner shot her a glance. "No."

"Then why haven't you made a move?"

Garner saw a Starbucks and pulled into the lot. He parked the car and looked at Hixson thoughtfully. "A move? You mean on you?"

"Your Honor," Hixson deadpanned, "Please instruct the witness to answer the question."

"Why haven't I made a move on you?" Garner repeated. "You mean aside from the fact that your best friend just died, and I'm defending her husband, who's accused of killing her?"

"Your Honor, the witness is being evasive."

"Carrie, I hope I'm going to say this right, because this is really important. Rafiq is my client and my friend. He is fighting for his life. I'm his attorney. I'm going to need your help – like today. And, I'm probably going to need to have you testify about what you and Ann were doing."

"Ann was my friend. I know Rafiq and consider him a friend. I *want* to help. Ann would want me to help."

"Fair enough, but I don't want you wondering if I'm pretending to like you to get you to help."

"Give me a break!" Hixson said, smiling. "I've got eyes. I can tell by the way you look at me that's there more going on between us than that."

Garner hesitated before responding. "Two things," he said. "First, what if it didn't work out between us, or we had an argument or something? If Rafiq gets convicted, I'm going to torture myself for a very long time, maybe for the rest of my life, with 'what ifs?' and whether I missed something or could have done something better. I don't want to wonder if I messed something up because of whatever might be going on between us – not now, but at some point between now and the trial."

Hixson said nothing, waiting for him to finish.

"And second, if – *when* – I put you on the witness stand, I don't want to risk having the prosecutor ask you if you're dating defense counsel and implying …"

Hixson shot him a big smile. "Tiffany Albern reporting live for Queen City News," she said, imitating the television news reporter. "Today, in the trial of Rafiq Medawar, we learned that Carrie Hixson, who testified for the defense, has been sleeping with Dr. Medawar's defense counsel, Lower Price Hill attorney Devin Garner. We contacted her parents at their home in Indian Hills for comment."

Garner grimaced. "Yeah, something like that. Let's just wait until after the trial, and see how we feel then."

Garner didn't mention it, but there was a third thing. Carrie Hixson was out of his league. He was the guy from the wrong side of town. Her family was wealthy, socially prominent. She was a socialite, destined to marry into another rich, socially prominent family. Even if she was interested in a bit of slumming, he was sure, in the end, he would get his heart broken.

TUESDAY, DECEMBER 8

9:45 A.M. – 10:15 A.M.

Summoned by Assistant Prosecutor William Bradford to discuss a new development in the Medawar case, Detective James Chilton drove downtown, parked his unmarked car near the courthouse, and headed to the nearby William Howard Taft building, where the Hamilton County Prosecutor's offices were.

For December, the weather was still surprisingly nice. By now, the skies would normally be gray and overcast, and except for the occasional bitterly cold day, they would usually remain that way until spring. But the weather this morning was mild and the sky bright blue. In short, it was a perfectly nice day. It went without saying, Chilton thought, the lawyer would find a way to ruin it.

Chilton waited a few minutes in the Prosecutor's reception area before Kemi Adichie, Bradford's paralegal, emerged and led him to Bradford's office. Bradford made him wait just long enough, Chilton thought, to establish who stood where in life's pecking order.

Bradford stood and greeted Chilton warmly and thanked him for coming so quickly. After the usual courtesies, Bradford sent Adichie to get coffee for Chilton. He then briefly recounted his meeting the day before with Devin Garner, the attorney for Rafiq Medawar.

After explaining that Ann Medawar's friend and the other students in her documentary class had put it together, Bradford played the video Garner left behind. To Chilton's surprise, the damn thing was rather impressive.

Bradford explained that he needed Chilton to check out the video and figure out what their response was. "Find out what we know about these women, and where you guys are on these cases," Bradford said. "They're probably unrelated, but if we've got a serial killer, we need to know it."

"I'll get right on it," Chilton promised. "The obvious first step is to contact whoever put this video together, to see if they have any other information that might be helpful. Okay if I start there?"

"No, I don't want you contacting them. They're working with Medawar's attorney. I don't want him to know we're playing catch up on this."

As Chilton headed back to the homicide squad, he turned the problem over in his mind. He couldn't imagine why some sicko would want to kill young Mexican women. If you were going to kill someone, there were so many more deserving targets. "Obviously," he decided, "we're talking about someone who's never had to deal with lawyers."

10:45 A.M. – 1:15 A.M.

After getting a fresh mug of coffee, Detective James Chilton spread out on his desk the copies of the reports that Kemi Adichie had given him – the reports Bradford was about to give Devin Garner, Medawar's attorney.

Chilton had run into Garner before. It was a routine case, but Garner wanted to be the next Perry Mason or Jack McCoy or something. During cross-examination, Garner made him look like an idiot. Actually, Chilton recalled, it was a case he had picked up at the last minute from another detective. He hadn't had time to figure out that the other detective had made some stupid mistakes. Garner had probably been right to call him on the mistakes, but that didn't mean he had to like the prick.

Chilton slid the DVD into his computer and watched the video again, this time stopping it frequently and taking notes. Ace Lindsey's daughter and her BFF identified four women who had been killed and one who was missing. All five, counting the missing woman, were Hispanic. According to the video, the four dead women had all been shot twice, at least two of them with a 9mm handgun.

It wasn't hard to tell why two Indian Hill girls playing out their Nancy Drew fantasies thought there was a serial killer on the loose. What they didn't know was that these days, the 9mm handgun was one of the most popular guns, actually *the* most popular gun, among your criminal class. Also, the way the dead bodies had been disposed of wasn't consistent. Two of the women had been tossed off bridges. If that had been the case with the other two, it would be a classic serial killer scenario. The homicide unit would have been all over it.

But the other two bodies had been disposed of differently – the first at a Hispanic social services center in Lower Price Hill and the other at the fairgrounds in Carthage. Those victims could have been killed by someone within the Hispanic community. Or by someone trying to send a message to Hispanics telling them they weren't welcome – to name just a couple of possibilities.

Chilton turned to the forensic reports. The crime scene reports didn't tell him much, except that in each of the four cases, the victim had been shot twice – once in the torso and once in the head. The head shots were classic "kill shots." At least, that's the way things went down in movies and in television shows – the perpetrator makes sure the victim is dead with a second shot to the head. He personally had never seen a case in which that had been done.

Well, damn it, except for Ann Medawar.

The crime scene reports indicated that two of the victims were apparently living at the Nuestras Casas Housing Co-Op in Lower Price Hill. That was in District 3, and he was unfamiliar with the place. But that was a tangible connection between two victims. Plus, both victims' bodies had been dumped nearby – the first had been tossed over 8th Street Viaduct and the other dumped in front of the Saint Toribio Romo Gonzalez Center. If those were the only victims, he'd bet the killer lived in the housing co-op. Either that, or the killer was someone from Lower Price Hill who didn't like the idea of Hispanics moving into the neighborhood.

The other two victims had driver's licenses listing the Sleep Cheap Inn in Clifton as their residences, and both had key cards for rooms there. One had been found in the Mill Creek, apparently tossed there from the South Ludlow Street/U.S. 127 overpass. The other had been dumped at the Hamilton County Fair Grounds. Neither location was in Clifton, but neither was terribly far from Clifton either.

Why the Hamilton Fair Grounds? He pulled up the investigating officer's report. Some Hispanic association was having its annual festival there that weekend. Again, that could mean someone within the Hispanic community had killed that victim, or it could mean someone was trying to send the Hispanic community a message that they weren't welcome.

Still, the fact was two women who claimed the Sleep Cheap Inn as their residence had turned up dead. That was interesting. The inn wouldn't have cleaning crew living there. So, those women probably were prostitutes or drug mules. Maybe a john had killed them? Or maybe they had tried to get away and the guy who ran the inn killed them?

Nothing was adding up. If the same person killed the two women from the housing project in Lower Price Hill, and somebody else killed the two women from the Sleep Cheap Inn in Clifton, then the way the bodies were disposed of should have matched up. The two from Price Hill should have been put where their bodies would send a message, and the two prostitutes – *well, who knew?* But it would at least fit a pattern if both had been thrown over a bridge.

The fifth victim was a medical student, and she was still missing. Chilton had been doing this long enough to expect her body would eventually show up.

So, what really was he dealing with? Four young Hispanic women had been killed in the same way and their bodies dumped somewhere else – all in less than six months. Two worked at a sausage company, and the other two were probably prostitutes. And now a medical student was missing.

Chilton turned to the autopsy reports. The autopsies confirmed what the crime scene reports said about each victim being shot twice and all that. But reading the autopsy reports back-to-back, he noticed something else. All four women had been killed in the middle of the night. Not surprising, really, but he'd chalk that up as another point in favor of the serial killer scenario that Nancy Drew and her BFF had come up with.

An email from Kemi Adichie forwarded the gun identification reports from the Hamilton County Coroner's office. In a case like this, they were probably going to be more helpful than anything else. He read the four reports.

Each report addressed only the slugs removed from the specific victim from whom they had been removed. Each indicated that the slugs removed from that particular victim were 9mm slugs fired by a Glock pistol. But the reports didn't address the obvious question: *Was the same gun used in all of these shootings?*

Chilton checked to see who had done the ballistics analyses. John Crackstone, the senior gun-identification guy in the Hamilton County Coroner's office, had signed each of the reports. Chilton had dealt with Crackstone before. He was meticulous almost to a fault, but damn good at what he did.

Chilton called the Coroner's office and managed to get through to Crackstone. "John, I'm looking at the reports you did on the slugs removed from several Hispanic women. There's a separate report for each victim."

"Yes," Crackstone said. "Did Bradford give you those reports?"

"Yeah, but I can't tell from these reports if the same gun was used in all of these killings."

"Well, not from the individual reports, no."

"What I'm wondering is, did you do a comparison to

see if all of the slugs came from the same gun?"

"Yes, let me pull it up."

Chilton waited.

"Yes," Crackstone said. "The slugs from the first and third victims matched. The slugs from the second and fourth victims matched too. So, two guns, both 9mm Glock semi-automatics.

"Why didn't Bradford give me that report?" Chilton exploded. "Not that it's your fault, John, but what the hell?"

"Bradford was upset I did that analysis," Crackstone explained. "He didn't want me to do anything that would undermine the Medawar prosecution. He said Warren would go ballistic if he found out about the report. He said I should lose it."

"He actually said that?"

"Yes. I ignored him, of course."

"Medawar's lawyer thinks that whoever killed these Hispanic women killed Ann Medawar. Did you do that comparison?"

"No, but I could."

"I think you should."

"Bradford will have a stroke."

"I can live with that. I'd rather have that on my conscience than have this doctor get away with murder. Or wonder if we convicted the wrong guy because Warren's running for office."

Crackstone said he'd think about it.

When he hung up, Chilton found the bottle of aspirin he kept in his desk drawer and swallowed four. He located the bottle of antacid pills and took a couple of them to deal with what the aspirin would do to his stomach. And then he went and got coffee.

As he poured the coffee into his mug, Chilton tried to calculate exactly how long he had until retirement.

Too long.

TUESDAY EVENING, DECEMBER 8

6:00 P.M. NEWS

Queen City News Live: Bringing you the news you want to hear.

News Anchor Bob Bunker: Hamilton County Prosecutor Richard Warren spoke this morning to members of the Cincinnati Academy of Medicine. His remarks prompted many of the physicians attending this morning's meeting at a downtown hotel to walk out of the meeting. Tiffany Albern is at the Hyatt and has this report.

Tiffany Albern: Thank you, Bob. I'm at the Hyatt Hotel, where more than half of the physicians attending this morning's meeting walked out in protest. Here's some of what Warren had to say:

Video Clip of Warren speaking plays: America is becoming a third-world country because of the things that are coming at us from across the border. We've got illegal drugs coming across the border. Everyone knows that. We've got Central American children of prime gang recruitment age. Plus, we've potentially got the Ebola virus. Now especially with Ebola, what happens when that starts happening down in Mexico and Guatemala and people just walk into the country?

Tiffany Albern: After the meeting, I asked Warren why he thought so many physicians walked out during his speech.

Video Clip of Warren speaking plays: Tiffany, we've got a lot of foreign doctors in Cincinnati, and a number of them came here this morning planning on pulling this stunt. You know some of them come from places that don't share our values.

Tiffany Albern: I've heard people in your campaign say that physicians are reacting to your prosecution of Dr. Rafiq

Medawar.

Richard Warren: Tiffany, they shouldn't be saying that. I know that there are some doctors who feel that way, but I don't know how many. As you know, Tiffany, some of these foreign doctors come from places where husbands can have multiple wives, and women are expected to remain in the home. But I don't know how many of these doctors think that way and how many just want to see us move to socialized medicine.

Tiffany Albern: Thank you, Mr. Warren. Tiffany Albern, reporting live from the Hyatt Hotel downtown.

WEDNESDAY, DECEMBER 9

10 A.M. – 1:30 `P.M.

The room was too warm, but Carrie Hixson wasn't going to complain. She had taken personally the news that another Hispanic woman had disappeared, and her interviews with the family of Camila Suarez had been heart-wrenching. After the session with Garner, she felt she needed to do something. This meeting might well be her one chance to alert the Hispanic community before yet another victim turned up.

She was meeting with the editor and a reporter for Cincinnati's Spanish language newspaper. The paper had a small paid subscription base, mainly Anglos, but was widely distributed for free at Hispanic groceries, Mexican restaurants, and other places Hispanics might be expected to gather. Along with the city's one Spanish-language radio station, it provided a voice for the area's Hispanic community.

Hixson had given a shorter explanation to get the appointment, but now she explained her concern in more detail. She and Ann Lindsey Medawar had been working, along with the rest of their film class, on a documentary about the undocumented in Greater Cincinnati. But somewhere along the way, she and Ann had begun to focus on the disappearances and slayings of several young Hispanic women.

"We were convinced that there was a serial killer, or killers, responsible for those murders," Carrie said. "And then, just as we thought we were getting close to figuring out who was responsible, someone killed Ann."

From their expressions and body language, Hixson could tell she had their interest. She slid a DVD into her laptop and played the video she and the team put together for Garner – but without mentioning him or the meeting with the prosecutor's office.

When the short video ended, the audience of two seemed mesmerized, then excited. The editor insisted everyone else in the small office come and watch the video. After she replayed it, the editor placed a call to someone at the Spanish-language radio station. Thirty minutes later, two people from the station showed up.

Hixson replayed the video twice more. The reporter from the radio station peppered Hixson with questions. Then, the reporters from the radio station settled in with their equipment and interviewed Hixson.

Hixson wasn't sure the interview went well. She thought her answers could have been more concise. The producer assured Hixson she handled the interview very well. The only thing that could have made it better would have been if she could speak Spanish.

Speaking in Spanish, Hixson asked the producer if he wanted to do the interview over in Spanish. The producer looked stunned, then animated. He immediately ordered the reporter to re-do the interview.

Hixson thought the second version went better.

Still astonished that this Anglo white-bread chick could speak Spanish, the producer claimed that it went better than that. His praise was so extravagant, Hixson wondered briefly if the guy was going to propose marriage. And that was before lunch arrived.

The producer watched in amazement as Hixson quietly ate a dish involving a strong Mexican pepper that most Anglos would have avoided – or if they had tasted it by mistake, would have caused them to cry for mercy.

"¡Dios mío, ella come como un Mexicano!" he said, in awe. *My God, she eats like a Mexican!*

A week later, the newspaper featured the story on its front page. The radio station held the story until the paper published, which gave it time to add some interviews and material of its own.

The stories attracted a great deal of attention in the Hispanic community, but aside from Univision, the more mainstream media did not pick up the story.

The story – and the fact the Anglo media did not pick it up – generated a great deal of discussion and argument within the Nuestras Casas community. One of the older men there, a serious man, did not participate in the discussions. But he carefully tore the story from the newspaper, folded it, and put it in his wallet.

FRIDAY, DECEMBER 11

10:30 A.M.– 11:15 A.M.

Devin Garner opened the package someone from the Prosecutor's office had just dropped off at his office. As he expected, it contained the materials Bradford agreed to produce concerning the abducted and killed Hispanic women.

Garner quickly read each report from beginning to end – he would read them again later, taking notes, and then he likely would read them a dozen more times. But for now, he returned to the reports prepared by the ballistics expert in the Hamilton Coroner's office. He pulled the similar report from Ann's file. On a fresh piece of paper, he jotted down the name of the victim in one column and the reports' conclusions in a second column – imaging how the information might look on a poster board he might someday soon show a jury:

Ann Medawar	Glock 9mm
Natalia Garcia	Glock 9mm
Valerie Zuniga	Glock 9mm
Isabella Ramirez	Glock 9mm
Sofia Flores	Glock 9mm

The information was infuriating and too important to sit on until trial. He called Bradford.

When Bradford picked up, Garner didn't bother to introduce himself or say Hi. "Bill, did you look the reports you just sent me?" he asked. "I mean, Jesus H. Christ, did you read the goddam forensic reports?"

"I read them," Bradford responded without emotion, revealing nothing.

"Every one of these women was shot with a Glock 9mm," Garner said, "the same as Ann Medawar."

"I read the reports."

"Did you read those reports before you told the judge they weren't material to my client's defense?"

"No," Bradford said, tersely. "I hadn't seen them yet."

"Okay, so now you've read them, and you know someone out there is abducting and killing young Hispanic women. You know Ann was investigating those deaths. Somebody got nervous and killed her. They shot her with a 9mm Glock, just like all the others. You know goddam-good-and-well my client didn't kill his wife. You know you're prosecuting the wrong person."

Bradford didn't respond.

"Here's what I want to know," Garner said, not trying to reign in his indignation. "I want to know if you are going to dismiss the charges against my client."

"I can't. I talked to Warren, and he's adamant your guy killed his wife. He says we're not dismissing."

"That's not a good enough reason to prosecute an innocent man. Warren's an idiot. Everybody knows that. Bill, I thought you were better than that."

At first Bradford didn't respond.

"Give me a minute," he said finally. "I'm going to call you on my cell."

Garner could hear Bradford's door close before the line went dead. He picked up a pen, scratched it on a notepad to see if it still had ink. It didn't. Garner threw it across the room and watched it bounce off the wall.

His phone rang. It was Bradford.

"You were going to explain," Garner said, before Bradford could say anything, "why you're going to prosecute an innocent man, a really decent guy — a friend of mine — for something you know he didn't do."

"Devin, I understand where you're coming from, but I don't know that your client is innocent. But it really doesn't matter what I think. Warren says he's not backing down on this. He says if I'm not willing to prosecute this case, he'll find someone who will. Someone who wants my job."

"He said that?"

"More or less."

"More or less? What does that mean?"

"Jesus, Devin. He said if I'm going soft, he'll find someone who still has a hard-on for the job."

"You should resign. Walk away while you still can. While you've still got your reputation. While you can still look at yourself in the mirror."

"And then who's going to pay my bills? You?"

"You're an experienced trial lawyer. The feds would jump at the chance to hire someone like you. Or, you can go into private practice. Any of the big law firms in town would pay you double what you're making – and wonder why you didn't ask for more."

Again, Bradford didn't respond.

Garner was sure he had more to say. "What's really going on?"

"I can't resign. Warren is running for Congress, and he's probably going to get elected. If I stick this out, I'm the obvious candidate to succeed him, and he's promised to back me."

Garner fought the urge to say something smartass.

"If I stick it out, I will be the first non-white to hold this job. I can make some real changes around here. If I quit, Warren will handpick some Tea Party asshole to run the Prosecutor's office, and – well, you know what that would mean."

Garner lost the fight against the urge to say something he would regret. "And that's why you're going to put my client through a trial, and maybe get him convicted and put him in prison?"

"Give me a break, Devin. I don't decide if your client is guilty or not. The jury decides if he's guilty, I don't. The judge sentences him, if it comes to that, I don't."

"You have discretion not to prosecute."

Bradford cut Garner off before he could say more.

"And the voters elected Warren to decide how to exercise that discretion. Not me."

"And now that he's in office, there's a reason everyone calls him '*the Dick*.' If you're not willing to tell Warren he's wrong, let me talk to him. Set something up."

"How about this?" Bradford said. "I'll do my job, and you do yours. If the evidence is as clear as you think, you'll get him acquitted."

"That's bullshit! No matter how good a job I do, no matter how clear the evidence is, there's no guarantee the jury won't convict. Juries figure if you went to all the trouble of prosecuting someone, he must be guilty. Everybody knows that."

"I can't help that. If there's no evidence he killed his wife, and the jury convicts him, the court will set it aside, or you'll get it overturned on appeal."

"Bill, we both know there's no guarantee of that. Besides, by then, his career, his reputation – his life – will be ruined."

"Look, Devin, I can't dismiss. I told you – it's not up to me. The case is going to go to trial. I'm not going to lay down and let you win. I'm going to do my job, so maybe you better do yours. The judge and jury can sort out who's right. Or God can. It's not up to me."

"This case is going to trial because *the Dick* thinks it's good for his campaign, and you aren't willing to call him on it."

"Give me a break, Devin," Bradford said. "This case is going to trial, because that's how the process works."

SATURDAY, DECEMBER 12

EVENING

The documentary group gathered for a late snack and drinks at Reya's Authentic Mexican Restaurant – arriving just after 9:00. Some had Coronas, others Margaritas, and the designated drivers had Mexican soft drinks. The group ordered burritos, enchiladas, tacos – plus some items most had not tried before. The restaurant provided lots of chips and fresh salsa.

Those who learned the least in their high school or college Spanish classes tried their language skills with the waitress – causing the waitress no end of confusion, but she giggled along with the group.

The group begged and were allowed to take pictures of themselves with the waitress. She produced a real Mexican sombrero, and they took more pictures and videos.

The waitress found Reya and brought her to the group for more pictures and laughs.

In all, the bill came to almost two hundred dollars. Hixson put it on her charge card – Garner had already given her a check for two hundred dollars. She would drop off the credit card receipt at his office next week – along with the photos. If the charge didn't show up on the cash register tape, they would be able to sign affidavits or testify at his uncle's divorce hearing.

The group left a very generous tip for the waitress.

6:35 P.M. - 6:45 P.M.

Carrie Hixson called Devin Garner. "They've killed another woman," Hixson said when Garner answered.

"Another Hispanic woman?" Garner asked.

"Yes," she said. "A waitress at Reya's. Her name was Alejandra Cruz."

Garner thought he recognized the name. He could feel his emotions welling up. He was angry.

"Where did they find her?" he asked.

"At the Turfway Park race track. According to the news, workers found her body when they arrived early this morning to care for the horses."

Garner let the news sink in.

"Devin," Hixson said, "we – my documentary class – were at Reya's last night, like we talked about. She waited on us. And now she's dead."

Garner let her give expression to her grief, before asking if she intended to try to track down the woman's family.

"I have to," Hixson said. "I owe it to her, to all these women, to Ann."

"I'll contact my uncle," Garner said, "and see if he can put you in touch with Alejandra's family."

When he finished talking with Hixson, Garner called his uncle. Hank had just learned the news from Reya's daughter, Maya.

"You met Alejandra," Hank told Garner. "She waited on you when you visited me at the restaurant."

"I was really sorry to hear about her death, and now I feel even worse," Garner said. "Do you know anything about the funeral arrangements?"

"You don't need to go. I knew her, you didn't."

"You know she's not the first young Hispanic woman

to be killed over the past several months? She's at least the sixth that I know of."

"I haven't heard anything about that."

"You heard about the U.C. medical student who went missing?"

"Yeah, that was terrible."

"Well, her body hasn't turned up yet, but she was the fifth victim. I've got a friend who is investigating these killings. She's making a documentary. She's explained to me that each of these women was killed the same way. I've seen the forensic reports. They've all been killed by the same type handgun. Some other similarities."

"You think there's a serial killer?"

"Yes."

"Oh, come on, if there were a serial killer, the police would be all over it. And the news people would be sensationalizing the hell out of it."

"You would think so. But these are Mexican women, and the police aren't connecting the dots."

"That doesn't make any sense."

"The early victims were undocumented, and a couple of them may have been prostitutes. In fact, you met one of the earlier victims. She was working at the Sleep Cheap Inn. You told me you drove her there from Reya's."

"You don't think Diego has anything to do with this?"

"I don't know, but my friend thinks the killer is caught up in all this anti-immigrant nonsense."

"That wouldn't surprise me. It's gotten bad."

"I want you to meet my friend, the one who is making the documentary about these killings. Her name is Carrie, Carrie Hixson. You'll like her."

"Okay."

"Carrie has interviewed the families of all these women, and she is hoping to interview the family of Alejandra."

"I don't know her family."

"Well, I'm going to find out when Carrie can meet us

for lunch. You two can work something out. Maybe you can call Reya's daughter. Or, if there is going to be a visitation, maybe Carrie can go with you, and you can introduce her."

"Carrie?" Hank asked. "Is she pretty?"

"Very."

"You dating her?"

"She's out of my league."

"Don't sell yourself short."

MONDAY, DECEMBER 14

Detective James Chilton learned about the death of a Hispanic woman in Florence from news reports. On Monday, he tracked down Samantha Farmer, the Florence police detective responsible for investigating the murder, and made arrangements to meet her at her office.

Farmer was a tall, athletic black woman, who was all business. From the plaques on her wall, Chilton learned that she had served in the Marines in Iraq and was a competition-level shooter.

Chilton explained that at least four, maybe five, young Hispanic women had been abducted and killed in Cincinnati. He was wondering if the murder she was investigating might be related.

"Here's what we have," Farmer said. "On Sunday morning, workers found the body of a young Hispanic woman, Alejandra Cruz, dumped outside Turfway Park. She was a waitress at Reya's Mexican restaurant."

"How was she killed?" Chilton asked.

"Shot twice. Torso shot, headshot. Killed somewhere else, dumped at the track. No signs of sexual assault. She still had her wallet."

"Why the race track? Any idea?"

"Lot of Mexicans work there," Farmer said. "They take care of the horses, the track. Lot of them live in an apartment complex not far from there."

"Someone could be trying to send a message that Mexicans aren't welcome," Chilton said, thinking out loud.

"Could be," Farmer allowed. "Not sure if it's related, but we had an anti-immigration group hold a rally here on Saturday at the Florence Park. Got some idiots all riled up about Mexicans and Muslims."

"A hate group?"

"Yeah, the League of Natural Born Citizens. They had

posters up around town for what they call a 'Make America White Again' rally."

Chilton snorted. "'Make America White Again'? I'm guessing not too many black folks there."

"Sure, Jim," Farmer said, "we be there with a booth selling sheets and hoods to all the nice white people."

Chilton laughed. He handed Farmer copies of the police reports relating to the Cincinnati cases.

"I'll send you the reports on our case as we get them," Farmer promised.

Chilton thought he had heard of the League of Natural Born Citizens, but couldn't recall where. Back at his own office, he checked the internet and found the group's website. It was full of anti-Mexican, anti-Hispanic, anti-Muslim, anti-Semitic, anti-black, and anti-Obama rhetoric. Nothing on the website, however, told him where he'd heard of the group.

Chilton checked with the intelligence units of the Cincinnati Police Department, the Hamilton County Sheriff's office, and the Ohio State Police. He asked Farmer to check with the Kentucky State Police's intelligence unit.

While waiting to hear back from them, he checked with the FBI. It must track these hate groups, he thought.

The FBI assured him that it did track hate groups and had the League of Natural Born Citizens on its radar. What could they tell him about it? *Nothing.* The FBI didn't share.

Chilton returned to the League of Natural Born Citizens website. It appeared to be a local thing without any obvious organizational ties to any national group. He identified its leaders and checked their police records. His check turned up nothing out of the ordinary.

He still couldn't recall where he'd heard of this group, but he decided he would have to interview its leaders. As he thought about that, he could feel indigestion forming in his stomach.

WEDNESDAY, DECEMBER 16

6:00 P.M. NEWS

Queen City News Live: Bringing you the news you want to hear.

News Anchor Bob Bunker: In our lead story, earlier today Cincinnati Police officers raided the offices of Obreros de Hoy, a staffing agency in Northside. Tiffany Albern was on the scene there this morning and filed this report.

Tiffany Albern: In another of a series of raids on employers suspected of hiring undocumented immigrants, Cincinnati Police arrived at the offices of Obreros de Hoy, here in Northside this morning, just after 8:00 a.m. As in other recent, similar raids, they left with books, records, laptops, email servers – the large computers that store emails – and other materials.

According to a statement released by the Hamilton County Prosecutor's office, Obreros de Hoy was on paper the actual employer of a number of the undocumented immigrants apprehended in other recent raids. According to the statement, Obreros de Hoy also supplied workers to several subcontractors used by local home builder, The Bauherren Company.

The Prosecutor's office said it is looking for evidence Obreros knew the workers used fake or forged identification papers. The Prosecutor's office said the police are also looking for the identities of other undocumented workers.

I have with me Carl Anwalt, the attorney for Obreros de Hoy. Mr. Anwalt, your reaction to this morning's raid?

Carl Anwalt: This raid was an outrage. Immigration is a federal matter. Congress has given responsibility for immigration enforcement to ICE, to the U.S. Immigration and Customs Enforcement agency. Congress did not give that responsibility to the county prosecutor in Hamilton County or any other county. What we have is a prosecutor, Richard Warren, who is abusing his office to drum up support for his run for Congress.

Tiffany, I've seen some of the documentation the Prosecutor's office claims are false papers. If they're fake, I've got to say, those papers would have fooled me. Like other Cincinnati employers, Obreros de Hoy works hard to check its employees' paperwork.

It should not be subject to harassment and disruption of its operations just because Warren is looking for publicity. You don't shut down a Kroger supermarket because one of its cashiers accepted a counterfeit $20 bill without realizing it. This really isn't that different.

This is just political grandstanding.

Tiffany Albern: Did the police take into custody any workers suspected of being undocumented?

Carl Anwalt: Not here, but what we've seen after past raids is the prosecutor's office uses the confiscated employment records to identify workers with Hispanic names and then harasses them. I expect we'll see more of that after this raid.

Tiffany, many of these individuals were born and grew up here. Frankly, it's really just a matter of time until we see a massive civil rights suit against Warren, with Hamilton County taxpayers picking up the tab for what he's been doing.

Tiffany Albern: Reporting live from Northside.

Co-Anchor Ashley Gelb: After the break, we have a special report: How much sugar is in your favorite Starbucks drink?

WEDNESDAY, DECEMBER 16

6:30 P.M. – 7:45 P.M.

Devin Garner watched the news of the raid on the Los Obreros de Hoy staffing agency. Seconds after the story ended, his cell phone rang. It was Carrie Hixson.

"Did you watch the news?" Hixson asked. "Did you see the story about Warren's latest raid?"

"I just saw it."

"The lawyer. Do you know him?"

"Afraid so. He's on the opposite side of my uncle's divorce case. Why?"

"I've got an idea. Can I come over to your office so we can talk about it?"

"Sure. What's this about?"

"I'll explain when I get there. In the meanwhile, is there any way you can find out if he has any connection to the Sleep Cheap Inn? Does he represent them?"

"Yes, he does."

"What about the other places Warren has raided?"

"That's usually confidential – unless he's represented them in litigation. I can check on that."

"Do what you can, and I'll see you in a little bit."

Garner did several searches of the local courts' electronic dockets and didn't see where Anwalt represented any of the companies in litigation. He also ran a search on the Secretary of State's corporation registry.

Garner pulled up the articles of incorporation for Diego's corporation – Aqua Caliente, Inc. The articles did not list Diego Olivar as the incorporator, which was no great surprise. It's not unusual for Articles of Incorporation to list the attorney who set up the corporation as the incorporator. That protects the identity of the owner of the corporation.

The incorporator – as well as the attorney for the corporation – was Carl Anwalt.

Garner searched the Secretary of State's website for the Articles of Incorporation for Los Obreros de Hoy. Carl Anwalt was its incorporator and attorney as well. The other companies the county had recently raided were long-established companies. Anwalt would not have been involved in their incorporation or representation. But Garner did find several other entities Anwalt had incorporated – including some of the subcontractors used by The Bauherren Company. Anwalt had also incorporated the not-for-profit housing Co-Op not far from Garner's own office.

Hixson let herself into his office.

"Carrie, it's not safe around here after dark. You should have let me know you were here. I would have been happy to walk with you from your car."

"We've had this conversation before," Hixson replied.

"I don't want anything to happen to you."

"Jamal and another of the watchers walked with me." Hixson was referring to the informal group of "watchers" who kept an eye on the neighborhood.

"He never escorts me," Garner complained in a mock pout.

"I'm better looking," Hixson said matter-of-factly. "But he *is* very protective of you."

Hixson set up her laptop. She pulled up the file she wanted him to see. "I don't know if you remember," she said as she was doing that, "but after Rafiq went into the inn, Ann moved the camera to get a better shot when he came back out of the inn."

"I remember that."

"Do you remember that as she was doing that, she made some practice videos of some men who happened to be coming out of the inn?"

"Let me see," Garner said.

Hixson ran the video. The first two men to leave the inn

meant nothing to him when he first saw the video, but that was no longer the case.

"Jesus," Garner said. "Can you run it again?"

Hixson re-ran it several more times.

"That's Anwalt, right?" she asked.

"Yes, and the guy with him is his buddy, Judge Richter."

"What's a judge doing in a place like that?"

"Good question," Garner agreed, "but I'm short on answers right now."

He handed Hixson copies of the articles of incorporation for Aqua Caliente.

"Agua Caliente is the company that owns the Sleep Cheap Inn. Carl Anwalt is the incorporator. That doesn't mean he owns the company. It just means he set up the corporation and used his name to hide the name of whoever does own it."

Hixson took a quick look at the document. It didn't reveal much.

"Anwalt is also the incorporator of the staffing agency the county raided today," Garner explained.

Finally, he handed Hixson the paperwork for Nuestras Casas Housing Co-Op. "My guess is, that's who gets raided next."

"I'm spending a lot of time there," Hixson said. "A lot of the people who live in the Co-Op technically work for Los Obreros. It finds them jobs with companies that don't look too closely at their documentation. After it deducts for a bunch of phony charges, Los Obreros doesn't pay them even minimum wage.

"Oh, and get this. Los Obreros has vans that pick them up at the Co-Op in the morning and take them to wherever they work. And then, the vans bring them back at the end of the day. Los Obreros doesn't want them trying to drive and getting picked up by the cops."

Together, Garner and Hixson re-watched the video Ann had inadvertently made of Anwalt and Richter leaving the

Sleep Cheap Inn.

"I'm wondering," Garner said, "if Anwalt thought Ann was closer to putting things together than she was."

"You don't really think he had Ann killed? I don't buy it. He's an attorney. He's not going to have someone killed. My money is still on whoever is killing the Hispanic women."

Garner shrugged. "Either way," he said, "you're going to have one hell of a documentary."

THURSDAY, DECEMBER 24 –
SATURDAY, JANUARY 2

The Christmas holidays always brought gifts: drug possession cases, domestic abuse cases and of course, shoplifting cases. Devin Garner spent much of the holidays working, mainly on cases other than the Medawar case.

Carrie Hixson went to Vail with her family for the holidays. Garner had never been to Vail, but it wasn't hard to imagine the social scene after the day's skiing was done. Lots of good-looking young men and women from wealthy families would congregate in bars. They would mention the colleges they had attended, the fraternities and sororities they had belonged to, and the vacations they had taken in Europe. There would be lots of hookups.

He missed having Carrie around. He tried not to think about how she might be spending her time, or who she might be spending it with.

It was probably Carrie's influence, but over the holidays he found himself thinking of the Hispanic immigrants in his neighborhood. If he felt he would never really be accepted into Carrie's world, what was it like for them – especially given the current political climate? They must feel even more like they will never really fit in, will never be truly accepted in the country.

He arranged to have a couple crates of oranges and some inexpensive boxes of chocolates delivered to the Nuestras Casas Co-Op. They arrived on Christmas eve.

On Christmas, he attended a family gathering hosted by a cousin and his wife. Afterwards, he had dinner and exchanged presents with Hank. He talked with Hank about how much he missed his father. Hank told him his father would have been proud of what he had accomplished and what he was doing.

SUNDAY, JANUARY 3 –
MONDAY, JANUARY 4

For Greater Cincinnati, the holiday weather was exceptionally nice, with lots of blue sky and warm days. On the weekend after New Year's Day, a dozen Sierra Club members took advantage of the nice weather to do clean up along the banks of the Whitewater River just across the state line in Indiana. Near where I-275 crossed the small river, the volunteers found the badly decomposed body of a woman and summoned the police.

The crime scene investigator believed the body had likely been thrown from the expressway into the river. Once in the small river, the corpse lodged in some vegetation near the shore, partially shielding it from view. He reported his conclusion up the chain of command, along with his suspicion that the body was that of the missing University of Cincinnati student.

To no one's surprise, on Monday, the Coroner's office confirmed that the body was indeed that of U.C. medical student Camila Suarez, who had gone missing after leaving a party near the U.C. campus seven weeks earlier.

Detective Chilton added Camila Suarez to the list of young Hispanic women who had gone missing and turned up dead. Six altogether, that he was aware of.

The fact that this woman had been thrown off a bridge supported the notion that he was dealing with two serial killers – one who had a thing for tossing dead women off bridges, and another who was trying to make a point about Hispanics not being welcome. But serial killers who struck in alternating months made no sense.

This woman had no ties to Lower Price Hill. Like a lot of students, she lived in Clifton, but had no apparent ties to the Sleep Cheap Inn.

He was no closer to identifying the killer or killers.

SATURDAY, JANUARY 9

EVENING

The more Sam Scherge thought about it, the more convinced he was that the reason his boss gave for firing him and his buddy, Roger Storrs, was bullshit. After spending time on the internet and having his eyes opened to what was going on in the country, it was obvious the company just wanted to get rid of them, to make room for more Mexicans it didn't have to pay as much.

It was true, he'd be the first to admit, that he and Storrs had a couple cans of beer and smoked a joint in the company parking lot during lunch. But since when was that a reason for firing anyone? They weren't on the clock.

And that whole thing about grabbing that Mexican woman's tits in the warehouse just made his blood boil. That was clearly a bullshit reason to fire someone. He was pretty sure Maria was an illegal. She had no right to be here, taking a job away from some American. What right did she have to complain, really, if he grabbed her tits?

The politicians talked big about deporting all the illegals, but no one was doing anything about that – except him and Roger. That was why he was standing where he was.

It was dark, cold and damp, which he didn't mind, but he was standing across the street from the Nuestras Casas Housing Co-Op, which made his skin crawl. The place was full of illegals. Every evening you could see them going down the street to that little Mexican grocery – and the cops weren't doing a damn thing.

He had his eye on one woman who lived in the Co-Op. He guessed she was about twenty. She was short and thin, with long black hair. She was actually kind of cute, for a Mexican, but in ten years, all those refried beans would catch up with her, and she wouldn't be a cute little enchilada any-more. She would be another chubby burrito. But by then, she'd be sitting at home with a bunch of kids living off wel-fare. *Why should he give up half his paycheck in taxes to support people like her and her kids?*

And her kids would be citizens! Guaranteed by the fourteenth freaking amendment. He'd read about that online. The politi-cians needed to get their shit together and change that.

The young woman emerged from the Co-Op. Like he knew she would, she started up the street, toward that little Mexican grocery. He crossed the street and began following her, walking a little quicker than she did. Storrs was waiting up the street, standing next to his pick-up truck. He needed to be sure he was just behind the woman when she got to where Storrs was waiting.

As the woman approached, Storrs said something, ap-parently trying to engage her in conversation. She replied, "No hablo Ingles." She was going to walk right by him. Storrs stepped in front of her and pointed to the open pas-senger-side door on his pickup. She shook her head "no" and started to turn around, to retreat, but by then Scherge was behind her and shoved her forward.

The woman started screaming. Scherge heard Storrs tell her to shut up – like talking to her in English was going to help. Scherge stepped closer and grabbed the woman and began to push her toward the truck. That's when, from freaking nowhere, some guy grabbed his arm from behind. As he turned, this Mexican dude landed a fist right in his face. Scherge stumbled backward, losing his grip on the woman.

The Mexican was short and thin, but muscular and dan-gerous looking. Scherge tasted blood and realized his nose was bleeding. Storrs was just standing there like an idiot do-ing nothing.

The Mexican dude shouted something at the girl, and she began running away. Before Scherge could grab her, the

Mexican attacked again, landing more punches to his face. Storrs intervened and knocked the asshole to the ground, but by then other men from the Co-Op were running toward them, and Storrs was shouting for him to get into the pickup.

The whole thing was fucked up! There was no sense hanging around now.

WEDNESDAY, JANUARY 13

6:00 P.M. NEWS

Queen City News Live: Bringing you the news you want to hear.

News Anchor Bob Bunker: Hamilton County Prosecutor Richard Warren spoke to the Fraternal Order of Police this morning. Tiffany Albern is at the FOP hall and has this report.

Tiffany Albern: Thank you, Bob. I'm at the Fraternal Order of Police headquarters where Hamilton County Prosecutor Richard Warren just finished speaking. Here is some of what Warren told the audience:

Video Clip Plays, Warren speaking: All Muslims in the United States should be legally obligated to register. We should have their personal tracking information in a database. I don't think we can rule out requiring all Muslims to carry special religious identification. I don't think we can rule out warrantless searches of their homes and places of worship. And yes, we may have to shut down some mosques. We're going to have to do things that we never did before. We're going to have to do certain things that were frankly unthinkable a year ago.

Tiffany Albern: After his remarks, I got to speak to Warren. I reminded him that after the last election, party officials said the party needed to do a better job of reaching out to minorities. I asked him if he disagreed.

Video Clip Plays, Warren speaking: After Mitt Romney lost the last presidential election, there were some in the party who wanted to change course and try to win the Hispanic vote, the Muslim vote. I don't agree. I'm just no great fan of identity politics.

Tiffany Albern: I asked Warren if he had any comment on Dr. Medawar's claim that he is not from Syria, that he is an American.

Video Clip Plays, Warren speaking: Well, I haven't seen his birth certificate. But if he's not from Syria, his family is.

Tiffany Albern speaking: He says his family is from Beirut.

Warren speaking: Come on Tiffany! Beirut is the capital of Syria. If you're going to cover this story, you need to know these things.

Tiffany Albern: Reporting live from FOP headquarters.

Co-Anchor Ashley Gelb: In other news tonight, a fire in Pleasant Ridge left a family homeless. Pictures when we return.

MONDAY, JANUARY 18

10:00 A.M. – 11:45 A.M.

Devin Garner was surprised when Jonas Trottel, the "slow" kid he had represented in the missing gun trial, showed up at his office. He had not seen Jonas since the trial. After the usual pleasantries, Garner asked Jonas what brought him in.

"You said if I got in trouble again, to come talk to you."

"That's right," Garner said. It had probably not been easy for Jonas to ask for help. He tried to keep his manner cordial and supportive.

"I think I'm in trouble," Jonas confided.

"What happened?" Garner asked.

Jonas looked frightened and didn't seem to know where to start.

"Where are my manners?" Garner said. "Do you want a soft drink?"

"No, thank you," Jonas said, looking sheepish.

"I'm going to get myself one," Garner said. "You sure?"

"Okay."

Garner returned a minute later with two cans of soft drink.

Jonas eagerly accepted one.

"What happened?" Garner asked again.

"You know that Mexican store down the street?"

Garner nodded. He knew the place. It was a Mexican "tienda" or grocery. It also had a small lunch counter or "taqueria" and was popular with the residents of the Nuestras Casas Housing Co-Op, a couple blocks further down the street. He had eaten there many times.

"This man, he was walking up the street," Jonas said. "I think he was going to go there. But somebody in the alley started yelling something. The man – he went running into the alley."

"What were they yelling?"

"'Help! Help! She's hurt.'"

"Did they say anything else?"

"They were yelling something else, but I couldn't understand it. I think it was in Mexican."

"And then what happened?" Garner was not naturally patient, but understood he had to be with Jonas.

"When the man ran past the dumpster, they hit him." Jonas fidgeted nervously. "With a board or something."

"And then what?"

"And then they started kicking and hitting him."

"Do you know who this man is?"

"No."

"How many men beat him up?"

"Two."

"Were they Hispanic?"

Jonas looked confused.

"The men who beat this man up, were they Mexican too?"

"No," Jonas said. He nervously drank some of the soft drink.

"Okay, so then what happened?"

"They drove away."

"What happened to the man they beat up?"

"He was bleeding. He threw up. They hurt him bad."

"Ok, Jonas, tell me what happened next."

Jonas shifted nervously in his seat. "Maybe I should go," he said.

"Jonas, do you trust me?" Garner asked.

"Yes, sir."

"Then just tell me what happened."

"I ran to that Mexican place. I told them to call an ambulance. I told them the man was hurt bad."

"You did the right thing. That was very good, Jonas."

Jonas fidgeted.

"And then what happened?" Garner pressed.

"And then the ambulance came and got him."

"Did the police come too?"

"Yes," Jonas said. He became agitated and began nodding his head up and down.

"You want some pretzels?" Garner asked.

Jonas shrugged his shoulders.

"Come with me," Garner said, leading Jonas to the little kitchenette at the back of his office. Garner lifted a large tin of pretzels from the floor and sat it on the tiny table.

"Can you open that?" Garner asked. "I'm going to see if I can find a bowl."

Jonas pried the can open, and Garner poured a generous portion of pretzels into a plastic bowl. He led Jonas back to his office and placed the bowl of pretzels between them on the desk.

"You were telling me about what happened when the police arrived," Garner prompted.

"They asked me if I saw who did it."

"What did you tell them?"

"I told them no."

Garner nodded and waited for Jonas to continue.

Jonas said nothing and seemed lost.

"Do you know who they were? The men who beat up that man?"

"Yes, sir."

"You do?"

"Yes."

"Who were they?"

"They live in the neighborhood. They went to Oyler." Oyler was the local public school.

"You knew them from school?" Garner asked.

"They were older than me. They used to make fun of me and make me give them my lunch money and stuff."

"Do you know their names?"

"Yes."

Garner took a deep breath. "What are their names?"

"Sam and Roger."

"Do you know their last names?"

"Yes."

"Jonas, what are their names?"

"Sam Scherge."

Jonas was bobbing his head up and down.

"And Roger Storrs," he said finally. "He's really mean."

"You say they live up the street from where you and your mother live?"

"Yeah, they live in that big apartment building."

"What else can you tell me about them?"

"Roger has a truck. The one with the flag."

"That red pickup truck with the Confederate flag you see around here sometimes?"

Jonas nodded yes.

"The police asked you if you knew who they were?"

Jonas nodded again.

"And you told them you didn't know."

Jonas shook his head.

"Why didn't you tell the police who they were?"

"I was afraid."

"You were afraid those guys would hurt you, like they did that man in the alley."

"Yeah," Jonas said.

"And now you're afraid the police will find out that you saw what they did, and that you know who they are? You're afraid you'll be in trouble with the police?"

"They said I'd go to jail, and you wouldn't be able to help me this time."

"Who said that?"

"They did. They were driving around yesterday and saw me, and they stopped and got out. They asked me if I told the police who they were. I told them I didn't. Sam told me that was smart, because if I told the police, they would do to me what they did to that man."

"Did they say anything else?"

Jonas nodded. "They told me not to tell anyone. They said if the police found out I lied, the police would put me in jail, and you wouldn't be able to help me this time."

"Jonas, I'm glad you came and talked to me about this."

"I'm afraid," Jonas said. "Are the police going to put me in jail?"

"Not if we go and talk to the police and explain what happened. If we don't, and the police find out you lied about not knowing those guys, you could be in trouble. The police may think you were involved."

"Will they arrest me?"

"No, if we explain what happened, the police will understand. I'll go with you, and we'll explain what happened."

"Will the police tell Sam I told on him?"

"I'll talk to the police and see if we can work something out so that doesn't happen." Garner hoped he wasn't overpromising.

"But here's the thing, Jonas. You have to be sure you don't say anything about going to the police to anyone. Just me and the police. And your mother, if you want to tell her. But nobody else, understand?"

Jonas nodded.

"What do you say we go to the police station right away and get this cleared up, so you don't have to worry about it."

"Okay."

"When we talk to the police, you have to tell the truth. That's very important, understand?"

"Yes, sir."

It took Garner only a couple of phone calls to learn which detective was responsible for the investigation and to arrange to meet him at the District 3 Station with Jonas.

***

Once at the station house, Garner explained the situation to the detective.

"Jonas," he said, "wants to 'amend' the statement he gave on Saturday."

The detective smiled and nodded.

Garner had Jonas tell the story in his own words.

The detective made notes and pressed Jonas for more information about where Scherge and Storrs lived and what kind of truck Storrs owned. Jonas was able to answer most of the detective's questions.

The detective thanked Garner for bringing Jonas in, but didn't seem terribly interested in following up.

"I'd like to talk to the man they beat up," Garner said, "to apologize for what happened and to see if I can help, but I don't know the man's name."

The detective gave Garner the man's name and address. "He's undocumented," the detective explained, "and doesn't want to press charges or testify. He's afraid he'll be deported."

"If he helped you, you wouldn't turn him into the feds, would you?"

"No. I tried to explain that to him, but he's afraid."

Garner thanked the detective and promised to let him know if he heard any more.

***

When Garner dropped Jonas off at home a short time later, he explained to Mrs. Trottel what had happened. He told Mrs. Trottel he doubted she would hear any more about it.

"It's so hard for Jonas," Mrs. Trottel explained. "I've helped him get a couple different jobs, but the jobs seldom last more than a couple weeks."

Garner glanced around the room and what he could see of the rest of her apartment. It was neat and tidy, but spare. The furniture and carpet were worn.

"He's working at McDonalds now," Mrs. Trottel continued, "about fifteen hours a week – cleaning up the stuff people leave on tables and the floor. He seems to like it. He's been there now for several weeks, so maybe this job will work out."

"That's progress," Garner said, trying to be encouraging, but not wanting to linger too long. He was sympathetic – he wasn't going to charge for his time, but he didn't want to be late for his next appointment. He glanced at his wristwatch. Mrs. Trottel didn't seem to notice.

"The problem," Mrs. Trottel went on, "is his job is just part-time. It doesn't consume enough of his time or energy. He's not the kind of kid, you know, who is going to sit around and read books. I'd get him a computer or Xbox or whatever those things are called, but I just can't afford it."

Mrs. Trottel wrung her hands nervously.

"I need to get him involved in something," she said, "or he's just going to keep getting into trouble."

Mrs. Trottel was a good woman, and Garner felt sorry for her.

"I'll think about it, Mrs. Trottel," he said. "I promise. But if you'll excuse me, I'm meeting someone for lunch, and I don't want to be late."

"You run along now."

Mrs. Trottel looked up as if she had just remembered something important.

"Devin," she said, "thank you for all your help."

12:30 P.M. – 4:30 P.M.

While he and Jonas were waiting to see the detective, Garner contacted Carrie Hixson and made arrangements to meet for lunch. Over lunch, he explained that two jerks from Lower Price Hill had beaten up a Hispanic guy – one of the Hispanics living in the Nuestras Casas Co-Op.

Garner said he wanted to tell the man how sorry he and others in the community were. But he needed her to translate for him. Besides, he thought she might want to talk to the man for her project. This might be a good way to introduce her to the man.

Hixson was willing to serve as translator, and she was interested in seeing if she could persuade the man to tell his story for her documentary. But she was also interested in Jonas. "I've got an old digital camera I never use any more. What if I give it to Jonas and teach him how to take pictures?" Hixson asked. "I wouldn't mind."

Garner had to make a brief court appearance, but called Mrs. Trottel. He told her that he was sending a friend over to her apartment with a new hobby for Jonas.

When Garner caught up with Hixson a couple hours later, she reported that she and Jonas had hit it off nicely. Carrie said she would check back in on him from time-to-time, during her follow up trips to Lower Price Hill to finish her work on the documentary.

Their visit with Jabari Chan did not go as well. He had just gotten out of the hospital and was still in pain. He was more Mayan than Mexican and spoke only a limited amount of Spanish, making communication difficult. Someone else from the Co-Op helped with translation, but Hixson was unable to convince him to tell her his story for her documentary. He would not even explain why the men had attacked him. He also flatly refused to cooperate with the police.

Garner and Hixson made their way back to his office and took up their usual places in his conference room.

"Do you have any idea what this is all about?" Hixson asked. "Why would those morons beat up that poor man? Is this just because he's an immigrant, and they're idiots with too much testosterone and too little gray matter?"

"Maybe," Garner said. "Probably, that's all it is. But I think we're missing something."

"What?"

"A body."

Carrie arched her eyebrows. "A body?"

"Carrie, your theory is the killers strike each month after the Make America White Again rally. That would have been a week ago."

"I'm hoping they've stopped."

"Me too, but what if the guys who beat up Chan are the killers?"

"I'm not following."

"What if those jerks tried to grab another woman from the Co-Op, and Chan stopped them?"

"That's just a hunch, right? You're not basing that on anything specific?"

"It's pure hunch," Garner affirmed. "If I had anything specific to go on, you and I would be talking with the police right now."

"I'll see," Hixson said, "if anybody at the Co-Op will talk to me about what's going on."

Garner wished Chan had been willing to talk. He assumed Chan was afraid he would be deported if he came forward.

But Chan had more than that to fear.

Devin Garner got a follow-up call from Adam Zhang, the ICE agent.

"It's been a month since we talked," Zhang said after the usual greetings. "Have you persuaded Hank to cooperate?"

"I've spoken with him several times, but I've not been able to persuade him," Garner responded. "Do you have anything additional I can use as leverage?"

"I don't have anything I can share," Zhang said. "All I can say is, I think we're getting really close. If your uncle wants to get out in front of this, time is running out."

With that, Garner decided it was time to have a "come to Jesus" talk with his uncle. After he finished with Zhang, he called Hank and arranged to meet him for dinner. "There's been an important development," he told his uncle, "but I don't want to discuss it on the phone."

That evening, after the usual pleasantries, Garner explained the call from the ICE agent.

"I know you think I should talk to them," Hank interrupted, "but I'm not going to help them build a case against Reya." Hank drank some of his beer. "I married her. I don't want to see her go to prison," he said. "What would her kids think if I helped put their mother in prison? I couldn't do that to them."

"This isn't just about Reya," Garner said. He tried not to let his exasperation show. "The government is going to bring a case against Reya with or without your help. It sounds like they are going to name you, and probably others, as co-conspirators."

His uncle was unmoved. Obviously, Hank evidently didn't believe that would happen. Or, he believed he would be able to talk his way out of it if it did.

Garner tried a different tack. "You know the police in

Cincinnati have raided several businesses, including the Heidelberg Sausage plant, and Obreros de Hoy?"

"Yeah, that prosecutor over there – Warren, the one that's running for Congress – he is behind that crap," his uncle complained. "He's just trying to get attention. Everybody knows that."

"You know," Garner said, "that Carl Anwalt prepared the incorporation papers for Reya's Authentic Mexican Restaurant."

"I told you Reya always uses Anwalt," Hank said.

"I know you did, and if that's all he did, we might not be having this conversation. Anwalt also incorporated the company that owns the Sleep Cheap Inn."

"Yeah, I'm sure Reya had him do that. Like I said, she trusts Anwalt."

"What I've discovered," Garner said, "is that Anwalt also set up the Los Obreros de Hoy staffing agency."

His uncle nodded.

"Anwalt also set up the Nuestras Casas Co-Op," Garner said, "not far from my office."

Hank nodded again.

"Here's what I think," Garner said, pushing ahead. "I think Anwalt has put together a network to traffic in workers from Mexico. Reya – and probably others – get them into the country. Most of them get hooked up with Los Obreros, the staffing agency, which gets them jobs. They get housing at Nuestras Casas. Los Obreros takes a piece out of what they make. Nuestras Casas takes another piece. Some of that probably goes back to Anwalt."

Hank said nothing.

"The ones that don't go to Los Obreros get sent to Diego. I haven't figured out yet whether they just work in the inn, or if Diego forces them into prostitution or drugs, but it's just a matter of time until somebody figures that out."

Hank said nothing, but he pushed back from the table and folded his arms defensively.

Garner opened his iPad and brought up photos of Sofia Flores and Isabella Ramirez. He showed the photos to Hank. "Some of the girls that worked at the Sleep Cheap Inn have ended up dead."

"Whoa!" Hank said. "I don't know anything about that."

"Remember," Garner warned his uncle, "if you get charged with a conspiracy, the government can hold you responsible for anything *anyone* did in furtherance of the conspiracy. If the government can prove that you helped bring in people from Mexico and knew they were going to be fed into this setup, then you could be convicted just the same as Anwalt. And if Olivar had some of these girls killed to keep them from going to the police, you could be in deep shit."

"Oh, come on," Hank said. "That's ridiculous. They're not going to come after me for something Anwalt or Olivar did."

"Hank, it happens all the time." Garner let that sink in before continuing. "Anyone who participates in a conspiracy is guilty of any crimes committed by a co-conspirator in furtherance of the conspiracy. That's the law, and prosecutors take full advantage of it. They *love* to bring conspiracy charges."

"Where are you going with this?"

"You need to talk with ICE and get immunity. You'll probably never have to testify. Reya will make a deal and give up Anwalt or her contacts in Mexico."

Hank studied his hands.

"I can't guarantee you won't have to testify against Reya. But my guess is, Reya is just another small fish, and they would rather catch the big fish."

"You're serious about this?"

"Hank, I love you more than some kids love their parents. But you're going to start leveling with me, and do what I think you need to do to keep out of prison, or I'm not going to represent you. I'm not going to have you go to prison because I didn't handle your case right – because I didn't manage your case the way I would if you weren't my uncle."

The waitress arrived with their meals, and neither said anything except to the waitress while she served their meals.

When she left, Hank spoke first. "I took one of those girls out to Diego's place – the Sleep Cheap Inn." Hank pointed to the photo of Isabella Ramirez. "She came into the country with Reya and me, but Reya didn't need her and said Diego had a job for her."

Hank didn't touch his food, but took a sip of beer.

"Sometime later, we heard someone had killed her. Reya was shaken up about it and dashed over to Cincinnati to talk to Diego. She said Diego didn't know anything about who killed her. I didn't give it much thought."

"Go ahead and eat your food before it gets cold," Garner told his uncle. "But keep talking. I want to hear everything you know. Or even suspect."

Over the next half hour, Hank explained that Anwalt provided the fake documentation for the people Reya brought in. He also arranged for them to be hired by the staffing agency, and for the staffing agency to place them with friendly employers. Hank told Garner, as he had previously, that Anwalt laundered the money Reya made from her "coyote" business through the restaurant. Or had until he and Reya married.

Hank said he also suspected Diego was using the inn for prostitution. "I've even heard rumors," he said, "that Anwalt takes Judge Richter there occasionally."

"To see a prostitute? The judge goes to the inn for sex?"

"Yeah. His wife's dead, and he's too old to be dating."

Garner shook his head.

"Can I tell the ICE agent you're ready to cooperate?"

"Let me think about it. Give me a few days."

SATURDAY, JANUARY 23

Carrie Hixson was spending a lot of time in the Nuestras Casas Co-Op, befriending the people there and listening to their stories. Beyond her current documentary project, she was toying with the idea of writing a book based on their experiences, or perhaps a novel with a setting and characters similar to the people she encountered there.

Paz Ramos, one of the women Hixson befriended at the Co-Op called Hixson, distraught. "Carrie, I don't know what to do," she said in Spanish. "I hope you can maybe give me some advice."

"What's the problem?"

"Besides my day job, I also work on the weekends, and sometimes during the week, for a caterer. The caterer, he supplies food and workers for fancy parties, receptions, and things like that. You know what I'm talking about?"

"Yes, sure. I've been to events like that."

"I'm supposed to work on Saturday night. But the job is a fundraiser. Some rich man is having it in his home."

"What's the problem?"

"It's for that *bastardo* Warren. They say he will be there."

"Oh great!"

"I don't know what to do," Ramos told Hixson, sobbing. "No one wants to work this job because that *bastardo* Warren will be there. But my boss, he says he will fire anyone who doesn't show up."

"That's harsh."

"I need the money, because you know they arrested my husband when they raided the sausage company. I need the money to pay for an attorney for him."

"What are the others going to do?" Hixson asked.

"They say they are not going to go. They are afraid they will be arrested. And they say Warren is a bad man, and they don't want anything to do with him."

"I've been to events like this," Hixson told the young woman. "I don't think you need to be concerned about being arrested. The prosecutor is only interested in arresting Mexicans when it gets him publicity. He's there to get money for his campaign. He won't want to embarrass his host."

"So you think it will be okay if I go?"

"Yes. Where is it?"

"It is in Indian Hills, at the home of the man who owns the sausage plant. I don't have the address. They will take us there in a van."

"I know where it is," Hixson assured the woman. "It's around the corner from where my parents live."

Hixson asked the woman for the name and phone number of the person who ran the catering business.

She called the caterer and introduced herself as a college student. "I heard you're working the Warren fundraiser this Saturday. I was wondering if you need any help?

"You want to work that?"

"I'm in college and could use the money. Besides, it's just around the corner from where my parents live."

"Yeah, sure," the man said. "I usually use some Mexicans for these things, but they learned that this is for Dick Warren, and most of my regulars don't want to show up. They're afraid of Warren. They hate him anyway."

Hixson asked for all the usual details: Would he provide uniforms? Where did she need to go? When did she need to be there? How much would the job pay?

The caterer had his own question. "Do you have any friends who might be interested in helping out for this party? The pay is crap, but I thought I'd ask."

"Do I know any college students who need some quick cash? Are you kidding?" Hixson laughed. "They all do. I'll talk to some of my friends and get back to you."

Several hours later, Hixson called the caterer back with the names and phone numbers of several friends who would be willing to help out for the Warren event. She assured him they were dependable and from good families.

Hixson saw no need to trouble the caterer with the fact that all of the volunteers were from her documentary class, or that Cam was scrambling to find tiny cameras they could use, discretely, to get footage from the event. *The poor man seemed to have troubles enough.*

The attendees, it turned out, included – among others – the owners or managers of several of the businesses the Cincinnati police had raided over the previous months. Carl Anwalt was there as well. Each delivered the requisite contribution to the host and got to shake hands and have his picture taken with Warren.

The host and one or two others made remarks about Warren's candidacy, about how important it was for the business community that the Congressional District have a representative in Washington who was sympathetic to the concerns of business, and who was committed not to raise taxes.

No one discussed with Warren the raids or his nearly completed investigations into their hiring practices. That would have been inappropriate. Instead, as the guests mingled, they discussed the Warren campaign, the economy, the weather, and football. Only occasionally, when neither Warren nor their host was within earshot, would someone make a sly reference to the raids, prompting snickers and murmurs.

Carl Anwalt, who had organized the event, was pleased with how the evening went.

MONDAY, JANUARY 25

Hank Bremen was happy to hear from Reya's daughter, Maya Sanchez, until he learned why she called.

"I had a big blow up with Mamá," Maya said. "On our last trip to Mexico, Mamá was bringing back three women who wanted to come into the country, okay? But that wasn't enough trouble. She insisted on bringing drugs too. Anyway, when we were getting close to the border, someone called Mamá and told her we were heading into a trap."

"What did you do?"

"Mamá made me take the drugs – they were in a knapsack – and leave the van with the women. I had to lead them through the desert on foot. It took two days."

Hank could tell from her voice that Maya was still upset.

"We had no food or water," Maya continued, "except what we grabbed from the van in a big hurry."

"You could have been arrested," Hank said, stating the obvious.

"I know, but I was more afraid that we would be found by the men who hang around the border. They would have killed me for the drugs."

"Do you want me to try to talk to Reya?" Hank asked.

"No, it wouldn't do any good. She says she has to bring back the drugs until she has enough money for the new restaurant.

"You know that's why I left. Are you sure you don't want me to try to talk to her?"

"No, she's still mad at you. It would make things worse," Maya said. "Besides, she just left for Mexico again. She tried to make me go with her, but I refused. We had a huge screaming match."

Hank tried to re-assure Maya she had done the right thing, but Maya was not consoled.

"Mamá said I would have to go with her next time, in

March. She said if I didn't, she would make Hector drop out of the university and go with her.

Hank thought Hector was too smart to give in to Reya's bullying, but he was concerned that Maya might give in to the emotional blackmail.

"Maya, listen to me," Hank said. "Do not go to Mexico with your mother again – not under any circumstances. Your mother isn't thinking straight, and she's going to get herself arrested or killed."

"But –

"Please," Hank insisted, "if you are even thinking about it, promise me you will call me or come see me. I don't want you getting arrested or killed. It's too dangerous."

When the call ended, Hank called his nephew.

"Devin, I've made up my mind," he said. "I want to meet with that guy you've been talking to – the ICE agent."

SATURDAY, JANUARY 30

11:30 P.M. – 11:40 P.M.

For Jabari Chan, after his beating by the two white Anglos, his honor was at stake – as was that of his friends and neighbors in the Nuestras Casas Co-Op.

If they did not respond, they would lose respect, and others in the surrounding Anglo neighborhood – who resented their presence – would recognize that the men in the Nuestras Casas community had no *cojones*, and they would attack. If they did not respond, more of them would be beaten. And more of their women would be abducted and killed. And if the women became afraid, it would not be long before the whole group gave up and were driven away.

That was the reasoning in conversations between Chan and his best friend, between the two of them and the other men, and soon, throughout the Nuestras Casas community. It was only a matter of time until someone spotted where the red pickup truck with the Confederate flag parked at night. From that point, it did not take much effort to identify where the pickup's owner and his friend lived and where they were most likely to be found. With that information in hand, the talk coalesced into planning.

When several men from Nuestras Casas finally cornered Roger Storrs and Sam Scherge leaving a bar late one evening, they more than returned the beating the two *cabrones* had inflicted on Jabari Chan. When the Nuestras Casas men were done, Storrs and Scherge were left on the pavement, beaten and bleeding. Both had to be hospitalized.

The most surprising thing, from the perspective of the Nuestras Casas men, was that the two *cabrones* seemed to be so surprised by this turn of events.

FRIDAY, FEBRUARY 5

Under the rules in state courts in Ohio, an expert witness for either side in a criminal proceeding must prepare a written report summarizing his or her findings, analysis, conclusions or opinions, and expected testimony. The report must also summarize his or her qualifications.

Each side must disclose its expert witness reports to the other side at least twenty-one days before trial, although the trial court may make exceptions. If an attorney doesn't disclose the written report to opposing counsel by the deadline, the rule precludes the expert witness from testifying at trial.

Garner expected to call only one expert witness, Professor Adams. He made sure he had her report in hand and disclosed it to Bill Bradford before the 21-day deadline.

Garner expected the prosecution would call John Crackstone, the senior gun-identification expert in the Coroner's office, but to be safe, Garner "disclosed" to Bradford the reports prepared by Crackstone with respect to the slain Hispanic women – even though he had gotten those reports from Bradford. Each report was specific to one victim and concluded that the slugs removed from that victim came from a Glock 9mm pistol.

Garner wanted to retain a ballistics expert to compare the slugs from the Hispanic women with the slug removed from Ann, but Rafiq had been unwilling to try to raise additional money to pay for that. Garner trusted Crackstone, but was concerned that Crackstone had not taken the obvious next step.

On Friday, Garner received from Bradford the reports of the several expert witnesses the prosecution expected to call. Garner would spend a lot of time poring over those reports, but his first step, as usual, was to read through all of them quickly. As he did, it was clear the pathologist's report would give him the most heartburn.

Garner expected – and was hoping – the pathologist would place the time of death late on Friday night or early on Saturday morning, when Rafiq was at the Trauma Center, trying to find Ann. He had a long string of witnesses lined up to testify to Rafiq's presence there.

Unfortunately, the pathologist placed the time of Ann's death between 10:00 a.m. and 1:00 p.m. Rafiq was at home in bed at that time – meaning he had no useful alibi. That timing was also more consistent with the prosecution's theory that Ann had confronted Rafiq over his supposed infidelity.

Garner called Rafiq and asked him to come to his office, so that they could discuss the pathologist's report. Rafiq had performed autopsies as part of his medical training, but he was not a pathologist. More importantly, it was unlikely an experienced pathologist would get the time of death wrong by twelve hours or more in a case where the body had been found twenty-four hours after the estimated time of death. Garner doubted Rafiq would be able to spot a hole in the pathologist's report, but he wanted Rafiq to work through that for himself.

Two other reports also troubled Garner. One was the report from Wendy Yang, the photographic expert. She concluded that Ann would have been standing further away from the entrance to the inn than Rafiq remembered. Her conclusions were also at odds with those of Professor Adams. He would work with Adams to figure out why she and Yang disagreed – and how to attack Yang's conclusions.

The other troubling report was that of John Crackstone. The report was simply another copy of the analysis of the slug removed from Ann, indicating that the slug had been fired from a Glock 9mm. So far as it went, that report was consistent with the possibility the "Make America White Again" killer or killers had murdered Ann. But it was worrisome that the report did not address whether the slug removed from Ann matched the slugs from any or all of the slain Hispanic women.

It was helpful, of course, that Crackstone had not con-cluded that different guns fired the slugs. But it was odd — and troubling — that Crackstone had not tested the slugs to see if they had all come from the same gun or guns. Presum-ably, Bradford had insisted that Crackstone not do that anal-ysis.

Of course, it was possible that Crackstone had in fact done the analyses, but Bradford didn't like the result and was withholding the reports. Garner had repeatedly requested any such analyses, and Bradford had repeatedly assured him there were none. Bradford was an honorable guy and thor-oughly professional. Garner didn't think Bradford would outright mislead him.

But Garner wouldn't be surprised if Bradford had asked Crackstone *not* to compare the slugs out of concern that the results would be bad for the prosecution. Jurors who had watched too much CSI would be bothered by the absence of evidence proving or disproving the theory that whoever killed the Hispanic women had also killed Ann, but Garner had no way of knowing if they would blame him or the pros-ecution.

He fired off another letter to Bradford seeking assur-ance that the Coroner's office had not done a comparison of the slugs.

WEDNESDAY, FEBRUARY 9

Devin Garner escorted his uncle into the Cincinnati office of the Immigration and Customs Enforcement agency and asked for Special Agent Adam Zhang. The ICE office was in the federal building, in the heart of the downtown Cincinnati business district. In short order, Zhang appeared and introduced himself. Garner and his uncle followed Zhang to a conference room.

After completing the paperwork to secure immunity for his uncle, Garner laid out what he had been able to piece together about the syndicate that brought undocumented workers from Mexico into the city and funneled them through the Obreros de Hoy staffing company into positions with several local employers – all orchestrated by a local attorney, Carl Anwalt.

Hank promised to tell what he knew about that syndicate, but first, he had a different concern. He explained that Reya Sanchez had gone back to Mexico a couple weeks ago. She would be returning in mid-March. When she did, she would likely be bringing with her some Mexican nationals who wanted to come into the country, but didn't have visas. She would also be bringing drugs into the country.

Hank explained that Reya was trying to get her kids to help with her drug smuggling. He wanted ICE, or the DEA, or somebody, to intercept Reya before she did.

The agent had plenty of questions.

Three hours later, as the session was wrapping up, the agent picked up an envelope.

"Before I forget," Zhang said, "here is the report on Angelica Rios. She left the country after Ms. Medawar turned up dead. And here is a certified copy of the record of her leaving the country. I'm sending a copy to Bill Bradford too."

"Do you know why she bolted?" Garner asked.

"It looks like she was here on forged papers. If we caught and deported her, she would be ineligible to return. Maybe she wanted to get out ahead of that, in hopes of being able to return legally at some point.

"Of course," Zhang added, "it may be that she was afraid of whoever killed your client's wife. She may have been afraid she was next."

FRIDAY, FEBRUARY 12

The Hamilton County Prosecutor's office quietly let it be known that it had completed its investigation of the Heidelberg Sausage plant and other local businesses and would not be filing charges. It put that information out late on Friday afternoon, ensuring it got scant media attention.

When they learned of the decision, Carrie Hixson and her classmates were glad they had the fundraiser videos to weave into their documentary. But they would not finish their documentary until near the end of the semester. That would be well after the March 15 primary.

Carrie Hixson wanted something sooner.

SATURDAY, FEBRUARY 13

5:25 P.M. – 5:35 P.M.

For Sam Scherge and Roger Storrs, it had been a miserable two weeks since the men from the Co-Op had ambushed them. Nursing beers and a serious grudge, they had spent the last couple hours at a bar and grill not far from where they lived. At 5:25 p.m. they ordered fried chicken, which required twenty minutes or more to prepare, and quietly slipped out the back door.

Just after 5:30 p.m. Saturday evening, as usual, Jabari Chan and his friend stepped out of the Nuestras Casas Co-Op. It was a mild evening, especially for mid-February. The men lit cigarettes. When they finished the cigarettes, they would walk to the evangelical church a few blocks away.

The red pickup truck with the Confederate flag screeched to a stop in front of them. Before either could react, a man kneeling in the bed of the truck opened fire. Chan fell immediately, and his companion a moment later. The truck took off, its tires squealing. The Confederate flag – the truck's most distinctive feature – waved in the wind.

At 5:35 p.m., Storrs and Scherge were back at their table, waiting for their fried chicken. The tavern's staff and patrons, they were sure, would swear that they had been right there all afternoon and evening. None of them liked the Mexicans moving into their neighborhood anyway.

By then, neither Jabari Chan, nor his companion was thinking about fried chicken, and neither needed an alibi. Chan was dead, and his companion was in critical condition.

SUNDAY, FEBRUARY 14

LATE MORNING

On Sunday morning, Devin Garner was at home eating brunch, when Jamal Muhammad called.

"I need to talk with you," Muhammad said. "About something important. You going to be in your office this afternoon?"

"I'll be there shortly." The Medawar trial was only two weeks away. Even though it was Sunday, he would be in the office to work on his trial preparation.

Moments after Garner arrived at his office, Muhammad, who had apparently been watching his office, materialized.

Muhammad was tall – easily over six feet. He wore a long black tunic or dishdasha, and a white cap or kufi, advertising his commitment to the Muslim faith he had adopted several years ago. He was an intense, no-nonsense man, but in his own way, rather charismatic.

"Did you hear about the shooting last night?" Muhammad asked.

"No, I went jogging this morning and then did chores."

"Someone shot two men coming out of the Housing Co-Op. One's dead. Not sure about the other. It was in the paper."

Garner had brought the Sunday paper with him to the office. He opened the paper, found and skimmed the story. He stopped when he saw Jabari Chan's name.

"Were your men involved?" Garner asked.

"No, but one of our watchers was nearby. He got out his cell phone and caught the shooters, or at least their truck, as they drove past, leaving the scene."

"Did he see the shooting?" Garner asked, wanting to be certain he understood exactly what had happened.

"Heard it," Muhammad said.

"He didn't see or get video of the shooting itself," Garner asked, "but he did get video of the shooter driving away from the scene?"

"You can't make out the shooter," Muhammad said, "just the truck, but otherwise, right."

"Did your man inform the police?" Garner was pretty sure the answer would be an emphatic "no."

"No," Muhammad confirmed. "That's why I'm here."

"Okay," Garner said. He knew Muhammad and the other men in his neighborhood watch group didn't trust the police. Some of them, he suspected, had concerns that went beyond distrust.

Garner wasn't sure what Muhammad wanted him to do. He asked to see the video.

Muhammad handed him a thumb drive. Garner plugged it into his laptop and ran the short video. It showed a red pick-up truck speeding by. It was impossible to make out the face of the driver, but the pickup was sporting a large Confederate flag.

Garner stopped the video just as the pickup passed the watcher, before it sped away. He enlarged the frame. The license number was clearly visible. Garner jotted it down.

"What do you want to happen?" Garner asked.

"My man doesn't want to get involved. I was thinking you could give this to the police without saying who gave it to you. Attorney-client privilege and all that."

"The video can't be used in evidence," Garner stated, "without a witness who can explain what it is and when it was taken."

"My man is not going to the police. He's not going to testify. He can't have anything to do with the police. You understand what I'm saying?"

Garner nodded. He assumed the man had an outstanding warrant or warrants.

"Besides, he doesn't want some white guys attacking him or his family. We thought you could figure something out."

"Let me think about it," Garner said.

"How are things with you?" Muhammad asked. "You're representing that Syrian doctor. He's Muslim, right?"

Garner said he was doing fine, and yes, he was representing Dr. Medawar, but no, Medawar was not Muslim. He wasn't Syrian either.

"He's not?" Mohammad said. "I thought that's what they said on the news."

"They did," Garner agreed. "The prosecutor has it in his head that Dr. Medawar is Muslim. His office keeps telling the media that Dr. Medawar is a Syrian Muslim, and every time the media repeat that, Warren's more sure than ever that it must be true. It's the only reason he's prosecuting him."

Mohammad shook his head. "You Christians," he said with a smile, "are fucking up this country."

MID AFTERNOON

Devin Garner called Carrie Hixson and wished her Happy Valentine's Day. "I've got something for you," he said, "but I'm afraid it's not a Valentine or box of chocolates. It's bad news."

"I'd rather have a Valentine," Hixson said.

"Someone shot Jabari Chan and another man as they came out of the Co-Op. According to the newspaper, the shooting was at 5:30 yesterday evening. Chan's dead, and it sounds like the other man may not make it either."

"Oh my God, that's awful. Do the police know who did it?"

"I don't think so. Actually, that's why I called you."

"Devin, do you think the guys who beat him up did this?"

"Yeah, I'm sure they did," Garner said. "Right after the shooting, someone in the neighborhood videoed their pickup truck speeding up the street, Confederate flag and all.

The person who got the video wants to remain anonymous. He gave it to a client of mine, and the client brought the video to me on condition I leave him out of it."

"What are you going to do?"

"Well, the reason I called was to see if you would like to have dinner with me and help me think through what to do. I mean, if you don't have plans for this evening."

"I don't have plans," Hixson made a point of saying. "There's this guy I like, but he won't ask me out."

"He's an idiot!" Garner joked.

"You think?"

"I'll make a copy of the video and we can talk about what I should do with it."

"You can email it to me," Hixson said.

"I thought about that, but I don't want to create an email trail just in case, at some point, the Prosecutor's office starts issuing subpoenas."

Well, if he were honest with himself, he thought, he would admit that it would be nice to see her.

Hixson agreed to dinner. She said she was glad he called.

WEDNESDAY, FEBRUARY 17

6:00 P.M. NEWS

Queen City News Live: Bringing you the news you want to hear.

News Anchor Bob Bunker: Hamilton County Prosecutor Richard Warren had an embarrassing "open microphone" problem this afternoon at a campaign stop in Mt. Healthy. Tiffany Albern, who is covering the Warren campaign for Queen City news, is in Mt. Healthy and has this report.

Tiffany Albern: Bob, I'm here at the Community Center in Mt. Healthy where Hamilton County Prosecutor Richard Warren addressed the Mt. Healthy Neighborhood Improvement Association. Warren told the group that immigrants come to this country to take advantage of our welfare programs. Here's part of what he told the group:

Video Clip Plays: Ladies and Gentlemen, I'm running for Congress because I think Congress needs to focus on the immigrants who are rushing across the border, because they've heard there's a bowl of food just across the border. These people aren't coming to this country because they want to become citizens. These immigrants come here because they heard there's free food, free drivers' licenses. I don't have to tell you that. Everybody knows that. But Congress isn't doing enough about it.

Tiffany Albern: But, as you said, Warren did have an open mike problem today. During a question-and-answer session following his speech, a member of the audience told Warren that several young Hispanic women from the area have been abducted and killed in recent months. She complained that it didn't seem like the police were doing anything to investigate those slayings. She asked Warren if his office could do anything to get the police to look into the slayings. Here's Warren's response:

Video clip of Warren speaking plays: Ma'am, I want you to know that my office is on top of that. Absolutely. In fact, I personally directed that a task force be set up to investigate what you're talking about. One of my best people is on that task force. But you have to understand, investigations are hard work and take time, and they don't make the evening news. But we're working on that, you have my word on it.

Tiffany Albern: But when the session ended, our recorder caught Warren talking with a campaign aide:

Warren's voice: What was that woman talking about? Hispanic women being grabbed and killed? This is the first I've heard of this —

Aide's voice: It was in some Spanish language newspaper. It wasn't in the Enquirer.

Warren's voice: Come on! You can't let me get caught with my pants down on something like that. Tell Bradford I need to speak with him. We've got to organize something.

Tiffany Albern: I asked to speak to Warren about the apparent discrepancy, but his staff told me he had to rush to make another appointment.

Tiffany Albern, reporting live from Mt. Healthy.

Co-Anchor Ashley Gelb: Coming up next, we interview a Cincinnati man who is in Ciudad Juárez, Mexico, where Pope Francis is visiting the Mexican-American border today to show solidarity with Mexican immigrants seeking to come to the United States.

THURSDAY, FEBRUARY 18

MORNING

Detective James Chilton heard the news reports of Dick Warren's gaffe, and so he was not entirely surprised when he got the call from Bill Bradford. Bradford wanted him to organize an inter-departmental task force to investigate the deaths of the slain Hispanic women.

Chilton pushed back. He told Bradford something like that had to come from high up in the Police Department. He couldn't do something like that on his own.

Shortly after the call from Bradford, his superiors in the Police Department confirmed the new assignment. The deaths of these Hispanic women were probably not related, his superiors assured him, but if the public became concerned that there might be a serial killer on the loose, the Department had to be on top it.

His superiors told him this was his top priority. They gave him the names of detectives in District 3 and District 5 who would be assigned to the task force. His superiors assured him they would get back to him shortly with someone from Indiana and possibly someone from Northern Kentucky as well. Chilton said he'd already been in touch with the detective investigating the Kentucky homicide and provided her name.

Chilton asked if he would get any additional resources. *Sorry, none were available,* came the answer. He asked if anything could be taken off his plate.

Sorry, no.

Chilton was angry and frustrated, but work was work, and if someone was killing young women, finding and stopping the killer was good work.

AFTERNOON

So, what really was he dealing with? Chilton asked himself, as he had so many times before.

His interviews with the leaders of the League of Natural Born Citizens were unhelpful, except for one thing: Each of the slain Mexican women had gone missing after one of the League's "Make America White Again" events. The event or rally would take place on a Saturday afternoon, and that night or very early on Sunday morning, a young Mexican immigrant or Mexican-American woman would go missing.

He couldn't explain the discrepancy in how the bodies were disposed of, but John Crackstone, the ballistics guy in the Hamilton County Coroner's office, assured him that the same two guns had been used in all six killings. One 9mm gun had fired the bullets that killed victims one, three and five. A second 9mm gun fired the bullets that killed victims two, four and six. Crackstone thought they might be dealing with two killers working together, taking turns.

And now, Chilton was going to have to deal with a frigging task force. And the press. Those jackals would have a field day. "Natural Born Citizens stalk illegals!" Or maybe, "The 'Make America White Again' serial killers!"

Chilton decided to wait for the names of the Kentucky and Indiana members of his task force to schedule a meeting. The longer that took, the longer until the full story leaked.

By then, he thought, maybe he would catch a break and be closer to solving the case.

FRIDAY, FEBRUARY 19

MORNING

Devin Garner sat in the federal courthouse, just outside the room where the grand jury was meeting. He sat there nervously re-checking his cell phone for messages and reading news headlines. His uncle, Hank Bremen, was inside the grand jury room, testifying to the grand jury concerning Carl Anwalt's network of businesses.

The grand jury is perhaps the strangest aspect of the whole American criminal justice system. A grand jury meets in secret to consider whether the evidence presented by the prosecuting attorney is sufficient to charge someone with a crime. It meets in secret to avoid damage to the reputations of persons it investigates but doesn't indict. The secrecy also protects witnesses from retribution.

To protect grand jury secrecy, a witness is not entitled to be accompanied by counsel in the grand jury room. If the witness believes the prosecutor is asking something improper – for example, something that invades the attorney-client privilege – the witness must ask permission to step outside to consult with counsel.

And so, Devin Garner sat outside the grand jury room, hoping his uncle would be forthcoming, but also hoping he wouldn't be afraid to ask for help if he felt uncomfortable with any of the questions.

Two hours later, Hank stepped from the grand jury room. "I'm done," Hank said simply.

Garner walked his uncle out of the federal courthouse and drove him back to his own office. There, he debriefed his uncle before taking him to lunch. As near as Garner could tell, it all went as expected.

Garner assumed the grand jury would hear from other

witnesses before it acted, but neither Zhang, nor the Assistant U.S. Attorney, who questioned Hank during the grand jury, would be able to tell Garner what, if any, action the grand jury took. Garner asked Zhang and the AUSA to alert him, as soon as they could, if he and Hank needed to take precautions.

They promised they would.

If the grand jury indicted, Garner assumed the feds would keep the indictment secret until Reya returned from Mexico in mid-March. He encouraged his uncle to plan a fishing trip with friends at that time.

TUESDAY, FEBRUARY 23

MORNING

Detective James Chilton had made a promise to Bradford – and to himself. He had promised that he would review all the evidence in the Medawar case one last time before the trial began. Bradford didn't want any surprises, and Chilton didn't want to be made to look foolish by Devin Garner again. With the Medawar trial starting in just a week, it was past time to do what he'd promised to do.

He began by reviewing the videos Ann Lindsey Medawar made on her cell phone the day she was killed. Those videos, after all, were the key to the whole case.

The first video showed Dr. Medawar and the nurse – Angelica Rios – walking briskly into the inn. Chilton re-ran that video again. Dr. Medawar was carrying a doctor's bag. *Damn!* He hadn't paid any attention to that before. *Well, maybe he was just carrying his doctor kit in case someone saw him. Maybe he had sex toys in it. Or, maybe Dr. Medawar was telling the truth about what he doing there.*

The next video showed two men leave the inn, then another man, and then another. The first two appeared to be businessmen of some sort. The other two appeared to be Mexicans, dressed casually. The inn had no record of any of them staying there the night before, and the manager, Diego Olivar, claimed not to know who any of the men were.

Next, there were a series of videos and stills of the inn, the parking lot, the traffic passing in the street, and the like. Chilton went through them quickly. It wasn't clear why Ms. Medawar took those shots. He couldn't see what they had to do with proving that her husband was banging the nurse. Maybe the reason she took those was just something stupid, like she was bored. Of course, if she really was making a video, like the defense contended, that might explain why she wanted them.

Chilton went back through the whole series again, lingering over the shots of the parking lot. He jotted down the license plate numbers and almost absent-mindedly checked the numbers. The late-model, silver Toyota with Ohio plates belonged to Dr. Medawar, and the really-old Chevy belonged to Rios, the nurse. A little further away, there was another late-model car with an Ohio plate. It belonged to Ms. Medawar. It hadn't been there the next day, when the police investigation began, and it still hadn't been found. The only other vehicle with Ohio plates was the piece-of-crap Honda that belonged the manager, Diego Olivar.

There were two late-model cars with Kentucky plates and two older cars with Texas plates. Chilton checked the cars with Kentucky plates first. One belonged to that judge whose car kept showing up in the surveillance logs. Chilton went online and found a picture of the judge. It was definitely him in the video. Chilton looked up the other man, and he turned out to be an attorney with an office in Covington. Again, when Chilton compared the guy's face with the video, it was a match. Neither had spoken with Ms. Medawar, and neither seemed like someone defense counsel would claim might have killed Ms. Medawar. So, nothing of interest there.

Chilton checked out the two vehicles with tags from Texas, but he found nothing interesting about their registered owners.

Chilton stood and stretched his legs. He had hardly drunk any of his coffee, but it was cold. That was reason enough to dump it out and get fresh. On his way back to his desk, he and another detective bantered about that night's basketball game matching top-ranked Villanova against the local favorite, Xavier.

Settling down again, Chilton watched the next video — the one that showed Dr. Medawar leaving the inn. Nurse Rios exited first and held the glass door, so it wouldn't slam in Medawar's face. Nothing exceptional there.

Chilton played the next video. It was the same as the one before it. He had always assumed it was simply an extra copy of the previous video, but when he compared the two, he could see small differences – just enough to be sure someone hadn't given him two copies of the same video.

But that was weird. Why would the doctor and the nurse leave twice? Did they forget something and go back for it? Maybe, but Dr. Medawar had his doctor kit in both videos, and the nurse hadn't been carrying anything.

Chilton stopped another of the Homicide unit's detectives, Gabriella Morales, who was passing by. She was a woman. Maybe she would see something he didn't. He explained the situation and re-ran the videos. Morales asked him to re-run the two videos again.

After he did, Chilton asked, "What do you think?"

"Well, for one thing, they don't look like they just had sex."

"How can you tell that?"

"Look at them. Especially the woman. Look at her hair. No way she just got laid."

"Yeah, maybe," Chilton said, unconvinced. "But why two videos of them leaving? What am I missing?"

"I think this looks staged. I think whoever made this video asked them to repeat the scene."

"What makes you think that?"

"I don't know. I guess because the two videos are practically the same. The only real difference is the angle. I think whoever made this video moved a little to get a slightly different angle."

Chilton thanked Morales. If she was right, Warren's theory didn't hold up, and the husband was telling the truth.

That completed the videos on Ms. Medawar's cell, but he still needed to review the videos found on her computer. He thought he could go through those quickly.

He was wrong. There were interviews with a whole series of people. Each had known one of the Hispanic women who had been killed. It took a couple hours to listen to all of the interviews. Ms. Medawar and her classmate — or friend, or BFF, or whatever — had done a good job with the interviews. He would share them with the Task Force.

When he finished with the interviews, he broke for lunch and ran some errands.

AFTERNOON

After lunch, Detective Chilton picked back up with the videos, beginning with a folder called "Meetings." If, as he expected, it contained videos of meetings about the documentary, he planned to skip it. That would help him pick up the pace. He didn't want to spend the whole week looking at videos.

Inside the "meetings" folder, there were subfolders. Ms. Medawar labeled the first subfolder "Aug. 2015." Inside it, there were several videos. He played the first video. It began with a shot of a handwritten sign indicating the subject of the video: "Make America White Again Rally Aug. 2015."

Chilton stopped the video and went to the next subfolder. Ms. Medawar labeled it, "Sept. 2015." The first video in that folder began with another handwritten sign. This one said, "Make America White Again Rally Sept. 2015." He repeated the process with the third and final subfolder. Its opening shot identified it as, "Make America White Again Rally Oct. 2015."

So, Ann Medawar had made the connection between the Make America White Again rallies and the deaths of the Hispanic women. Chilton could feel his stomach sour. He found the antacid tablets in his desk and swallowed a couple.

He watched the videos.

When he finished, he took a couple more antacids tablets. And went and got more coffee.

He needed to tell Bradford what he'd found, but he decided to wait. He needed time to figure out what exactly he'd seen. Or rather, what it meant.

What if there really were something to the theory the defense was pedaling? What if the scumbags killing Mexican women thought Ms. Medawar was on to them? Or thought she was getting too close – and killed her?

But why would they have waited a week?

And what did the inn have to do with it?

What if the inn didn't have anything to do with it? What else was going on the day Ann Medawar went missing?

He checked his notes. The Cincinnati police raided that sausage company that day. What if she went to check that out after she left the inn and bumped into the killers there? But if she went there, wouldn't she have taken pictures?

He couldn't put the pieces to the puzzle together. That probably meant he was missing some pieces. He needed to find them. *But where?*

He let his supervisor know that something had come up, and he was probably going to be spending a lot of time over the next week getting ready for the Medawar trial. That and working on the Task Force.

11:00 A.M. – 11:45 A.M.

No matter how the men from the Nuestras Casas Housing Co-Op tried to persuade him, Diego Olivar could not see any reason to get involved. But to demonstrate that he was taking their concerns seriously, he had invited them to move to one of the inn's empty rooms. There, again to show them respect, he asked the appropriate questions. But with so many men trying to answer, it was all rather confusing.

"Let's begin at the beginning," Olivar said. He pointed to the man who seemed to be the most reliable narrator – an older man, short, dignified and serious. "I want *you* to tell me," Olivar said. "How did this whole thing get started?"

The man described how the two *cabrones* had tried to grab a young woman who lived in the Nuestras Casas Housing Co-Op and how Jabari Chan had stopped them. Chan believed, the man explained, that the two Anglos were going to kill her – just like someone had killed two other women who had disappeared from the Co-Op.

"And two others," someone else volunteered, providing what little he knew about how those women had been found dead.

The latter two women, the designated narrator knew, had worked at the Sleep Cheap Inn, but he saw no purpose in saying so. If Olivar had killed them, there was no point in blaming their deaths on the Anglos. But if he hadn't, maybe this was an angle that would interest him.

"It said in the newspaper," the old man continued, "that all four of these women were shot with a 9mm Glock." The man pulled from his wallet a copy of the article he saved from *La Jornada Latina*, Cincinnati's Spanish language newspaper. He offered Olivar the newspaper article.

"That," he added, "is the same kind of gun that killed

Jabari Chan."

"The same *cardones* who have been killing my women shot your friend?" Olivar asked, his attention now fully engaged.

"*Sí, Sí,*" the men agreed, now that they knew what it would take to get Olivar and his cartel friends to act. "Los mismos *hombres!*" *The same men!*

"Why didn't you say so?" Olivar asked.

"¡Todos saben eso!" the old man explained. *Everybody knows that.*

PART III: THE TRIAL

TUESDAY, MARCH 1

8:30 A.M. – 5:00 P.M.

Today, at last, the trial would begin.

As Rafiq Medawar approached the courthouse, he wished that today, of all days, Ann were by his side. But that was the whole point of this, wasn't it? Someone killed Ann, and justice demanded that someone be punished for that crime.

The Hamilton County Courthouse loomed before him. Before his indictment, he had never given any thought to the building. But since his indictment, this courthouse had become a brooding presence in his life, and he had taken the time to learn something about it. Constructed in 1915, it was a massive limestone structure, fronted by Ionic columns that stood several stories tall. With an interior of more than half million square feet, the courthouse occupied a square block in downtown Cincinnati.

A quotation in block letters ran along the top of the front side of the building. He had read the quotation before, but stopped and read it again:

THE PURE AND WISE AND EQUAL
ADMINISTRATION OF THE LAWS
FORMS THE FIRST END AND BLESSING
OF SOCIAL UNION

He hoped that he would be the beneficiary of that first end and blessing of social union. But his experience thus far did not inspire confidence. He was being prosecuted, he believed, because the prosecutor thought, at least initially, that he was from Syria, or was the son of Syrian immigrants, and a Muslim. And now, the prosecutor was unwilling to admit his mistake or back off. Medawar thought that was a far cry from the pure, wise and equal administration of the law.

Garner had told him the quote was from a huge tome written by a British windbag a couple decades before the United States was formed. Medawar wondered if it was time to sandblast that inscription from the face of the building and replace it.

Maybe, he thought, it should say: *If you're white, you're right. If you're black, get back. Face Mecca to pray, you're going away.*

Medawar walked inside the building and took the elevator to the appropriate floor. As he did, he replayed in his mind something else Garner had told him. One of those earlier courthouses had been destroyed in the courthouse riot of 1884. On that occasion, the citizenry, inflamed by the local press, took exception to the news that a defendant had been convicted only of manslaughter, not murder, and therefore would not be hanged. When the ensuing riot ended, the courthouse was smoldering rubble.

He had no illusions that feelings ran quite so high over his own fate, but the thought gave him little comfort.

He found the courtroom assigned to the Honorable Benjamin Seiler. As he stood by the door, he thought: This is where my future will be decided. Not in medical school. Not in the hospital where I did my residency. Not in the operating room at the trauma center. Not in the little church where Ann and I were married.

He pushed open the door and entered the courtroom. He spotted Garner already seated at counsel table. He strode down the center aisle. Some in the courtroom hushed as he walked by, others took no notice.

Garner saw him and jumped to his feet. Garner opened the low gate and invited him into the cordoned off area at the front of the courtroom, the area reserved for parties to the proceedings, their counsel, the bailiff, and jurors.

Garner pointed to the table assigned to the defense. On the table stood the paraphernalia Garner had arranged for use during this first phase of the trial – jury selection. He had even thought to put a legal pad and pen on the table for him.

Medawar sat next to his attorney, the place reserved for the accused, and waited. He could feel his impatience rising. As a physician, he understood that adrenaline was coursing through his veins. As a man accused of killing his wife, that knowledge was of little help.

At exactly 9:00, the bailiff stood and commanded, "All rise." He called out the name of the case, *The State of Ohio versus Rafiq Anthony Medawar*, and its case number. As he did, Judge Seiler entered the courtroom, briskly climbed three stairs to the dais, and seated himself in the tall swivel chair behind the large, ornate desk universally referred to as the "bench."

"Please be seated," Judge Seiler instructed.

Assistant Prosecutor William Bradford stood and announced, "Ready for the prosecution." As he did, Medawar felt nothing but rage. The only reason he had been charged was that Hamilton County Prosecutor Dick Warren, who was nowhere to be seen, thought he was a Muslim from Syria. Assistant Prosecutor William Bradford knew that, but was pursuing the case anyway.

His own attorney, Devin Garner, stood and proclaimed, "Ready for the defense."

The emotions this stirred were more complex. He felt real gratitude for all the effort Garner had put into his defense. Even so, he could not help but wonder if he had made a mistake hiring a friend to represent him, instead of someone more experienced. *Was that a decision he would always be glad he had made? Or one that he would regret the rest of life?*

The attorneys turned to the business of selecting the jurors who would decide his guilt or innocence. As they did, his thoughts shifted to a new question.

What sort of juror, he wondered, would be most likely to vote to acquit someone they likely thought of as a hot-headed Syrian whose wife caught him cheating with a nurse?

The lawyers asked questions, and the jurors responded. Hour after hour, the process dragged on.

Everything seemed completely familiar. Courtroom dramas are, after all, a staple of television, movies and literature. And, at the same time, everything seemed utterly surreal.

He loved Ann. How could he be on trial for her murder?

FRIDAY, MARCH 4

9:00 A.M. – 4:35 P.M.

On Friday morning, the attorneys finished selection of the jurors and alternates. Opening statements were next, but first the court had to decide a motion that threatened to take away one of the most important issues Devin Garner intended to raise.

Bradford had filed a motion "in limine" – a motion filed "at the threshold" of a trial. Bradford wanted to exclude any evidence of the slayings of the several Hispanic women whose deaths Ann had been investigating. The court sent the newly sworn jurors to the jury room and invited Bradford and Garner to make their arguments on the motion.

Bradford argued that the court should confine the evidence to the one homicide charged in the indictment. The court should not allow the trial to get bogged down in details of other crimes, and speculation about who was responsible for those crimes.

As he had in his earlier motion to prevent discovery into the deaths, Bradford suggested that at least some of the women may have been illegal immigrants, and for all anyone knew, may have engaged in prostitution, drug use, or other behaviors that put their lives at risk. There was no proof they had all been killed by the same person or persons, let alone that their killer or killers had murdered Ann Medawar. Getting into the details of their deaths would be a sideshow and a distraction.

Garner had arranged for Carrie Hixson to be present in the courtroom for the hearing on the motion. When it was his turn to respond, he explained that Ann Medawar's classmates put together a short video about the slayings Ann Medawar and her classmate, Carrie Hixson, were investigating when Ann was killed. He asked permission to play the video, so that the court would have a better understanding of the evidence the prosecution wanted to keep the jury from hearing. He offered to have Ms. Hixson testify about how the video had been put together, if the court would find that helpful.

"I'll watch the video," Judge Seiler decided. "It won't be necessary for Ms. Hixson to provide foundational testimony. I'm going to treat the video as part of your argument, not as evidence."

"Your Honor," Bradford interjected, "if you're going to watch this, it may be more convenient to do that in chambers. Besides, this video – if it's the same one I've seen – is pretty graphic."

That prompted some dissatisfied murmuring by the press corps and others in the courtroom.

"Your Honor, what Mr. Bradford is trying to say, I believe, is that it would look bad for his office, for his boss, if the media and the community at large were to see the details of these slayings of Hispanic women his office ignored – while they were busy raiding legitimate businesses around town looking for immigrants to harass."

Garner turned away from the bench momentarily, found two of Hixon's classmates in the audience and nodded. As Cam Willey and Nancy Wong stood, Garner faced Judge Seiler again.

"Your Honor, classmates of Ann Medawar have copies of this video and are distributing them to any reporters interested. So, I think we can put that issue behind us."

Bradford was clearly angry, but said nothing.

"Let's proceed," Judge Seiler said.

Garner turned to Hixson. "Ms. Hixson, if you will."

Hixson projected the video onto the screen she and Cam put up before the hearing began. The video was essentially the same as the one she had presented months earlier to Bradford. It had, however, been updated with information about Camila Suarez, whose body had been retrieved from the Whitewater River, and the new victim, Alejandra Cruz, whose body had been dumped at Turfway Park.

When the video ended, Garner argued that Ann Medawar and Carrie Hixson had been investigating the abductions and murders of those women — and may have come too close for comfort for the perpetrator or perpetrators.

He argued that it was essential for the defense to show the similarities in how the women had been killed and how their bodies had been disposed of, because that evidence — while circumstantial — was compelling evidence the same killer or killers had committed all of the slayings.

Bradford responded that the video demonstrated his own point — allowing evidence of the other slayings would embroil the court in half a dozen trials.

Judge Seiler denied Bradford's motion. He would allow the defense to present evidence of the slayings of the Hispanic women. He would also allow testimony about Ann's investigation into who was killing those women and why. But he required Garner to be efficient in presenting evidence of those other slayings and to tie them to the shooting death of Ann Medawar.

With that, Judge Seiler had Scott Greene, the bailiff, bring the jury back. Counsel presented their opening statements. The prosecution would begin calling witnesses first thing Monday morning.

FRIDAY, MARCH 4

6:00 P.M. NEWS

Queen City News Live: Bringing you the news you want to hear.

News Anchor Bob Bunker: Today, in the homicide trial of Dr. Rafiq Medawar for the slaying of his wife, Ann Lindsey Medawar, attorneys finished selecting jurors and made their opening statements.

From a well-known Cincinnati family, Ann Lindsey Medawar was active in Cincinnati's social scene and an advocate for a number of causes. Before being indicted, Dr. Medawar was a Trauma Center surgeon.

Tiffany Albern has this report.

Tiffany Albern: Thank you, Bob. I'm here at the Hamilton County Courthouse with Professor Gregor A. Eitel, who teaches criminal law at the University of Cincinnati law school and has been following the case for us.

The victim, Ann Lindsey Medawar, was apparently last seen at the Sleep Cheap Inn in Clifton. On her cell phone, police found videos of Dr. Medawar and a Filipino nurse entering and leaving the inn. The prosecution asserts that Ms. Medawar confronted her husband, and he became angry and killed her.

Professor Eitel, how do you see the case so far?

Professor Eitel: Well, Tiffany, as the trial gets underway, I think both sides have significant problems.

The prosecution does not have an eyewitness or other direct evidence that Dr. Medawar killed his wife or that otherwise contradicts Dr. Medawar's version of events. The police haven't found the murder weapon. With no eyewitnesses, no confession, and no murder weapon, the prosecution has no direct evidence that Dr. Medawar killed his wife. The prosecution's case is at best circumstantial.

The defense has its own problems. The Filipino nurse, who met Dr. Medawar at the inn, disappeared. We learned today during opening statements that she was in the country on forged papers, and after Ann's body was discovered, she fled back to her home country. Apparently, she feared that if the police started looking into her background, she would be deported. Her absence deprives Dr. Medawar of an eyewitness whose testimony might have exonerated him.

It also doesn't look like the defense has any evidence to back up Dr. Medawar's claim that there was an undocumented woman at the inn with sick kids. Obviously, it would be hard to get someone in that situation to come forward, but that is a big problem for the defense. We also learned today during opening statements that the prosecution has found someone – a gang member named Jay-Jay Moore – who claims to have given Dr. Medawar the handgun used in the crime. That will go a long way with the jury.

Tiffany Albern: Professor Eitel, what can you tell us about trial counsel?

Professor Eitel: Tiffany, on that score, the advantage goes to the prosecution. As you know, the prosecutor's office has assigned Bill Bradford, its most seasoned attorney, to try the case. As a prosecutor, Bradford has tried a dozen prior homicide cases – and over a hundred felony cases of all sorts. He is widely regarded as the heir apparent if Dick Warren is elected to Congress.

Tiffany Albern: I understand you taught Devin Garner, the attorney defending Dr. Medawar?

Professor Eitel: I did. It was several years ago, but Devin Garner is a bright young guy – a very hard worker. I feel like he's a real up-and-comer, Tiffany, but at this point in his career, he doesn't have Bill Bradford's experience, and he doesn't have the resources the Prosecutor's office can bring to bear on a case like this.

Tiffany Albern: Tiffany Albern, reporting live from the Hamilton County Courthouse.

Co-Anchor Ashley Gelb: Scientists at John Hopkins School of Medicine and the University of Nebraska report discovering a virus that infects human brains and makes people act stupid. Our investigative reporter has the details after this.

SATURDAY, MARCH 5

MORNING

For Devin Garner, the weekends during a trial often meant catching up on work for other clients. This morning, he had an appointment with Carl Anwalt to discuss the property division between Hank and Reya. He had agreed to go to Anwalt's office.

Anwalt had refurbished one of the many stately old homes in Covington – just across the river from Cincinnati – and used it as his law office. He showed Garner into a room that may once have been an elegant parlor or sitting room, but which now served as a small conference room.

While he turned on his computer and it loaded, Garner began with a short – and clichéd – statement about how it was foolish for two former spouses to spend a lot of money on attorneys arguing over a property division – especially where the two had been married only a few years. Just before he married Reya, Garner explained, Hank sold the business he had run for years. Hank was clearly entitled to have that money allocated to him.

"Hank's bottom line is simple," Garner said. "Hank just wants his money back. He needs it to hold him over until he's eligible for Social Security.

"And, since Reya is making this litigation more protracted than it should be, he needs her to pay his attorney fees. If the case goes to trial, he's almost certain to get that much – and possibly more.

"Reya should settle and move on," Garner concluded.

Anwalt pushed back. "Reya no longer has Hank's money," he argued. "It was invested, along with her own money, in the new restaurant. If Hank stuck it out, when the new restaurant opened and was a success, he would have claimed that the new restaurant was part his. He'd be claiming that his money and input helped make it possible. Hank can't have it both ways. Just because there are some problems with the building permits doesn't give him the right to bolt and demand his money back."

Anwalt tapped his fingers on the table impatiently. "Reya," he said, "doesn't have the money to pay Hank what he's demanding anyway."

"She can easily borrow that much," Garner replied.

"If she borrows to pay Hank what he wants, she won't be able to refinance the new restaurant," Anwalt countered. "She'll lose everything she has invested in it."

Garner made his best arguments, asserting that, under the case law, the court would have no choice but to award his client at least that much – and maybe a good deal more. "She can't keep everything," he said, "and leave Hank penniless."

Anwalt scoffed. "I've known Dirk – Judge Richter – for a long time. He's not going to buy that. Besides, you've seen the restaurant's financials. Revenues and profits went down after Reya and your uncle got married."

"If you push this thing to trial," Anwalt continued, switching from elder statesman mode to intimidator, "I'm going to go after your uncle about his drinking problem. Reya will testify that your uncle was falling down drunk most of the time and was driving away business. The waitresses will back her up on that."

Anwalt smirked. "When I get done, your uncle is going to be lucky if Richter lets him keep the shirt on his back."

Garner opened his briefcase and extracted a document. "Since you, or your office, do Reya's bookkeeping, here's a notice for your deposition and a subpoena requiring your attendance."

"You're not going to take my deposition," Anwalt snapped. "I've given you the restaurant's records. The records speak for themselves. You don't need to depose me."

"You're responsible for preparing her financials, so I'm entitled to take your deposition. And as soon as I have the transcript of your deposition, I'm going to move for an order disqualifying you as trial counsel. You cannot represent Reya at trial, because you're going to be a witness."

"You're never going to get away with that," Anwalt said, running his hand through his hair. "Richter will quash the subpoena. There's nothing you need from me. You can read the P&L's, and so can he."

"Oh, I think there's plenty to cover in a deposition."

"Bullshit! Name one thing." Anwalt was on his feet.

"Well, for starters," Garner said, "since Hank left, it looks like Reya has been doing a lot of business off the books. So, I'm thinking I need to find out if you know that she's been closing the cash register every night at 9:00, and everything that comes in after that is off the books?"

"You can't prove that, and even if she is, I don't know anything about that."

"There are thousands of dollars of credit card receipts, but no corresponding cash register entries, so I think we can cover that in your deposition." Garner smiled and tried to relax his voice. "Besides, I want to ask about how you were laundering money from Reya's coyote business through the restaurant until she married Hank and you got skittish."

"You'll never prove that."

"I'll leave it to the forensic accountants to tell me what I can prove."

Garner thought he saw Anwalt's right eyelid twitch. Anwalt moved away from the table and began pacing.

"And then, of course, I'll want to ask how many times you brought Judge Richter to Reya's for a free lunch," Garner said, speaking calmly. "Was it just about every week for the last three years? Four years? Yeah, I think that's something we need to cover."

"That's penny-ante bullshit."

"Well, it will go into my motion to recuse Richter."

"Richter will piss all over your motion."

Garner pulled another folder from his briefcase. He removed from it the articles of incorporation for Reya's Authentic Mexican Restaurant, Agua Caliente, Los Obreros de Hoy, Nuestras Casas Co-Op, and the several companies that regularly did subcontract work for the home builder, The Bauherren Company. Garner slid the documents across the table.

"When I take your deposition, I'm also going to ask you about the relationships among these companies. I'm going to ask how Reya fits into things, and how you do. Frankly, it looks like maybe you're running a human trafficking ring."

"Number one," Anwalt said, "the judge is never going to allow you to take my deposition." Anwalt picked up the papers Garner had put on the table and tossed them back across the table.

"Number two, your uncle went to Mexico with Reya. If she brought any illegals into the country, he was an accomplice or co-conspirator. You're not going there, because you don't want your uncle to end up in prison. You're wasting my time."

"Is Reya really willing to say Hank was drunk all the time and driving away customers?" Garner asked, shaking his head in mock disbelief.

"She'll say any fucking thing I tell her to say. And knowing Reya, probably more."

Garner pulled another document from his briefcase and tossed it across the table to Anwalt.

"It's a deposition notice for Judge Richter. I want to ask him if Hank was falling down drunk every week when he was in the restaurant with you for his free lunch."

Anwalt glanced at the document and then angrily batted it away.

"You're out of bounds, and that deposition notice is just a stunt. If you go through with it, you're going to end up in front of the bar association."

"My client says you like to take Judge Richter to the Sleep Cheap Inn," Garner said, giving Anwalt a smile. "He says Richter likes the Mexican working girls there. It seems to me that I have professional obligation to ask the judge about that. I mean, if you're arranging prostitutes for him, that ought to go into my motion asking His Honor to recuse himself, don't you think?"

Garner had heard people say that someone was so angry they looked like they were about to have a stroke. He may have even used the expression himself. But he had never before seen anybody look so much like they might actually be about to have a stroke as Anwalt. His face was red, he was perspiring, and he was pacing up and down the room. He was rubbing his chest just below his right shoulder.

"The girls who work there," Garner bluffed, "say that Richter is into some pretty weird stuff. His trips there must be expensive."

Anwalt stopped and glared at Garner. "I've never been to that place in my life, and neither has Judge Richter. Either you're making this up, or your uncle is suffering from alcoholic psychosis."

Garner hit several keys on his laptop and brought up a video. "Ann Medawar made this video at the Sleep Cheap Inn the day she was killed," he explained.

He played the video.

"As you can see," Garner said, "it shows you and Judge Richter leaving the Sleep Cheap Inn. This was just before someone killed Ann."

Anwalt said nothing.

"Or to say the same thing a different way," Garner said, "just before someone had her killed."

"What are you implying?" Anwalt asked.

"On the video," Garner said, "you don't seem all that happy to see Ann making a video of you and the judge coming out of this sleazebag inn. What's the expression, 'If looks could kill'?"

"You're in way over your head. You know that? You're messing with things that are out of your league. Way out of your goddam league!"

"Don't threaten me. Just tell me: Do we have a settlement? Or do I need to put my concerns in filings with the court? If I do that, I think the media will find them rather interesting. Don't you?"

Anwalt sat down. "Okay, okay. You've got your settlement. I'll work it out with Reya." He rattled off the figure Reya needed to pay Hank. "Just that and your attorney fee, right?"

"That's right," Garner said, rising from the chair and snapping his briefcase closed.

"What are we talking about for the fee? Five hundred dollars?"

"More."

"You want a grand? You're unbelievable, you know that?"

"Five grand."

"That's blackmail! You do shit criminal cases for peanuts. You've never gotten a fee that big in your life. $1,500 tops."

"Haven't you heard?" Garner said. "I'm playing out of my league on this one."

Anwalt laughed. "Okay, okay. Just send me the papers. Reya's out of the country, but I'll find her and have her sign them. She'll need some time to raise the money, so go do your trial. I'll have Richter approve the paperwork, and we'll settle up when you're done."

Garner nodded.

"But if one word of any of this leaks," Anwalt said, "you're going to be sorry. Worse than sorry. Tell your uncle too. Tell him not to drink so much. He could have an accident."

LUNCH

Garner headed from Anwalt's office to the restaurant where he was to meet Hank.

"The good news, I guess, is that Anwalt agreed to settle," Garner told his uncle after they placed their lunch orders. "Reya will repay the money you got when you sold the bar, and she'll cover my fee. The divorce will be finalized, and you'll get your money once all the papers have been signed and Judge Richter approves them."

Hank looked at Garner skeptically. "I don't know how you got Anwalt to agree to that, but what about Reya? There's no way in hell she is going to go along with that."

"Anwalt said he would handle her."

"Good luck with that," Hank scoffed. "Tell me. How did you get Anwalt to come around?"

"Basically, I blackmailed him."

"You threatened to make public his relationship with Judge Richter? The free meals and all that?"

"Yeah. He denied it all."

"I told you he would."

"I also said I would put in my motion papers that he pays for Richter to have sex with the prostitutes at the inn."

"You can't prove that."

"I know, and he denied it. He said Richter has never been there in his life."

"Then, why did he agree to settle?"

"Remember us talking about the Medawar trial?"

"Yeah. It's all over the news."

"Well, when Ann Medawar was making her videos, she took some practice shots of people coming out of the inn. I don't think she knew who they were, but she videoed Anwalt and Richter walking out of the place. I showed Anwalt the video, and he caved."

Hank raised his eyebrows. "He didn't want it getting out about Richter and the prostitutes?"

"I'm sure that was a big part of it, but it got really weird."

"What happened?"

"On the video, Anwalt looked angry. I think he was upset that Ann caught him and Richter on video coming out of that place."

Hank laughed. "I guess he was."

"But just to leverage the video as much as I could, I made some smart-ass remark about how this was just before Ann was killed."

"You said that?"

"Actually, what I said was more like, 'Look at that expression on your face. *If looks could kill.*' And then I said something about this being shortly before someone *had* Ann killed."

"You don't actually think Anwalt had anything to do with that woman being killed?"

"I didn't until I saw how Anwalt reacted. Now I'm wondering."

Hank studied Garner for a long moment. "Are you going to be able to bring that up in your trial?"

"I've got a *huge* problem," Garner said. "If I don't bring it up, it would be malpractice. Worse than that, if I don't go after Anwalt, Rafiq may be convicted."

"I don't understand. What's the problem?"

"Anwalt said you've got your settlement only if nothing about him and the judge comes out. He says if any of that gets out, the deal's off, and you won't get a penny. He implied that Olivar, or whatever cartel has its hooks into Olivar, are liable to pay you and me a visit."

Garner stood. "Excuse me," he said. "I'm going to be sick."

Hank followed Garner into the restroom and watched as his nephew vomited. Garner rinsed out his mouth and splashed water on his face. When they returned to their table, Garner's face was white.

The waitress delivered their food. Garner ignored his.

"You okay?" Hank asked.

"No, I'm not okay. I've got a *huge* conflict of interest. If I bring this stuff up in the trial, you lose your settlement. And, for all we know, maybe Olivar or someone from the cartel will try to kill you. But if I don't bring it up in the trial, Rafiq could be convicted." Garner hesitated, processing what he had just said. "I'm going to have to withdraw as Rafiq's attorney."

"Won't that look bad for him? And you?"

"For him, for me. It's a disaster all the way around."

"Devin, I don't like this. You have to do what's right for your client in that trial. Don't worry about me."

"How can I not worry about you? The settlement will blow up, and maybe he tries to have you killed."

"We'll work out my divorce. If you bring this stuff up in your trial over in Cincinnati, it'll be all over the news. You'll be able to force Richter off my case – if he's still on the bench."

Garner nodded. *That was true.* "You sure?"

"Yeah. I don't want it on my conscience that this doctor got convicted so I could keep a settlement. I wouldn't feel right. Besides, I don't want you to withdraw. This case will make your career."

"Aren't you afraid Diego will come after you to retaliate against me?"

"Look, I don't think Anwalt has any intention of honoring the deal he just made with you. I think the minute you walked out of his office, he was on the phone to Diego. I think you're the one who should be worried."

Lost in his own thoughts, Garner said nothing.

"Besides," Hank said, "I think the Feds are going to indict Diego and Anwalt. If they do, it's not going to take those two very long to figure out who pointed the finger at them. I've already crossed that bridge. Publicity may be our best protection."

"You're still living out of your trailer at the club?"

"Yeah, but I'll leave town, go fishing somewhere, until

this blows over."

"Where?"

"Doesn't matter. Probably one of the lakes down state – Dale Hollow, Lake Cumberland, somewhere like that."

"Be careful."

Hank shook his head. "I'll be careful, but you're the one we need to worry about."

MID-AFTERNOON

Carl Anwalt insisted on talking with Diego Olivar outside the inn – out of concern that the feds might be bugging it.

"This young lawyer that's representing Hank in his suit against your mother," Anwalt said, handing Diego a slip of paper. "His name and address are on there."

"What about him?"

"He knows too much. He threatened to go public with what he knows if Reya didn't settle with Hank."

"You want me to take care of him?"

"Yeah, but he's involved in the Medawar trial. He's representing that doctor. They're friends or something."

"So what?"

"If you do something now, the media will be all over it. You need to wait until the trial is over. See if you can get to him right after the trial and try to make it look like a suicide."

"You think he's going to lose?"

"Of course, he's going to lose. That schmuck doctor hasn't got a chance."

"So, this lawyer guy, he loses the case, his friend the doctor gets convicted. He feels responsible, and he kills himself? I like that."

"Just don't screw it up."

AFTERNOON

Garner was in the office on Sunday, preparing for the next day's witnesses in the Medawar trial. Somewhat to his surprise, Professor Adams had agreed to come to his office. He thought she would make him meet her at her office on the University of Cincinnati campus.

Professor Adams arrived a little after 1:30, escorted by Jamal Muhammad and Raeshaun Bowman. Bowman was another of the men in the informal "neighborhood watch" group. Apparently, some teens had approached Professor Adams a bit too aggressively, and Muhammad and Bowman intervened.

Muhammad stepped into Garner's office with the professor, while Bowman left to keep an eye on her car.

Garner thanked Muhammad for watching out for Dr. Adams.

"No problem. How are you doing?" Mohammad asked.

"Fine," Garner replied reflexively. "No, actually, to be honest, I've got a problem I'd like to discuss." He motioned to Muhammad to step outside, so Professor Adams would not hear what he had to say.

"I'm handling a divorce case. I represent the husband. The wife is Mexican and apparently doesn't approve of how I'm handling the case. She sent me a box with a couple chickens and a couple baby chicks, all with their necks wrung. She apparently thinks I have a wife and kids. So, it's a threat against my whole family."

Mohammad flashed a wry grin. "That Christian woman's putting some heavy voodoo on you."

"Maybe."

"And then, yesterday," Garner said, "her attorney threatened me. Or at least implied that this woman or her family might try to kill me."

"Maybe you should stick to representing criminals," Mohammad said, "and stay away from that domestic relations stuff. Might be safer, you know?"

"This family is into some bad stuff," Garner said. "I was hoping you and your guys could keep a close eye on my place over the next couple weeks as that plays out and I finish this trial."

"We can do that. I'll talk with all the guys."

"I'm especially worried about any Mexicans who don't belong in the neighborhood."

"We will be alert. We won't let them hurt you, my friend. Inshallah."

MONDAY, MARCH 7

9:00 A.M. – 11:15 A.M.

To open the prosecution case, Assistant Hamilton County Prosecutor William Bradford called as a witness "Indy" Induprakash Bannerji, a soft-spoken thirty-two-year-old Cincinnati Police Department crime scene specialist.

The choice, Garner thought, was inspired. By opening with a dead body and no explanation, the prosecution was sure to capture the jury's interest. Plus, from the prosecution's point of view, the subject matter was safe – meaning, it didn't risk getting the prosecution's case off to a shaky start. On top of that, Bannerji was smart and well educated – maybe the only person in that role in the country with Ph.D. He wasn't going to undermine the case by saying something stupid.

Ann Medawar's body had been found at the overlook in Eden Park – ordinarily a beautiful spot with a view of the Ohio River and the Kentucky basin on the other side of the river. Bradford had Bannerji describe the crime scene in detail. Bannerji laid it on heavy with photographs, drawings, and extensive minutiae.

The point of the exercise, Garner knew, was to bulk up the amount of evidence in the prosecution's weak case – and of course, to satisfy any jurors who had watched too many "CSI"-type television dramas and expected lots of forensic testimony.

After more than an hour of the impressive, but largely irrelevant testimony, Bradford had Bannerji testify to finding the decedent's cell phone in her pocket. From a substantive standpoint, that exchange was the real point of putting Bannerji on the witness stand. Bradford was nailing down the chain of custody for the cell phone. Bannerji had also been the one to find the videos of Dr. Medawar and the Filipino nurse entering and leaving the Sleep Cheap Inn. The foundation for the videos coming into evidence was airtight.

When Bradford completed his direct, Garner requested a sidebar conference with Judge Seiler – a whispered conference at the side of the bench. He asked for permission to withhold his cross-examination of the witness until the defense case. Bradford objected that would be inefficient. Garner thought the objection sounded too much like it was based on nothing more than opposition to anything the defense wanted.

Judge Seiler asked Bannerji if he would be available the following week. Bannerji responded that he was leaving at the end of the week for a long-planned trip to India to visit family. He apologized profusely. Judge Seiler denied Garner's request.

Before taking his turn with the witness, Garner had the court reporter mark several exhibits and gave copies of the exhibits to Bannerji, Bradford, and Judge Seiler. The exhibits were crime scene reports detailing the sites where each of the slain Hispanic women had been found. Garner had expected to call each of the crime scene specialists as a witness and have each testify only to the report he prepared. But Judge Seiler had pressed the attorneys on both sides to expedite the case by having one witness cover all of the crime scene reports.

Before turning to the exhibits, Garner asked Bannerji a question that went to whether the court had jurisdiction over the slaying of Ann Medawar:

"Dr. Bannerji, where was Ann Medawar shot?"

"Well, as I testified, she was shot in the chest and in the head."

"I'm sorry, Indy – strike that. I apologize, Dr. Bannerji. I meant geographically. Did the shooting occur in Ohio, where her body was found? Or, across the river in Kentucky? Down the road in Indiana? Somewhere else?"

"I can't answer, except to say that we found no evidence that the gunshot wounds were inflicted at the site where the body was found."

Garner let a moment elapse before resuming his questioning – just enough to let that sink in and to signal that he was moving to a new topic.

"Dr. Bannerji, I just gave you a report identified for the record as Defense Exhibit No. 1. Are you familiar with that document?"

Bradford rose and objected that the exhibit – and the related line of questioning – did not pertain to the decedent and was irrelevant and prejudicial. Judge Seiler overruled the objection for the "reasons previously stated."

Bradford requested that the record note his continuing objection to all questions related to the subject of the exhibit.

"So noted," Judge Seiler responded.

Garner repeated his question, and Bannerji acknowledged being familiar with the exhibit. It was a crime scene report he had prepared.

"What sort of crime?" Garner asked.

"A homicide."

"When and where was this crime scene investigation?"

"This was on June 13 of this year. The situs of the investigation was the railroad yard under the 8th Street viaduct."

"Please tell the jury what you found there."

"The body of a young Hispanic woman."

"Were you able to ascertain the woman's name?"

"Yes, sir. She still had her wallet and identification papers." Bannerji studied the report. "Her name was Natalia Garcia."

"Your report indicates that the woman had been shot?"

"Yes, sir."

"Actually, she had been shot twice? Once in the chest and once in the head?"

Bannerji glanced briefly at the report, before responding, "That's correct."

"Did you determine how this young woman's body came to be on the railroad tracks?"

"Yes, sir. Someone dropped her body from the bridge."

"Was Ms. Garcia roughly the same age as Ann Medawar?"

"She was nineteen, so she was younger."

"Dr. Bannerji," Garner said as he picked up the next exhibit. "Let's turn now to the report identified as Defense Exhibit No. 2. Are you familiar with that document?"

"Yes, sir."

"And just to speed things along, this is another crime scene report that you prepared – again, involving the body of a young woman?"

"Yes, sir."

"This woman's body was dumped in front of Saint Toribio Romo Gonzalez Center in Lower Price Hill?"

"That's correct."

"This report is from July 12?"

"Yes, sir."

"The dead woman was Valeria Zuniga?"

"Yes, sir."

"She had been shot twice – once in the chest, and once in the head?"

"Yes, sir."

"The actual shooting took place somewhere else?"

"That's correct."

"She was roughly the same age as Ann Medawar?"

"Yes sir."

"In just a few months' time, you documented the locations where the bodies of three young women – including Ann Medawar – had been dumped?"

"That's right, but –"

"And you found that each of those young women had been shot twice – once in the chest, and once in the head –

and then dumped somewhere where they were likely to be found?"

"That's correct."

Using the same questions, Garner took Bannerji through the crime scene reports detailing where each of the other bodies of young Hispanic women was found. Defense Exhibit 3 was the crime scene report, dated Sunday, August 9, detailing the site where the body of Sofia Flores, age twenty-two, had been found. Her body had apparently thrown from the South Ludlow Street/U.S. 127 overpass into the Mill Creek.

Defense Exhibit 4 recounted that the body of Isabella Ramirez, age twenty-one, had been found September 13 at the Hamilton County Fairgrounds. It was the weekend of the annual Hispanic festival.

Defense Exhibit 5 was an Indiana State Police report. It stated that Sierra Club volunteers found the body of U.C. medical student Camila Suarez on December 30 – six weeks after her disappearance. Based on the report, Bannerji testi-fied, "she was dumped into the Whitewater River from I-275, where it crossed over the river."

Finally, relying on a report by the Florence Police, Ban-nerji recited the bare facts concerning the discovery of the body of Alejandra Cruz, age twenty-five. Workers found her body on Sunday, December 13, at the Turfway Park racetrack in Florence, Kentucky.

In each case, the woman had been shot twice – once in the chest or torso and again in the head. Geographically, each woman had been shot someplace other than where her body was found. Each of the women was Hispanic.

Garner mounted a large Google map of the Greater Cincinnati area on a tripod and asked Bannerji to mark the approximate locations on the map where each body had been found.

Bannerji left the witness stand and marked each site with a small circle. Next to each circle, he wrote the last name of each victim and the date of death.

While Bannerji remained next to the map, Garner asked another question, as breezily as he could, hoping Bradford would not object. "It's not unusual, is it, for a serial killer to select victims, or at least to leave victims, in multiple jurisdictions to confuse the police?"

"No sir, that's not unusual."

As Bannerji returned to the witness stand, Garner reviewed his notes. "One last question," he announced.

Before posing his wrap up question, Garner scanned the jury. The jurors seemed to be paying attention, but as usual, they tried to keep their facial expressions neutral. He glanced at the judge. Judge Seiler was working on the instructions he would give the jury at the end of the case. He apparently sensed the pause in the usual drone of questions and answers and looked up. Garner looked back at Bannerji, who waited expectantly.

"Dr. Bannerji, does this evidence suggest the same person or persons killed all these women –"

"Objection!" Bradford shouted. "Argumentative."

Judge Seiler hesitated a moment and announced, "Overruled." Turning to the witness, he added: "Dr. Bannerji, you may answer."

"I can't answer," Bannerji responded, addressing Judge Seiler. "I mean – I don't *know* if the same person killed all of these women."

Bannerji turned to Garner and added, "Just like I don't *know* if that really will be your last question. But I know what my experience tells me. My experience tells me it would be unusual for a serial killer to vary his victims the way we see here – six Hispanic women, all apparently low-income or poor, and then an upper socio-economic class Anglo."

Garner shot a glance at Bradford, who had a smirk on his face.

"Dr. Bannerji," Garner asked, trying to recoup, "did anything you noted in these reports, or anything you observed at the scenes you examined, rule out the possibility that the same person killed all seven of these women?"

"No, sir. Nothing in these reports, and nothing I observed, ruled out that possibility. But, sir, nothing established that possibility either – nothing established that the same person killed all of these victims."

Garner hadn't expected Bannerji to give him more than that. The question was intended for the jury. Garner checked his notes, thanked the witness, and announced he had no further questions.

Bradford hesitated before announcing he had nothing further.

Judge Seiler excused Bannerji and wished him a safe trip.

11:15 A.M. – 12:00 P.M.

Bradford rose to call his next witness. But before he could announce, "The prosecution calls ...," he got a surprise.

At that moment, Weary Dunston burst through the doors at the rear of the courtroom, bellowing, "Your Honor! Your Honor!" The septuagenarian spieler proceeded down the center aisle of the courtroom just as fast as his spindly legs could carry him. As he did, he continued to exclaim, "Your Honor! Your Honor!" as often and as loud as his brittle lungs would permit.

In his wake followed a woman of some bearing, who appeared to be embarrassed— maybe even annoyed—by the commotion. Garner had no idea who she was.

For the occasion, Dunston wore what may have been the finest suit in his closet. Except for age and wear, it was equal in every respect to those on offer at the gentlemen's apparel stores with the deepest discounts. Judging by its style, Garner figured he had been in college when Dunston bought it. But by Dunston's standards, that made the suit almost contemporary.

It was hard to tell, but Dunston had apparently even

polished his shoes. *True*, a hole had worn its way through the sole of the right shoe. But when his shoes were firmly planted on the courthouse floor, as they were now—Dunston had stopped and was coughing violently into his pocket handkerchief—that small imperfection did not detract in any meaningful way from his over-all appearance.

Dunston's client—the woman in his wake—was dressed in a nicely-tailored and obviously expensive suit. Beneath her suit jacket, she wore a shimmering pearl-colored silk blouse. Her necklace and earrings were custom-made. Completing her outfit, the woman wore pearl-colored Manolo Blahnik pumps that went perfectly with her outfit.

All in all, the woman presented herself exactly as might be expected of someone equally at ease in a corporate boardroom or in a social gathering in the toniest east side neighborhood.

How old Weary Dunston came to represent such a client was a mystery to Garner. Although Dunston sometimes drew an appointment to a more serious matter, he typically practiced in traffic court, where he specialized in those cases that required the least effort. But today, the ancient litigator was exerting himself to the fullest.

"Your Honor," Dunston wheezed as he made his way past the tables reserved for trial counsel and pressed resolutely forward, "may I approach the bench?"

"Mr. Dunston," Judge Seiler responded, bemused at the ancient barrister's grand—and grandstanding—entrance. "We're in the middle of a trial."

"Precisely, precisely," Dunston agreed, as if that had been the very point he had come to press upon the court. "I wish to address the court, if I may, in a matter of great urgency and importance. It is a matter which cannot wait, Your Honor, if the court is to avoid a serious miscarriage of justice in this proceeding."

"Fifteen-minute recess," Judge Seiler sighed. "Let's do this in chambers."

When Judge Seiler, the court reporter, counsel, and the well-dressed woman were all seated in the judge's chambers, Dunston—who remained standing—attended first to an important formality. "Your Honor, if I may," he said, "I would like to introduce my client, Ms. Emily Goessel."

The judge nodded politely in the woman's direction.

"My client has become aware, Your Honor, that the defendant in this matter, Dr. Rafiq Medawar, claims that he and a certain nurse—a modern-day Florence Nightingale, if you will—went to the Sleep Cheap Inn, on the morning in question, to care for the two desperately ill children of a woman believed to be an undocumented alien.

"It is Dr. Medawar's contention, as my client understands the situation, that this poor woman feared she would be deported if she took her children to the hospital.

"The State, on the other hand, contends that Dr. Medawar and this nurse went to this inn to attend to a very different sort of physical need. The prosecution, Your Honor, would have the jury believe that there never was a Madonna with child, hiding from the authorities – from the modern Herod, if you will – in this humble place, caring as best she could for two desperately ill children.

"On that very point rests this gentleman's honor and liberty," Dunston proclaimed, warming to his peroration. "And so, Your Honor, my client has asked me – *insisted*– that she must come forward."

"Mr. Dunston," Judge Seiler chided the bombastic old barrister. "You are not addressing a joint session of Congress. Can you get to the point, please?"

"Exactly, exactly," Dunston agreed wholeheartedly. "On the morning in question, Your Honor, Ms. Goessel's own child was also ill. The child's school contacted Ms. Goessel and demanded that she come immediately and take her sick child home."

Judge Seiler cleared his throat in warning.

"As you would expect, Your Honor, Ms. Goessel left

work immediately and went to pick up her ailing child."

At this point in his oration, Dunston lowered his voice and looked apologetically at his client for what he had to say next. "You might, Your Honor, say that she *sped* to her child's side, because—as it happened—a police officer pulled her over for speeding."

"Unfortunately, Your Honor, while Ms. Goessel may have been in too great a hurry to reach her poor, sick child, the young patrolman who pulled her over was in no hurry at all. As Ms. Goessel sat in her car, waiting for him to approach, this young patrolman and a lady cop chatted and flirted and what have you – as if Ms. Goessel and her dear, sick child had all the time in the world."

"Mr. Dunston, if you don't get to the point soon," Judge Seiler threatened, "I am going to have the bailiff take you into custody and deposit your sorry old carcass next door in the Detention Center."

"Well, yes, getting to the point, Your Honor. As Ms. Goessel sat there, she became frustrated, as I'm sure you would have been if the tables had been turned. In this state of high dudgeon, Your Honor, my client retrieved her cell phone from her purse and began recording these two young police officers chit-chatting and romancing and what-have-you. In short, she began making a video of their flagrant neglect of their duties."

"You've got thirty seconds," Judge Seiler warned, "before I call the bailiff."

"I'm sorry, Your Honor, I have been in such a rush to get to the crux of the matter, that I have completely forgotten to mention a crucially important detail. When, in response to the patrol car's siren, Ms. Goessel pulled her vehicle over, she happened—purely by chance, Your Honor—to pull into the parking lot of the Sleep Cheap Inn there in Clifton.

"As I was saying, Your Honor, and hurrying along now,

my client was making a video of these young officers chatting and flirting and delaying her from reaching her precious child. As she was doing this, Your Honor, all of sudden, without warning, several foreigners walked right in front of her, between her and these young cops. Right into the picture, so to speak."

His patience exhausted, Judge Seiler turned to Ms. Goessel. "Ma'am, assuming this is why we're here, who were these people?"

"There were two men and a woman," Goessel replied crisply, "and two young—very young—children. They all appeared to be Mexican, or at least Hispanic. The two men looked tough – scary actually – and the young woman looked frightened. Because they walked right in front of me, in front of my cell phone camera, they're on the video I was making. You can see them for yourself."

Goessel produced her iPhone, opened the camera, brought up the video, and handed the phone to the jurist.

"When was this?" Judge Seiler asked.

"Friday, October 16, about 9:12 a.m.," Goessel replied. "You can see the time and date on the video."

Judge Seiler watched the video and then handed it to Bradford, who watched it and passed the cell phone to Garner.

"If I may," Dunston interjected—to belabor what was now obvious. "Barely fifteen minutes after Dr. Medawar left the premises, these two desperados strong-armed this poor mother and her toddlers from the inn, and it's all right here on video."

Perhaps brought on by the powerful emotions this image stirred up, another violent coughing spell overcame Dunston.

"Your Honor," he rasped, when he could breathe again, "in view of the parties' contentions here, and in view of the fact that this kind man's life, liberty, and honor are in jeopardy, I think you will agree that it is imperative the jury see this video for themselves."

"Mr. Dunston," Judge Seiler inquired, "did you advise counsel you had this video?"

"No, Sir, I came directly to the court. I didn't want to put defense counsel in the position of having to argue late-discovered evidence, and risk —"

"Don't you think," Judge Seiler interrupted, "that you should have contacted the Prosecutor's office and explained what your client had come forward with?"

"The Prosecutor's office? Oh, good God, no, Your Honor."

Dunston coughed again, a deep and bone-rattling cough.

"With all due respect, Your Honor," he explained when he regained his composure, "you know how they are in that office. On the rare occasion when they happen upon evidence of real importance, their first instinct is to hide it. No telling, Your Honor, what pressure they might have brought to bear to silence my client."

"Your Honor!" Bradford objected. "There is no basis for that accusation. It's ridiculous! He owes the Prosecutor's office an apology."

"Actually, Your Honor," Dunston responded, "now that you focus my attention on the issue, I *did* bring this to the attention of the Prosecutor's office — in traffic court. When my client appeared on the matter of her traffic citation, I explained to the young Deputy Assistant Prosecutor that my client had this video and why it was significant. Your Honor, she refused to have me send it to her. I think it could be said she did not want to come into possession of evidence that might exculpate this poor man."

"Okay," Judge Seiler persisted, "if you don't trust the Prosecutor's office, did you disclose the existence of this video to defense counsel, to Mr. Garner?"

"No, Sir, like I said, in the interests of justice, I came directly here."

"You didn't answer the thrust of my question, Mr. Dunston," Judge Seiler scolded. "If you don't trust the Prosecutor's office, why didn't you let defense counsel know what you had?"

"He's just a youngster," Dunston responded, dolefully. "What if he were unable to convince the court that he had not been sitting on this evidence, hoping to surprise his more experienced adversary at the last moment? What then – God help us! – if the court were to exclude this important evidence? My conscience, Your Honor, would not permit me to put justice at so precarious a risk."

Judge Seiler rolled his eyes at the garrulous old goat's explanation, but turned his attention to the video's admissibility.

Five minutes later, after hearing from both counsel, Judge Seiler had his bailiff call court back into session. He then summoned Ms. Goessel to the witness stand as the court's witness.

When Emily Goessel was sworn and seated in the witness box, Judge Seiler led her through how she came to make the video of the woman and children leaving the Sleep Cheep inn. At Garner's in-chambers suggestion, Goessel had emailed the video to counsel. From her laptop at counsel table, Kemi Adichie projected the video onto the large screen set up for videos. The jury watched the video with obvious interest.

***

Weary Dunston was pleased with his client and the dramatic impact her testimony would make. But he was not so completely focused on his client that he was unable to congratulate himself. He had, after all, every reason to feel satisfied – and not just with how things were playing out in court.

The day's dramatic turn of events in the trial would get prominent play in the evening's local news broadcasts. His name would surely be mentioned.

With that in mind, more than a month earlier, he had arranged – with what he thought to be commendable fore-sight – to have commercials for his practice run during the week's local news broadcasts. *They would complement the news stories,* he thought, *just as nicely as his client's shoes complemented her outfit*

.

MONDAY, MARCH 7

6:00 P.M. NEWS

Queen City News Live: Bringing you the news you want to hear.

News Anchor Bob Bunker: The court began hearing testimony today in the trial of Dr. Rafiq Medawar, who is charged with the slaying of his wife, Ann Lindsey Medawar. Tiffany Albern is at the Hamilton County Courthouse and has this report.

Tiffany Albern: Thank you, Bob. I'm here with Professor Gregor Eitel, who teaches criminal law at the University of Cincinnati law school and has been following the trial for us.

Professor Eitel, have there been any surprises so far?

Professor Eitel: Yes, and that in itself is surprising, because it's just the first day of testimony. The big surprise was a witness that neither side saw coming. Things had barely gotten underway this morning, when an attorney, Weary Dunston, interrupted the trial. Dunston announced that he had a witness who videotaped a woman and two toddlers being ushered from the Sleep Cheap Inn, shortly after Dr. Medawar left the inn.

Tiffany Albern: We obtained a portion of the video she played for the jury. [Video plays.] What can you tell us about the witness?

Professor Eitel: The surprise witness was Ms. Emily Goessel, Executive Director at the Blue Chip City Foundation. She was pulled over for a traffic ticket the morning Ms. Medawar disappeared and videoed the woman and her children being escorted from the inn. Her testimony and video undercut the prosecution theory of the case.

Tiffany Albern: You said there was another surprise?

Professor Eitel: Yes, it is the defense strategy. As you know, Dr. Medawar retained Devin Garner, who's only five years out of law school. Garner has been the second chair in three prior murder cases, but this is the first time he has tried a homicide case as the lead attorney for the defense. I like Garner. I think he's a terrific young lawyer, but Tiffany, I think we're seeing evidence of his relative inexperience already.

Tiffany Albern: In what way?

Professor Eitel: Well, from what we've seen so far, the government's case is not as strong as the prosecution would like. Remember, the government must prove its case beyond a reasonable doubt. All the defense has to do is poke holes in the government's case.

Garner is trying to present a different scenario than the one presented by the prosecution. He presented evidence today that several young Hispanic women have been killed over the last year in the Greater Cincinnati area. He apparently intends to argue that Ms. Medawar was investigating those killings in connection with a documentary she was making. I think he is hoping the jury will conclude that whoever killed those other women became concerned about her documentary and killed her. That's a risky strategy.

He should be reminding the jury that the prosecution must rule out any other reasonable alternative scenario. By presenting this specific scenario, he runs the risk that the jury will vote to convict if it rejects the particular scenario the defense is presenting.

Tiffany Albern: Do you think Dr. Medawar would have been better served by retaining more experienced defense counsel?

Professor Eitel: Well, Tiffany, Dr. Medawar's future is on the line here, and experience is important. The trial isn't over yet, but I think that would have been the safer bet.

Tiffany Albern: Tiffany Albern reporting live from the Hamilton County Courthouse.

Co-Anchor Ashley Gelb: Coming up after the break,

a special report you won't want to miss if you drink iced tea. Tea has many health benefits, but the beverage you get in your favorite restaurant may contain a surprising number of bacteria — as our investigative reporter reveals after this word from our sponsors.

On Tuesday morning, Assistant Hamilton County Prosecutor William Bradford called as a witness Cincinnati Police Detective James Chilton, the lead detective on the Medawar case. Garner had tangled with the pugnacious cop once before, in a different case, and he wasn't looking forward to the rematch.

Bradford began by questioning Chilton at length about his training and experience, his many years on the force, and the numerous homicides he had investigated during his career. Only then did Bradford have Chilton detail the investigation into the murder of Ann Medawar.

By describing the police investigation, Chilton effectively provided an overview of the prosecution case, so the jury would be able to put into context the more detailed and specialized testimony to come. Throughout his testimony, Chilton used the stilted language with which police detectives narrate such matters – giving his testimony an official and authoritative air.

When it was time for him to cross-examine, Garner felt he only needed to focus on a few points, but hoped to accomplish more.

"Detective Chilton," he began, "in the course of your investigation did you find an eyewitness to the shooting of Ann Medawar?"

"No," Chilton conceded, "but we also weren't able to find any witness who could confirm where Dr. Medawar was at the time of the murder of his wife."

The answer was well rehearsed and combative, confirming Garner's concerns that this was going to be a difficult cross.

"You couldn't find a witness to confirm that Dr. Medawar was at home sleeping after working the night shift?" Garner asked sarcastically.

"That's where he says he was, but like I said, we couldn't find anyone who could confirm that."

"You were able to confirm that he worked the night shift?"

"Yes."

Garner shook his head. "Did you find an eyewitness to the dumping of Ann Medawar's body in Eden Park?"

"No."

Moving to a new topic, Garner asked: "You searched Dr. Medawar's home and car the day Ann Medawar's body was found?"

"Yes."

"Were you able to find the gun used to kill Ms. Medawar?"

"No, but —"

"Your Honor, I would ask that the Court instruct the witness to answer the questions he's asked and not give a speech."

"Just answer the questions, Detective," Judge Seiler responded, but without any sign of optimism that his direction would be heeded.

"You tested Dr. Medawar's hands for gunpowder residue?"

"The technician did."

"Did you find evidence that Dr. Medawar had recently fired a gun?"

"The test was negative, but that doesn't mean anything. You want to do that in the first three hours. Sometimes you can find something after six hours, if the suspect hasn't washed his hands. But it had been much longer than that when we did the test, and Dr. Medawar had taken a shower. No telling how many times he'd washed his hands."

"Based on the videos recorded on Ann Medawar's cell

phone, you theorized that she suspected Dr. Medawar was having an affair with the nurse, Angelica Rios?"

"We found a video of a doctor – a surgeon – and a nurse going into a hot sheets inn." Chilton turned to the jury and smirked. "Yeah, we thought that was a reasonable theory to pursue."

"In the course of your investigation, did you find anyone to whom Ann Medawar confided concerns that her husband might be cheating on her?"

"No, but that's not unusual. A woman like that doesn't want people to know she can't keep her husband."

Garner stole a glance at the jury. Some of the women on the jury appeared irritated.

"The police department was able to examine Ann Medawar's emails?"

"Yes. Again, that's standard procedure."

"Did you find any emails in which she discussed concerns that her husband was cheating?"

"None that I recall."

"You also seized Dr. Medawar's computer?"

"Yes, again, that's standard procedure."

"Because he was the victim's husband?"

"Yes, along with other factors."

"And were you able to search Dr. Medawar's email?"

"Our computer guys were."

"Did you find any evidence that he was having an affair?"

"Not in his emails, but he's a smart guy. That could just mean he was careful."

"As you know, the defense contends that Ms. Medawar was making – along with others – a documentary about the plight of undocumented immigrants in our community?"

"Yeah, I've been told that."

"Were you able to find eyewitnesses who could corroborate that?"

"Sure, we found people who knew she was taking a class

about documentary filmmaking. But no one could say that's why she was making a video of her husband and this nurse going to a hot sheets inn."

"On Ann Medawar's computer, there were a number of videos she took in connection with the documentary she was making?"

"Yes."

"You found no evidence to support your theory that she suspected her husband of cheating, and no evidence that he was in fact cheating, but you were able to confirm that she was working on a documentary?"

"Asked and answered," Bradford objected. "And argumentative."

Judge Seiler told Garner to "move along."

"In the course of your investigation, did you learn that students in this class Ann Medawar was taking were using their cell phones to capture video for their documentary?"

"Yeah, that's what we were told."

"Before this case, did you know people were using cell phones to make documentaries?"

"No, not documentaries, but every police officer in the country knows people use cell phones to make videos."

"In the course of your investigation, did you learn that the students in this class also used, as standard practice, a second camera, typically one mounted on a tripod, both as a backup and to get a different angle?"

"Yeah, the professor told us that."

"Did you find a second camera?"

"No, we didn't. We thought that cut against the idea that the decedent was making a documentary about illegal immigrants when she was filming her husband and this nurse going into a hot sheets inn."

Garner sighed and looked to Judge Seiler. "Your Honor," he said, "I'm afraid the witness has forgotten your instruction."

The judge encouraged the witness to limit his answers

to the question asked and not to give a speech.

"Detective," Garner asked, picking up his cross again, "you're aware that the defense contends Ms. Medawar was investigating – in connection with the documentary she was helping to make – the murder of several undocumented immigrants?"

"Yes."

"And you're aware the defense contends that whoever was responsible for those murders may have become concerned about her snooping around and killed her?"

"Yes, I'm aware of that. I've been around long enough to know that defendants and their lawyers come up with all sorts of theories."

"Detective, if the defense theory is correct, would it be logical to assume that whoever is responsible for these murders would have wanted to make Ann Medawar's camera disappear?"

"Yes, but that's a big assumption."

"Don't you think Ann's husband would know she was using her cell phone to capture video for this documentary she and classmates were making?"

"I don't know what he knew."

"To sum up, if Ann Medawar was using a camera and a tripod, they're missing?"

"We never found them."

"But the killer left her cell phone in her pocket?"

"Yes."

"And from that you concluded her husband must have killed her, as opposed to a stranger concerned about the documentary she was making?"

"Argumentative," Bradford objected – using a weary, *Do-I-even-have-to-point-this-out?* tone of voice.

Judge Seiler upheld the objection. "Save it for your closing," he told Garner.

"The camera may have been in her car," Detective Chilton volunteered even though Judge Seiler had sustained the objection.

"And, as you testified on direct, you were not able to find Ann Medawar's car. Correct?"

"That's right."

"Is it your theory that Dr. Medawar killed his wife, drove her car somewhere and hid it, and then – what? Walked back? Took a taxi back to his own car?"

Bradford objected again. This time Judge Seiler overruled the objection.

"We weren't able to determine how he got rid of the car, unless the nurse helped him. Obviously, it would have been helpful if we could have found the car."

"In the course of your investigation, Detective, did you determine where – geographically – Ann Medawar was shot and killed?"

"No, not precisely."

"You ruled out the Medawar home?"

"Yes."

"Did you rule out the rooms in the Sleep Cheap Inn?"

"No, of course not. The inn has over a hundred rooms."

Garnered hesitated a moment and then said, "Sixty-four, actually."

Bradford jumped to his feet. "I object to counsel testifying."

Garner smiled and said, "Withdrawn." He looked at his notes, and looked back at the witness. "Did you attempt to determine if there was a woman with two children staying at the inn?"

"Yeah, we checked on that."

"What did you do to check on that?"

"We talked with the manager, and he told us there was no one there like that. And he gave us a printout of the inn's registered guests. There were no women on the printout."

"The manager was Diego Olivar?"

"Yeah."

"You didn't get a search warrant to search the inn?"

"We had no probable cause for a search warrant."

"You're aware that Ms. Goessel testified yesterday and brought with her a video of a mother with two toddlers leaving the inn about fifteen minutes after Dr. Medawar left?"

"Yeah, but at the time, we didn't know anything about that."

"Is it possible that the manager, Diego Olivar, lied to you when he told you there was no undocumented woman at the inn?"

Chilton stared at Garner and shrugged noncommittally.

"Yes or no, Detective: In the course of your investigation of Ms. Medawar's death, did you touch base with the patrolman who ticketed Ms. Goessel?"

"No."

Garner glanced back at the list of points to cover in his outline. The pause signaled that he was about to move to a new topic.

"Detective Chilton," he asked when he was ready to resume his cross, "you weren't able to establish that the shooting occurred in Ohio, were you?"

"Look, we didn't rule out the far side of the moon, but the decedent resided in Ohio, she was last seen in Ohio, and her body was found in Ohio. There's no reason to think she was killed anywhere else."

Garner put the large Google map of the Greater Cincinnati area back on the tripod. It was the map on which Dr. Bannerji had marked the locations where the bodies of six Hispanic women had been found. Garner presented Chilton with the six crime scene reports.

Garner did not actually want to spar with Chilton over whether the deaths of the six Hispanic women and the death of Ann Medawar were related. He was sure Chilton would be well-rehearsed and ready with damaging responses. But he also didn't want to leave the issue of the other deaths off the table. His strategy depended on keeping the issue in the jury's mind.

He needed a safe question that reminded the jury of the other women, but that didn't give Chilton a chance to try to explain away those slayings.

"Detective Chilton," he began, "we've heard testimony that seven young women, if you include Ann Medawar, have been brutally killed in the Greater Cincinnati area since June, and that each of those women, including Ann Medawar, was shot twice – once in the chest, and once in the head – and their bodies dumped somewhere away from where they were killed. You're aware of that?"

Chilton's response was uncharacteristically monosyllabic: "Yes."

"Dr. Bannerji was kind enough to mark this map with the locations where each of those young women's bodies was found. Can you see the map from where you seated?"

Another monosyllabic response indicated that he could.

"Detective Chilton, you have in front of you the same reports as did Dr. Bannerji. Do you have any issue with where Dr. Bannerji marked those locations on this map?"

"No. I'm sure Indy – Dr. Bannerji – marked the map just fine."

"Sir, as everybody learns from reading the newspaper, or watching television crime dramas or going to the movies, when there's a serial killer, the police sometimes form a task force or some form of concerted effort to identify and stop the serial killer. In your experience, is that true?"

"Yeah, sure, *if* there's reason to believe there is a serial killer." Chilton stressed the word "if."

"Has the Cincinnati Police Department formed a task force or some other form of concerted effort to identify and arrest the person or persons responsible for killing the women whose bodies were dumped at the locations indicated on this map?"

"Yes and no," Chilton responded. He turned to the jury before continuing. "There is an inter-departmental task force looking at the deaths of the six Hispanic women," he said directly to the jury. "That task force includes law enforcement officers from Kentucky and Indiana as well. But that task force is not looking into the death of Ms. Medawar. We already know who killed her."

Garner felt like he'd just been sucker punched. He had seen the news coverage in which Hamilton County Prosecutor Warren had claimed to have set up a task force to look into the possibility that the deaths of the Hispanic women were related. He had followed up by requesting that the prosecution produce any records relating to that investigation.

Bradford had responded there were no records. As the news reports indicated, Bradford said, Warren had made up the story about having established a task force.

Bradford misled him. Garner was furious.

But he was also standing at the podium with the jury watching. Searching for something quick – and he hoped safe – he asked: "Are you a member of that task force?"

"I'm heading it up," Chilton beamed.

"You're heading it up?" Garner repeated.

"That's right."

Garner looked at his notes. After a long pause, he turned back to Chilton. "You're heading up the task force looking into the slayings of these Hispanic women?" he asked again.

"Yes," Chilton replied, obviously relishing the moment.

"Then, can we assume," Garner said, "that the task force has no clue who the serial killer is?"

Several of the jurors broke into smiles. Chilton's face turned red, his jaw clenched, and his body tensed. He glared at Garner.

"That's what I thought," Garner said. "Not a clue." Turning to Judge Seiler, Garner announced, "No further questions."

"Your Honor," Chilton stammered, turning to Judge Seiler, "I'd like a chance to answer."

"Go ahead."

"We've determined that each of those abductions occurred following a rally by an organization called the League of Natural Born Citizens. They've had these rallies on a monthly basis. The locations vary. They've been in Price Hill, in Clifton, across the river in Florence. They call them 'Make America White Again' rallies. They have speakers ranting about blacks, illegal immigrants, Muslims. They get people all riled up.

"Each of the abductions and killings has occurred after one of those rallies, later that night or in the very early morning hours. For example, they had one of the rallies in Florence in December. The abduction and murder of the waitress from that Mexican restaurant occurred that night.

"We believe there are two killers, working together — some kind of sick buddy thing. We believe one is killing Hispanic women because he wants to send a message that Hispanics aren't welcome in our community. That's why we see bodies dumped at that Center in Lower Price Hill, at the Hispanic festival, at the racetrack over there in Kentucky.

"We believe that the other person in this pair is just a sick freak who wants to kill women and toss their bodies off bridges.

"So, it's not like we don't have a clue. We are on this, and we're going to find out who these killers are."

When Chilton finished, Judge Seiler looked at Garner. "Further cross?"

"Yes, Your Honor. Just briefly." Garner returned to the podium, walking slowly, trying to collect his thoughts. He realized he had been too dismissive of Chilton.

"Detective Chilton," he asked, the question still forming in his mind. "You reviewed the videos and photos that Ann Medawar took in connection with the documentary she and the rest of her class were making?"

"Yes, I know how to do my job, and I did it."

"Ann went to several of the 'Make America White

Again' rallies and caught some of the action on video?"

"That's right."

"She also panned the crowd and took stills of some of the vehicles that people came in?"

"Yes."

"She and her partner in the class even interviewed some of the people at those rallies?"

"Yes."

"Based on your review of her work and based on your own experience investigating this case, was Ann Medawar pursuing the same theory? And by the same theory, I mean that the killer or killers were regulars at the 'Make America White Again' rallies."

"We got there a little differently, but yeah, it looks like she was pursuing the same theory."

"She got there a little before you?"

Chilton stared at Garner. "Actually, she got there well before we did."

"And then somebody killed her?"

"Yes, or we wouldn't be here, but —"

"Detective Chilton," Garner said, cutting the detective off. "Thank you."

Bradford asked a number of follow-on questions about the task force's efforts. His questions were largely aimed at trying to draw distinctions between the "Make America White Again" killers and the murder of Ann Medawar.

And then, switching direction, he asked if the Task Force had been able to determine if Dr. Medawar knew, or had contact with, any of the victims, "besides his wife."

Chilton said they had not been able to determine that.

Bradford also elicited testimony that – unlike Ann Lindsey Medawar – four of the six Hispanic women had been "illegals." Those questions, Garner was certain, were intended more for the media than the jury.

Garner seldom requested permission to conduct further

examination after the prosecution did rebuttal, but Bradford's rebuttal covered new ground. As a rule, Garner also made a point of not asking questions on cross-examination to which he did not know the answer. He decided to break that rule too.

"Just to clarify," he began, "Dr. Medawar is not a suspect in that investigation, correct?"

"Not at this time," Chilton said, twisting the knife.

"When Isabella Ramirez was killed, Dr. Medawar was on duty at the Trauma Center?"

"Yes, he worked that night," Chilton said.

"In fact, at the time someone was killing Ms. Ramirez, Dr. Medawar was operating on Jay-Jay Moore, who the prosecution intends to call as a witness?"

Chilton shifted in his seat. "That's right."

Garner was surprised. It had not occurred to him that Chilton would have checked to see if Medawar was working on the dates of the other slayings — let alone make the connection with the surgery on Moore. Once more, Chilton moved up a couple notches in his estimation.

Garner looked at his notes.

"We touched on this before, but just to be certain we're on the same page. Ann Medawar was apparently focusing on the 'Make America White Again' rallies in an effort to identify the killer, or killers, responsible for murdering these Hispanic women?"

"Asked and answered," Bradford objected.

"Go ahead and answer," Judge Seiler said, "and then I'm sure Mr. Garner will move on."

"Yes, that's what it looks like."

Garner smiled and said, "Thank you, Detective. No further questions."

With that, several reporters dashed out of the courtroom, rushing to be the first to air the latest developments: The police were looking for a pair of serial killers, the "Make America White Again" killers, who were responsible for the string of murders of young Hispanic women. Ann Medawar had been pursuing the same theory, and may have been close to identifying the killers when she was murdered.

11:00 A.M. – 11:05 A.M.

Moments after Detective Chilton left the witness stand, Garner caught up with him in the hallway, just outside Judge Seiler's courtroom.

"What do you want?" Chilton snapped.

"First, I want to apologize," Garner said. "I was angry at Bradford, and I took a cheap shot at you. I shouldn't have done that. I'm sorry."

"And, second, let me guess, you want a favor?"

"No. I wanted to share something with you."

"Go ahead."

"I can't prove it, but I think I know who your killers are."

"You do, huh? A police task force hasn't been able to solve this, but you figured it out on your own."

"These guys ride around in a red pickup truck with a Confederate flag. You can see the truck in the videos Ann took at the rallies."

"There are a lot of pickup trucks at those rallies."

"Detective, I've got to get back in the courtroom. Just take these names, and if you want to know why I think they're the killers, call me later, after I'm out of court."

"Give me the names."

"Sam Scherge and Roger Storrs. The truck belongs to Storrs. They live in an apartment building in Lower Price Hill."

"You seem pretty sure about this," Chilton said, this time without the attitude.

"You don't need me to tell you how to do your job," Garner said. "But if it were me, I'd find out which cell phone towers their cell phones were pinging around the time of the abductions and killings. And around the time the bodies were dumped. I believe these two jerks will show up in all the right places."

"And if it checks out, what do you want in return?"

"I want you to catch them before they kill someone else."

"That's it?"

"That's it," Garner said. He turned and headed quickly back into the courtroom.

TUESDAY, MARCH 8

6:00 P.M. NEWS

Queen City News Live: Bringing you the news you want to hear.

News Anchor Bob Bunker: We report tonight startling, new revelations concerning the police investigation into the brutal murders of at least six young Hispanic women.

Detective James Chilton, who heads the task force investigating those murders, testified that police believe a pair of serial killers is responsible for the murders. Detective Chilton also revealed today that each of the murders took place following the monthly rallies of the League of Natural Born Citizens, suggesting that the killers may have attended those rallies.

Those disclosures came today during testimony in the ongoing homicide trial of Dr. Rafiq Medawar for the slaying of his wife, Ann Lindsey Medawar. During cross-examination, Detective Chilton conceded that Ms. Medawar was investigating the same theory that police are now pursuing and may have been closer to identifying the killers than previously disclosed.

Tiffany Albern has this report.

Tiffany Albern: That's right, Bob. We've prepared this map that shows where each of these murders occurred and the location of the League of Natural Born Citizens rally earlier in the day. The most recent in this string of murders occurred in Florence, after a Natural Born Citizens rally there.

Detective Chilton also disclosed that Ms. Medawar appears to have been pursuing the same theory before her murder and may have been close to identifying the killers. In his testimony, Detective Chilton maintained that there was no evidence linking the League of Natural Born Citizens killers to Ms. Medawar's murder. It is expected, however, that defense attorney Devin Garner will hammer at that possibility in his arguments to the jury at the conclusion of the case.

News Anchor Bob Bunker: Thank you, Tiffany. In other news, today Kentucky Senator Rand Paul proposed an amendment to the Constitution to preclude children born in this country to undocumented immigrants from becoming citizens. More on that after this.

WEDNESDAY, MARCH 9

Bradford called Wendy Yang to testify on Wednesday morning. She would be the day's star witness. Yang was a short, thin woman of about forty-five, with black hair that was prematurely turning grey at the temples. She ran a forensic consulting business and testified frequently for the Hamilton County Prosecutor's office.

The prosecution wanted her to lay the foundation for admission of the videos Ann Medawar took of her husband and the nurse. Yang's expert witness report indicated she would also testify about her reconstruction of where Ann was standing when she took those videos.

As soon as Yang had been sworn in and stated her name and occupation, Garner stood and interrupted. "The defense," he announced, "will stipulate that Ms. Yang is qualified to testify as an expert on the matters detailed in her report."

Garner knew, of course, that Bradford actually wanted to have the witness testify at length about her education, training, experience, and areas of expertise – the better to impress the jury not only with her expertise, but with the importance of the case. His own offer to stipulate was simply meant to let the jury know that Bradford was dragging things out unnecessarily and was wasting their time.

Bradford ignored Garner and proceeded to question Yang at length about her background, before beginning what promised to be a lengthy series of questions intended to lay the foundation for admission of the videos. He was obviously planning to have Yang say she examined Ann Lindsey Medawar's cell phone and verified that the video had not been tampered with.

Garner rose again and offered to stipulate to the admissibility of the videos. It was obvious they were going to be admitted anyway, and he wanted the jury to know the defense wasn't hiding from them.

Once again, Bradford ignored him and returned to his planned questions, but this time Garner pressed his objection. "Your Honor," he complained, "the witness examined the decedent's cell phone and found the videos Ann Medawar made on the day she died. I don't think there is any reason to waste a lot of the jury's time having the witness testify at length about how she found the videos. Everybody knows how to open a cell phone and look at the videos or photos stored on it."

Bradford bristled, but this time Judge Seiler urged him to "move along." In short order, Yang identified and played two video clips – one showing Dr. Medawar and the Filipino nurse entering the inn, the other showing them leaving. Yang testified to the time lapse between the two videos. As she testified, the videos were projected onto a large screen so the jury could see them.

With that, the jury had seen the prosecution's most damaging evidence. But Bradford wasn't done.

"Ms. Yang, were you able to reconstruct from the video approximately where Ms. Medawar was standing when she made these videos?"

"Yes, Sir."

"Please explain how you did that."

"I approached this in two ways. The decedent used an iPhone. The specifications for the iPhone camera give you detailed information about how wide the camera opens up, measured in degrees. As with most digital cameras, it's possible to adjust the focus – to make the image look closer. That affects how much of the scene the camera's lens can take in. With that information, it just took some trigonometry to determine how far away the camera was, depending on the degree of magnification."

"Did that approach pinpoint how far away the decedent was?"

"No, sir, it only provided a range, because you would also need to know where she had the camera set in terms of magnification."

"You also employed a second method?"

"Yes, sir."

"Can you explain that for us?"

"Yes, sir. It was basically trial-and-error. I had two crime scene specialists walk toward and away from the inn entrance, just as the defendant and his companion did in the videos the decedent recorded. I used an iPhone of the same model the decedent used and recorded the scene from a number of angles, until I was able to match the image size and angle on the videos the decedent recorded."

"And did that enable you to determine where the decedent was standing when she made the video of her husband and his companion entering the inn?"

"I was able to approximate that, yes."

"Okay, that was *entering* the inn. Were you also able to determine where the decedent was standing when she made the video of her husband and his companion as they *left* the inn?"

"Yes, sir. Again, I was able to make a close approximation of that."

"And did you prepare a diagram showing those locations?"

"Yes, sir."

Bradford nodded to his paralegal to project a new exhibit on the screen.

"Does this diagram show the approximate locations where the decedent was when she made these videos?"

"Yes, sir. The exhibit shows where the cell phone camera had to be positioned to get the same angle and image size as the videos she made. The locations are indicated by the camera icons, and the distance and angle by the arrows."

"Are those locations within the range of possible locations you determined mathematically?"

"Yes, sir. In both cases, the location is roughly in the middle of the ranges I calculated."

"Would someone entering the inn have been able to see the decedent making this video if she was in the location indicated on the exhibit?"

"No, sir, not if they were looking where they were going. Of course, if they turned or were looking around, they could have seen her. But we don't see them do that in the video."

"Looking at your diagram, your reconstruction placed the decedent in the parking lot of the inn when she made these videos?"

"Yes, sir. Actually, in the area where there are the usual spaces marked off for cars to park in."

"Could she have been standing next to a car or other vehicle in such a way that it would be more difficult or impossible for the defendant to have noticed the decedent making these videos?"

"Yes, sir. In fact, the decedent took several stills and videos of the inn and its parking lot while her husband was inside. If you look at those, you can see that there was a car right in front of where we placed her." Yang gave an exhibit number.

Kemi Adichie, the paralegal from the Prosecutor's office who was operating the projector, brought up the still shot. Yang pointed to where she determined Ann Medawar had been standing.

Bradford turned to Judge Seiler and said, "No further direct, Your Honor."

Garner was impressed. A less experienced attorney, hoping to dazzle the jury with his expertise, would have taken far longer with the witness. In doing so, he might well have gotten mired down in minutiae that would have bored – and quite possibly confused – the jury. In walking Yang through the reconstruction, Bradford had been surgical. For Garner, that meant he had to be as concise or risk giving the jury the impression that he didn't know what he was doing.

He stepped to the podium. He wanted to begin his cross with a question that somehow cut right to the heart of what he needed to show, but it wasn't possible. He decided to start with something safe.

"Ms. Yang, you have been referring to Ann Medawar as the decedent. Can we assume that when she took these videos, she was still alive?"

The witness smiled. "Yes, of course."

"Would it be all right with you if I refer to her as Ann?"

"Yes, sir."

"Ann had an attachment for her cell phone, an adapter lens, isn't that right?"

"Yes, sir. That's in my report."

"And you describe this gadget in your report as a 1.33x Anamorphic Adapter Lens for iPhone, made by a company called Moondog Labs?"

"Yes, sir."

"This device is used to get a wider view, more like what we're used to seeing on television or in the movies?"

"Yes, sir, that's correct."

"And she also had some software on her iPhone that worked with this gadget to squeeze that larger view down and to give her a better-quality picture?"

"Yes, sir. That's in my report as well. The software is called FimicPro, version 5."

"When you went to the inn to re-enact these videos, you stated that you didn't use Ann's cell phone, you used another iPhone provided by your lab?"

"That's right."

"Did you have the same model adapter lens and software on the iPhone camera that you used for this reenactment?"

"Yes, sir. Well, actually we did it both ways — with the adapter and without it."

Garner could see that the witness was beginning to tense. Her face flushed slightly, as if she sensed — or perhaps feared – where Garner was going next with his questions.

"Ms. Yang, you showed the jury an exhibit that shows where – approximately – Ann must have been standing when she made the videos you've shown us."

"Yes, sir."

"Did you make those approximations – the ones shown in your report and on this exhibit – using the camera with the adapter lens?"

"No, sir, those approximations were made with just the iPhone, without the adapter lens."

Yang's face now had noticeably more color. She rubbed her nose.

"You said you also did the re-enactment with the adapter and the extra software?"

"Yes, sir, that's right."

"And were you able to determine where Ann would have been standing if she was using the adapter when she made this video of her husband and the nurse, Angelica Rios, entering the inn?"

"Yes, sir."

"That's not in your report?"

"No, sir. That's not in my report."

"And you didn't include that determination on this diagram either?"

"No, sir."

Garner stood at the podium staring at the witness for a long time – maybe long enough to have counted to thirty under his breath. He could see Yang was uncomfortable.

"If Ann was using the adapter lens, she would have had to stand much closer to the entrance to get the images found on her cell phone camera. Isn't that correct?"

"Yes, sir. If she was using the adapter lens, yes."

"Based on your education, training, experience, and observations, were you able to form an opinion as to whether Ann was using the adapter lens when she made these videos?"

"I was able to do that, yes."

"What opinion did you form?"

"It's my opinion she was using the adapter lens when she made those videos."

"Are you confident about that?"

"Yes, sir, it's actually pretty easy to tell."

That admission was huge, but its importance probably wasn't apparent. Garner glanced at the bailiff to see if his face revealed any reaction. It didn't. Greene was concentrating on a crossword puzzle. Garner glanced at the jury. While the jurors seemed interested, he couldn't tell if they understood the importance of what Yang had just conceded.

"Please show us on your diagram where Ann would have had to have been standing when she made these videos of her husband and Angelica Rios entering the inn?"

Yang stepped down from the witness stand and moved to a spot where she could point to the locations on the image projected on the screen.

"She would have been here for the video of them going into the inn, and here for the exit video."

"At those locations," Garner asked, without waiting for Yang to return to the witness stand, "would it have been easy for Dr. Medawar to see his wife taking the video?"

"Yes, sir. It would have been pretty hard for him not to have seen her."

"Is there a reason you left this out of your report?"

Yang shot a plaintive look at Bradford. The jurors followed her glance and watched Bradford for some reaction. Bradford kept his head down and stared at the legal pad in front of him on counsel table, as if he were deep in thought and unaware of the eyes focused on him.

Garner repeated his question. "Ms. Yang, was there a reason you left this out of your report?"

"Yes, sir."

"And what is that reason?"

"Mr. Warren discussed that with Mr. Bradford and me.

Mr. Warren told me not to include that. He said it was up to you to develop your own expert witness testimony."

Garner took a moment to look at his notes. As he did, Yang returned to the witness chair.

"Ms. Yang, you showed us a clip of Dr. Medawar and Angelica Rios entering the inn, and another one of them leaving the inn. Correct?"

"Yes, sir."

"You actually found two videos of Dr. Medawar and Angelica Rios leaving the inn, didn't you?"

"Yes, sir. They're almost identical."

Turning to the prosecution table, Garner asked, "Ms. Adichie, can you bring up the video the prosecution showed again?"

Adichie complied, and once again, the jurors watched the short video of Dr. Medawar and the nurse leaving the inn.

Garner asked Adichie to show the second video.

She complied, and the jury watched the video on the projection screen.

"Ms. Yang," Garner asked, turning everyone's attention back to the witness, "is this the second clip, the one you and Mr. Bradford didn't show the jury?"

"Yes, sir. As I said," Yang volunteered, "they are almost identical."

"Ms. Yang, you understand that the prosecution claims that Ann suspected her husband of cheating and was hiding outside this inn to collect evidence that he was being unfaithful?"

"Yes, sir. Absolutely."

"And you're aware, the defense contends Ann was there to get some video for the documentary she and her class were making?"

"Yes, sir, I know what the case is about."

Garner had two lines of questions left to ask. He decided to ask first the one the witness was prepared for.

"Ms. Yang, would you agree that using the lens adapter and Filmic software would be consistent with the defense contention that Ann was gathering footage for her video project?"

"Yes, sir, I agree it would be *consistent* with that, but once she had this equipment available, there was no reason for her not to use it if she was trying to get video of her husband having an affair with the nurse. I don't think you can say one way or the other, just from the fact she used this equipment."

Garner was sure Bradford had rehearsed that answer with her in advance. He just wanted to get it out of the way, rather than leave it for Bradford to elicit on re-direct.

"Ms. Yang, can we agree that if Ann were trying to video her husband without being seen, she should have used a regular camera with a telescopic lens, so she could have stood further away."

"Yes – if she knew what she was doing and had a camera with a telephoto lens."

"Ms. Yang, as we just discussed, Ann made two videos – two takes – of her husband and Nurse Rios leaving the inn. Is it customary, when you're trying to video someone without their knowing it, to ask them re-do the scene?"

Bradford jumped to his feet and objected. "Argumentative!"

Without waiting for a response from Garner, Judge Seiler overruled the objection.

"No, obviously, you don't do that if you don't want the subject to know you're making a video."

"In your professional opinion, if Ann asked her husband and Nurse Rios to walk back into the inn and come out again so that she could get a better shot, would you say it was likely that she was attempting to get video for her documentary?"

"Yes, sir, if that's how she got the two videos."

"In your professional opinion, would the fact that Ann

was standing where her husband could see her when he entered the inn and again when he left the inn, also be consistent with making a documentary and inconsistent with a hidden video?"

"Yes, sir."

"Did Mr. Warren ask you to leave those opinions out of your report?"

"Yes, sir."

"Thank you, Ms. Yang," Garner said. "I think we've got the picture."

THURSDAY, MARCH 10

MORNING

On Thursday morning, the prosecution resumed its case with its diciest, but perhaps most essential witness – Jasper "Jay-Jay" Moore. The witness was a gang member, frequent drug user, and sometime drug dealer – which put him in the class of people who regularly arrived by ambulance at the Trauma Center.

Before getting to the point of his appearance, Bradford elicited from Jay-Jay Moore testimony that Dr. Medawar had operated on him twice – once when Moore had been stabbed and more recently when he had been rushed to the Trauma Center with a life-threatening gunshot wound.

Moore testified that, following his most recent surgery, Dr. Medawar asked for help obtaining an unregistered gun. Moore said this happened while he was recovering from his gunshot surgery – which, if true, placed the conversation in the month before Ann Medawar had been killed.

Under a grant of immunity, Moore claimed he had found a Glock 9mm pistol for Medawar. He bragged that he did not charge the doctor for the gun, but had given it to him, because, "you know, the doctor, he saved my worthless ass."

"You didn't make Dr. Medawar pay you for the gun," Bradford restated Moore's testimony in more courtroom-appropriate language, "because you felt grateful to him because he saved your life?"

"Not just once, man," Jay-Jay Moore replied. "He saved my worthless ass twice."

To take the sting out of the expected cross-examination, Bradford led the colorful witness through his prior convictions and a well-rehearsed explanation that in exchange for his testimony, the prosecution had agreed not to charge him in connection with the transfer of the weapon. The prosecution had also agreed to reduce his sentence on unrelated drug charges.

There were almost no specifics in Moore's testimony. When it was his turn to cross-examine, Garner decided to focus on the lack of detail. He began by asking, "Where, specifically, were you when gave this gun to Dr. Medawar?"

"I think it was there at the hospital," Moore responded.

"Where exactly in the hospital?"

"I don't remember."

Garner flipped through the papers he brought with him to the podium, as if looking for one in particular. He pulled a document out and glanced over it.

"Mr. Moore, are you sure it was in the hospital? Are you sure you didn't tell the police that you met Dr. Medawar in a chili parlor to give him the gun?" The paper in his hand said nothing about that.

"Yeah, maybe. Maybe that's where it was." Moore scratched his head. "Like I said, I don't remember."

"You testified that you gave the gun to Dr. Medawar sometime after the surgery for your gunshot wound. Can you be more specific?"

"About what?"

"About when you supposedly gave this gun to Dr. Medawar."

"No. It was after I was released from the hospital. I musta still been on painkillers. It's all kinda a blur, man."

"How did you get this gun?" Garner asked.

"I bought it."

"How much did you pay for it?"

"Five hundred dollars, maybe. I don't remember."

"Where did you get five hundred dollars?"

"It might not have been that much. I don't really remember."

"Who did you buy this gun from?"

"The gun dude." Moore smiled.

"Who is the 'gun dude'?"

"The gun dude? He be the man brothers go to when they need a piece."

"What's his name?"

"I don't know."

"Does he have a nickname? A street name?"

"I guess."

"What does he go by?"

"I don't know."

"What does the 'gun dude' look like?"

"Like a brother."

"He's black?"

"Yeah, man. He be black."

"Was he short? Tall?"

"I don't remember."

"You can't recall if he was short or tall," Garner repeated in disbelief. "Was he in a wheelchair?"

"I don't think so."

"Was he fat or skinny?"

"Fat, I guess."

Garner brandished another document as if ready to contradict Moore with it. "Didn't you tell the police he was skinny?"

"Maybe, I don't recall." Moore hedged.

"How did you contact 'the gun dude'?"

"I went where he be."

"And where was that?"

"I don't remember. Like I said, I was on painkillers, man."

"You have no idea at all where you found the 'gun dude' and purchased the gun?"

"It might have been in Lincoln Heights, the West End, someplace like that."

Out of frustration as much as anything, Garner asked Moore if he might have gotten the gun at the Sleep Cheap Inn.

"No way!" Moore replied. "No way I be going there."

"And why is that?" Garner asked.

"If a brother went there, those Mexicans would shoot his ass."

Garner suspected the last response was Moore's way of getting back at the prosecutor without reneging on his deal, but he couldn't rule out the possibility Moore was trying to help Dr. Medawar.

Of course, it was also possible, just that once, Moore had seen no reason not to tell the truth.

AFTERNOON

After the lunch break, the prosecution presented elaborate testimony by the pathologist from the Hamilton County Coroner's office who performed the autopsy on Ann Lindsey Medawar.

The pathologist testified that he removed a 9mm slug from her body. He described the location of the slug and the likely angle from which it had been fired. He also testified that a second slug had ripped through her body and exited the other side. The pathologist concluded his testimony by stating that in his opinion, the gunshots were the cause of death and that death would have been essentially instantaneous.

The pathologist also testified that he believed the time of death would have been between 10:00 a.m. and 1:00 p.m. on Friday. Bradford had him explain in detail the basis for his opinion.

Aside from establishing the time of death, the testimony was unnecessary, but provided a suitably gruesome conclusion to the substantive portion of the prosecution case — a conclusion calculated to leave an indelible impression on the jurors.

Garner had no basis for disputing the time of death and so had nothing to gain from an extended cross-examination. "Doctor," he asked when he took his turn at the podium, "did your autopsy reveal the identity of the person who shot Ann Lindsey Medawar?"

"No," the pathologist responded, condescendingly, "that's not the purpose of an autopsy."

"Then, I don't see any point in wasting more of the court's – and jury's – time." Turning to the judge, Garner added, "No further questions."

As he returned to the defense table, Garner could see Bradford smirk.

FRIDAY, MARCH 11

9:00 A.M. – 10:00 A.M.

John Crackstone, the gun identification or "ballistics" expert from the Hamilton County Coroner's office was an experienced witness. He had a reputation of being meticulous almost to a fault, but honest and objective. In his own past encounters with Crackstone, Garner had always found him to be that way.

Almost sixty-five years old, Crackstone was tall and lean, with salt-and-pepper hair. He was soft spoken and old-school polite. When he entered the courtroom, he wore, as usual, gray dress slacks and a tweed sports coat. The jacket had leather elbow patches. Crackstone came across as a beloved, if perhaps overly fastidious, college professor.

In the prosecution's pretrial materials, Bradford listed the subject of Crackstone's testimony simply as identification of the weapon or bullets that killed Ann Medawar. As his expert witness report, Bradford produced the report concluding that a 9mm Glock pistol fired the slug removed from Ann Medawar.

Juries expect CSI-like evidence, and Crackstone could provide some of that. He could also tie in Jay Jay's More's testimony about giving Medawar a 9mm Glock to the crime.

Garner expected to counter that by questioning Crackstone about his reports identifying the slugs from the Hispanic women as all having been fired by a Glock 9mm pistol. In short, Garner did not expect Crackstone's testimony to change the trajectory of the trial.

But when Bradford announced he was calling Crackstone as his next witness, he handed Garner a new report. Garner raced through the report as Crackstone took the oath and seated himself in the witness box. As he did, Garner saw he had a huge problem.

Bradford began by walking Crackstone through his credentials and extensive experience. Garner tried to head that off. He offered to stipulate that Crackstone was well qualified as an expert witness. Bradford wasn't having it. He laid it on thick.

Bradford also anticipated the usual defense line of attack. He had Crackstone acknowledge that he had testified for the county in a great many cases. To balance that, he also elicited that Crackstone had testified for the defense in other cases.

When he turned to the substance of the ballistics testimony, Bradford had Crackstone describe in detail the procedures he followed in identifying the slug removed from Ann Medawar.

Bradford then turned to a new topic.

"Mr. Crackstone, just so you know where I'm going with this next series of questions, the defense has made much in this trial of the fact that several young Hispanic women have been shot to death over the past year. You're aware of those shootings?"

"Yes, I believe so," Crackstone said.

"The defense," Bradford continued, "has even gone so far, in its effort to deflect attention from Dr. Medawar, as to suggest that whoever shot those women may have also shot Ms. Medawar. You're aware of that?"

"So you've told me," Crackstone replied.

Garner knew Bradford could care less whether Crackstone was following the trial. He was simply setting the stage for the jury, but had to frame his scene setting in the form of questions.

Bradford pointed Crackstone to the map showing where and when each of the slain Hispanic women was found. The map showed the names of the victims and the dates of their deaths.

"Mr. Crackstone, have you and your team in the Coroner's office examined the slugs taken from the six Hispanic women identified on that chart?

Crackstone carefully checked the names against the reports in front of him. "Yes, we have," he said.

"Did you supervise and participate in that work yourself?

"Yes."

"What, if any, conclusions, did you draw about the guns used in those shootings?" Bradford asked.

Garner rose. "For clarification," he asked, "are you asking the witness to testify at this point just about the slugs removed from the Hispanic women?"

"That's correct," Bradford replied.

"You're not asking, at this juncture, for him to compare those slugs with slugs removed from anyone else?"

"Correct," Bradford said in a clipped, almost curt, response.

Crackstone had compared the slugs removed from the Hispanic women to determine if the same gun had fired them. That was not disclosed before trial, but Crackstone's conclusions were actually helpful to the defense. Garner would not object to *that* testimony. He would save his objection for Crackstone's other, more damaging, new analysis.

Crackstone testified that the slugs removed from the several Hispanic women had been fired by two different guns, both 9mm Glocks. Bradford had Crackstone address each victim separately.

Then, moving to the defense's map, he asked, "Mr. Crackstone, you've testified that whoever killed these young Hispanic women used two different guns of the same type in these murders. Did you find a pattern in the way the killer, or killers, used these guns?"

"Yes, I did," Crackstone replied, answering only the precise, yes-no question Bradford asked.

"What was that pattern?"

"The killer or killers," Crackstone responded, "used these weapons in alternating months. In other words, the killer, or killers, used one gun in the months in which the victims' bodies were tossed off a bridge. The killer or killers used a second gun in the months in between.

"This suggests," Crackstone explained, "that there were two killers, working together, each with his own Glock 9mm. It looks like they took turns killing these young women and deciding how to dispose of their bodies."

"Turning now to my final topic," Bradford said, letting Garner know he was now moving to the critical new material. "Have you—"

Garner jumped to his feet, shouting, "Objection!"

Judge Seiler glanced in his direction, waiting for Garner to state the nature of his objection.

"Your Honor, as Mr. Crackstone was about to be seated in the witness chair, the prosecution handed me a new expert witness report. I believe the prosecution is about to inquire into matters disclosed for the first time in that new report.

"The issue," Garner suggested, "is one the court may want to consider outside the hearing of the jury."

"Is that correct, Mr. Bradford? Are you intending to question the witness about matters not covered by your pretrial disclosures?"

"Yes, Your Honor," Bradford said. "I'd like the opportunity to explain."

Judge Seiler sent the jury out with the usual admonition not to discuss the case until all the evidence was in and he had instructed them on the legal issues.

Garner argued first.

"As Mr. Bradford was calling Mr. Crackstone to the witness stand, he handed me a brand-new expert report. This new report indicates Mr. Crackstone has done an analysis comparing the slugs removed from the Hispanic women with the slug removed from Ann Medawar."

"My specific objection," he told Judge Seiler, "is to Mr. Crackstone testifying to this new analysis. Your Honor knows the rules and your own pretrial orders. The prosecution was required to disclose that *before* the trial began. The prosecution didn't follow the rules. It is now barred from having Mr. Crackstone testify to the new matters covered in today's report. As Your Honor knows," Garner said, "the rule says conclusions not disclosed before trial 'shall' be excluded. It's mandatory."

Garner broadened his objection. "There's a larger issue here," he said. "The prosecution is deliberately disregarding the rules. It clearly did that with Ms. Wang's report. She testified that Warren had her prepare a report that left out material that was clearly exculpatory. And now, he wants to hand me a new expert witness report as the expert is taking the witness stand. The rules are intended to do away with trial by ambush, but that's we have here."

"If the defendant is to get a fair trial," Garner insisted, "it's essential that the court exclude Crackstone's testimony."

Garner glanced sideways at Bradford, before continuing. "There is no exception to the pretrial disclosure rules," he concluded, "for cases in which the prosecutor thinks the defendant is a Syrian or a Muslim. Nor should there be."

Bradford rose, obviously angry, and made his counterarguments in a voice louder and more emotional than usual for him.

"The prosecution did not anticipate — and could not have been expected to anticipate — the defense strategy of blaming some supposed serial killer," Bradford began. "The prosecution had no way of knowing the defense would try to blame the murder of Ms. Medawar on whoever is responsible for killing these young Hispanic women. The theory was just too absurd. Ms. Medawar, after all, was not Hispanic."

"Besides," Bradford said, "it's obvious who killed her. Her husband. The rest of this is a red herring."

Judge Seiler looked as if he was about to say something,

but didn't.

"It was only after it became clear," Bradford went on, "that this strange argument was central to the defense, that we asked the Coroner's office to determine if the argument had merit."

"Mr. Crackstone's report," he summed up, "isn't late. It is late-breaking news."

Bradford also heatedly rejected the allegation that the prosecution had not played by the rules or had not timely divulged potentially exculpatory materials. "But even if that were true," he argued, "the evidence Mr. Garner wants to exclude is too important to keep from the jury. It would put the criminal justice in a bad light if the jury were to decide this case without hearing what Crackstone has to say. The public would lose whatever faith it still has in jury trials."

"One final point, Your Honor," Bradford said. "The Coroner's office had trouble completing the report sooner, not because it wanted to ambush the defense, but because of its workload. As Your Honor knows, there has been an upswing in heroin overdoses this year. There has been an upswing in crime in certain minority and immigrant communities."

Garner was livid. He had to measure his words carefully to be sure he didn't lose the argument by overacting. He ran his hand through his hair and took a deep breath.

"Your Honor, four months ago, just after Thanksgiving, I met with Mr. Bradford in the Prosecutor's office. I showed him a version of the same video I showed the court before the trial. Ms. Hixson was there, just as she was when I showed the documentary here. Ms. Adichie was there as well.

"That video laid out the defense theory that a serial killer was responsible for the murder of these Hispanic women, that Ann Medawar was pursuing that story in connection with her documentary, and that the serial killer, or killers, may have killed her to avoid exposure. I spelled all that out for him.

"I'm at a loss to understand how the prosecution could be surprised that we would present that theory at this trial. The prosecution cannot claim surprise. Mr. Bradford – quite literally – has seen this movie before."

After further back and forth, Judge Seiler indicated he was ready to make his ruling. He opened his copy of the Ohio Rules and flipped the pages to the rule governing discovery in criminal cases.

"Mr. Bradford," he began, "I am profoundly troubled that the prosecution waited until now to disclose this report. As you know, the purpose of discovery is to provide both parties with –." Judge Seiler paused to read from the rule book – "the information necessary for a full and fair adjudication of the facts."

"The easy thing for me to do would be to exclude the testimony because the report is late. But the rules also stress that they should be interpreted to protect not just the parties, but to –." Again, Judge Seiler read from the rule book, "'to protect the integrity of the justice system.' I don't think it protects the integrity of the justice system, or respect for the courts, if the jury were to decide this case without knowing what Mr. Crackstone has determined."

Turning to Garner, Judge Seiler continued. "The rule also stresses that the obligations it creates are mutual. While I believe the prosecution could have, and should have, produced this report sooner, the defense could have retained its own ballistics expert.

"I am going to allow the testimony," he concluded, "but will consider other measures, if necessary, to assure that we have a fair trial."

The bailiff brought the jury back.

"With your permission, Your Honor," Bradford said, making sure Judge Seiler was ready for him to resume.

Judge Seiler looked to make sure the court reporter was ready. "Proceed," he said.

With that, Bradford moved in for the kill.

"Mr. Crackstone, have you," he asked, "compared the slugs removed from the bodies of these young Hispanic women with the slug removed from the body of Ann Lindsey Medawar?"

"Yes, sir," Crackstone said. "I have."

"Based on your examination, your training and your experience, were you able to form an opinion as to whether the slug removed from Ms. Medawar's body was fired by either of the guns used in the shootings of these Hispanic women?" Bradford asked.

"Yes, sir," Crackstone responded.

"And what conclusion did you draw?"

"The slug found in Ms. Medawar was not fired by either of the guns used to kill those other women. Different weapons fired them. Another Glock 9mm, but not the guns used to kill these young Hispanic women."

Bradford had Crackstone explain in elaborate detail the basis for his conclusion. The explanation was something any "CSI" fan on the jury would be sure to enjoy.

But from Garner's perspective, the explanation was anti-climactic. The prosecution had already put a bullet in the heart of his most dramatic argument.

10:00 A.M. – 10:30 A.M.

Garner had been careful not to tie his defense exclusively to the theory that the "Make America White Again" killers had killed Ann. But he had not devoted as much trial time to any other theory. The jury might well believe that he had put all his eggs in that basket.

Nothing he could ask Crackstone was going to solve that problem. Garner decided to limit the focus of his cross-examination. He would not attack Crackstone's conclusion. He had no basis for doing so, and he knew enough about Crackstone's meticulous work to trust his conclusions — even if he didn't like them.

Instead, he decided to probe why Crackstone had not made the comparison sooner. He would begin with a foundational question: *When had he first compared the slugs from the Hispanic women with the slug from Ann's body?* Then, he would chip away at why that comparison had not been done sooner.

The tactic conceded the validity of Crackstone's opinion and risked reinforcing it. But Garner hoped he would be able to lay the basis for a subsequent motion aimed at Bradford's failure to produce the report sooner. And, he wanted to have a solid record for appeal if the jury convicted.

"Mr. Crackstone, good morning," Garner began. "I'd like to say it's a pleasure to see you again, but given the nature of your work, I hope you'll pardon me if I don't."

Crackstone smiled politely.

"When did you first compare the slugs from—"

Garner stopped, excused himself, and returned to counsel table. He took a drink of water. He probably needed the hydration, but his purpose had been to rethink his question. He decided not to go immediately to the comparison with the slug from Ann. He needed to go in smaller steps.

"Mr. Crackstone, when did you first compare the slugs removed from these Hispanic women? In other words, when did you first consider the possibility that these Hispanic women might have been shot by the same weapon?"

"Well, informally, right away. But the slugs from the first two victims didn't match up. Later, we were able to compare the slugs from the first four victims. That's when we knew we were on to something."

"Did you write up a report to that effect?"

"Yes, sir."

"That would have been – what, in October or November?"

"Yes, sir."

"Did you give that report to Mr. Bradford?"

Crackstone grimaced. "I was hoping you weren't going

to ask me that."

"My client wishes someone hadn't murdered the woman he loved, Mr. Crackstone. Did you give that report to Mr. Bradford, or let him know you had done that analysis and what your results were?"

"Yes, I gave him the report. He read it and gave it back to me. He was upset. He said I should not have put my conclusions in writing. He said Warren would be angry and that I should lose the report."

Bradford objected and moved to strike Crackstone's answer.

Judge Seiler overruled the objection.

"Did you lose the report?" Garner asked

"No, of course not. I don't work for Mr. Warren."

"Mr. Bradford did not disclose your report. Do you know why that is?"

Bradford objected.

Judge Seiler overruled the objection. "Mr. Crackstone," Judge Seiler counseled the witness, "the question is: Do you know?"

"I don't know anything about that," Crackstone said, "other than that he didn't take the report with him."

"Do you remember when that was," Garner pressed, "or the circumstances of that encounter?"

"I don't recall the date. Mr. Bradford just said he had to produce any reports relating to the slain Hispanic women. He was making the rounds, making sure he had everything."

"Did Mr. Bradford instruct you not to compare the slugs from the slain Hispanic women with the slug from Ann Medawar?"

"Yes. He was quite emphatic about it."

"And did you agree not to do that comparison?"

"Not exactly."

"I don't know what that means," Garner said. "How did you respond to Mr. Bradford?"

Bradford objected. Judge Seiler summarily overruled

the objection.

"I told him to go shit in his hat," Crackstone said. He turned to Judge Seiler. "I'm sorry about the language, Your Honor."

"Entirely understandable, under the circumstances," Judge Seiler replied, looking at Bradford.

"When did you first compare the slug from Ms. Medawar with the slugs from the Hispanic women?"

"Shortly after that exchange."

"In early December?"

"That sounds right, but I don't recall the exact date.

"Did there come a time when Mr. Bradford reversed himself? In other words, did there comes a time when he asked you to do that comparison?"

"Yes, sir."

"And when was that?"

"That would have been last week."

"And did you do that comparison in response to Mr. Bradford's request?

"Yes. We went back and redid everything and prepared a new report."

"Were your conclusions the same?"

"Yes, but these slugs were all fired from 9mm Glocks. It was worth redoing, just to be sure."

Okay, Garner realized, that was the proverbial one question too many, but he'd had to ask it. Garner advised the court that he had no more questions. He added that he wished to renew his earlier motion.

"I will take your motion under advisement," Judge Seiler said. "We can discuss it later."

"Mr. Bradford," Judge Seiler asked, "do you have any further questions for the witness?"

Bradford did not.

10:45 A.M. – 11:55 A.M.

The prosecution ended its case with the parents of Ann

Medawar, who testified about what a wonderful and loving daughter Ann was. Evidence rules did not permit the Lindseys to testify to their suspicion that Rafiq Medawar was somehow responsible for their daughter's death, but the fact that they testified for the prosecution told the jury everything it needed to know.

Garner saw nothing to be gained by attempting to cross-examine the grieving parents, and a lot to lose. He waived cross-examination.

As Mrs. Lindsey, still wiping away tears, left the witness stand, Bradford announced that the prosecution rested.

After lunch, the court reconvened – without the jury – for the inevitable motion to dismiss the charges.

Garner moved for dismissal, arguing passionately that the prosecution had not presented anything like enough evidence to convict his client. The prosecution established that Ann Lindsey Medawar was shot to death, but had presented no evidence demonstrating that his client had committed that crime. He also argued that the prosecution had not established that the killing took place in Ohio, and thus had not established that the court had jurisdiction.

Garner made a second motion as well. He argued the prosecution failed to honor its obligation to disclose potentially exculpatory materials. Worse, he argued, the prosecution had instructed Yang to withhold conclusions that undermined the prosecution's theory of the case. On top of that, the prosecution had failed to produce – and had actively tried to suppress – the analysis Crackstone had done, demonstrating that the shooting deaths of the several Hispanic women were related.

The prosecution had also instructed Crackstone not to compare the slugs from those cases with the slug from Ann Medawar – out of concern that the analysis would show that Dr. Medawar was innocent.

The prosecution had failed to disclose the inter-departmental task force looking into the murders of the Hispanic women. And it also failed to disclose any documents the task force may have generated.

"That's what has come to light so far," Garner concluded. "What else has the prosecution withheld?"

Responding to the motion to dismiss, Bradford argued that the prosecution had presented evidence of motive, means and opportunity. "We have shown" he said, "that Dr. Medawar had a motive – his wife caught him going into a sleazy hotel with another woman. We have shown that he had the means to commit the crime – our witness, Jay-Jay Moore, testified to giving him a 9mm Glock. And he had opportunity. Dr. Medawar was the last person to see his wife alive. Issues of credibility and the weight to be given the evidence are for the jury."

Bradford also argued that any irregularities with respect to the murders of the Hispanic women were meaningless, as the prosecution had shown that those killings were unrelated.

Bradford angrily rejected the assertion that the prosecution had withheld exculpatory evidence. The prosecution, he argued, had no obligation to prepare expert testimony for the defense. The defense could have retained its own experts to analyze the slugs. The same was true of the camera images.

The interdepartmental task force was not looking into Ann Medawar's death. It was completely irrelevant.

Judge Seiler said he wanted to reflect on this decision and announced that the court would be in recess for fifteen minutes.

While Judge Seiler was in chambers, Garner told Medawar that the court should dismiss the case as too weak to go the jury. But he also warned that courts don't dismiss high profile cases on motions to dismiss. Judges in Ohio are elected. No elected judge dared risk being perceived as weak on crime. With all the publicity the case had received, Judge Seiler would deny his motions to dismiss.

When Judge Seiler returned, he denied the motion to dismiss for insufficient evidence without explanation. But to Garner's surprise, Judge Seiler did not rule on the motion to dismiss for prosecutorial misconduct. Instead, he announced he was holding his ruling on that motion until the trial ended.

Garner would be forced to put on a defense case.

1:05 P.M. – 1:35 P.M.

After the lunch break, Devin Garner began the defense with Father Joseph Zaidan, the pastor of St. Anthony of Padua Church on Victory Parkway, in East Walnut Hills.

Father Zaiden testified that, according to the church's meticulously kept records, Rafiq Anthony Medawar was baptized in the church two weeks after his birth. When Rafiq was an eighth grader, the Maronite Catholic bishop confirmed him. On a more light-hearted note, Father Zaidan said that when Rafiq graduated from the eighth grade, the pastor at the time gave Medawar a special blessing – to protect him from the Jesuits at St. Xavier High School.

Father Zaidan testified that he personally presided at Rafiq's wedding to Ann Lindsey. And yes, sadly, he presided at Ann's funeral.

The purpose of Father Zaiden's testimony was to humanize Rafiq Medawar – and to make sure the jury did not believe that he was a hot-tempered Syrian immigrant hellbent on imposing Sharia law.

Bradford waived cross-examination for much the same reasons Garner had not wanted to cross-examine Ann's parents.

Judge Seiler had other matters he needed to deal with and recessed the trial for the weekend.

FRIDAY, MARCH 11

6:00 P.M. NEWS

Queen City News Live: Bringing you the news you want to hear.

News Anchor Bob Bunker: The prosecution completed its case today in the homicide trial of Dr. Rafiq Medawar. The former Trauma Center physician is charged in the shooting death of his wife, Ann Lindsey Medawar. Tiffany Albern is at the Hamilton County Courthouse and has this report.

Tiffany Albern: Thank you, Bob. I'm here with Professor Eitel from the University of Cincinnati Law School.

Professor Eitel, from your perspective, where do things stand now that the prosecution has ended its case?

Professor Eitel: The main thing is, the prosecution got past the defense motion to dismiss. I think that's the headline. The defense has raised significant questions about the prosecution theory that Ann Medawar was secretly videoing her husband. As the defense pointed out, if you're trying to video someone without their knowledge, you don't ask them to re-do the scene.

Tiffany Albern: Have there been any other surprises?

Professor Eitel: Well, the defense got a big surprise today. The defense was pointing to the recent string of murders of young Hispanic women. Defense attorney Devin Garner was attempting to suggest that Ms. Medawar was looking into those slayings and that whoever is behind those slayings became nervous and killed her.

The prosecution shot that down with testimony from John Crackstone, the gun identification expert. He testified the slugs removed from the Hispanic women do not match the slug removed from Ann Medawar.

Tiffany Albern: Defense counsel also moved to dismiss the charges against Dr. Medawar based on what Mr. Garner called prosecutorial misconduct. Can you explain what that's about? Is Devin Garner simply whining?

Professor Eitel: Tiffany, we hold prosecutors to a high standard, but too often, we see prosecutors cut corners. In particular, we sometimes see prosecutors withhold exculpatory evidence. And that certainly seems to be the case here.

What we've seen so far, is that the prosecution has withheld important exculpatory evidence. That evidence throws into question the whole decision to prosecute Dr. Medawar. It also creates possible grounds for appeal if Dr. Medawar is convicted. It's not like Bill Bradford to do that. But what puzzles me more is that some of this was pretty obvious stuff. You have to wonder if Hamilton County Prosecutor Dick Warren is calling the shots on this.

Tiffany Albern: Professor, will Dr. Medawar testify on his own behalf?

Professor Eitel: The conventional wisdom is you don't put the defendant on the witness stand unless you have to. But that stems in part from the fact that the usual defendant may have a criminal record or may have some other problem. Dr. Medawar has no record. He's a smart guy. But even so, one mistake by the defendant on the witness stand can be fatal. So, it will certainly be interesting to see if the defense has Dr. Medawar testify.

Tiffany Albern: Reporting live from the Hamilton County courthouse.

Co-Anchor Ashley Gelb: We'll be back after this.

SATURDAY, MARCH 12

11:35 A.M. – 11:55 A.M.

It was Saturday morning, and Diego Olivar was sitting with a companion in the Tienda y Taqueria, or grocery and eatery, on State Street in Lower Price Hill. His companion, Felix Pérez, was one of the men from the cartel. A very dangerous man.

Olivar was waiting for the call from the two women who were watching the apartment building where the Anglos lived. The Anglos were the *cabrones* who had been killing Mexican women.

Today, Olivar swore to himself, those *cabrones* would have to account to God for what they had done.

About noon, as Olivar was stirring a new cup of coffee, the women called to say that the Anglos were leaving.

Olivar and his companion left the Taqueria, got into a van, and drove quickly the few blocks to the apartment building. Olivar pulled to a stop directly in front of the building. The two Anglos were still standing there talking. They looked up, wary.

Olivar quickly jumped from the van and shouted, "¡Hola! ¡Hola, *amigo*s!" His companion got out on the passenger side, smiled and waved. Olivar and his companion opened the rear doors to the van. Each pulled out a bag of groceries and wrapped an arm around it. Each reached back into the van and with some effort pulled out a large Mexican sombrero.

"These are for you!" Olivar shouted to the two Anglos standing not far from the door to the apartment building. "We – your neighbors – we heard what happened to you," Olivar said. "*No Bueno, no Bueno!*" Olivar said, shaking his head, heading toward the Anglos.

"We wanted you to know that the community is not like

that," Olivar continued. He walked toward the two Anglos. "Please accept these," he said, offering the bag of groceries to the taller man.

Despite the crutches he was using, Roger Storrs – looking somewhat confused – reached for the bag. Later, when the police tried to piece together what happened next, they were uncertain. Maybe Sam Scherge saw something. Maybe he had better instincts. But he didn't accept the bag of groceries offered by Diego Olivar's companion. Scherge reached instead for the gun stuck in his belt.

Better instincts or not, Scherge did not get to use his gun. Before he could, Olivar and his companion fired the handguns they carried, concealed by the sombreros. The Anglos were dead before their bodies hit the ground. Not satisfied, Olivar pulled the trigger to his revolver twice more – firing a kill shot to each man's head. He wanted to make sure both were dead, and he wanted to avenge the two women they had taken from him.

Olivar muttered a curse, and then he and his companion dashed back to the van they had come in. Olivar guided the van through Lower Price Hill and turned up the steep hill to Mt. Echo Park. When they reached the pavilion, Olivar parked the van. He wiped his fingerprints from the steering wheel and door handle. He and his companion switched to Olivar's Honda sedan.

Olivar drove toward the expressway, being careful not to speed or run a red light. He had agreed to drive the cartel guy to Lexington, where he would catch a flight to Mexico. The cartel guy refused to fly out of the Cincinnati airport. The police, he said, might be looking for any Hispanic male trying to leave from there for Mexico.

Olivar thought that gave the police too much credit, but he didn't argue. This cartel bastard was not someone you argued with. Besides, for all he knew, there might be another reason he wanted to go to Lexington. He might be picking up money in Lexington and taking it back to the bosses in

Mexico.

Olivar pulled his Honda onto the expressway and turned the car radio on. He switched it to 97.7, the local Spanish language station. The station was playing an oldie – Rubén Blades singing "Pedro Navala." Olivar turned the volume up.

1:35 P.M. – 1:40 P.M.

On Saturday afternoon, when Mrs. Trottel called, Devin Garner was in his office working with Rafiq Medawar and Carrie Hixson.

The prosecution had blown a large hole in the case Garner expected to put on. Crackstone, the ballistics expert, destroyed the argument that the "Make America White Again" killers shot Ann. Aside from the fact that she and Ann were working on a documentary about undocumented immigrants, that also rendered useless any testimony Carrie Hixson could provide.

Hixson argued that the men who were killing the Hispanic women may have simply used a different gun when they killed Ann. *Who knew how many guns they had?*

Medawar returned to his argument that he should testify. He wanted to tell the jury how much he loved Ann. He felt he could handle any cross-examination Bradford threw at him.

Garner wasn't sold on either approach. When Mrs. Trottel called, he welcomed the diversion.

Mrs. Trottel said she read in the newspaper that Carrie was going to testify on Monday. "Was that true?" she wanted to know.

Garner looked at Hixson, who couldn't hear what Mrs. Trottel was saying. "We haven't decided yet."

"She's such a lovely girl," Mrs. Trottel said.

"Yes, Ma'am," Garner said, smiling at Hixson. "I think she's a lovely young woman too."

"She's still single, isn't she?" Mrs. Trottel asked. "I don't know why some eligible young bachelor hasn't married her."

"Yes, Ma'am. That is surprising, isn't it?"

"Well, I was wondering," Mrs. Trottel asked, "if it would be all right if I brought Jonas down to the courthouse to hear Carrie testify. He just thinks the world of her, you know."

"Yes, Ma'am. If she testifies, that would be fine."

Garner glanced at Hixson. "I'll tell Carrie that there is going to be an eligible bachelor in the courtroom rooting for her."

"Now, Devin, you know who I had in mind. Shame on you!" Mrs. Trottel laughed. "But I should tell you the real reason why I called. Did you hear that someone shot those two men – the ones who beat up that poor man. You know who I mean, that man who lives down the street in the Co-Op?"

"No, I hadn't heard. When was that?"

"Just a little bit ago. It was terrible! The police are still there. Killed them in broad daylight. I knew those two were nothing but trouble. I told Jonas not to have anything to do with them. You heard me!"

"Someone shot the two guys," Garner repeated for the benefit of Carrie and Rafiq, "who beat up Jabari Chan."

"You told Jonas, too!" Mrs. Trottel said. "Maybe he listened to you. Well, thank goodness he wasn't with them."

"Where was Jonas when this happened?" Garner asked.

"Jonas," Mrs. Trottel asked, "what were you doing when those men were killed? Come here and tell me."

Garner waited for Mrs. Trottel.

"He says he was up in the park, making his videos like usual." Mrs. Trottel said.

Garner smiled. "I'm glad he wasn't with them."

"He wants to know when he can see Carrie and show her his 'documentary'? I swear, if you don't do something about that girl, Jonas just might!"

"Mrs. Trottel, why don't you and Jonas come here now.

Carrie is here. I think we'd all like to see the video Jonas made."

1:40 P.M. – 2:15 P.M.

When the Trottels arrived, Carrie Hixson connected the digital camera she had given Jonas Trottel to her laptop so the group could see his videos.

"The videos are from this morning," Jonas wanted everyone to know. "I was making a documentary about the squirrels."

"Where were you when you shot these?" Hixson asked.

"In the park," Jonas said.

"Mt. Echo Park," Mrs. Trottel explained. "He likes to go there. He's got young legs. I'd never make it up that hill."

"They're just squirrels," Jonas said, ignoring his mother. "Except for the bad men."

"What bad men?" Hixson asked.

"They were saying bad words," Jonas explained.

"When was that," Hixson asked, "so we don't watch that part? Is it near the beginning?"

"It's at the end, just before I came home."

"Okay, I don't think we'll get that far anyway."

"It was right after the shooting," Jonas said, bobbing his head up and down nervously. "I heard the shots, and then a couple minutes later the bad men showed up."

Hixson glanced at Garner.

"What did they do?" she asked.

"Nothing," Jonas said. "They just got out of the van, and then they got into a car. But the one man was saying bad words."

"How many men were there?"

"Two," Jonas said. "The one that was driving and saying the bad words, and the one that had the gun."

"Jonas," Hixson asked as she sped to the last of the videos Jonas had taken. "Do you mind if we see that?"

"If you want to, Ms. Hixson."

2:15 P.M. – 4:45 P.M.

Minutes after watching the video, Garner reached Bill Bradford on his cell.

Assistant Prosecutor William Bradford reached out to Detective James Chilton and briefed him on the call from Garner. It wasn't clear to Detective Chilton why Bradford had called him. He had the day off. Bradford should have called whoever was on duty in the Homicide squad.

But Bradford had called him, so now it was his problem. Chilton called the Homicide squad. It took only a minute to determine that Gabriela Morales was the detective who responded to that mess. He spoke with her and told her she needed to go to Garner's office, to look at some video he had, and see if it was useful.

Ninety minutes later, Morales called Chilton at home and thanked him for putting her in touch with the lawyer. "He was very helpful with today's shooting," she said. "But that's not the main reason I'm calling."

Chilton waited for the other shoe to drop.

"I'm actually calling because I may have solved the killings of those Hispanic women you're investigating. I think my shooting victims were the killers."

"You think?"

"There's a lot that has to be done to confirm it, but I'm almost certain."

Chilton headed into the office and found Morales. He followed her to a cramped, government-issue conference room. While she set up her laptop computer, he went and got coffee.

"Here's what we have," Morales said. "A month ago, on February 13, we had two men shot coming out of the Nuestras Casas Housing Co-Op. Both Hispanic. One died on the scene, the other later. Nobody is saying anything about who did it. And then, as you know, today, we had two Anglos shot."

Chilton grunted. He wasn't sure what that had to do with the Hispanic women.

"I met with the lawyer you told me to go see" – Morales looked at her notes – "Garner."

I know who the prick lawyer is, Chilton thought. Just get to the point.

"He had this young guy with him in his office. Real slow kid." She checked her notes again. "Trottel. Jonas Trottel. He lives in the neighborhood."

"The lawyer, Garner, he says there was bad blood between my vics and the Co-Op guys. He says my vics beat up one of the guys who lived in the Co-Op, a guy named Jabari Chan."

"How would he know *that*?" Chilton asked.

"Well, this kid saw it."

"And he's just now getting around to telling you? I guess he is slow."

"No, actually, the lawyer took him to District 3 and had the kid give a statement. Chan didn't want to prosecute, so the statement just went in a file drawer.

"Next thing you know, somebody beats the crap out of my vics. Of course, they claimed they didn't know who beat them up or why. But it's not hard to figure out that it was retaliation by the Co-Op guys."

"Where's this going?" Chilton complained.

"Well, like I said, then somebody shoots Chan and another man coming out the Co-Op. But nobody in the neighborhood was willing to tell us what was going on."

"Of course not," Chilton said.

"The lawyer helped me out on that too. It turns out one of his clients caught my vics on video driving away from the Co-Op after the shooting. I mean *right* after."

"So, your vics beat up someone from the Co-Op," Chilton summarized. "That guy and his buddies beat up your vics. Your vics turn around and shoot two guys coming out of this Co-Op. And now, somebody has killed your vics, evening the score."

Morales nodded to indicate Chilton's summary was correct.

"So," Chilton asked, "what's that got to do with the Hispanic women?"

"The lawyer says he thinks that's what started all this. He thinks my vics, the Anglos, tried to grab one of the women from the Co-Op, back in January. He thinks Chan intervened and started this whole tit-for-tat thing."

"How does Garner know that?" Chilton asked.

"He wouldn't say," Morales said. "But I talked to some people in the Co-Op, and that's what they said too. They all said the same thing – '¡Todos saben eso!' – 'Everybody knows that!'"

"He said to tell you that these were the guys he told you about."

Chilton processed what she was telling him. "Do we have any evidence," he asked, "linking your vics to those other killings?"

"Maybe. My vics had guns. Didn't get to use them, but they were 9mm Glocks."

"That's promising," Chilton agreed. "Thanks." He made a mental note to call John Crackstone, the gun identification guy in the Coroner's office. Chilton stood and prepared to leave.

"I got something else you need to see," Morales said.

Chilton remained standing, but didn't leave.

"That kid with the video – the one that's slow," Morales said. "Well, he was in Mt. Echo Park Saturday, videoing the squirrels. It looks like he may have also caught on his video the guys who killed my vics."

"It's Lower Price Hill," Chilton grumbled. "No matter where he points his camera, he's going to see something squirrely."

"Anyway," Morales continued, "he was trying to video squirrels, got distracted, and ended up videoing two guys ditching a van and switching to a car. We checked it out, and the van was stolen."

"The shooters were hiding their tracks," Chilton said, letting Morales know he understood what she was telling him. "That sounds more like pros than some neighborhood tit-for-tat."

"That's what I thought too. Unfortunately, the kid didn't get a license number for the Honda. And he says he's never seen the men before."

Morales brought up the video and ran it. The video clip showed two men get out of a van and into an old, blue Honda. It was impossible to see the men's faces.

"Run that again," Chilton ordered.

Morales complied.

Chilton grunted.

"You recognize them?" Morales asked.

"No, but the Honda looks familiar."

Chilton wasn't sure, but he thought he remembered the car from the surveillance runs at the Sleep Cheap Inn. *Maybe, just maybe*, he thought, *I'm going to catch a break.*

4:45 P.M. – 6:30 P.M.

Chilton sat a mug of fresh coffee on his desk before re-running the video of the two men changing vehicles in Mt. Echo Park.

Chilton pulled up the police surveillance videos of the Sleep Cheap Inn and its parking lot – the ones the District 4 patrolmen had been making for him. Just as he recalled, a beat-up, blue Honda was a regular in the surveillance videos. He was sure it was the same one.

He called Morales over to look at the videos. She agreed. The Honda in the Mt. Echo video and the Honda in the Sleep Cheap Inn videos appeared to be the same vehicle.

The fact that the Honda was in most of the Sleep Cheap Inn videos meant it belonged to someone who worked at the inn. Unlike the squirrel kid, however, the patrolmen had gotten the Honda's license plate number. Chilton ran the number. It was registered to Diego Olivar, the guy who ran the inn.

Chilton figured he could probably get a search warrant based on the change of cars near the scene of the shooting in Price Hill. But a search warrant based on just that wouldn't allow him to search for everything he wanted.

He was also supposed to be investigating the shooting deaths of the Hispanic women. Two of the Hispanic women had papers showing the Sleep Cheap Inn as their residence. Chilton pulled up the file with the information he had been collecting on the Hispanic women. Those two were Sofia Flores and Isabella Ramirez.

Chilton set out the basic facts in the form of an affidavit. First, he recounted the barest facts of the shooting in Lower Price Hill. He explained that minutes after the shooting, two men had been captured on video, not far from the scene of the shooting, changing from a stolen van to a beat-up blue Honda. A vehicle meeting that description belonged to Diego Olivar. Although it was not possible to make out his face on the video of the men changing vehicles, one of the two men – the driver – met the general physical description of Diego Olivar. Chilton concluded by indicating that Olivar was the manager of the Sleep Cheap Inn in Clifton, and the Honda had frequently been observed there.

Next, Chilton sketched out that he was investigating the abduction and murder of two Hispanic women, Sofia Flores and Isabella Ramirez. Both had identification papers listing the Sleep Cheap Inn as their residence. That, he argued, provided probable cause to search the inn's business records. He should be allowed to search for evidence concerning whether the women had in fact resided at the inn and for how long, and whether the two women had been employed by the inn or were relying on drug trafficking or prostitution. To buttress that contention, he recited that routine monitoring of the inn had revealed patterns of traffic consistent with prostitution. Chilton thought that might be thin, but combined with the possibility that Olivar had been involved in the killings in Price Hill, he thought it would be enough.

He contacted the judge on duty that weekend and secured two search warrants – one covering the inn and the Honda, authorizing a search for weapons, and the other covering the inn's customer and employment records.

He began making arrangements to conduct the search first thing Monday morning.

SATURDAY, MARCH 12

6:00 P.M. NEWS

Queen City News Live: Bringing you the news you want to hear.

Co-Anchor Ashley Gelb: Two men were shot and killed today in Lower Price Hill. According to police, the men were leaving the apartment building where they lived about noon, when they were gunned down. Tiffany Albern was on the scene and filed this report.

Tiffany Albern: Ashley, I'm standing in front of the apartment building here in Lower Price Hill, where earlier today two men were gunned down. Police are withholding the names of the victims, both white males in their early twenties, pending notification of next of kin. Neighbors describe the two as having grown up and lived their whole lives in Lower Price Hill. Neighbors also tell us there has been other violence in the neighborhood in recent weeks, which they blame on the influx of Hispanics into the neighborhood. In fact, several neighbors told us that Hispanics recently beat up the two men.

Tiffany Albern, reporting from Lower Price Hill.

Co-Anchor Ashley Gelb: Are those magazines in your doctor's waiting room safe to touch? A local student wanted to find out. More about that, sports and weather after this.

SATURDAY, MARCH 12

EVENING

On Saturday evening, Devin Garner attended the Cincinnati Bar Association's Annual Dinner. Hamilton County Prosecutor – and Congressional candidate – Richard Warren was the keynote speaker. Ostensibly, Warren was to speak to concerns raised by the legal community about his raids on various employers. Garner suspected that instead, Warren would simply give some version of his campaign stump speech.

Garner decided to go only because Carrie Hixson had given him a "heads up" that she and several of her classmates would be there – and not just to video Warren's remarks for their documentary. Hixson had somehow finagled to present a mini-documentary they had prepared for the occasion. She had persuaded the meeting organizers that the video would balance Warren's expected remarks. Bar Association officials pre-viewed the mini-documentary and agreed.

Warren went first. He vented about immigration. As he usually did, he spoke as if the government of Mexico was deliberately sending people to the United States.

"They're not sending us their finest people," Warren bellowed. "And there are also people coming in from countries other than Mexico.

"We have drug dealers coming across, we have rapists, we have killers, we have murderers. I mean, it's common sense. What – do you think they're going to send us their best people, their finest people? The answer is no."

When Warren finished with his remarks, the evening's host asked if anyone had any questions – in a tone that suggested he was asking merely to be polite, but did not actually expect or want questions.

One of the attendees accepted the challenge. "Was it true," the man asked, "that the police have detained over 200 individuals in connection with your raids on employers, but only about thirty-five of those individuals actually turned out to be undocumented?"

"Where did you get that?" Warren asked.

"From your office," the questioner replied. "Actually from statements your office has issued."

"I'm not sure why you're asking that if you already know the answer," Warren said, combatively.

"Well, my actual question is, have the people who were arrested, who weren't undocumented, sued yet?"

"Why would you ask something like that?" Warren grumbled. "You want to represent them? Let me tell you, that's one ambulance you don't want to chase."

"Has the Justice Department launched an investigation into your office *yet*?" the next questioner asked. "And if not, when do you think we can expect that?"

"No," Warren replied. "Not going to happen. Next?"

Garner decided to join the queue and was next. "Is your office," he asked, "going to be prosecuting any of the employers you raided?"

"You're the clever young fellow defending that Syrian doctor who killed his wife?" Warren parried.

"You've got me mistaken for someone else," Garner said. "I represent an American physician, a devout Catholic, who loved his wife very much and is being maliciously prosecuted by an out-of-control prosecutor, who thinks, mistakenly, that my client is Muslim. Not that that should matter."

"I heard you had a smart mouth," Warren said. "But to answer your question, my office has looked hard at those employers, and we have concluded that there isn't enough evidence to prosecute."

Warren glanced back at the host, who took the hint, and announced that he was going to have to curtail further questions to keep the evening on schedule.

The host introduced Carrie Hixson, and she in turn gave a two-minute introduction to her group's mini-documentary. Cam Willey projected the video onto the large screen workers moved into place.

The five-minute long video did not deal with the Hispanic women who had been abducted and killed. Although that would be an important part of the final class project, Hixson had promised Garner not to get into that while the trial was still underway. Neither thought the Bar Association would agree to show that anyway.

Instead, this version of the documentary dealt with the fact that the undocumented are often taken advantage of by employers. The video explained that when "coyotes" brought undocumented immigrants into the Greater Cincinnati area, they often ended up in the employ of Obreros de Hoy and lived at Nuestras Casas Co-Op. The documentary showed vans with the Obreros logo picking up workers at the Co-Op and dropping them off at the Heidelberg Sausage Company and several other employers.

The video presented interviews with immigrants and others who explained that the employers paid Obreros for providing the workers. On paper, Obreros paid the workers the legal minimum wage.

But the workers – some were disguised – explained that in practice, Obreros deducted from their paychecks excessive charges for transportation, housing, and a variety of other items. The workers received very little. The workers believed that some of the money they paid went to cover the expense of procuring phony documentation, and some – the workers believed – was kicked back to the employers.

The video switched to scenes of law enforcement officers raiding those employers and Obreros and hauling away e-mail servers and file cabinets full of records. A clip of Warren followed, telling reporters his office would follow the evidence wherever it went.

The Bar Association officials hadn't seen what the documentary showed next – Carrie and her friends added it at the last minute. The new footage showed a beaming Warren at the fundraiser hosted by the owner of the Heidelberg Sausage Company. He was shaking hands with other attendees. As their faces appeared on the new footage, voice-overs identified the owners and senior officials of the companies raided at Warren's request and the dates on which their companies had been raided.

The short documentary ended with the previously released statement from Warren's office asserting that his office would not pursue charges against the employers whose offices Warren had directed the police to raid.

In a final note, the documentary stated that the employers' contributions went to a PAC supporting Warren's campaign. The amounts of the donations did not have to be disclosed. Thus, how much it had cost the employers to escape prosecution was not available.

An angry Warren stood up, threw his napkin down in disgust, and walked out. The audience applauded as he left.

Warren wasn't the only one unhappy. As Garner was leaving the meeting, Carl Anwalt found him. "I told you we had a deal only if none of this got out," Anwalt said. "I'm tearing up the agreement between Hank and Reya. You and your uncle will never see a dime."

"I had nothing to do with Carrie showing that documentary," Garner said. "I tried to talk her out of it."

"I don't believe you. You're lying." Anwalt hesitated and made sure no one was listening. "But I'll tell you something that is true. When Diego and his cartel friends find out about this, they're not going to be happy."

"So?"

"So, you might want to make sure your will is up to date."

SUNDAY, MARCH 13

MORNING

On Sunday morning, as he sat in his office at the Sleep Cheap Inn, Diego Olivar had time to think about things. One of the things he thought about was the subpoena. It said he was supposed to be at the Medawar trial tomorrow, Monday, and testify. Not that he had any intention of showing up.

That whole trial, Olivar decided, was a problem. It was putting the inn in a bad light. They just needed to convict that doctor and stop talking about the woman and her camera.

The lawyer, Hank's nephew, he was definitely a problem. *What was his name? Garner? Sí, that was his name. Garner.* He kept talking about how somebody was killing Hispanic women and how that woman and two others had disappeared from the inn. He was making it sound like the *cabrones* killing the Hispanic women had something to do with the inn. *¿Qué mierda! What bullshit!*

He, Diego Olivar, had taken care of the *cabrones* killing Hispanic women. That lawyer should just shut up about them.

Instead, Garner was stirring up a lot of talk about prostitution and drugs at the inn. That was bad for business. All that attention was making the cartel guys upset.

Anwalt said they would convict that doctor, but it sounded to him like maybe that lawyer, Garner, was going to get him off.

The more Olivar considered things, the more it seemed foolish to wait any longer to take care of Garner.

Maybe, Olivar thought, he should take care of Anwalt as well. If the feds ever caught Anwalt, Olivar told himself, he'll sing like a parrot in mating season. Besides, why should

Anwalt get a cut of everything? He wasn't the one taking all the chances and doing all the work. Maybe after he took care of Garner, he just might visit Anwalt as well. *Kill all the effing lawyers!*

His cell phone rang. It was Anwalt.

"Last night," Anwalt said, "I went to a bar association dinner, and it was a disaster. First, Hamilton County Prosecutor Dick Warren speaks."

"I hate him!" Olivar said.

"Yeah, well, then they had some woman show a little documentary. She was working with the Medawar woman – the woman with the camera."

"So?" Olivar asked.

"She shows a documentary that accuses Reya of bringing illegals into the country. It didn't name Reya, but it showed her restaurant."

"She'll be pissed when she finds out," Olivar said.

"It gets worse," Anwalt said. "This video says a syndicate arranges for the illegals to go to Obreros. It says Obreros sends them to employers that don't look too carefully at their paperwork. It says the syndicate sends the illegals to live at the Co-Op, or sends them to your place. It didn't mention me by name, but it says an attorney put this syndicate together and provides phony documentation for the illegals."

"How does this woman know all this?" Olivar asked, accusingly.

"It has to be Garner – Hank's nephew. She's real friendly with him. He put it together for her."

"Who knows about this video?" Olivar asked.

"Everybody! She showed it at the Bar Association dinner, and the media were there."

"Oh, fuck."

"Yeah, well, the video ends with that fundraiser for Warren I put together," Anwalt continued. "It implies Warren decided not to prosecute the companies the police raided after they contributed to his campaign."

"No Bueno," Olivar offered.

"No shit! The media went nuts. They all showed parts of the video on the news last night. I'm sure they'll be doing follow-ups."

"I am going to kill him," Olivar said.

"Hang on a second," Anwalt said. "Reya is calling me. I need to talk to her. I'll call you back."

When Anwalt called back, he had worse news. The feds had arrested Reya. They caught her coming into the country with three illegals and a kilo of heroin. Anwalt said he would find an attorney down there to represent her, but it didn't sound good.

Olivar was beside himself. His mother had been arrested. The media were focusing on things that were none of their business.

His rage focused on Hank's nephew, Devin Garner. That prick was behind all this, he was sure.

He, Diego Olivar, would make Garner wish he'd minded his own business.

10:30 A.M. – 1:00 P.M.

On Sunday morning, Devin Garner jogged for the first time since the trial began, showered, and wolfed down breakfast before heading into the office.

Once there, Garner was supposed to accomplish several tasks. He needed to review his outline for Professor Adams. She was going to testify on Monday morning. He also needed to call her, to make sure she knew when to arrive and to make sure she didn't have any last-minute questions.

And he needed to outline the testimony he would elicit from Medawar. Garner still wasn't happy about needing to put Medawar on the witness stand, but he didn't see where he had a choice. On the whole, Garner thought Medawar would do fine, but he had expected the defense case to be so airtight, it would not be necessary. Then, he would have felt more secure about Medawar testifying. But having the defense turn on how well the defendant held up on cross-examination was never a good idea.

Finally, Garner needed to re-work the outline for his closing argument. He could do that, if necessary, after Medawar rehearsed his testimony.

But as he sat in his conference room, surrounded by trial exhibits and diagrams, witness outlines and other trial paraphernalia, he did none of those things. Instead, he stared at a blank, yellow legal pad.

He wanted to subpoena Anwalt and get him on the witness stand, but Anwalt lived and worked in Kentucky. He was beyond the subpoena power of an Ohio court and certainly would not testify voluntarily.

Should he have Hixson testify about the documentary and about what she had learned about the network Anwalt had put together? Could he even get her testimony into evidence, or would it all be rejected as hearsay? And if he could get her testimony in, would he be exposing her to retaliation?

On the legal pad, he wrote one question: *What am I missing?*

1:00 P.M. – 3:30 P.M.

Diego Olivar drove to Lower Price Hill. He was not expecting the lawyer to be working on a Sunday afternoon. Mainly, he thought he would familiarize himself with things.

But as his car approached the office, he saw a man enter Garner's office. Olivar wasn't sure, but he thought the man was that Syrian doctor, the one on trial for killing his wife. Olivar pulled over and waited a few minutes. The man did not come back out.

Olivar drove by the office slowly and headed to a Mexican restaurant further up Price Hill. He ate lunch and returned. He brought a bottle of tequila with him.

He parked where he could see the entrance to the lawyer's office, but not too close. He waited for the attorney to finish his meeting with whoever the hell he had in his office with him.

Then, he would make the lawyer pay.

1:00 P.M. – 3:30 P.M.

At one o'clock, Medawar arrived at Garner's office with Chinese takeout.

Over lunch, Garner and Medawar chatted about what they should cover when he testified. As they finished lunch, Garner said he had something he needed to say. "Rafiq, I want you to know that I'm really sorry for the way things went at the end of the week. I didn't see Crackstone's new report coming, and the judge shouldn't have let him testify to the new stuff. I feel responsible."

"It wasn't your fault the ballistics guy didn't confirm that those nut jobs killed Ann. We discussed the risks before the trial began, and we both agreed it made sense to point to those killers as someone who may have killed Ann. Besides, I still think they may have been responsible."

"Thanks," Garner said. "I appreciate your saying that."

"I'm waiting until the trial is over," Medawar said, smiling, "before I complain about ineffective assistance of counsel."

Garner didn't think gallows humor was a good sign, but at this point, it was better than an angry argument. He put his fortune cookie aside and cleaned up the debris from lunch. After a short break, he took Medawar through a practice run of his direct examination. Then, he conducted a mock cross-examination. Everything went as well as could be expected.

Medawar prepared to leave so Garner could finish his other trial preparation.

Garner walked out with his friend, absent-mindedly prying open the fortune cookie. It was turning into another beautiful spring day. The sky was a radiant blue with just a few wispy clouds. The air was cool, but warmer than usual for mid-March. Garner popped a piece of the cookie into his mouth and read the neatly typed message that came in the cookie.

The message said: "Good Fortune will visit you."

But it was not Good Fortune waiting to pay Garner a visit.

3:30 P.M. – 3:32 P.M.

Diego Olivar perked up as Garner and his visitor stepped from Garner's office.

Olivar opened his car door, slid out, and stood next to his car, waiting for the visitor to leave.

The visitor said something to Garner and walked off, toward his own car.

Olivar pulled the pistol from his waistband. Holding the gun behind his back, he walked toward the young attorney.

"Señor Garner!" Olivar called out. "I need to speak with you."

Garner turned and looked in his direction.

"Por favor!" Olivar said. "We need to talk."

Garner opened the door to his office to duck inside, but hesitated.

Olivar continued walking toward Garner. He walked slowly, not wanting to startle his prey. "I need to speak to you about the subpoena," he called out. "The one that says I have to testify in court."

"What about it?"

Olivar delayed answering and continued to close the distance between himself and the lawyer. "I don't know nothing. Why you need me to testify?"

"He's got a gun!" a voice called out from behind Olivar.

Olivar cursed. He was still further away from Garner than he wanted to be, but he had no choice. He raised his gun, aimed, and pulled the trigger. The gun fired, the sound echoed off the buildings, and Garner stumbled and fell.

Olivar spun around to see who was behind him. He

turned just in time for the iron pipe to crash into his face.

Everything went dark.

3:33 P.M. – 3:39 P.M.

Rafiq Medawar was about to get into his car when he heard the shot and turned. He saw Garner go down, and then he saw the shooter spin around and go down. A tall, thin, African-American man in a black gown was standing over the unconscious shooter.

Medawar ran to where Garner was struggling to get up, bracing himself against the door jamb.

"Stay down," Medawar called out.

Garner lay back down.

Medawar could see blood on Garner's shirt. It appeared to come only from his upper arm or shoulder.

"Did the force of the impact knock you down?" Medawar asked.

"No," Garner confessed. "When I saw the gun, I tried to get inside the door, but my brain was moving faster than my feet. I tripped over myself."

Medawar took that as good news. He assisted Garner up and helped him remove his shirt. The bullet had gone through Garner's upper arm, at the shoulder, doing mainly superficial damage.

"You're going to be okay," Medawar assured Garner, "but you need to go the hospital and get that taken care of." He insisted Garner remain seated.

Medawar used his cell phone to call 9-1-1. He asked for both police and an ambulance.

That done, he left Garner's office and approached the man prone on the pavement. He carefully kicked the gun away before beginning his examination. The man was already waking. Medawar told him to lie still and gently pressed on the man's nose.

The man cursed and tried to push himself up.

"Lie still," Medawar ordered in a commanding voice,

"or I'll have my friend here hit you again." Medawar pressed hard on the man's nose.

The man let out a cry.

"Lie real still," Medawar insisted, "and I think you'll live."

The man – who appeared uncertain what had happened or how badly he was hurt – rested his head on the pavement.

Medawar heard sirens. Someone had apparently called for help even before he had. A police car arrived, followed in quick succession by two more police cars and an ambulance.

Later, at the hospital, Medawar gave Garner a stern warning. "When the adrenaline wears off," he said, "you're going to feel wiped out. You're going to need to get some rest."

"The police are going to want to talk to me."

"That's fine," Medawar said, "but call the judge and see if you can get the trial postponed a day. Or at least until after lunch tomorrow, so you can sleep late in the morning. Trust me, you'll need it."

Garner called Bradford, who agreed to call the judge.

EVENING

It was Sunday evening when Detective James Chilton stepped into the police interrogation room. Chilton remained standing for a moment, sizing up Diego Olivar.

Seated at the table and wearing cuffs, Olivar had a splint over his nose. His left eye was puffy and swollen. By morning, it would be black-and-blue. The other eye might be as well.

The doctor at the Trauma Center said Olivar had sustained a broken nose, fractured occipital bone, and a concussion. At the time of his arrest, Olivar also had an elevated alcohol level.

There had been a bottle of tequila in Olivar's Honda.

Evidently, Olivar had been fortifying his courage. But Chilton figured by now the blood alcohol level would be lower, and a hangover not far off. All-in-all, Chilton decided, Olivar was a stupid bastard.

Chilton settled into the seat across the table from him and introduced himself. "I know they already read you your Miranda rights," Chilton said, "but I'm going to do it again."

Olivar said nothing.

A second detective entered the room. Detective Gabriela Morales introduced herself and placed a laptop computer on the table.

Chilton recited the familiar statement of rights.

"You have any questions?" Chilton asked.

"How much I have to pay you?" Olivar said. "What is it going to cost for you to let me go?"

"Things don't work that way here, *amigo*," Chilton responded. "You're not in Mexico."

Olivar scoffed.

"You know where you are?" Chilton said. "You're in a whole lot of trouble."

"I barely nicked that stupid lawyer."

"Around here," Chilton said, "being a bad aim is not much of a defense."

Olivar didn't respond.

Chilton looked at his watch. "You want some coffee?" he asked.

"*Sí*, gracias," Olivar said.

"Black?"

"*Sí.*"

"You want anything?" Chilton asked the other detective. She declined.

When Chilton returned with the coffees, he was more relaxed. This was one part of the job he enjoyed. Just him and the perp.

Chilton removed his jacket and draped it over an unused chair. He loosened his tie.

"You know I'm getting overtime for this?" Chilton asked. He sipped his coffee.

"Good for you," Olivar retorted.

"I was hoping you could me help me with something. Not about the lawyer. I know him. He's a prick. I want to talk with you about something else."

"You want me to help you?" Olivar followed his question with a contemptuous laugh. "Why would I do that?"

"Look, *amigo*, we're just killing time until the prosecutor gets here. He makes all the decisions. But while we're waiting, there's just something I'm curious about. Nothing to do with the prick lawyer you shot."

Olivar drank some of his coffee.

Chilton could see that Olivar seemed to think he was in control, at least for now.

"We've had a lot of excitement in Price Hill this weekend," Chilton said. "Besides you shooting the lawyer, someone shot the two assholes responsible for killing several Hispanic women."

Olivar looked at the detective suspiciously.

"We think those assholes killed a couple of the girls working at your place, at the inn."

Olivar glared at Chilton.

"In any event, yesterday morning, somebody killed those two assholes. Shot them right in front of their apartment building. You probably heard about it on the news."

"I don't watch the news," Olivar said. "It's all garbage."

"Can't say I blame you," Chilton said amicably.

Chilton took another sip from his own coffee. "Witnesses say two Hispanic guys did it," Chilton bluffed. "These guys — '*hombres*' — right? Isn't that how you say it?"

Olivar didn't respond.

"Like I was saying, these *hombres* shoot the two guys who have been killing all those women. Saves everybody the trouble and expense of a trial. Know what I mean?"

"I don't know anything about that," Olivar said.

"Well, these *hombres*, they have big *cojones*," Chilton continued. "They shot those jerks right there in broad daylight. One of these *hombres* even takes the time to shoot them a couple more times. Making sure they're dead, you know. Then, these *hombres* stroll over to this van they came in. They drive off, nice and slow, like they're in no hurry at all. Like I said, big *cojones*."

"What's this got to do with me?" Olivar asked.

"I was just hoping you could help us out with that. I thought maybe you knew something about who did it. Maybe you heard something."

Olivar snorted and shook his head derisively. "I told you. I don't know anything about that."

"I had to ask," Chilton shrugged, still all friendly and chummy. "You didn't hear about that on the news?"

"I told you," Olivar said, "I don't watch the news. It's all garbage."

"Then you probably didn't hear what these *hombres* did next. They drove around the corner to Mt. Echo Park." Chilton paused. "You ever been up there?" he asked. "Mt. Echo Park, I mean. Nice little park, up on top of the hill. Great view of the river and downtown."

Olivar looked at the second detective. "He always talk this much?"

Detective Morales smiled and shook her head. "Not usually," she said. "I think he's had too much coffee."

"You want some donuts?" Chilton asked. "This time of day, they won't be fresh, but there must be some around here."

Olivar looked at Chilton in disbelief. "I don't want no fuckin' donuts."

"Okay, then where were we?" Chilton asked. "Oh, yeah. These *hombres* go up to the park there and ditch the van. They get into a car and drive off. Like real pros. Like I was saying, these *hombres* have big *cojones*."

Olivar allowed himself the smallest hint of a smile.

"*Cojones* the size of coconuts," Chilton said. "But brains the size of pinto beans. The park on a Saturday is full of people, and somebody got them on video."

"You're lying," Olivar said evenly. "I watch television. You cops lie all the time. You try to trick people."

Chilton shrugged his shoulders. "The video was on all the news programs," he said.

Olivar stiffened. It was barely noticeable, but Chilton had seen it before. He'd seen plenty of suspects give the same tell when they realized they were in trouble.

"You got the video?" Chilton asked Morales.

Detective Morales cued up the video. She turned her laptop so Olivar could see it. She ran the video, then re-ran it a second time.

"Here's what I was hoping you could help us with," Chilton said, "Who is the other guy? The guy there with you?"

"You can't see their faces," Olivar said.

"Well, you can't see your face very well, but you can see your *amigo* good enough. The forensics guys will clean it up real nice on Monday."

"You trying to pin this on me?" Olivar asked, challenging Chilton. "You can't tell who that is. You're trying to frame me."

"Relax, Mr. Olivar. Nobody's trying to frame you." Chilton turned to Detective Morales and asked her to play the video again, but to stop it when she got to the get-away car. When she complied, Chilton asked if she could enlarge the car any.

"That's fine," he told Detective Morales. "Show it to Mr. Olivar."

Detective Morales complied.

"Mr. Olivar, that piece of shit is your car."

Olivar was no longer smiling.

There was a knock on the door. Chilton was irritated, but barked, "Come in."

A patrolman stepped into the room and handed Chilton a folder. Chilton opened the folder and studied the document inside.

After a moment, Chilton looked up at Olivar and smiled.

"Congratulations, *amigo*," Chilton said to Olivar. "Ballistics says your gun is a match for some of the slugs in those assholes. The ones I was just talking about. Your car, your gun. That's murder and conspiracy to commit murder on Saturday, and attempted murder tonight." Chilton looked at Olivar and shook his head. "You've had quite the weekend."

Olivar glared at Chilton, but said nothing.

Chilton looked back at the document in the folder. He took the ballpoint pen from his pocket and circled pastrami with Swiss on rye, before handing the folder to Morales. She circled ham and cheddar. She also checked baked beans. She handed the folder back to the patrolman.

The patrolman took the folder and left the room.

"We've got you on video, we've got your car, we've got the ballistics report," Chilton said. "And we've got this shooting this afternoon. A couple of solid witnesses to that, plus gunpowder residue on your hands, your fingerprints on the gun."

Chilton stretched his neck.

"There's something you need to know about the prosecutor who's coming in," Chilton continued. "He's a real hard ass. Know what I mean? And, he's pissed about having to come down here on Sunday night.

"I'd say, you're looking at the death penalty. Unless you've got something really good to give us, your number's up, *amigo*."

Olivar responded with a vulgar expletive.

"Your friend there in the video. I'm thinking he's with one of the cartels. That's something the prosecutor might be interested in."

Olivar repeated the expletive.

"I know, I know. You figure if you give him up, the cartel won't like it. That's why Detective Morales here thinks I'm wasting my time. She told me that before we even got started."

Olivar remained defiant and said nothing.

"In fact, I bet you're already worried about what the cartel thinks. Maybe they think you're keeping your mouth shut, and you're okay. Maybe they think you're talking, cutting yourself a deal, and you're in deep shit. Maybe they don't care. Maybe they just want to be on the safe side."

Chilton shook his head and sighed. "That's a lot to worry about, *amigo*. That's a lot to have on your mind."

The sneer returned to Olivar's face.

"Here's the thing. I don't want you worrying about which way that might go. So, I'm going to step out of the room here and fix things so you don't have to worry about what the cartel might be thinking."

"How you going to do that?" Olivar asked. His tone was openly skeptical.

"Well, see, I know some reporters," Chilton said. "Sometimes, you know, we share information. I mean, sometimes I do them favors, and sometimes they cut me some slack. I think this might be one of those times."

Olivar appeared confused.

"Here's what's going to happen," Chilton explained. "I'm going to leak to some reporters that you gave up your accomplice and that we're looking for him. That way, you'll know where you stand with the cartel."

Olivar jumped up. "No! Don't do that, *por favor*."

LATE EVENING

Detectives James Chilton and Gabriela Morales briefed Assistant Prosecutor Bill Bradford.

Morales went first. She had gotten to Price Hill that afternoon well before Chilton. She described how Olivar tried to shoot the lawyer, Devin Garner.

Bradford already knew in general terms what had happened with Garner, but was glad to get the details.

Morales also gave Bradford the basics on the other shooting, the one on Saturday morning, of the two men in front of the apartment building in Lower Price Hill.

"This is where it gets interesting," Chilton interjected.

"Our suspect," Morales said, "just confessed to participating in that. He says he shot one of them, and his partner shot the other one. He won't say who his partner is, just that he is with one of the Mexican cartels."

Then Chilton got his turn.

"You're not going to like this next part," Chilton warned Bradford. "He says the cartel guy is the one who shot Ann Medawar."

"He said that?" Bradford asked.

"Yeah. He says after her husband left, she came in and offered him some money. Olivar wanted the videos she took, and she refused to turn them over.

"They were trying to decide what to do when Anwalt called.

"Who is that?" Bradford asked.

Chilton explained who Carl Anwalt was. "I don't know if you remember," Chilton added, "but when Ms. Medawar was at the inn, while she was waiting for her husband to come back out, she got video of some men leaving the place."

Chilton watched as Bradford struggled to make the mental leap from the evening's shooting back to the trial.

"The two businessmen she got on video," Chilton continued. "One was a judge from Northern Kentucky. The other is an attorney. That's Carl Anwalt."

Bradford nodded.

"Anwalt represents the inn. He pays for the judge to have sex with the girls at the inn, and the judge calls all the close ones in his favor."

"This judge sits in Kentucky?" Bradford asked.

"Yeah," Chilton said. "Anyway, the attorney, Anwalt, calls Olivar. Anwalt's all pissed off that some woman videoed him and the judge coming out of the inn. He was afraid the woman was a reporter or something. He was all bent out of shape that she was going to blow the whistle on the judge. He wanted Olivar to get the video from the woman and scare her off."

"I think I'm following," Bradford said.

"Olivar finds the woman's camera and tripod in the trunk of her car and threatens her. But then, according to Olivar, that's when things went hinky. The cartel guy shows up. He says he's seen this woman around some of the places the police raided, getting video.

"The cartel guy calls Anwalt, and Anwalt's shitting bricks. They decide the woman is trouble. The cartel guy up and decides to kill her. Olivar claims he doesn't like that, but admits it was his idea to try to make it look like whoever abducted and killed the two women from his place killed Ms. Medawar too."

"The guy you're holding," Bradford asked. "That's Olivar, the manager of the inn?"

"Right," Chilton said.

"Where's the cartel guy?"

"Mexico. Or, at least that's what Olivar says. Says he flew out of Lexington yesterday."

"How do we know Olivar's not lying?" Bradford asked. "How do we know he didn't kill Ann Medawar?"

"We don't," Chilton said.

"I don't like this," Bradford said. He muttered an obscenity and headed into the interview room, flanked by the two detectives. He had Olivar repeat his story. When he'd heard enough, he stepped out and signaled for the detectives to follow him.

"I'm not cutting him a deal just on his say-so."

"Not that anyone's asking my opinion," Chilton said, "but there's no need to make a decision tonight. He says the gun that killed the Medawar woman is in the safe in his office at the inn. We've got a search warrant for the inn. We'll know more in the morning after we conduct the search."

Bradford weighed that option. "Okay, yeah," he concluded. "Let me know right away if you find the gun. In the meanwhile, let's hold this nonsense real close. I don't want Garner finding out. He's taken us on enough wild goose chases."

Another thought occurred to Bradford. "Before you go in on the search warrant," he said, "call Warren's spokesperson. Pam Sprecher. You met her." Bradford gave Chilton Sprecher's number.

Bradford looked directly at Chilton. "I'm going to tell her to play this as another of Warren's raids, looking for illegals. If reporters ask you about the search, you need to be singing the same song as Sprecher. Got it?"

Chilton grunted.

Chilton was angry and frustrated. They now knew Dr. Medawar didn't kill his wife. But Bradford didn't want anyone to know. He was going to continue the prosecution.

That wasn't right. It just wasn't.

MONDAY, MARCH 14

7:58 A.M. – 8:25 A.M.

Bright and early the next morning, detective James Chilton pulled his car into the parking lot of the Sleep Cheap Inn. He immediately called Pam Sprecher, Warren's PR person.

Sprecher would notify the media that the police were raiding another business suspected of harboring illegals. With the primary the next day, Warren was hungry for the publicity. Chilton didn't care about that. What he cared about was that as soon as Sprecher did her thing, the news jackals would show up and complicate his life.

He slid out of his car and waited as a dozen others arrived – each in his or her own official vehicle. A minute later, he led a group of the law enforcement officers into the inn's lobby, while others spread out looking for anyone trying to bolt.

The team included Detective Gabriela Morales, several other detectives, patrolmen, crime scene investigators – and for good measure, a locksmith. Ignoring how Prosecutor Warren preferred to do things, Chilton had even invited ICE. To his surprise, Adam Zhang, the local ICE special agent, had agreed to come along.

Chilton stormed into the inn, approached the front desk, and demanded to see the manager or owner. The clerk behind the desk spoke little English, but managed to communicate with Detective Morales.

"Señor Olivar no está aquí! Él estará de regreso pronto." The clerk insisted.

"He says, Olivar isn't here," Morales translated, "but will be back shortly."

Chilton handed the search warrants to the clerk and pointed to a couple of computer forensics guys. "They need to see the computer files containing the records of your guests," Chilton said. "And the files identifying your employees."

Even before Morales could tell the frightened clerk what he wanted, Chilton shouted, "Get moving!"

While Morales worked out the logistics with the clerk, Chilton kept an eye on the detectives and patrolmen who were searching for weapons. *No one wanted to get shot executing a search warrant.*

The search for weapons didn't take long. There was a handgun under the counter, a shotgun in the manager's office next to the desk, and another handgun in the manager's desk. The locksmith opened the safe in the manager's office. Just as Olivar said, there was yet another handgun – a 9mm Glock.

Chilton found Peter Browne, the young patrolmen who had been monitoring the inn and time-and-again had photographed the old Honda. Chilton tasked him with taking the guns to the Hamilton County Coroner's office.

"Don't stop on the way," he told the young patrolman, "and don't get lost. And whatever you do, don't mess up the chain of custody. Got it?"

"Yes, sir," the good-looking young patrolman said.

"Repeat it," Chilton commanded. "Don't stop on the way, don't get lost, and don't mess up."

The young patrolman rolled his eyes. "I was first in my class, Detective. I won't let you down."

As Browne headed toward the door, Chilton called out to him.

Browne swung around, apparently thinking the detectives had found something else.

"Don't stop," Chilton said. "Don't get lost. And don't mess up the chain of custody."

Browne saluted and headed out of the door.

Chilton followed Browne through the door and stepped

to the side, out of the way of the police and reporters dashing in and out of the inn. He called John Crackstone, the gun identification guy at the Coroner's office. He had an urgent request.

Then, he called Bradford and left a message that he found the Glock in the safe, where Olivar said it would be.

11:30 A.M. – 11:45 A.M.

When he got up, about 8:30 Monday morning, Garner contacted Bradford and Scott Greene, Judge Seiler's bailiff. Bradford had made arrangements to postpone resumption of the trial. It wouldn't start until after Judge Seiler's usual noon lunch break. But Garner wanted a brief meeting with the judge before court resumed. Greene scheduled that for 11:30.

When Garner got to the courtroom, Bradford and O'Malley were already there. They told him the judge was waiting.

Judge Seiler expressed what struck Garner as genuine concern for his condition, asking Garner if he was ready to continue the trial. He offered to postpone resumption of the trial until the next day.

Garner downplayed the extent of the damage to his arm. He assured the judge he was eager to get going.

"If you need more than one recess this afternoon, or if you need to end the day early," Judge Seiler said, "I'm going to understand."

Garner cleared his throat. "Thanks, Judge. I may need to take you up on that, but right now, I feel okay. My concern has to do with the man who shot at me last night."

"We've got him on multiple charges, including murder and attempted murder," Bradford said. "He's not going anywhere."

"The man who tried to kill me last night," Garner explained to Judge Seiler, "is Diego Olivar, the manager of the Sleep Cheap Inn. The last time my client saw his wife alive, she was headed into the inn to see him. He's under subpoena to testify today."

"When did you serve the subpoena?" Judge Seiler asked.

"Before the trial began," Garner said.

"He's in custody," Bradford said. "He's not going to stroll in here this afternoon looking to testify."

"Judge," Garner said, "I want you to order the county to bring Mr. Olivar here this afternoon. Like I said, the last time my client saw his wife, she was going to into the inn to see Mr. Olivar. Last night, he came to my office complaining about the subpoena and tried to kill me. I have the right to put this man on the witness stand and ask him about what happened to my client's wife."

"I don't know if I can get him here this afternoon," Bradford said, "but even if I can, he's going to refuse to testify. His attorney will tell him to exercise his right against self-incrimination."

"He's right," Judge Seiler told Garner. "He'll take the Fifth."

"That's his right," Garner conceded. "But my client has the right to have the jury see him do that."

Bradford objected. The jury would read too much into his refusal to testify.

Garner and Bradford went back and forth several times on that, before Judge Seiler made his ruling. He directed Bradford to make arrangements to have Diego Olivar brought to his courtroom mid-afternoon. He also suggested Bradford come up with an appropriate cautionary instruction to the jury.

Bradford turned to O'Malley. "You heard the judge," he said. "We need a jury instruction."

1:00 P.M. – 1:45 P.M.

At one o'clock sharp, his arm and shoulder beginning to ache, Devin Garner sat at counsel table alongside Rafiq Medawar, waiting to resume the defense case. It seemed like a very long time since Friday, when Crackstone's testimony had rocked the defense case.

The bailiff stood and said, "All rise."

Judge Seiler entered from his chambers and climbed the stairs to the bench at his usual brisk pace. He glanced around the courtroom, taking in the surprising number of reporters and spectators present.

Taking a cue from the judge, Garner allowed himself a glance at the audience in the courtroom. Evidently, the fact that someone had tried to kill him had generated renewed interest in the trial. The press, he thought, smelled blood.

"Please be seated," Judge Seiler said.

"Ready for the prosecution," Bradford announced.

"Ready for the defense," Garner replied.

"Proceed," Judge Seiler said.

And with that, Garner called Professor Joan Adams to testify.

Professor Adams briefly described her course on making a documentary and Ann Medawar's participation in the class. She testified that the class decided to make its documentary about the challenges immigrants faced in the Greater Cincinnati area. She mentioned the various aspects the class participants elected to concentrate on.

Garner had Professor Adams describe the equipment the class members decided to use. She discussed the reasons they wanted to use their cell phones, including the flexibility and informality cell phones allowed. She also discussed her insistence that, whenever possible, they use a camera mounted on a tripod. The camera, she explained, served both as a backup and provided a different angle on the action.

To lay a foundation for his next series of questions, Garner re-played – for Professor Adams and the jury to see – the video Ann made of Rafiq Medawar and Angelica Rios leaving the inn.

Even though the prosecution's expert had conceded the

point, he elicited Professor Adams' opinion that Ann had been using the adapter and special software the class had agreed to use. *Yes*, she agreed with Ms. Yang, Ann had to be standing quite close to capture the images on her videos. *Yes*, she also agreed that if Ann had been trying to video her husband unobserved, she would not have asked him to re-stage his exit from the inn.

"Professor Adams, have you examined the videos of Dr. Medawar and Nurse Rios leaving the Sleep Cheap Inn?"

"Yes, in detail."

"Were you able to determine why Ann wanted to make the second video?"

Bradford objected that the question, as framed, called for the witness to read the decedent's mind.

Garner withdrew the question and re-phrased it. "Did you find a problem with the first video?"

"Yes, I did."

"Can you show the jury what the problem was?"

"Yes, I think so." Using an iPad, Professor Adams brought up the video and played it, stopping partway through. She froze the video with Rios already out of the inn but holding the door open for Medawar.

"I'm going to focus on this area of the door," Professor Adams said, "and enlarge it."

The image on the large screen changed. The jurors studied it intently.

"If you look closely at the glass door, you can see a reflection of a camera on a tripod. If that video was in the class documentary, I don't think anyone would have noticed it, but Ann was a perfectionist."

Bradford limited his cross-examination to what struck Garner as some rather surly questions –

Had Ann discussed with her why she was going to the inn to film her husband and his hot little nurse-friend?

Isn't it a fact that Ann could have used the attachment and special software not only to capture the complaints of people in the country illegally, but also to capture evidence of a cheating spouse?

Did she have any reason to believe, based on her own personal knowledge, that Ann had been killed by a serial killer and not by a spouse upset at having been caught having an affair?

The last question was one too many.

Professor Adams stiffened her back, arched an eyebrow, and responded. "Well, if Ann had been trying to video her husband surreptitiously," she said, "she was smart enough to know to use a telescopic lens – not a lens designed for a wide-angle view. And if she had been trying to video her husband surreptitiously, she certainly would not have asked him to redo his exit from the inn."

Professor Adams removed her glasses. "And, as to my personal knowledge, well, the day before she disappeared, Ann discussed with me –"

Bradford interrupted. "Please limit your response to the question posed."

"You asked about my personal knowledge," Adams responded in her most professorial tone. "My personal knowledge is that the day before she disappeared, Ann discussed with me a trip to Lebanon she was hoping to take with Rafiq next summer. It was to be a surprise, to let him see where his family had come from back when."

"Your Honor," Bradford said, "I move to strike. Non-responsive. And hearsay."

Judge Seiler did not wait for Garner to respond. "Counsellor," he admonished Bradford, "you invited that. Overruled."

Garner wasn't sure he would have ruled the same way, but he wasn't going to complain.

Bradford thanked Judge Seiler – something experienced litigators sometimes do, hoping the jury will think the judge just ruled in their favor.

"No further questions," Bradford announced — apparently deciding further questioning risked more damage.

Judge Seiler announced a brief recess.

1:45 P.M. – 2:00 P.M.

During the recess, Garner used the restroom. While still in the restroom, he allowed Medawar to check the bandaging on his arm and shoulder.

"There's some bleeding," Medawar said. "Not a lot, but you need to get the wound checked and re-bandaged. And you need to rest."

"I can't," Garner said. "I begged the judge to have Diego Olivar brought here for me to question him. He should be here by now."

"You should ask for the trial to be postponed until tomorrow," Medawar urged his difficult patient. "The judge can have him testify then."

"I'm okay for now." Garner insisted. "Let's just see how things go."

Detective Chilton entered the restroom. Even though they hadn't been discussing anything sensitive, Garner and Medawar immediately stopped talking.

Chilton appeared angry.

"I need to speak with your lawyer," Chilton said to Medawar. "In private. Police business. About last night."

"I'll be right outside," Medawar said.

"Make sure nobody comes in," Chilton directed Medawar. "We're just going to be a minute."

Three minutes later Chilton emerged.

Medawar re-entered the restroom and helped Garner put his shirt and jacket back on. "What was that all about?" Medawar asked as he did.

"I promised not to say."

"Carrie is here. She's worried about you," Medawar told Garner. "She's in the courtroom. But if you think you might need her to testify, she says to let her know, and she'll wait in the hall."

"She's fine. I want her to see this. Let her know."

On his return to the courtroom, Garner gave Hixson a quick smile, but continued to the bailiff's desk. Greene confirmed that Diego Olivar was in the holding cell, ready to be brought into the courtroom.

2:00 P.M. – 2:30 P.M.

When police officers escorted him into the courtroom, Diego Olivar was dressed in an orange jumpsuit. A chain ran from the cuffs on his wrists to his waist, where it connected with the chain around his waist. From there, it ran down to the chain connecting his ankle cuffs. Olivar was also sporting a nose brace, and his eyes were black-and-blue. Altogether, he looked brutish.

The Public Defender office had assigned an attorney – a shy, introverted young man in the wrong profession – to protect Olivar's rights. He protested that Olivar should not be compelled to appear as a witness. Olivar would refuse to answer any substantive question, he argued, on the grounds that doing so might tend to incriminate him in violation of his rights under the Fifth Amendment. There was no purpose in even calling him as a witness.

"He has the right to refuse to answer counsel's questions," Judge Seiler ruled. "And the defendant has the right to have the jury hear him do it."

Olivar had the wary expression of a cornered animal, but took the oath and seated himself in the witness box. As Garner took his place at the podium and glanced at his notes, Olivar stared at him menacingly.

In response to questions from the court reporter, Olivar gruffly stated his name and address for the record.

"Mr. Olivar," Garner asked in a matter-of-fact voice, "before we get into anything that you might regard as incriminating, I hope we can cover a few preliminary matters, just so we can all get to know you a little better. Just some simple background stuff."

Olivar continued to glare at Garner.

"Can we agree that you manage the Sleep Cheap Inn in Clifton?" Garner asked.

"*Sí*," Olivar said.

"I think everyone understands your answer, Mr. Olivar," Judge Seiler interjected, "but we need you to try to answer in English."

Olivar nodded. "Yes," he said, switching to English. "I am the manager."

"In fact," Garner said, again in a low-key, familiar manner, "you're also the owner or part-owner?"

After some hesitation, Olivar conceded that he was.

"Mr. Olivar, this case concerns the death of Ann Lindsey Medawar. The prosecution refers to Ms. Medawar as the 'decedent.' Would you mind if I just call her 'Ms. Medawar'?"

Olivar stared darkly at Garner, but didn't respond.

"The jury has heard testimony in this case, testimony that on the morning of Friday, October 16, Ms. Medawar was outside the Sleep Cheap Inn. According to the testimony, Ms. Medawar videoed her husband, a nurse, and others, entering and leaving your inn."

Olivar continued to stare at Garner, saying nothing.

"I want to show you one of the videos Ms. Medawar made that morning," Garner continued. He turned to Kemi Adichie, the paralegal at the prosecution table. "Ms. Adichie, would you play Prosecution Exhibit 27?"

Adichie played the video, projecting it, as usual, onto a large screen for the jury to see. The video showed two men exit the inn, followed by another man, and then another. The first two men were businessmen or professionals, dressed in suits and ties. The next two men were Hispanic and were dressed as manual laborers.

Garner asked Adichie to replay the video, stopping on the first man to exit the inn.

When the video froze, Garner turned to the witness. "Mr. Olivar, this gentleman is Carl Anwalt, the attorney for the inn. Have I got that right?" Garner asked.

Bradford jumped to his feet, saying, "Objection, leading."

Garner flashed an angry glance at Bradford. He shook his head in frustration and turned back to face the witness.

"Mr. Olivar," Garner said, "there are rules about how things are done in a trial. For example, suppose I call someone as a witness. When I question that witness, that's called 'direct examination.'

"Generally speaking," Garner continued, "on direct examination, a lawyer is not allowed to ask questions that are framed in such a way as to suggest the answer that the lawyer expects or wants the witness to give. We call that a 'leading question.' That's because we don't want a lawyer giving hints to a friendly witness.

"When the other attorney gets his turn to question the witness, that's called 'cross-examination.' Generally speaking, on cross-examination, a lawyer can ask all the leading questions he wants.

"But in a trial, sometimes things get turned around, and a lawyer calls as a witness someone who is actually a hostile witness. When that happens, the judge will usually allow the attorney to question the witness as if he were conducting cross-examination."

Bradford rose and objected. "Your Honor, counsel is supposed to be questioning the witness, not lecturing him on the rules of evidence."

"Do you have a question for the witness?" Judge Seiler asked Garner.

"Yes, Your Honor," Garner said. "I do." Garner slid his suit jacket off and pointed to the large bandage around his shoulder and upper arm. Near its center, the bandage was stained pink, indicating that Garner had moved his arm too much and had experienced some bleeding.

Garner had the jurors' attention.

"Mr. Olivar," Garner said, "yesterday afternoon, I stepped out of my office, and someone shot me. I'm not going to ask you if you did that, because I know you would assert your right not to incriminate yourself. At least, I assume you would."

"If Mr. Garner is going to testify," Bradford objected, "he should be sworn and seated in the witness box."

"My question for you, Mr. Olivar, is this," Garner said, ignoring Bradford. "Did the police arrest you outside my office yesterday afternoon, and charge you with shooting me?"

"Objection!" Bradford thundered.

"Mr. Bradford," Judge Seiler responded, "if you don't want Mr. Garner to get into what happened yesterday, perhaps you would like to stipulate that the witness is hostile."

Bradford threw up his hands in protest and responded, "So stipulated." Bradford sat back down.

Garner had never seen Bradford show his temper in court in that way. In the courtroom, Bradford was generally ultra-cool, the consummate professional, never showing more emotion than necessary.

"Thank you," Garner said to Bradford, acknowledging the stipulation. Garner slid his jacket back on. It hurt when he did.

Garner turned back to the witness. "Now, Mr. Olivar, getting back to the man in the video. Who is that man?"

Olivar looked at the Public Defender lawyer. The lawyer nodded, and Olivar answered, "Carl Anwalt."

"Is Mr. Anwalt an attorney, if you know?"

"*Sí.* I mean, yes."

"Does Mr. Anwalt represent the Sleep Cheap Inn?"

"*Sí,*" Olivar said. Correcting himself again, he added, "Yes."

Garner asked Adichie to advance the video to show the next man.

"Mr. Olivar, I believe this man is also well-known. Do

you recognize him?"

Olivar looked to the Public Defender, who nodded.

"I know who he is," Olivar said.

"Who is he?" Garner asked.

"Judge Richter," Olivar said, speaking in a low voice — as if hoping that no one would hear.

"Judge Dirk Richter?" Garner asked in a voice as loud as Olivar's had been soft. "Judge Dirk Richter of the Boone County Circuit Court in Kentucky?"

"*Sí, Sí.*"

"Is Judge Richter a frequent guest at the Sleep Cheap Inn?"

"Objection," Bradford yelled. "Not relevant. It's unfair to drag a public official's name, a judge's name, into this. He's not a party here. He's not able to defend himself against Mr. Garner's accusation. This has absolutely nothing to do with this case."

Once more, Garner thought that — coming from Bradford — the objection was a bit too emotional.

"It has everything to do with the case," Garner responded. "Judge Richter—"

"Sidebar, Your Honor," Bradford interrupted. "I think we should do this at sidebar."

Garner moved to the side of the judge's expansive bench.

Two minutes later, Garner returned to the podium, Bradford returned to the table for the prosecution, and the Public Defender returned to his post near the witness.

Garner turned toward the prosecution team. He noticed that O'Malley was back. No doubt she had brought a jury instruction, which — if adopted by the court — would tell the jury to develop acute amnesia.

"Ms. Adichie," Garner said, "if you would be so kind as to return to the frame with the attorney, Mr. Anwalt."

Adichie backed up the video. The screen showed Carl

Anwalt exiting the Sleep Cheap Inn. He appeared to be looking directly into the camera. He appeared upset.

For effect, Garner decided to keep Olivar and the jury in suspense a few moments longer. "Mr. Olivar, before we get to that," Garner said, "you were born in México?"

The question appeared to catch Olivar off guard. "*Sí*," he answered. "I mean, yes."

"Did you learn to speak Spanish as a child?"

"Yes."

"You only learned English later, right?"

"Yes."

"Will you let me know if you don't understand any of my questions?"

"*Sí*," Olivar said. "Yes," he corrected himself.

"Mr. Olivar, I want to direct your attention to the image of Mr. Anwalt there on the screen," Garner said.

The image of the angry lawyer had remained on the screen, glaring at the jurors, while he and Olivar discussed Olivar's familiarity with English. Now that Garner indicated he was about to ask about the angry lawyer, all eyes focused on that image.

Garner hesitated.

"I'm sorry, but before I ask you about Mr. Anwalt, let me ask you this," Garner said. "Are you familiar with the expression, 'If looks could kill?'"

Bradford exploded out of his chair. "Objection!" he shouted.

Judge Seiler waited for Bradford to state the nature of his objection.

Collecting himself, Bradford asked "to approach" – that is, to approach the bench for another sidebar conference.

The lawyers huddled with Judge Seiler and then broke, like players just given a new play by their coach.

"Mr. Olivar," Garner said on returning to the podium, "I am not your attorney, and I cannot give you legal advice. But I am now going to ask you some questions that you may regard as sensitive – as more than just background information."

Olivar appeared deeply suspicious under the best of circumstances, and these – for him – were not the best of circumstances. Even so, the warning somehow made Olivar, nose brace and all, seem even more suspicious.

"Mr. Olivar," Garner said, "as I mentioned, the evidence in this case is that Ms. Medawar made this video of attorney Carl Anwalt and Judge Richter leaving the Sleep Cheap Inn on the morning of Friday, October 16." As he spoke, Garner gestured to the image of Carl Anwalt on the screen. A sharp pain in shoulder punished him for gesturing. The pain quickly subsided, returning to the dull ache he had experienced most of the day.

"Mr. Olivar," Garner asked, "were you at the Sleep Cheap Inn that morning?"

The Public Defender stood. "Your Honor," he protested.

Olivar took the hint. Reading from the slip of paper the Public Defender had given him just before he had entered the courtroom, Olivar recited: "I invoke my rights under the Fifth Amendment and respectfully decline to answer, on the grounds that my testimony may tend to incriminate me."

"On that morning, at the Sleep Cheap Inn," Garner asked, "did you encounter Ms. Medawar?"

Reading from the paper, Olivar again asserted his right against self-incrimination.

"Did you speak with Ms. Medawar?"

Olivar again refused to answer.

"After he left the inn that morning, did the attorney, Carl Anwalt, call you?"

Again, Olivar refused to answer.

"Judge Richter comes to your place about once a month, doesn't he?"

Olivar smirked, but refused to answer.

"Judge Richter comes there for the prostitutes, doesn't

he?"

Again, Olivar refused to answer. The smirk remained.

"Does the attorney, Mr. Anwalt, have an arrangement with you to cover the expenses Judge Richter incurs with these prostitutes?"

Olivar refused to answer, but the smirk remained.

"When he called you that day, was Mr. Anwalt upset that Ms. Medawar videoed him and Judge Richter leaving your place?"

To Garner's surprise, Olivar answered. "Furioso! Fuera de su mente."

"In English," Judge Seiler urged.

"He was pissed," Olivar said, apparently already having second thoughts about the wisdom of answering the question.

Olivar's loud response had jolted the introverted Public Defender into action. He asked and was given permission to consult with his client.

Garner was sure the poor guy was telling Olivar he could not pick and choose which questions to answer. If the questions were such as might incriminate him, he could refuse to answer all of them, across the board. Or, he could answer all of them. But aside from purely non-substantive questions, he couldn't choose to answer some questions and refuse to answer others.

Sixty seconds later, Diego Olivar, duly advised, returned, chains rattling, to the witness stand.

Garner asked: "Did you take Ms. Medawar's camera?"

Olivar refused to answer, reading again from the paper the Public Defender had given him.

"Did you threaten Ms. Medawar if she exposed Judge Richter?"

Olivar again refused to answer, but it was apparent he was upset with the direction the questions were taking. He looked, Garner thought, like a giant orange sausage about to explode.

"Excuse me, Your Honor," Garner said. He walked back to counsel table and took a drink from a bottle of water.

Judge Seiler asked if Garner needed a break.

"After this witness," Garner replied. "Thank you."

Garner slowly returned to the podium and glanced at his legal pad. It was blank. But Olivar didn't need to know that. Neither did the jury.

"Mr. Olivar, your mother is Reya Sanchez?" Garner asked.

"*Sí*," Olivar said.

"She owns Reya's Authentic Mexican Restaurant in Florence?" Garner asked.

"*Sí*," Olivar said, then corrected himself, and responded in English. "Yes."

"Does Mr. Anwalt represent your mother and her restaurant?"

Bradford objected, and another sidebar followed. When it ended, Bradford made a point of thanking Judge Seiler.

"Mr. Olivar, does Carl Anwalt represent your mother and her restaurant?" Garner asked, repeating the question to which Bradford had objected.

"Yes," Olivar said.

"Is your mother, Reya Sanchez, involved in bringing undocumented individuals from Mexico into this country? Helping them get across the border?"

Bradford objected on relevancy grounds.

To Garner's surprise, Judge Seiler overruled the objection. Garner sensed the judge was unhappy with Bradford, but he was watching Olivar as the exchange between Bradford and the judge played out.

Olivar, Garner thought, was one of those people whose emotions show on their faces, as plain as the news scrolling across the bottom of the screen on CNN. It was also obvious Olivar went a little crazy at the mention of his mother's illegal activities. He would probably react that way, Garner thought, at any derogatory reference to his mother.

Garner repeated the question.

Olivar refused to answer, again reading the statement the Public Defender had given him.

"Mr. Olivar, is it true that the people your mother brings into the country go to various businesses that Mr. Anwalt has relationships with?"

Olivar angered, but once more read from the slip of paper, refusing to answer.

"Does Mr. Anwalt provide phony documentation for the people your mother brings into the country?"

Olivar refused to answer.

"Some of the women your mother brings into the country end up at your place, where they are forced into prostitution?"

Olivar refused to answer, but Garner could see that Olivar was again close to exploding. This time, Garner did not intend to let up, even momentarily.

"Are you aware, Mr. Olivar, that on Saturday night, at a bar association meeting, a woman who was a friend of Ms. Medawar showed a documentary about what happens to the people your mother brings into this country?"

"I'm not a goddam lawyer," Olivar said angrily. "I don't go to no bar association meetings. I don't know anything about that."

"Mr. Anwalt is a lawyer, and he called you and told you about the documentary, didn't he?" Garner asked.

Garner was no longer relying on anything Chilton had told him. He was going on pure instinct. It didn't really matter what his questions accused Olivar off, as long as Olivar refused to answer on the grounds that his response might be incriminating.

Olivar read the slip of paper, refusing to answer.

"Mr. Anwalt blamed me for the documentary, didn't he?"

Olivar declined to answer.

"And then, yesterday, after you talked to Mr. Anwalt, you came and parked outside my office?"

Olivar refused to answer.

"When I showed Dr. Medawar out of my office yesterday, you approached me? You called my name?"

Olivar again refused to answer.

"You were upset about having to testify about Ms. Medawar's death. Isn't that right?"

Medawar squirmed in his seat, but refused to answer.

"And then you shot me?"

"Why are you asking me all this," Olivar responded, "when you know I'm not going to answer?"

"The last time my client saw his wife she was walking into your inn to see you. I want the jury to get to know what kind of person you are." Garner replied, drawing another objection from Bradford.

Judge Seiler upheld the objection and admonished the jury to disregard Garner's statement.

"Directing your attention back to the day when Ms. Medawar was at the inn," Garner said, going back to the question he had approached, but backed away from earlier. "Did Mr. Anwalt discuss killing Ms. Medawar with you?"

Olivar hesitated before responding, "No."

Judge Seiler cautioned Olivar that he could not pick and choose which questions he would answer. If he was going to answer some of the questions in this line of questioning, he would need to answer all of them.

Not wanting to allow Olivar time to retract his answer, Garner immediately shot another question at him. "After Mr. Anwalt and you talked, you shot and killed Ms. Medawar. Isn't that right?"

"I told you, I'm not going to answer your questions," Olivar said in an angry voice.

"Mr. Anwalt told you to try to make it look like the murder of the young Hispanic women somebody has been killing. Isn't that right, Mr. Olivar?"

"He didn't tell me to kill her," Olivar snarled, his voice loud and menacing. "He just told me to get the videos she made of him and that judge."

"This morning, the police found the gun you used to kill Ms. Medawar in the safe at the inn? Isn't that right?"

"You stupid bastard!" Olivar said. "I didn't kill that woman, and that's not my gun. Anwalt told—"

Olivar seemed to realize he'd gone too far. Garner waited to see what Olivar would do.

Garner wasn't the only one. Everyone in the courtroom seemed to be focused on the volcanic witness's struggle with himself. The judge watched him. The jurors were looking directly at him. Scott Greene, the bailiff, watched with disgust on his face. Even the long-dead judges in their portraits on the courtroom's walls seemed to be waiting to see what the witness would say.

"Anwalt talked to someone else," Olivar said finally. "That gun belongs to the man who killed her. That man told me to get rid of the gun, but I hung onto it in case I needed it to prove I wasn't the one who killed her."

Olivar stood up and started to navigate his way out of the witness box, chains rattling as he moved.

"Mr. Olivar," Judge Seiler said, "you haven't been excused."

"This is all bullshit," Olivar responded. "I told the police all this last night." He pointed to Bradford. "I told him too." Olivar struggled out of the witness box, trying to not to trip.

"Mr. Olivar," Judge Seiler said.

"I'm not saying anything else until I get a deal." Olivar said. He marched from the witness stand toward the police officers, who moved forward to intercept him.

"I'm done," Garner said, smiling.

Judge Seiler looked at Bradford. "Do you want to question him?"

Bradford shook his head. "I've had my fill of him."

2:30 P.M. – 2:45 P.M.

After Diego Olivar's abrupt departure, Judge Seiler announced another brief recess, sent the jury out, and invited the attorneys into chambers.

When the lawyers were seated in front of him in chambers, Judge Seiler looked at Bradford. "Bill, have you considered dismissing the prosecution against Dr. Medawar?"

"I talked with Warren this morning," Bradford replied, surprising Garner. "He said 'no.' He was adamant."

"I want you to talk with him again," Judge Seiler said. "Bring him up to date on this afternoon's events. Tell him, I don't see how you can get a conviction."

"I'll see if I can reach him," Bradford said and excused himself.

Judge Seiler asked Garner how he was holding up. "You look white as a sheet."

"To be honest, I'm feeling a little drained right now, but as long as the wound doesn't start bleeding again, I'm okay. I want to get through this next witness."

"You sure?"

"Absolutely sure," Garner assured the judge. "But, if I may, Your Honor, I'd like to step out a minute. Dr. Medawar went to get a soft drink for me. I'd like to get a little caffeine and have him check my bandage again."

"By all means."

Garner made his way through the courtroom, waved off a reporter with a question, and stepped into the hall.

Medawar hadn't returned with the soft drink yet, but he saw John Crackstone, his next witness.

Garner approached Crackstone, exchanged greetings, and apologized for making him testify again.

"I knew you would," Crackstone said, "when you saw my report."

"Your report?" Garner asked.

"I gave Bradford a new report today." Crackstone said.

"Didn't he give it to you? I gave Bradford extra copies for you and the judge."

"Not yet."

"Well, I'm sure he will."

"John, what does your report say?" Garner asked.

"I examined the slugs removed from those men killed on Saturday in Price Hill. One of them matches the slug removed from your decedent. From Ms. Medawar."

"Excellent!" Garner said. "Have you found the gun?"

Bradford emerged from the small attorney conference room he had used to call Richard Warren. At the same time, the elevator opened and Medawar stepped off.

"Let's go talk to the judge," Bradford said to Garner. He seemed upset that Garner was talking with the prosecution's expert witness.

"What did Warren say?" Garner asked.

"He said 'no.' We're not going to dismiss."

"I'll join you in chambers in a couple minutes. I need to have the good doctor check my bandage."

Bradford ushered Crackstone into the courtroom.

Garner reluctantly headed to the restroom with Medawar.

Five minutes later, when Garner entered chambers, it was apparent neither the judge nor Bradford had discussed the case while they waited for him. Bradford had left O'Malley in the courtroom to chaperon Crackstone.

"Everything okay?" Judge Seiler asked.

"I'm okay. Thanks."

Judge Seiler turned to Bradford. "What did Warren say?"

"He said the jury should decide the case," Bradford responded.

"Why doesn't Warren want you to dismiss?" Judge Seiler asked. "Because of the election tomorrow?"

"That, and he's mad at Devin over the stunt at the bar association dinner Saturday."

Bradford paused, choosing his next words carefully.

"Plus, he still thinks Dr. Medawar had something to do with his wife's death. I think his exact words were, 'You can't tell me that Syrian son of a bitch didn't have something to do with it.'"

Judge Seiler shook his head. "Do the polls still say Warren's going to lose the primary tomorrow?"

"Yes. As you can imagine, he's in a pissy mood."

"Let's get started again," Judge Seiler said, shaking his head.

2:45 P.M. – 3:00 P.M.

After the recess, John Crackstone seated himself in the witness box. Judge Seiler reminded him that he was still under oath.

Garner stood at the podium. For a brief second, he felt woozy and wondered if he was going to faint, but the moment passed. Deciding he might not have the stamina for a long examination, he decided to go to the heart of the matter.

"Mr. Crackstone," he said, "when you were last here, you testified about the slugs removed from several young Hispanic women. Specifically, you testified that those slugs did not match the slug removed from the decedent in this case, Ann Lindsey Medawar. Have I got that right?"

"In summary, yes," Crackstone allowed.

"Have you since found slugs that do match the slug removed from the body of Ann Lindsey Medawar?"

Bradford objected, arguing that Garner had not laid a proper foundation for the question.

Judge Seiler overruled the objection.

"Yes," Crackstone responded, "I have. Well, not slugs," he corrected himself. "A slug."

Garner rephrased the question to be sure the answer would be admissible. "Mr. Crackstone, have you found a slug taken from another gunshot victim which – based on

your analysis, experience, and professional judgment –
matches the slug removed from Ann Lindsey Medawar?"

"Well, actually I didn't find it," the ever-meticulous
Crackstone clarified. "The pathologist in the Coroner's office found it. He removed it from the body of a man killed
on Saturday."

"That man was Roger Storrs?"

Crackstone pulled a small notebook from the inside
pocket of his sports coat. He thumbed through the pages,
found the page he wanted, and studied it. "Yes, sir," he said.
"That's right."

"He and a companion were shot and killed on Saturday
morning, outside the apartment building where they lived in
Lower Price Hill?"

"That's the information I was given."

"You examined the slugs removed from Mr. Storrs and
his companion?"

"Yes, I did," Crackstone said. He adjusted his glasses,
glanced at the jury, and waited for the next question.

"What did you find," Garner asked, "when you examined those slugs?" To himself, Garner said, *it didn't take me
this long to get shot.*

"There were four slugs, two from each victim. I determined that three of the slugs were fired from the same Smith
& Wesson .38 revolver. The fourth slug was fired from a
9mm Glock."

Garner had no idea if the jury followed that.

"If I can elaborate," Crackstone said, "it appears there
were two shooters. One shooter shot the first victim in the
chest with a Smith & Wesson, and a different shooter, armed
with a Glock pistol, shot the second victim, also in the chest.

"Then," Crackstone continued, "it appears that the first
shooter fired twice more. He fired a bullet into the head of
the first victim, and then he fired a bullet into the head of
the second victim."

Garner appreciated the explanation, but he still wasn't

sure how much of it was getting through to the jury. What Crackstone was saying was this: Diego Olivar and some other thug shot Sam Scherge and Roger Storrs, the men responsible for the "Make America White Again" slayings. Olivar and his companion each put one shot into his victim, and then one of the shooters – probably Olivar – fired an additional shot into each victim's head.

But unless the jurors were clairvoyant, none of them would understand that.

Judge Seiler asked a question. "Mr. Crackstone, do you have the weapons that fired those shots? Or are you just working from the slugs removed from the men shot to death in Price Hill on Saturday morning?"

"At the time I did this analysis and prepared my report, Your Honor, I only had the slugs removed from the victims."

Judge Seiler leaned back in his chair, indicating that was the extent of what he wanted to ask.

Garner took the hint.

"At the time you did your analysis and prepared your new report," Garner repeated the always-exacting witness's testimony, "you did *not* have either weapon? Did I understand your response to Judge Seiler correctly?"

"That's correct," Crackstone confirmed.

"Have you come into possession of either of those guns since you did the analysis reflected in your report?"

"Yes," Crackstone said. "I was hoping you would ask me that."

Jesus H. Christ! Garner thought to himself. *Why didn't you just come out and say you had the gun?*

To the witness, Garner said, "Please tell the jury about that."

"Well, late yesterday afternoon, there was another shooting in Lower Price Hill. Someone shot –" Crackstone pulled the small notebook from his jacket pocket again and thumbed through it.

"Please continue, Mr. Crackstone," Garner said, forcing a smile. "I don't know about everyone else, but I'm very interested to learn who got shot in Lower Price Hill late yesterday afternoon."

The jurors got the joke and smiled.

"Well, yes, I suppose so," Crackstone said, realizing his gaffe.

"After last night's shooting, the police brought you the gun used by last night's shooter, Diego Olivar?"

Crackstone checked his notebook. "Yes, from a Mr. Olivar. That's right."

"And did that gun match the slug removed from Ann Lindsey Medawar?"

"No, it did not," Crackstone said. "But the gun did match three of the slugs from the shooting on Saturday morning."

Garner wondered briefly if he was still in the hospital, having a nightmare.

"Mr. Olivar's gun was the Smith & Wesson?"

"Yes, that's right."

"Mr. Crackstone," Garner asked, exasperated, "have you come into possession of a gun that *does* match the slug removed from Ms. Medawar?"

"Yes, I think so," Crackstone said. "Yes."

"Please tell us about that."

"Well, this morning the police searched the premises of the Sleep Cheap Inn and found several weapons. One of those was a 9mm Glock."

Crackstone looked at his notebook again. "According to what I was told, that gun was found in a locked a safe in the office at the inn. The detective on the scene asked me to give it priority."

Crackstone looked up from his notebook. "I would like to have more time," he added, "but based on my preliminary analysis, it's the weapon that fired the slug found in Ms. Medawar's body."

"In your professional opinion," Garner reframed Crackstone's answer, "the pistol found this morning in the office of the Sleep Cheap Inn, in a locked safe, is the weapon that killed Ms. Medawar?"

"Yes," Crackstone said. "That's correct."

"Thank you," Garner said. Turning to Bradford, he said, "Your witness."

Bradford looked defeated. He said he had no questions.

Judge Seiler announced that the court would be in recess for five minutes. "Ladies and Gentlemen of the jury," he cautioned the jurors, "you should retire to the jury room, but don't get too comfortable. We're going to need you back out in a few minutes."

3:00 P.M. – 3:15 P.M.

When Judge Seiler and counsel were seated in his chambers, he had a question for Bradford. "Are you familiar," he asked, "with the First Rule of Holes?"

Bradford looked uncertain what the judge was asking.

"The First Rule of Holes goes like this," Judge Seiler said. "When you find yourself in a deep hole, stop digging."

Bradford smiled.

"Will the prosecution dismiss?" Judge Seiler asked.

"My hands are tied, Your Honor. Warren will not authorize me to dismiss. He's adamant."

Judge Seiler removed his glasses and cleaned them with the edge of his black judicial robe. "You know I haven't ruled on Mr. Garner's motion to dismiss for prosecutorial misconduct."

Bradford shifted in his seat.

The judge let Bradford stew.

"Did I understand Olivar right?" Garner asked. "Some cartel guy talked to Anwalt and then decided to kill Ann?" Garner was angry that Bradford had not disclosed that, but he pressed the point not to vent, but to increase the pressure on Bradford.

Judge Seiler looked at Bradford.

"Yeah, that's what he claimed, but I didn't believe him. I thought he was making it up to get a deal on murdering those idiots in Price Hill."

"That's exculpatory, even if you didn't believe it," Garner pressed. A prosecutor is required to divulge any exculpatory evidence – that is, evidence that suggests the defendant might not be guilty. Sometimes, lawyers and judges can argue about whether or not a given piece of evidence is exculpatory. But a confession? Garner was certain that was exculpatory in anybody's book.

Bradford kept his thoughts on that to himself.

Judge Seiler looked at Bradford for a long moment without speaking.

"Look," Bradford said finally, "I don't know if the defense intends to call any more witnesses. But I can offer this. If the defense were to rest at this point, the prosecution will not call any further witnesses."

"In other words," Judge Seiler said, "if the defense stops now, the evidence is closed. Mr. Garner can renew his motion to dismiss. And then either I dismiss, and Mr. Warren blames the dismissal on me, or I can let the case go to the jury, and Mr. Warren blames the jury when it acquits?"

Bradford shrugged his shoulders.

"Devin," Judge Seiler said, "I'm prepared to have Warren blame the outcome on me. Are you ready to put an end to this?"

"Yes, sir."

"We need to do this in open court," Judge Seiler said, getting up.

3:45 P.M. – 4:00 P.M.

Thirty minutes later, accompanied by his client, Devin Garner stepped from the gloomy interior of the Hamilton County Courthouse into the bright daylight outside.

The abrupt end to the trial was a dramatic plot twist sure

to get prominent coverage in the night's newscasts and in the next morning's newspaper. The reporters and camera crews waiting on the courthouse steps rushed forward to get a comment.

Garner squared his shoulders and made the brief statement that would be shown on every television news program in the Greater Cincinnati viewing area that evening.

"Dr. Medawar and his family are grateful to the court for its ruling bringing this trial to a close," Garner said. "But this is a case that never should have been brought. There was never any evidence that Dr. Medawar killed his wife.

"This case was based on the theory that Dr. Medawar was a Syrian Muslim who was cheating on his wife. In fact, he is a life-long resident of Cincinnati and a practicing Catholic. He went to the inn to visit an undocumented woman with two desperately sick children. His wife was there to get material for the documentary she and her class were making. Thanks to a witness who came forward at the beginning of the trial, the evidence included a video of the woman and her children being rushed from the inn shortly after Dr. Medawar and Nurse Rios visited them.

"And thanks to heads-up police work by the Cincinnati Police Department, the evidence demonstrated that the murder weapon was in a safe in the Sleep Cheap Inn. The manager of the Sleep Cheap Inn testified that an associate of his killed Ann Medawar, and why. The prosecution knew this, but continued to press for a conviction anyway.

"The bottom line is clear: Dr. Medawar did not kill his wife, Ann Medawar. He loved his wife. He was prosecuted because of his ethnic background and presumed religion. That's the story you should report."

Several reporters tried to ask questions at once, but Garner ignored them.

"There is another story here – an important one. I hope you will report it as well.

"For months, a pair of killers stalked young Hispanic

women in our community. Fear and ethnic hatred animated them – emotions stoked for their own ends by politicians and extremists.

"Those thugs killed at least six young Hispanic women, maybe more. Those murders occurred over a relatively short period of time, all under remarkably similar circumstances.

"But the victims weren't white. They weren't wealthy or socially prominent or politically powerful. They were Hispanic. Most were poor and immigrants. Some of them may have been undocumented.

"And so, the media didn't notice. For months, there were no headlines.

"The Hamilton County Prosecutor didn't notice.

"But Ann Medawar noticed.

"She devoted her considerable energy and talents to trying to find who was killing those women. In doing so, she came close to identifying the killers.

"She also came close to unraveling the web of businesses and individuals who take advantage of immigrants in this community. Yes, the victims were undocumented. But they were desperate people who came to this country believing that we offered something better than the violence and the corruption where they were born."

"You should report that story."

Garner looked at Medawar to see if he wanted to add anything. Medawar shook his head.

"Are you accusing the Hamilton County Prosecutor's office," a reporter asked, "of prosecuting Dr. Medawar when it knew, or at least had reason to believe, he didn't kill her?"

"The evidence speaks for itself," Garner parried.

"Judge Seiler says he is going to ask the Department of Justice to investigate the Hamilton County Prosecutor's office, to see if it uses national origin and religion in deciding who to prosecute. Do you agree with him?"

"Judge Seiler is far wiser than I am," Garner replied,

smiling. "I'm not going to second-guess him."

"Dr. Medawar," a tall, attractive, blonde reporter called out. "Do you see your acquittal as a victory for Muslims in this country?"

Dr. Medawar stepped forward.

"You're Tiffany Albern?"

"Yes, from Queen City News."

Garner put a cautioning hand on his friend's shoulder.

"The Muslim religion is an old and honorable faith," Medawar said evenly, being careful to look at the television camera.

"But I am not Muslim. I am a Catholic. As Father Zaidan testified, I have been all my life.

"My parents came to this country from Lebanon, before I was born, to escape sectarian violence. I am disappointed to see some in this country trying to pit one group in this country against another – to pit 'us' against 'them.'

"Given my family history, given what happened in Lebanon, I am all too aware where that can lead. All you have to do is look at what happened in Lebanon, or at what is happening now in Iraq and Syria.

"Let me answer your question this way. To the extent that the prosecutor and public believed that I am a Muslim, no, I don't see my acquittal as a victory for Muslims.

"I see my acquittal as a victory for our country."

EPILOGUE

Determined to arrive on time, Devin Garner picked up his pace as he hurried across the University of Cincinnati campus. Professor Adams was hosting a special "premiere showing" of her class's documentary on the challenges facing undocumented immigrants. It would be a classy affair, with wine and cheese and a formal introduction of the film.

He reached the massive building just before 8:00 p.m. Carrie Hixson was standing in front, waiting for him. She wore a deep red evening gown with a plunging neckline.

"Wow! You look gorgeous," Garner said.

"Thanks! Just try not to drool when you meet my folks."

"Your folks?"

"My parents are going to be here, of course. I want you to meet them."

"I look forward to it," Garner said, adding just to himself, "like a root canal." He feared his concern was too obvious.

Carrie smiled and said, "You'll be fine." She hooked her arm through his and led him inside and toward the small auditorium.

"Professor Adams doesn't usually do this," Carrie explained on the way, "but she says she was so impressed with our documentary, she wanted to do something special."

"This showing is just for family and friends, right?"

"Mostly, but she's invited some VIPs from the community, mainly people who are interested in immigration issues. She's also corralled some people who are interested in documentaries. And, of course, the usual campus bigwigs."

"I'm impressed," Garner said.

"Don't be," Hixson laughed. "After all the publicity Rafiq's case got, those people are probably more interested in meeting you than you are in meeting them."

"I'm pretty sure my fifteen minutes of fame are over."

Hixson responded with an eye roll.

"Were you able" Garner asked, "to get the big indictment into the documentary?" He was referring to the federal indictment of Carl Anwalt and the rest of his syndicate on human trafficking and other charges.

"Yeah, it really helped to give us an ending to the story we were telling. I think that's why Professor Adams is so happy with what we did. If they hadn't indicted, I think she would have been afraid of getting sued or something." Hixson hesitated. "How's your uncle?"

"He went out to Texas and reconciled with Reya." Garner shook his head in mild disbelief. "She's agreed to cooperate with the Feds. She thinks she's going to get off easy, but Hank thinks she's being unrealistic. While all that sorts itself out, he's back in town, helping Reya's daughter, Maya, run the restaurant. So, he's happy."

Hixson placed her hand on Garner's arm and stopped. "I've got some news I've been dying to tell you," she said, "but I wanted to tell you in person."

Garner stopped and turned to face Hixson. He wondered if she was going to tell him she was engaged to some rich guy.

"Two things, actually," Hixson said. "First, WCET – the public television station – is going to broadcast our documentary. Professor Adams is going to announce that, so don't tell anyone until she does."

"That's terrific!"

"And WLW News has offered me a job as a news producer – well, assistant to the associate producer, or something like that. I think I'll be in charge of getting coffee, but it's a start."

"Congratulations!"

"How is Rafiq doing?" Hixson asked.

"He's going to do a stint with Doctors without Borders. I think it will do him good to get away. It will also give him a chance to decide what he wants to do long term."

Ann nodded. "He talked about Doctors without Borders before all this came up, but I thought he and Ann would have kids, and he'd find it impossible to get away."

Garner sighed. "I would have preferred that."

"Me too," Carrie said. "I think you know this, but we dedicated the documentary to Ann."

"Speaking of Rafiq," Garner said, "I'm taking him to dinner Friday. It's a going-away party. I'd like for you to come." He added, "as my date."

Hixson gave him her goddess smile.

"I'd like that," she replied, pulling her blonde hair back and shaking it.

Now, Garner thought, *now, I'm in trouble.*

AUTHOR'S NOTE

This novel is not based on, inspired by, or otherwise intended to be a representation of the current Hamilton County Prosecutor or any of his predecessors. It is also not based on, inspired by, or otherwise intended to be a representation of any current Circuit Court Judge for Boone County, Kentucky, or any of their predecessors. If any of those real public officials were to read this novel, they would be as appalled by the behavior of their entirely fictional counterparts as any reader.

The quotes attributed to the fictional Hamilton County Prosecutor are for the most part based on — and sometimes are nearly exact quotes from — various actual candidates for political office. A billboard paid for by a politician running for Congress in Tennessee suggested the notion of "Make America White Again."

If this novel was inspired by anyone, it was inspired by the politicians attempting to scare people with xenophobic concerns about immigrants. Typically, those immigrants left their native countries to escape violence and corruption. This country's insatiable demand for illegal drugs directly contributes to that violence and corruption. And, this country's gun manufacturers and gun dealers often provide the weapons the drug cartels and dealers use.

Finally, I wish to thank my beta readers and the members of the Covington Writers Group and the Boone County Writers Group. This book is better for their suggestions and constructive input.

ABOUT THE AUTHOR

Before retiring and taking up writing, Gary Reed had a successful and interesting legal career. He ended his active practice as Associate General Counsel for Humana Inc. in Louisville, Ky., where he led the team that handled the company's internal investigations and litigation across the country.

Before that, Mr. Reed created the legal department for ChoiceCare Health Plans, Inc. in Cincinnati, Ohio. He is the author of a number of professional articles and presentations.

He began his career with a large law firm in Cincinnati, where he handled product liability and insurance coverage litigation in courts around the country.

Mr. Reed grew up in Covington, Kentucky. He got his undergraduate degree from Xavier University in Cincinnati, where he wrote for and edited the campus newspaper, *The Xavier News*. He obtained his law degree from The Catholic University of America in Washington, D.C.

He is also the author of *Things Could Get Ugly*, set in the summer of 1939.

PRAISE FOR
Things Could Get Ugly
By Gary Reed

Great read. Loved it!

Mr. Reed has constructed a complex story that tantalizes the reader by weaving the individual threads into a story thick with the ambiance of the era.

John Bercaw, author of A Pink Mist

Crackling Good Novel

Reed has a knack for writing well researched mysteries that shine a spotlight on relevant social issues used to fuel a cracking good plot. He makes us care about those caught in the grinding wheels of oppression. But Reed gives us a bonus: a love story that deeply humanizes the hero. Yes. I loved Things Could Get Ugly.

Virginia L. Shephard, Ph.D.

Well Developed Characters and Interesting Geography

Enjoyed this book because of its characters and its setting. The cub reporter, an invincible young man in his twenties, and Woody, the former professor, are my favorites. I have heard about the reputation of Newport and Covington, KY., and this story gives them life.

Terri Bonar-Stewart, Ph.D., author of
Just a Couple of Women Talkin'

PRAISE FOR
Things Could Get Ugly
By Gary Reed

A Fun Read!
Really enjoyed reading this book.
It was fun to read about the local places I remember
around Northern Kentucky. It inspired me to look
into the history of Covington and what the Syndicate
had to do with our politics.
Blue Grass Reader, Amazon Customer Review

Historically Accurate and Exciting Storyline
I had heard many stories of that time period from my
parents and grandparents, and the events were accurate to the time and environment. The characters were
vividly portrayed and the book kept my interest from
beginning to end.
Amazon Customer Review

Excellent Reading
Wonderful historic novel. Well written, and well
researched. I can't recommend this book highly
enough.
Amazon Customer Review

Enjoy this book?

Your opinion is important! As an indie author, my success depends in large part on readers taking the time to post a constructive review on Amazon or GoodReads.

Please take a moment and share your opinion with potential readers!

And if you enjoyed this novel, check out my newest novel, *Things Could Get Ugly*.

Gary Reed